Lost Landscapes

Utah's Ghosts, Mysterious Creatures, and Aliens

By Linda Dunning

Lost Landscapes

Utah's Ghosts, Mysterious Creatures, and Aliens

By Linda Dunning

CFI
Springville, Utah

ISBN 13: 978-1-59955-058-9

Published by Council Press, an imprint of Cedar Fort, Inc., 2373 W. 700 S., Springville, UT, 84663
Distributed by Cedar Fort, Inc. www.cedarfort.com

LIBRARY OF CONGRESS CATALOGING-IN-PUBLICATION DATA
Lost landscapes : Utah's ghosts, mysterious creatures, and aliens / by Linda Dunning.
    p. cm.
Includes bibliographical references.
ISBN 978-1-59955-058-9
1. Ghosts--Utah. 2. Haunted places--Utah. 3. Monsters--Utah. 4. Extraterrestrial
beings--Utah. 5. Utah--History. I. Dunning, Linda, 1949- II. Title.

BF1472.U6U83 2007
001.9409792--dc22

                                        2007008248

Cover design by Nicole Williams
Cover design © 2007 by Lyle Mortimer

Printed in the United States of America

10 9 8 7 6 5 4 3 2 1

Printed on acid-free paper

This book is dedicated to my husband, John M. Dunning, whose fascination with history, nature, and the tales of his Native American heritage helped him survive an unpopular war while serving in combat as a hospital corpsman in Vietnam.

My thanks also to my sister Karen Loos, who did a great editing job, with additional help from Betsy Thompson.

Table of Contents

Book One

Lost Landscapes

The Sacred Four Corners

Ancestors and Spirit Beings

Much has been written about the land here and how it came to be. One cannot pass through this area without feeling the mystical quality of such vast and desolate spaces. There are so many voices, so many layers, and so many hauntings. One can touch not only ancient ruins but land formations which have seen centuries pass before, and feel only a minute part of what the land knows and sees and feels. It lives on without us and we are mere trespassers, viewing with our own individual interpretations, places, and times that we do not as yet fully understand. The ancestors, as the Navajos call them, left behind evidence of their spiritual beliefs. Hopis think the Anasazi left the land because of supernatural beings. The Navajos view themselves as having been enslaved by the Anasazi after having been given corn. They were then freed by holy beings that came down from the sky and destroyed their enslavers or brought drought and pestilence to them.

Many versions of this story center around a place called Chaco Canyon in New Mexico. Other versions say that the Anasazi were killed by a strong wind that sucked the air out of their lungs or that a great fire swept through the canyons and left black streaks or desert varnish on the rocks and dwellings. Still others claim that an ice storm crushed the people and drove their homes into the ground or that a flood destroyed everything in its path. All of these versions assume the Anasazi had offended the gods by abusing supernatural powers that had been given to them. The stories all tell that the sites left by the ancestors hold strong supernatural powers because of the events that occurred and the spirits that still reside there.

Many of the tribal groups in the Four Corners area are warned to stay away from these ancient ruins because evil spirits are believed to still reside there. Several months after I visited Mesa Verde, a dream came to me. At the time, I did not understand the dream, though I knew that it had followed me home from Mesa Verde. In the dream I was shown a small handicapped boy crying for his mother. His little remains were buried under his parents' bed where they slept each night. As I watched the boy, I realized that he was hydrocephalic or, as they called it in the old days, having "water on the brain." This large swelling of the head could have been considered evil in many tribes. In the dream it made perfect sense when a small spring appeared to flow from his head deep into the earth, which in turn made the land around him green again. When I visited Mesa Verde a second time several summers later, I happened to overhear some people talking about what they thought was a custom among tribes in the area. A stillborn or lost child would be buried under the parents' bed to make them fertile for another child. I could hear that child even then, just wailing away to his new brother and parents, though they had of course moved on to another place and time without him.

Older Navajo tribal members warn their younger counterparts against any kind of bad behavior by telling them that if they do not live in harmony with nature and display a profound respect for the land and its creatures, then bad luck could befall them. Most of the Navajos avoid sacred and mystical places. Medicine men or holy men, who know how to work with the powers in these places, know how to use these powers to heal, protect, and bless people, animals, and other things in nature. It's possible that "part of the ruin may become a place of worship, old arrowheads are used in medicine bundles, ancient pot shards are crushed for temper in newly formed pottery, replicas of Anasazi gourds and rattles are shaken during ceremonies and a piece of Anasazi bone may be used in the Enemy Way ritual to exorcise evil from a patient. None of this can be done without the proper ritual knowledge, which maybe as simple as a prayer or as complex as a lengthy ceremony."[1]

Navajo beliefs center around respect for the ancients, so that to walk in these ruins, touch them, or even see any of the mentioned artifacts can result in bad luck in one's own life or even poor health. These things may require supernatural rituals or cures which the holy men must perform for the person to rid him of bad luck, ill health, or just plain evil spirits. Therefore most of these ruins were left very much alone until the white man came into these areas and started discovering and exploring them. The robbing and ransacking of these sacred places caused many of the artifacts to disappear forever. People thought that not only could they get money and notoriety for finding such things, but they could also make new discoveries about these ancient peoples. There was a romanticized view of the Native American people that lead to a fascination, especially at the turn of the century and on into the 1930s.

White men have many theories about why the Anasazi disappeared in the space of only a thousand years; some of them are that there was a great drought or a natural calamity or many wars and battles or even that the people just decided to leave their cliff dwellings and move on. Native Americans believe that when visitors take things from these places, they take the spirits of these places with them. I cannot help but think of a friend of mine in another state who had a huge collection of such stolen and purchased Native American artifacts. Others who knew about his collection robbed him. He also suffered from a disease that killed him early. Some speculate that he had been cursed by holding onto his collection of sacred objects and artifacts.

My brother is a paleontologist whose job it is to excavate these sites to learn about the past. While he is fascinated by his work, he is certainly respectful of what he finds. He has told me stories of getting into fights in his younger days when some of the scientists drove into town for a drink at the local bar and some local tribal members confronted them about digging around in sacred sites. Things escalated and then the fight was on. This was before the repatriation law; now a tribe can claim the bones of their ancestors and give them another burial on the land of their choice. Conflict over desecrating ancient ancestral burial grounds is less likely now as most museums and universities are turning over the remains to those who feel that these remains are rightfully theirs.

I can remember going down to one of my brother's digs when I was in college. Three of us climbed down into a deep trench where they had just uncovered three tiny bodies. Their knees were pulled up to their chins. The middle mummy was slightly above the other two. While it seemed to be routine to everyone else, my college roommates were a bit grossed out by the scene, and it was anything but routine to me. While everyone else went about their business, I stood there watching the mummies. The spirit face of the real man stood out from the head of the mummy and turned towards me. He then let out a deep sigh or moan as though he were staring right through me to someplace way beyond me or perhaps way behind my time in the scheme of things. I thought that I had imagined it since I had a vivid imagination, but now I know better. Whether it was real or not did not matter. The important part was that the vision had occurred and it had happened to me. At that moment this man and I shared the same space in time and he had spoken to me but I had not understood. Nowadays I would have paid attention to the vision, and I would have tried to listen to this man whose silent grave had been opened after thousands of years' sleep in the ground—a grave opened to kindergarten researchers and uninitiated intuitives who did not understand what the man was trying to tell us.

Spiritual beings of all kinds reside everywhere in this country and especially in the Four Corners area. The Utes believe that the land is endowed with all sorts of spirituality, as are all the creatures which live upon it. Blue Mountain, Standing-alone Mountain or Navajo Mountain, and the LaSals are all sacred places in Utah. Spiritual beings also reside all over the mesas and canyons throughout the Southwest, just as they did when the Anasazi were here. Their petroglyph drawings depict larger than life, ripple-lined figures that appear behind the real people as ghostly outlines. Undulating lines depict these spirits as being different from the others and coming from the spirit world, although many of the experts say that we have no way of knowing what these figures really are, just that they are just different from the others.

Most Native Americans who practice the old ways believe that if one sees spirits, a gift must be left for them, especially if they have helped a hunter to find meat or a holy man to find particular herbs and healing plants. Saying nothing about having seen this spirit ensures good fortune. This makes it hard to hear about the spirit stories from many such tribes. Utes held healing rites in special places empowered with supernatural beings such as Babylon Pasture, Peavine Canyon, and the Bear Ears. The Navajo have four sacred mountains that surround the Four Corners area: Blanca Peak in Colorado, Mount Taylor in New Mexico, the San Francisco Peaks in Arizona, and the Hesperus Peak in Colorado. They also have four sacred rivers as boundaries: the San Juan, Colorado, Little Colorado, and the Rio Grande. Everything that lives within the boundaries of these four mountains and four sacred rivers is blessed and protected by holy beings.

Within the Utah borders of the Four Corners area there are many land formations that tell a story passed down through the generations through either the Navajo or Ute tribes. Navajo Mountain is supposed to be the head of a woman; her body is formed of Black Mesa and her feet are the Baluki Mesa. One of her hands grasps a wool twine with El Captain as her fist. Her partner's head is Chuska Peak or Tohatchi Mountain, and his body is the Chuska-Tunicha range. His lower extremities are the Carrizo Mountains with his feet in Beautiful Mountain in New Mexico. He holds in one hand a bow or sacred pouch called the Shiprock. The entire formation is called Pollen Mountain. Blue Mountain is female and often called Furry Mountain. Her partner mountain is known as the LaSals. Both ranges house various healing plants. Navajo medicine men talk of how the plants have been there since the beginning of time. There is also a male horse head on one side and a female horse head on the other side of the Shiprock peak, which connotes excellent wild horse herds, as well as good luck with domestic ones.

In Valley of the Gods or Monument Valley, rock formations are seen as guardian warriors frozen in time. Also called Valley of the Rocks, Monument Valley is said to be a storage place for the gods because the formations there look like giant barrels or pots to store water in. One formation is called Rain God Mesa and has four springs associated with healing and the making of rain. Totem Pole Rock is another frozen spirit held up by lightning. The "mittens" in the valley are two hands that lie dormant, left behind by the gods as a sign of great power. It is believed that someday these holy beings will return and rule from this place.

Nearby Eagle Mesa is a sacred site where the spirit of a dead person may go after burial. One can hear the voices of both children and adult spirits and see bones and footprints everywhere. This is not a site to wander alone in unless a person is blessed for such a mission, as spirits wander there without regard to those who hike this land; night camping might be quite a scary affair.

Sleeping Ute Mountain is another interesting place on the southwest boundary of these sacred lands. This mountain was once a god who became angry with his people and collected rain clouds to keep in his pocket. When storms come, the Utes say that the clouds are coming out of the rain god's pocket. When the end of the world comes, this god will wake up and fight off the people's enemies. Experts describe these stories as examples of "Spiritual Creationism," a belief in which every tree, rock, river, creature, plant, or land formation has a spirit and holds a place in the universe. Yet there are layers of existence here, the residue of past places and peoples, as well as very real present day conversations with spirits who may wish us to hear them.[2]

Whenever I go to such a place I feel as if I have come home, though I am a white woman without a drop of Native American blood in me and have to carry the guilt of my own ancestors over the terrible deeds they carried out to conquer the West. A vision I had at the age of twenty-one has come entirely true now, except for the ending. At the time, I was quite startled by having a Native American dream as a result of asking for help in knowing what I wanted to do with my life. I went to see a counselor in the last quarter of my senior year of college because I was not sure that my chosen major, teaching, was what I wanted to do. I asked her what I was to do with my life, and of course she was unable to answer me. That night I had a technicolor dream of a place I had never been, a cliff dwelling somewhere in the Southwest in my imagination I presumed. I did not understand then that such dreams are symbolic of our true callings in life, neither did I understand my true calling. The dream did answer all my questions, although I had no idea at the time what those answers were. I had no awareness of my own innate gift from my mother and it took a series of events to awaken me.

In the dream I climbed a grassy hill to a grass-covered shack where I met a tall, thin Native American man with long black hair. He took me into the shack and we made love. Then I walked with him out the back of the shack. As we walked in slow motion, he turned into a giant crow and flew away. I walked on up the hill alone and above me on the mesa was a huge ancient cliff dwelling city. It took me forever to get there and when I did, I seemed to float through the many stone rooms hearing voices, smelling fresh bread and berries, and seeing sights in my mind's eye none of which were actually there. As I floated through the rooms, I realized that I was looking at and sensing things from a distant past. Finally I came to the middle of the village and went into a kiva room and sat down on the other side of a roaring fire, which was odd for the middle of summer. Across from me, through the flames, I could barely see an ancient wrinkled man with a fish net tied around his head and white frizzled hair sticking out from it. He began talking to me, and I could not understand a word he said, not only because he was speaking in a foreign tongue, but also because the wind began to howl down through the rooms and grew louder and louder until it roared over his voice. I desperately wanted to understand because I knew he was laying out a blueprint for my life. Instead, I woke up crying and trembling all over, unable to understand what I was suppose to do.

Years later a Paiute student teacher in my classroom, whose grandmother was a dream interpreter, interpreted the dream as representing the many years or rooms with my students. She said that I was going to spiritually influence many children in my years on this earth. However, it was not until much later that I understood the dream in its entirety. My husband is tall and thin, once had long black hair, and has a great grandmother who was a six-foot tall Northern Cheyenne. When he was a hospital corpsman in Vietnam, he had to burn grass shacks like the one in my dream that represents what the war had done to him. Crows are considered mystical seers who can see through just about any kind of mischief or tragedy, and they follow him everywhere he goes. Crows can also mean death, and we both know that he will die first and I will live alone for a great while after him. I have since come to realize that I have guided many who were taken early and walked the shores of the river of death as a bridge between the living and the dead.

I looked for the mesa city from my dreams in all of my travels and finally decided that it was from the past and not a place I might see again until my own death approaches. The sights and sounds, sensations, and touches I experienced in the dream were a way of telling me about my gifts as an intuitive, although I didn't fully understand this until over twenty years later. The old man was one of my teachers, and that was why I was so desperate to understand him and could not. I now know most of the answers from this dream except for one: what the old wise holy man will tell me when I approach my own death. For that is when I will see him again, of that he had assured me even then. In the meantime, I continue my own journey as a teacher of children, trying to fit myself into a teaching world that is often inflexible and cold. I have become a subversive, whose island offers refuge to those children able to swim to it with their own intuitive souls. I am also an interpreter for those who have crossed over with unfinished business on this side, and for those on this side who wish to understand those lost to them more clearly. Death follows me or I follow it, noticing over the years that I had done preparation work with some who then passed on. It still startles me when it happens, as I am not a predictor of death, merely a healer for those left behind.

White people who believe this sort of thing are probably considered balmy by quite a few, unless of course the person is a writer, and then he or she has a good excuse, being an artist with a vivid imagination. There have been many writers from the Four Corners area who wrote about the spirits that roam this land. Albert R. Lyman, Frances Gillmor, Everett Reuss, Marie Ogden, Joseph Wood Krutch, Frank Waters, Wallace Stegner, Zane Grey, and Louis L'amour were among them. In later times there have been others such as Tony Hillerman, Paul Pitts, David Lavendar, and Terry Tempest Williams. All of them wrote about the mystical quality of this area, although Everett Reuss' story is the most interesting. It's an intriguing mystery of a twenty-year-old who disappeared in this area in the 1930s. Some say he was murdered, others that he just wandered off, fell, and died. Still others say that he just faked his disappearance and lived out his life in some other place. He left behind his journals and art prints, and these are his claim to fame.

An *empath* soaks in the land and people around her and absorbs a brief understanding of all cultures from the pictures, symbols, and sensations that bombard her, often without warning and sometimes with great pain or sadness for what she must feel. I spent a great deal of my life being frustrated by others' inability to feel or see such things, thinking that they refused to do so. Once I understood that some people just couldn't do this for whatever reason, I lost the anger and frustration and began to find my path in life. No regular counselor then or now would have said to me, "Perhaps you are a clairvoyant healer who has visions that can help other people," or suggested that I was perhaps able to see across or behind the veil that separates the dead from the living. No one would have thought to tell me to write these experiences down because I was probably just imagining them or making them up. The holy man in the dream came to answer my questions without the barriers of belief systems or time itself. I was just too young, and certainly not equipped, to either listen to or see the spirit world.

Some tribes call this the ability to walk within the spirit lodges of others. It is an isolation, which is both marvelous and sad, and it is a journey that Carl Jung would have described as a slow walk into an undiscovered country of the mind. While others call it a journey of the spirit, I like to think of it as a marvelous and yet sometimes painful walk into countries, cultures, and dreams of others into which I have the opportunity to travel without leaving my home. I assist others to understand and heal from both the living and the dead, and they assist me to understand more and more about the journey.

In Chaco Canyon, I felt healed and energized. In Mesa Verde, I was given stories to tell. At Canyon de Chelly, I was mesmerized by visions. At the age of twenty-one, I was given my direction dream without understanding it. When I searched for the mesa city in all of these places, I could not find it. I could only find it in my mind and fortunately my age, wisdom, experience, and even a little education have pronounced me sane, although perhaps a little deluded in some people's eyes. I walk through the spirit lodges of others carefully, quietly, and with great reverence and caution. Most important, now I am alive and not dead with a hole in my soul like I was for so many years. I had determined people just had to live like this. My soul and identity are complete now, so it is simply a matter of the journey. The whole world is alive in a way I never thought possible, and I hear the spirit beings and sometimes even see them. The world breathes, and I now know to breathe with her. There is a tapestry to things on this planet, a warp and weave to everything. Spirits of the Four Corners are everywhere and anywhere.

The one hundred and twenty-fifth anniversary of the Four Corners Monument was a historic gathering.

> At the Four Corners National Monument on Wednesday, tourists, locals, stamp collectors and two tribes gathered to celebrate the anniversary of this site. People sat on the concrete slab that marks the four corners to have their picture taken while others lined up to buy the commemorative postmarks from four directions, released

with the seals of both the Navajo and the Ute Mountain tribes on them. The Ute Mountain and the Navajo Nation tribes jointly own this site. Ceremonies included tribal dances and a reenactment of the marking of the Four Corners in 1875.

This area gets an average of 250,000 visitors each year, many of which are from other countries. The original monument was built in 1912 and the present one has steps leading up to where the four states touch as well as a flag flying for each state and a state seal on each corner. This is our culture and part of our heritage the Native American peoples say. It is spiritually touching and it's something for us to feel good about. Every day potters and jewelers line up along the area to sell their goods. The very first monument placed there 125 years ago was nothing more than a stick in the dirt held up by large rocks.[3]

Notes

1) McPherson, *A History of San Juan County*, 39.
2) Ibid., 2–6.
3) Associated Press, "Gathering Marks 125th Anniversary of Site Where Four States Touch," July 13, 2000.

Saltair
The Grand Lady of the Lake

From the beginnings of a small yet ornate building full of lattice-work and a few bathhouses called the Lake Park Resort, a grand resort was being planned. On what was known as Black Rock Beach, just north of the ruins of an old and very tiny resort called Lake House, the larger and more magnificent structure was rising into the sky. Dr. Jeter Clinton built Lake House in 1871. He expanded the resort to a three-story hotel and renamed it the Short Branch in homage to the famous New York watering hole, the Long Branch. A magnificent Moorish palace originally christened Saltaire (until the *e* was later dropped) was being constructed up the beach. This name fit; fifty tons of salt were produced each day in the area by the Inland Salt Company. The same railroad line that transported the salt also transported patrons who frequented the resorts on the south shore of the lake, long before Saltair outdid the competition.[1]

Garfield Beach was the most visited spot when the *Deseret Evening News* announced in 1893 that a new bathing resort would be built on the shores of the lake with a mammoth dancing hall. The resort boasted "promenades, elegant parks, club and bath rooms, and pure water and a sandy shore."[2] The new pavilion would be four thousand feet long. It would be built on pilings and stretch at least five feet out into the water. The first floor housed the main pavilion with a series of smaller pavilions for restaurants, refreshment stands, and comfort rooms. The second floor contained the dance hall, dressing rooms, clubrooms, and ladies' and gents' parlors. The suspension roof was constructed of three hundred tons of steel. The third and fourth stories were encircled by promenades, and the fifth floor was a massive cupola with an observatory room to view as far as Salt Lake City to the east and Tooele to the west.

John D.C. Gad of the *Utah Historic Quarterly* proclaimed, "The company will illuminate the great pavilion, towers, bath houses and approach with thousands of electric lights the rays of which on the gaily painted and many colored buildings and on the silvery waves will present a scene of grandeur and dazzling beauty which can scarcely be equaled even in the writings of Oriental story tellers."[3] People from both the city of Corinne and Salt Lake City came across the lake to swim, dance, and visit this growing resort. Opening day was planned for Memorial Day of that year, but vital construction postponed it for a week. On June 8, 1893, the new resort that had cost $250,000 opened just six months after the announcement of its construction. Special trains carried people to the event from Provo and Ogden, as well as Salt Lake City and the surrounding areas. Dignitaries spoke, a banquet was served, and people danced to the strains of Pedersen's Band. Its first season closed on Labor Day with a masquerade ball and carnival.

First owned by The Church of Jesus Christ of Latter-day Saints, Saltair hosted the world famous Tabernacle Choir in concerts several times a year. In its second year of operation, a huge statehood celebration was held there on August first. Political parties began to hold their rallies at the resort, and the YMCA held its gymnastics tournaments there. Garfield Beach began to feel the crunch from their next-door neighbor to the north and hired the Tabernacle Choir and the Logan Tabernacle Choir for a series of concerts, hoping to outdo the new resort. The first fatality at the new resort happened on July 8, 1896, when Charles Manca died of heart failure while swimming in the lake. One amusing event, reported in the *Salt Lake Tribune*, happened on July 13, 1897, when two young men entered the water at Saltair on Sunday without suitable swimming attire and were sent to jail for thirty days. By 1901, controversy had begun to arise concerning the moral atmosphere of Saltair. Beer was being sold openly, and it was becoming evident that Saltair's family image was on the wane. The Church began thinking of selling the property but did not want the resort to fall into the wrong hands. In 1902, the stockholders found their solution by transferring the property to a group of local businessmen who were members of the Church, often called Latter-day Saints. Saltair then became a gathering place for a diverse and interesting crowd of people.

While my mother's side of the family rarely went out to the beach resort, my father's family went there all the time. They came from Magna, Riverton, and even Santaquin to spend time at Saltair. The Cushings were my grandmother Madsen's family, and they laughed a lot and liked to have a good time. My grandmother chorded on the piano and harmonized with a friend, singing to the silent movies as her only job before she married. She and her friend once performed at Saltair on amateur night. We have family photos of my father's parents with their friends or relatives with their toes up in front of them floating in the very buoyant Great Salt Lake. My grandmother used to tell Danish stories, such as the one about a time when all the relatives were standing around waiting for an uncle to pass on. He was very old and his death was expected. Finally, after a long silence on the part of her dying uncle, one of the women leaned over him and pronounced him dead. Everyone began mourning, wailing, and crying. The woman interrupted all this noise to say something like, "Yah, de brudder has passed on." In the momentary quiet of the room, they heard a strong, deep voice say, "Not yet."

By 1905, the illegal sale of liquor was still a problem, the water level was becoming an issue, and the winds were hurting business at the resort. The management responded by dredging the lake, trying to enforce the beer sales problem, and enclosing the dance floor to protect against the winds. The lake had receded so far that they had to build a cable from the pavilion to deeper water so that rafts could be attached to it and towed out. In 1909, a new attraction was constructed alongside the pier. It was called the Ship Cafe. This cafe was two hundred feet long, ninety feet wide, and seventy feet high. The first floor contained the kitchen, the second floor housed the cafe, and the third floor was another promenade. A contest was held to name the cafe, and the winning entry was the Leviathan. The daughter of the governor at the time christened the ship with a bottle of champagne. By 1909, two bands played on the dance floor, one at each end, and it was now called the Hippodrome. That year, the *San Francisco Examiner* called Saltair the Coney Island of the West. As proof of this status, a team of flying ballerinas performed in the Hippodrome that year. President William

Howard Taft also visited the resort that year but only stayed for a few minutes at the very end of the season.

In 1910, the first prizefights were held at Saltair. Jack Johnson and Jim Jeffries were the first to be booked to fight there, but when Johnson said that he would fight only if President Theodore Roosevelt would referee, even the governor and other state officials halted the proceedings and the fight was held somewhere else in Utah. On May 13, 1910, a mass of fans had been to Saltair to see Pete Sullivan get punched out by "Cyclone" Johnny Thompson. After the fight, people surged up the stairs en mass, eager to catch the first train home. The stairs crashed down from the weight, toppling people into the gaping hole below them and into the lake. Hundreds of people fell into the lake and dozens were injured, seven of them seriously, but no one was killed.

> Broken limbs, bruises, and sore throats from swallowing the brine were reported. As they struggled in the cold water, some people panicked and became hysterical. One fellow even cried out, "Where is my baby?" As it turned out, the tot was actually at home. The *Salt Lake Telegram* took the resort to task, decrying its poor maintenance on a building that held so many people. The bathhouses and the pier at Saltair had been destroyed by high waves on April 3 of the same year, and while that wasn't a factor reported in the story of the accident, it might account for what happened.[4]

That year, ten thousand people went to the resort, and several improvements were made. A freakish sixty-mile-an-hour blast of wind destroyed two bathhouses and some of the railroad trestle in February. In April another violent gale helped to wash away 325 bathing houses ,and this time a hundred yards of railroad trestle were torn up. Custodians had to cling to rocks and girders and anything else that they could find to keep from being carried off by the wind. Another bad storm hit the resort in July of that year. For the next few years, continuing storms began to cost the owners a lot in repairs. Allegations were made that the owners were not spending the money needed to do the repairs or were not doing them properly for the safety of their patrons. In fact, the whole place was falling into disrepair.

The owners of Saltair pulled some elaborate stunts to bring in the crowds. Before July 24, 1911, the owners had been advertising for weeks their weekend spectacular involving a real bullfight. They brought in real matadors, picadors, banderilleros, and toreadors from both Spain and Mexico. They built a bullring and had full-page ads about this event in the papers. One article was even dedicated to the bull and proclaimed him a magnificent beast with very good blood-lines. A huge crowd showed up from Salt Lake City and all the surrounding towns. However, the owners did make one concession, that wooden practice swords and staves would be used instead of the real thing. There would be no killing of the bull at the end. So while the bull lived, he managed to gore four men. He was proclaimed in the newspapers as the winner, and they boasted in detail of his prowess with his horns. The more sensitive Americans turned out not to be that sensitive at all and newspaper accounts seem to show that everyone reveled in the event and had a good time watching the bull gore the men. The bull emerged victorious and was rewarded for his skill by being allowed to live.[5]

The golden years of Saltair were in full swing during the 1920s when half a million people came to the resort each year. By then the resort housed a funhouse, a ferris wheel, a roller coaster, a roller rink, pool halls, a ping pong parlor, a shooting gallery, a tunnel of love, a midway, and the largest ballroom in the West. Another grand stunt to pull in the crowds happened in 1924. This was when Rudolph Valentino and his wife, Natacha Rambova, visited the resort as one of the stops on their national dancing tour. As the couple tried to get to the resort for their concert, they were stuck in a traffic jam three miles from Saltair. They sent word to the resort to send a train and Rudy and Natacha were an hour and a half late for their performance. Rudy got up on stage in his street clothes and managed to calm the crowd with his amazing charisma and he and Natacha then swept the crowd away with their performance. Another time when they visited the resort, they tried to bathe in the waters. There was such a crowd that they had to graciously ask them to move back. They eventually had to leave because of the thousands of people trying to catch a glimpse of them.

Meanwhile, Saltair continued to be plagued with liquor problems as well. The *Salt Lake Telegram* reported another story during this time about several officials, including probation officers, were concerned about the morals of young girls and were trying to get Saltair's liquor license revoked. They claimed that young girls could easily get a drink out there with no problem and they would fall into bad company and eventual "moral decay." One probation officer reported that one of his cases had gone from bad to worse due to her visits to the resort. The girl's behavior had forced him to send her to the State Training School for Juveniles in Ogden. About this same time, an eighteen-year-old girl attempted to commit suicide in one of the bathhouses by trying to swallow an unidentified drug. The Grand Army of the Republic, veterans of the Civil War, held their convention out at Saltair that year. By this time, Saltair had lost its wholesome family image for good.

Saltair also had a series of fires over the years, which added to the site's woes. The first fire was in 1916 when hot coals spilled from a steam engine. By 1919, they were working on switching to electric trains rather than steam. The second big fire at Saltair happened on April 22, 1925, starting in the Ali Baba Cave. This time the fire burned in only one section and the other areas continued their business as usual. It consumed the roller coaster, burned the Leviathan to the water line, and destroyed most of the pavilion. The midway became charcoal and some of the bathhouses, piers, and railroad tracks were destroyed. Damage was estimated at $750,000 and, unable to find investors willing to take a risk on the resort, it shut its doors. Aside from financial problems and issues with the lake, a new resort, Lagoon, in Farmington, was beginning to take away a major portion of Saltair's patrons. In 1929, Saltair again opened its gates with several local financial backers. Two more resorts had opened on the south shore and Saltair was still wanting for customers.

The third big fire was in July of 1931 when the south pier caught fire, destroying seven amusement areas and ending with a gust of wind that pushed the blaze through the Giant Racer roller coaster, the biggest draw at the park. This time the blaze had started on the roof of the Fun House, and it took ten lines from two water pumps to finally put it out. This particular fire was the real start of Saltair's decline. The very next year another tragedy struck workmen who were on the scaffolding ,trying to repair the damage from the fire on The Giant Racer. In only three minutes' time, another gale force wind blowing at seventy miles an hour collapsed the scaffolding. It crashed down with the workers on it and below it. It carried twenty-foot planks more than one hundred feet to the pavilion below and many workers fell into the lake. Two of the men were killed while six others were seriously injured.

Saltair continued to decline during the 1930s as various sewage companies used the lake for disposal and contaminated the shore and lake, especially near Saltair. The worst receding of the lake waters took place in 1933, and Saltair stood on its pilings on a desert landscape far from the shore of the lake. All that garbage and the stinky brine shrimp made the place extremely uninviting. By the beginning of World War II, Saltair's gates were closed again as the war years were draining money from investors and patrons alike. It did not open again until the early 1950s. In June of 1951, still another fire destroyed bathhouses and caused $50,000 dollars of damage. Yet at the same time, the managers were thinking of ways to attract larger crowds and came up with diving mules as a publicity stunt.

The resort reopened in May of 1955, and developers even built a small lake around the resort to give the illusion of water, because by this time the lake had receded far from where the resort stood. Still another fire occurred in June of 1957. This time it broke out in the boiler room. Piers, bathhouses, and some of the concession stands were damaged and cleared away while the owners kept operating the rest of Saltair. The final tragedy happened on August 30, 1957, when a sudden gust of wind blew down what was left of The Giant Racer. The freakish seventy-mile-per-hour wind reduced the hundred thousand dollar structure to a pile of wooden rubble. It had been shut down at three p.m. when the storm began with slight winds and rain, so fortunately no one was injured. Big name bands and singers had propelled the revitalization of the resort in the fifties but after this final fire, Saltair shut down for good on Labor Day of 1958.

The old shell of Saltair was put to good use in the cult movie *Carnival of Souls*, a low-budget horror movie that a group of young filmmakers from Kansas thought would give them a start in the film industry. While it didn't really go anywhere at the time, the 1962 release filmed in black and white has become a Twilight Zone-like classic and has fans from all over the world. The film copies the basic outline for one of the 1960 Twilight Zone episodes that starred Inger Stevens. It was filmed in four weeks, half in Lawrence, Kansas, and the other half in Salt Lake City and at Saltair. The story goes that the young director, Herk Harvey, was driving alone from California on his way back to Kansas when, just as the sun was going down on the Salt Flats, an eerie Moorish castle rose up before him. He was immediately drawn to it and stopped his car, jumped the fence, and went to explore the old abandoned amusement park. The amusement park still had all the trappings of its former glory days strewn about its grounds and buildings. The director, Herk Harvey, intimated that the place was so scary that he felt as though the ghosts of the place that had been partying there had just left for the night. Having found this eerie place totally by chance out in the middle of a desert, he raced back to his friends, raving that he had found the perfect spot to build a horror story around. Perhaps Harvey had his own experiences there . . .

The little production company filmed the church scenes, pipe organ factory, and boarding house scenes in Kansas, but the city and shop scenes as well as the Saltair scenes were filmed here in Utah. What a treat to not only see downtown Salt Lake City and the old county courthouse in the fall of 1961, but especially to see scene after scene of old Saltair and all of her out buildings. The story is about a young woman and her two high school friends who drown in a car accident when they go off a bridge while trying to drag race with another car. Three hours later, as the people are trying to locate the car, the young woman comes walking up out of the water in shock but perfectly fine. She decides to move away from this sad event and because she is a professional organist, she gets a job in Salt Lake City at some church (the church used for filming is, of course, actually in Kansas). On her way to Salt Lake City, she also sees the old deserted Moorish-looking amusement park on the lake and stops to look at it. She keeps seeing a zombie-like face in her car window that seems to be associated with the old amusement park. The same face starts to appear in the windows of the boarding house she is staying in and, as the story goes along, she begins to have periods of time when no one can see or hear her and she doesn't know why. She goes to a therapist thinking she is going crazy and these zombie creatures start popping up everywhere.

Eventually, she ends up at Saltair feeling that she is going mad. The zombies chase her around Saltair and finally catch her. It seems she was dead all along but was running from death. This explains the periods of time when no one could see or hear her. It was sort of like a light bulb going on and off, only it was her soul's light and the dead were demanding her return. These fledgling filmmakers were out to make a Bergman film in the horror genre, and in many respects, they did just that. However, no one noticed this film when it came out and it ended up at the drive-in theatres. As an intuitive person, however, what fascinates me is how the director and film editor were able to evoke the mysticism and eeriness of old Saltair. The film is essentially built around two characters: the young woman of the walking dead whose spirit had momentarily escaped death and the "spirit" of a place whose soul was at that time caught in a place between the living and the dead. The scene in the ballroom with the dancing spirits of Saltair was something that I think went beyond a filmmaker's vivid imagination and borders on what people in the esoteric world would call a possession.

If you ignore some of the overacting and concentrate on the lead actress who carries the film, along with Saltair, the film is pretty good. After several re-releases, a two DVD volume was released. The set includes the original trailers, the film released to the theaters, and a later version with added footage. It also, among other things, includes an old postcard slideshow of Saltair, a brief written history of Saltair with photographs by Nancy D. McCormick and John S. McCormick, and a half hour of outtakes that show a lot more of Saltair. For anyone with their own memories of visiting the resort, or for anyone just entranced with the beauty of the old pavilion and its out buildings, this footage and the old postcards are a real treat. In what some consider a hokey old black and white horror film, others will see as genius and enjoy how these young filmmakers wove the death of this girl's spirit and the death of this castle on the lake's soul together in a tapestry of images dedicated to an esoteric history. A sort of low budget version of *The Mask of the Red Death* near the remnants of an ancient lake that is also dying a slow death of its own.

These young filmmakers made a film full of beautiful and haunting images whose storyline made very little sense. The film was carried by a brilliant young actress, Candace Hilligross. The eerie organ music also carried the film and added to its spooky ambience. However, there was something else of greater importance in this film, something that the director managed to capture on film at the old amusement park. When the crowd of flour-pasted zombies chase the heroine through the pilings below the park, or when they dance in the old ballroom decorated with cheap crepe paper and the more expensive 1920s hanging lamps shredded by years of wind and abandonment, the creepiness of the place comes to life.

Ghost hunters of today would have had a heyday there, reviewing Electronic Voice Phenomenon (EVP) recordings and taking pictures of the orbs and streaks and ecto-mists that this director somehow captured along with his fake zombies who danced among the real ghosts in that ballroom. Without knowing it, or perhaps he did know it, Harvey managed to capture on film the very essence of old Saltair and the many layers of her history as these "fake" spirits danced together or gazed out at the sunset from the long porches overlooking the lake. Herk Harvey only directed two low budget horror films before going on to produce over four hundred educational films. I would agree with those who laud *Carnival of Souls* that perhaps we lost a genius filmmaker along the way. This Moorish castle, Saltair, is the real reason that the film is a cult classic today. The essence of ghost hunting was captured in a film that was long before its time, by a man who perhaps didn't even know what he was doing, and a young actress who didn't even know that she was possessed.

I first saw Saltair in the late 1960s. I don't have any memories from its former glory days. At the time, all sorts of committees and government and private groups were attempting various ways to save the resort. Even Walt Disney was contacted for advice on how to revive the resort. His response was that Saltair had seen its last ticket days and its last tourist. It lay dormant until March of 1965, when several groups joined forces to restore Saltair. This attempt fell through due to lack of funds and various other difficulties. In 1966, I went out to Saltair with a friend to paint her for our art class. We had our own eerie experiences there in a fortunate chance to see Saltair before her demise only a year later. In September of 1967, a final fire occurred after several years of rotting and decay. This marked the end of this Grand Lady of the Lake. On September second of that year, the *Salt Lake Tribune* wrote, perhaps prematurely, of its final demise. "Great Salt Lake's tired but once proud lady—had her skirts charred early Friday morning. Fire swept through much of the elevated apron leading to the resort but firemen were able to prevent the flames from destroying the main pavilion with its large ballroom . . . Flames from the fire lighted the sky over the lake and the glare against the clouds could be seen over Salt Lake and Davis and portions of Weber and Tooele counties."[6]

Arson was never suggested, but by this time Saltair had become a place for teenagers to hang out. They often went inside even though signs were posted everywhere. It was of interest to me that the 1967 fire happened in September, as it was the very summer after my friend and I made a trip out there to paint the magnificent structures for our watercolor and oil classes at the high school. But we knew no Saltair history then. We had no idea that we were seeing something that would soon be gone forever, nor did we know that it was between renovations so some of what we saw was old and some of it was new. We were just two high school kids out for a fun day at the beach, unaware then of our later intuitive interest in the place. We only knew that when we went out there to paint our oils and watercolors, the place was abandoned and easy to walk to.

We got lovely sunburns and painted all day without a single memory of brine shrimp bothering us as we floated in the lake. We did our own tour of the building on not-so-steady floorboards and stairways. Both of us felt the cold spots and emotions that in those days we could not put names to. None of the other buildings were there then, just the main structure that was being renovated. Knowing nothing of Saltair's history, we heard music we were not supposed to. But we did hear it and nothing was around to have produced it, because we checked everywhere. It was a sort of old-fashioned dance music. Neither of us knew then that we were seeing Saltair for the first and the last time, or that our little oil paintings and watercolors would be a last remnant of something real about it. They were not good paintings and certainly there are many wonderful pen and ink drawings of the old Saltair that do it more justice than the colored and painted ones do. Most important for me was that I did not know then that these two little paintings would become something that I would treasure. It was because we got to see Saltair in the last moments of its life and hear its mysterious dance bands. Neither of us will ever forget the experience. My only regret is that had I known what I know now, I would surely have heard and seen much more than I did.

A last renovation and revival was attempted in about 1982, but this too was doomed to failure. Once again, Saltair had a small fire like the many others she had experienced over the years. The fickleness of the Great Salt Lake had also doomed the building as the lake rose and fell at its own whim, no matter what the politicians mandated that the lake should do. In 1970, what was left of Saltair burned to the ground. In 1982, rebuilt and refurbished, Saltair opened only to be flooded into oblivion in 1984. Several smaller fires have since destroyed the last remaining building completely, collapsing the pavilion into a pile of rubble and debris on the dry desert sand of a receding lake.

A tiny replica of Saltair was built in 1994, and it is made of cement and painted in a garish yellow and blue and gold. It is only an echo of the front arches of the main building and was obviously built to gain tourist monies from both visitors and rock concert participants. To the north of this much smaller pavilion is some of the debris from the original building, which makes an artificial shoreline on the lake. There are remnants of a miniature steamboat gift shop in front of the tiny concert pavilion and three old train cars supposedly from the original trains that carried the crowds out to Saltair. There is also an odd square cement building called the Camel-lot, whose purpose is a mystery to me, unless they actually intended to keep camels for rides along the lake. A few camels were reported in the late 1800s wandering the area, having escaped from their military units out west somewhere. It's a short walk to either side of the building and out the back double doors down to where the lake is. Look to the north, and there, along the shoreline of the rocks and beach, you will see a literal fence of rubble and debris that was once the Grand Lady of the Lake, Saltair, washing in and out with the waves.

Inside the building is a concession shop, a gift shop, and a grand staircase, which might actually echo the original one. On summer evenings, rock bands and other concerts blared through the night with no neighbors to complain about the noise. The new owners probably planned this to avoid lack of parking space and neighbors who might complain when the music starts. Out on the edge of the lake, there was no one to disapprove or complain of the noise. Or was there? The spirit neighbors to the north might not have liked the commotion, although they are only apparitions and don't seem to have much of a voice in things. On the other hand, even without the so-called Grand Lady of the Lake still standing there, these spirits probably did like it. After all, didn't Saltair in its hayday, house quite a rowdy force, the family-like atmosphere dissipating when the Church gave up its ownership? With the turn-of-the-century partying and the wild twenties, Saltair probably had quite a party going on all the time, at least during the summer months. The spirits and apparitions are probably rocking too! Recently, another fire, probably started by arson, burned the little riverboat gift shop, completely destroying it, and the rock concert enterprise went under too. I don't even know who owns it now, but all is quiet again out where the original Grand Lady of the Lake once resided.

A low-budget science fiction movie called *Neon City* starring Michael Ironside was later filmed here. It was also filmed mostly at the new Saltair and out on the Salt Flats. I haven't heard any specific ghost stories, although now that I am writing about Saltair, I might. But then I don't need to; empathic pieces of the past fly at me without warning. It is as if the lake will always have the last word on this. Spirits of the resort still populate the sands where it once stood in all its glory. They walk through and around you at every turn, especially when the place is quiet and deserted. There are unconfirmed rumors of a few suicide attempts and even one or two successful ones, but I imagine that many emotions linger there from the war years or soon after them and from those who found themselves alone in a contagiously happy crowd. Rumors of some kind of accident on the dance floor also persist, but don't seem to be given any credence with those who research Saltair's history. But there were certainly enough deaths, injuries, and tragedies for spirits to want to linger here, as well as enough joyous events for those few apparitions that might not wish to leave. Although Saltair is no longer there, the site of this beautiful and magnificent structure is. These spirits might simply be neighbors to those who frequent the tiny pavilion and gift shop next to where Saltair once stood, a disappointing echo of the main structure's magnificence. A few tourists stop by to look at the water and pick up a souvenir or two, wondering what all that rubble is along the shoreline to the north of them.

I remember Saltair now like most of us do, a memory that has been preserved as surreal pictures in my mind. There are spirits who dance on the lake, concession barkers who still sell foods and rides, and long ago bands and orchestras that still play their tunes as couples sway to their music. Swimmers and non-swimmers bob side by side in the salty lake that can support them both. Sunbathers recline on the hot sand after rinsing off the salt and tiny brine shrimp that sting and irritate their skin. There are whisperings of young lovers lost to more than one world war. Children's voices can be heard laughing and screaming as they dive into the salty water. Carnival music and dinner conversation can be heard as the clinking of glasses is heard clearly as it reverberates through the water. The smells of amusement park foods permeate the air and the voices of people long past can be heard along the board-walks. These are all sights and sounds gone forever now. All of these echoes and shadows are gone to the lingering history of a place and yet they paint their stories in our minds or speak to us in soft voices which the night wind cannot cover. Those of us able to see or hear them, miss our chances to do so as the rising waters engulf the shoreline debris. The few visitors to the site talk quietly among themselves, probably disappointed by the ruins, debris, heat, and brine shrimp that are all that remains of Saltair today.

On a quiet evening, however, you can imagine just what it might have been like to stand on one of those balconies overlooking the Great Salt Lake and watch the sun's magnificent reflections spread out over it like a golden sheath of light. You can imagine the ghostly images of Rudy and Natacha, as they danced to an appreciative and overflowing crowd in the grand ballroom or floated in the lake roped off from the crowd. You can see all the long ago actors and actresses, boxers and entertainers, who once performed there and the big bands which appeared nightly. You can feel all the pathos and drama that huge crowds bring with them, see amusement park rides, and feel the sudden winds which swept up from nowhere and either destroyed or amused. You can picture the brilliant strings of lights, trains arriving and departing, and people out for a good time, ten thousand of them arriving on Saltair's opening day. You can spy a Moorish castle, unique for its time and place, built on or sometimes near, depending on her whims, Utah's own Dead Sea. The Grand Lady of the Lake that I never got to see in her glory days has left behind an essence of her being, although the buildings are gone forever.

Gregory Navarro commented on Saltair in a letter dated September of 1984. He isn't writing about when the place was alive with music and people, but about its twilight years, alone and abandoned and yet still beautiful against the lake setting. "From the abandoned pavilion on any evening excepting those in the dead of winter, one could see the most beautiful sunsets to be had anywhere. There was almost a mystical quality to the experience, to watch the sun sink into the lake at a distance, casting the waters into the same salmon color as the pavilion itself."[7]

Notes

1) Bagley, "Utah Territorial Politician Was the Wellspring of Many Scandals," February 15, 2004.

2) Gad, "Saltair, Great Salt Lake's Most Famous Resort," 1968.

3) Ibid., 200.

4) Cecil the Librarian, "Expanding Your World," radio broadcast, May 18, 2001.

5) Ibid., July 27, 2001.

6) Cecil the Librarian, "Expanding Your World," transcript, *Salt Lake Tribune*, September 2, 1967.

7) Gregory Navarro, September 7, 1984, quoted in McCormick, *Saltair*, 35.

Legends of Mount Timpanogos

Many, many years ago, the Native Americans who lived on the mountain gave a yearly human sacrifice to the great god, Timpanogos. One year the season was very dry, the crops would not grow, and the people were afraid. The people thought that Timpanogos was angry with them, so they chose several young girls who were very beautiful and from important families. They were blindfolded and each drew a pebble from a pottery dish. In this way, they hoped the one who drew the black pebble would appease the angry god. It was the chief's daughter who drew the black pebble. It was the well-loved and kind princess Utahna who was fated to climb the mountain and be sacrificed. Everyone was upset by the news and wanted someone else to go, but it was too late. Princess Utahna made her farewells to everyone and ascended the mountain. She was to wander the trails alone and then, when she got to the highest peak of the mountain, was to leap to her death into the crags below.

A young brave who had fallen in love with her followed her up the mountain and watched as she fasted and chanted and prayed. She cried out to Timpanogos, asking him to bring rain to her people. The young man watched her for a very long time and when it looked as if she were readying herself to leap to her death for the last leg of her journey, he jumped out from where he was hiding and begged her not to jump. Utahna believed that he was the great god himself and went with him to a beautiful cave in the mountain where she fell in love with him. They lived together in the cave for a year or two. Then one day, a bear wounded the young man and his princess bride knew for certain that he was mortal and not a god. She helped the wound to heal, and when she was certain that he was all right, she waited until he had fallen asleep that night. Very early the next morning, she ascended the last leg of the mountain alone.

Utahna waited for the sunrise as she stood on the highest peak. When the beautiful morning sun rose over the peak, she stretched her arms out and leapt into the crags below. The young man woke up, and finding her gone, followed her trail up the mountain to where she had leapt to her death. He climbed down to where her body lay broken and mangled and carried her back to the cave where they had lived together so happily. He then lay down beside her and took his own life too. As their two bodies slowly entwined and soaked into the earth over time, the cave in which they had dwelled so happily grew into something most beautiful. It was in this cave, among the beautiful formations and rainbow colors, that their two hearts grew into one and became the great heart of the Timpanogos Mountain. The legend of the Sleeping Lady has been told in various forms and genres over the years, the story always ending with a description of her gentle form which can be seen if one looks at the outline of the mountain at daybreak, her long hair draping down to the north and her face, breasts, and thighs forming the continuous outline of peaks across the top.[1]

Another version of the legend of Timpanogos goes like this. A great drought came upon the Nez Perce tribe. The powerful chief called a council fire and announced his plan to alleviate the famine. He would send one of his four sons in each of the four directions to ask for peace with other warring tribes so that the Nez Perce could hunt on their neighbors' lands. Each son drew his lot. The fourth son, Timpanac, was sent to the south. He was told to go beyond the Great Salt Lake to where a great mountain pass would provide a crystal clear fresh water lake under its snow-capped peak. He was to go down through the mountain pass to this lake and talk with the "Fisheaters" there. As he descended, he was aware of being followed by a young maiden. He met with the great chiefs. Then he was to journey around the valley to be shown the abundance of their land. His guide was to be the chief's beautiful daughter, Ucanogos, but there were those who were jealous of the couple—young braves who wished to court the beautiful Ucanogos and young maidens who wished to have a chance to know the handsome young stranger, Timpanac. Many voices were raised in protest at their union.

The old chief called a council fire of his own to decide what to do. He announced that anyone who wanted to marry his beautiful daughter would have to enter a contest that he had conceived. It would be a series of events that would last for three days and the young brave with the highest score would win the hand of his daughter in marriage. Each brave would travel alone with no weapons and little clothing. The first test would be who could return with the most game by that evening. Timpanac returned that evening dragging a big bear and won the first day's event. The second day was a race around the crystal lake and the first to return would win. Timpanac was first of course. The third day's contest was to climb east to the highest mountain peak and return before the setting sun. Ucanogos stood waiting for him by a cottonwood shelter near the stream where they had first met. She assured him that she would be waiting for him and warned him of the jealousy of the other braves and their expected treachery on this last day. Timpanac climbed on until a band of braves who had lain in wait for him attacked him. In the ensuing struggle, he took a misstep and fell to his death from the mountain. Realizing what they had done, they climbed down the mountain and partially confessed their crime. They said that Timpanac had attacked them and then slipped and fell by accident.

Ucanogos listened in silence, and the next morning she could not be found anywhere in camp. She followed the signs and climbed to where the attack had taken place. She chanted and cried to the Great Spirit to be allowed to follow her lover into eternity, where he surely must have gone into the beautiful high mountain emerald pools. Suddenly she saw her lover's face reflected there in the water. The Great Spirit's answer was a terrifying storm full of great thunderbolts and lightning that streaked across the whole valley and over the people down below. The Native Americans in the valley fell to their knees in terror and placed their faces into the earth. When the storm was over, Ucanogos was nowhere to be found, but in her place was the gentle outline of her body as she slept across the mountaintop. The Great Spirit told the people that from now on the two lovers would be seen towering above the people side by side. The twin peaks of Timpanac and Ucanogos joined together as one. Their name was to be from this time on Mount Timpanogos.[2]

The truth about Mount Timpanogos's name, however, is a lot less romantic than the legends, although probably just as interesting. Chamber of Commerce member Eugene L. "Timpanogos" Roberts is credited with starting the whole legend of Mount Timpanogos. It was 1922 and the Timpanogos Cave National Monument was about to be dedicated. Mr. Roberts thought the story might further the monument as a tourist attraction for the area, which of course it did. The great heart of Timpanogos cavern was incorporated into the story and the first version of the legend was published in a book by Mr. Roberts called *Timpanogos Wonder Mountain*. The stories inside were told at the caves for years and years and became mistaken for an authentic Native American legend.

The actual meaning of the word *Timpanogos* comes from various sources. One source is from the Tumpipanogosots, meaning "rocky canyon people," and refers to the Pagonauts (fisheaters) who were the two tribes of Utes who occupied the valley long before the white man. The Provo River was called the Timpanoquint and Utah Lake was called the Timpanogo. The original name for Mount Timpanogos was Paakaret or "very high mountain." Various components of the word's meaning itself have been offered by local historians, such as *tim* meaning peg or rock, *to-yab-by* meaning mountain, *tumpi* meaning rock, *panogos* meaning water mouth, *noquint* or *pah* meaning running, which led one historian to come up with the name Rocky Running River. Years later, another historian claimed that with the Ute names *tiimpana* meaning mouth and *nuu-ci* meaning people, it was therefore the word *Timpana-nuu-ci* or the canyon mouth people. When the Spanish came through the area, they named the mountain Sierra Blanca de Los Timpanogos or White Mountain of the Timpanogos. The present name, Timpanogos, was first recorded on Captain Howard Stansbury's 1849 maps. Even in the naming of the Timpanogos caves, there were several suggested titles such as Cave of the Crystal Chimes, Cave of Crystal Cliff, Fairy Caves, and Cave of Elves. Finally Timpanogos Wonder Cave was chosen and a bit later, the word *wonder* was dropped.[3]

I was born in Provo and lived on Cherry Lane until I was six years old. At that time, my father left his post at Brigham Young University, and essentially left his religion as well. Our house stood under the same mountain range, only a little farther south of Mount Timpanogos. We lived right above the towns of Highland and Alpine. We visited the caves more than once when I was small, taking the long climb to the top where the caves are located. There was nothing in those days between our backyard and the foothills in Provo. We children climbed about in those foothills all the time, returning to our cherry orchards whenever we tired of the mountain's entertainments. In the winter, we would watch the deer come down from the mountains early in the morning and eat the leftover carrots in my mother's vegetable garden outside the kitchen window. It was a magical time for a child, being the late 1950s before all of the stresses and responsibilities of our modern day technological world. In the end, we all grew away from not only our parents' roots, but also away from the mountains. Our parents had both grown up with the mountains and left them as time went on. They left a world where nothing was ever questioned, and everything seemed to be in its rightful place. So to me, Mount Timpanogos represents a time before anything was changed or challenged, a comforting and magical land where everything was in its place and there was nothing frightening or strange to contend with. Ghosts and spirits have roamed those foothills and mountains for over a hundred years, the ghosts of men and women who came to this valley and others to settle the West, and the ghosts of the Native Americans before them.

In 1922, Timpanogos Cave National Monument was established. The caves are located above American Fork and the Timpanogos Storytelling Festival is held under their shadow every year. The first cave, Hansen Cave, was discovered in 1887. Timpanogos Cave was discovered in 1915 and Middle Cave was discovered in 1921. In the 1890s, an onyx company stripped the Hansen Cave of all of its mineral deposits and the Forest Service and other concerned groups began working to preserve its beauty. Tunnels connecting the three caves were dug in the 1930s to make it easier for visitors. The caves truly are a wonder. Long before the white man supposedly discovered them, the native peoples held them as quite sacred and therefore left them entirely alone. So it is no surprise to me that people have experienced all sorts of mystical phenomena within them. With a little stretch of the imagination, it's not hard to believe that these caves were born of a great love between a man and a woman just like the legend says.

There is a steep mile-and-a-half-long trail that takes visitors to the beginning of the cave tour. The hike takes about an hour. Tours sell out by early afternoon in the summer and as the day lengthens, the wait to climb lengthens. Stalactites, stalagmites, draperies, flow stone, and helicites cover floors, ceilings, and walls everywhere in these caves. The Chimes Chamber is full of helicites. The giant cave called The Great Heart of Timpanogos is full of stalactites joined together by draperies, as is the Camel Room. There are special flashlight tours, historic tours, and pool tours. The whole experience takes about three and a half miles of walking and three hours to complete. For thousands of years, these caves stood silent and hidden away from the outside world, a wonderland of nature's forces at work creating great, colorful beauty never seen in daylight.

Speleologists, the modern term for cave experts, devote their lives to exploring the mysteries of caves such as these. The white settlers were not the first to discover these caves, although they might think so. The fact that nothing was left behind is not proof that no one had been there. Native Americans, having strong beliefs about not disturbing sacred places, are good at this. They often visit a place and leave no signs of having been there. But the belief in not disturbing such sacred places may not have deterred the occasional wanderer or a Native American on a vision quest to find his spiritual path. Some of these people might have stumbled onto at least one of these caves long before any settlers had set eyes on these particular mountains.

When I sought to know if anyone had been to these caves before the settlers discovered them, this was the image that I received. A young Native American man had explored at least the first cave, completely awed by his own very personal vision quest there. Why I would see this particular young Native American is beyond me, although I see him clearly wandering about in the darkness, occasionally making some kind of light to see the various formations and in the mean time finding out his path in life. I also saw that his life was tragically cut short by a great world war. I don't often know the connection in a historical vision, but I strongly feel that there always is one. Whatever the young man wanted me to see, I was seeing through his eyes all those many years ago. Perhaps he had a message to deliver to someone who was close to him, or perhaps he simply wanted me to know that he, or at least a part of him, was there right then. Sometimes an answer comes to me, and sometimes I never do understand.

In 1887, forty-year-old settler Martin Hansen, took a hike up the mountain to cut timber. He followed the tracks of a mountain lion to a high ledge and discovered a small entrance to a cave. He did not go in that day but came back later with others to explore. He and his friends hacked out a steep trail straight up the mountainside so that others could explore the cave. Within a few years though, people had stripped the cave for souvenirs that they either took home or sold to museums and universities. In 1913, a group of families from Lehi, Utah, came for a day's outing to explore the cave. Two of their teenage sons went off by themselves and stumbled onto another cave entrance after climbing around a steep slope. These two boys, James W. Gough and Frank Johnson, and a man named John Hutchings filed a mining claim in 1915 on these caves, naming it the Lone Star Lode Claim. However, for some reason James Gough walled off the entrance and forgot about the caves. Timpanogos Cave was explored by various other brave souls, but general knowledge of it remained a secret until August of 1921 when an outdoor club from Payson rediscovered the cave.

Verl J. Manwill was a member of this club and the first to take an interest in preserving these two caves from more vandalism while making them more accessible to the general public. The night that they rediscovered the cave, the people around their campfire dedicated themselves to finding a way to keep this cave from being ruined like the Hansen Cave had been. That fall, George Heber Hansen and Wayne E. Hansen, son and grandson of Martin, found the third cave, eventually named Middle Cave. They had been deer hunting and looking through binoculars when they discovered another entrance. In 1922, several groups of citizens and the U.S. Forest Service urged the United States government to do something to preserve the caves. That year, President Warren G. Harding issued a proclamation establishing the caves as a national monument.

During this period of time, a trail was constructed and electric lights were installed. In 1923, a telephone system was installed to connect the base with the cave entrance. In the 1930s, the three caves were joined together for easier access. From 1922 to 1934 the Forest Service ran the caves, although they were actually operated by the Timpanogos

Outdoor Committee, a local group of businessmen that Verl J. Manwill helped put together. In 1934, the National Park Service began taking over operations and assumed complete control in 1947. Today the caves are open from May to October. Thousands of visitors from all over the world visit Timpanogos.

Drop by drop, over thousands of years, water leaked into the caves to form these natural wonders. Scientists predict that in another two hundred years, some of the ceiling and floor formations will join together. One of the mysteries of the cave is the helicites, the colorful, needle-like structures. Scientists have debated for years on just how these structures form against the force of gravity. Are the spiral crystals formed from mineral deposits on a spider web or fungi? Are they the result of electrical forces in the cave or cave winds? Or do they form from earth tremors? They could also be formed from water forces, as modern-day scientists believe. This theory states that water is pushed and pulled up the helicites' tiny central canal by hydrostatic pressure that goes against the force of gravity.

An intriguing highlight of the caves is the largest stalactites and stalagmites that are joined together in the Hansen Cave in a thirteen-foot column. Some of these various formations have quite colorful names: Cascade of Energy, Chocolate Fountain, Frozen Sunbeam, and Cave Popcorn. Then there are the underground pools like crystal clear mirrors reflecting the cave formations around them in the lighted caves. There are thirty such pools and lakes that have been discovered within the whole system of caves. Special tours take visitors to see them. Cave divers would love discovering more of them if they were allowed.

These natural wonders are indeed something to be awed by. I don't think that we have been the first to see them, nor will we be the last. I also feel that one more cave is yet to be discovered in the area. The mystical quality of the earth's treasures assures that we will never solve all of her mysteries, or come to understand our existence among them, at least not for a very great while. When I was there as a little girl, the darkness frightened me too much for me to enjoy myself. But as an adult, I find the caves fascinating, surreal, and certainly mystical. I feel as though beings other than the live ones are walking around, coming up to touch me on the shoulder and assure me that the place is still being guarded. I feel that the natural wonders there attract those, both living and not so "living," who love great beauty. I believe that spirits are around us in those caves at every moment. I am surrounded and enraptured by things both otherworldly and of this world. As I walk through such caves, I wish for the silence that would surely bring me more knowledge than I can receive in a crowd.

Things have changed for me since the days of my childhood, as they have for all of us. Yet when I stand in those caves, I remember my first time there, how our family climbed together to the top, back when my mother and I could take such a climb. We walked down into the deep dark bowels of the mountain to see nature's great beauties and wonders. The darkness frightened me, but when the lights went on and I could see the formations and the colors, it was wonderful. All of this came long before I knew that I could feel or see in the dark. I thought then that everyone else was feeling and seeing what I was and how wonderful it all was. I did not know then that only a few could see those shadows in the dark, though the basic ability is available to all of us. Our eyes have to be opened and our hearts have to beat in rhythm with the heart of the cave.

I later saw a documentary in which a group of researchers brought in several well-known psychics to "read" the same woman. She had six people in mind that she wanted to hear from who had passed on, although she had absolutely no experience with this kind of thing before and was somewhat skeptical. All five psychics identified and gave accurate information about each of the six people. The psychics weren't allowed to see each other or talk to each other beforehand and each one read separately with the woman. Both the subject and the psychics had their vital signs monitored. The only clues that could have been given would have been in the tone of voice as the subject was instructed only to answer yes or no and the psychics were not allowed to ask any questions.

The findings were impressive and the psychics were overjoyed to have participated in one of the first carefully structured and monitored lab tests to understand what happens during these exchanges. Most impressive was that all of the psychic mediums' brain wave patterns went into a sleep-like state and matched like overlays on a graph. The psychics' brain wave patterns also matched those of the subject. The researchers found strong evidence that the heart beat of every psychic was soon beating in exactly the same rhythm as the woman's heart. In other words, they had literally established a heart-to-heart connection that remained until the reading stopped, at which point the heart rhythms returned to their normal rates.

It is in the balance of things that we can feel and see both the terrors and the great mysteries while being humbled before them. Both the mountain and the caves will always hold a special place as one of the symbols of my own awakening mind and heart. As for the spirits, we all need to go to the caves to have our own experience, because they are definitely there waiting.

Notes

1) Thompson, *Indians of Utah*, 41.

2) Walker, "The Legend of Timpanogos."

3) Horrocks, "Timpanogos Cave: The Origin of the Word and the Name."

Spirits of the Deserts

Canyonlands National Park

Canyonlands National Park is located southeast of Moab and directly west of the La Sal Junction off Highway 191. Newspaper Rock can be seen from the Canyon Rims Recreation Area on Route 211 about thirty-six miles into the Canyonlands National Parks area. Continuing on down the highway past Blanding but before Bluff, there is a turn-off on Highway 262 for Hovenweep. Monticello is almost exactly in the middle between Moab and Bluff on Highway 191, where the turn off for the former Highway 666 goes east into Colorado. Not only do the local Native Americans consider the entire area sacred, but legend has it that there is a definite balance between good and evil here. It's the sort of place where a person can make choices, choosing which path to go down. Both skin walkers and followers of the black arts supposedly wander this area. One can see crows everywhere. Crows are a considered to be very mystical creatures. They are always fascinated by their own shadows and are said to be a favorite form of shape shifters.

Crows are considered the gatekeepers of the mystical world. They are the guardians of ancient records or sacred laws for many tribes and have the special talent of being able to be two places consciously during a single moment of time. Therefore, they can observe what is going on without others observing or noticing them. My part–Northern Cheyenne husband seems to attract them. We have noticed over the years that whenever we are traveling together in wide-open spaces, crows are everywhere along our path. Apparently crow medicine people are masters of illusion and if we obey the sacred laws of the crow in life, we are promised a good medicine death with a clear memory of one's past. Crows also have the ability to look into the future. If they allow the dark side to overtake them, they can become spoilers and breakers of the sacred laws and use their abilities to bring about great harm to others. If they break their own self-truths, they can cause themselves and those around them great emotional pain. Start watching when you go to such a sacred area and you will see crows everywhere watching and observing you.[1]

Canyonlands is filled with sacred sites from the Valley of the Gods to the Valley of Goblins. Just like Bryce and Zion National Parks, many a nature lover or New Ager will travel to this area to meditate among all of the canyon's natural wonders, especially in Chesler Park in the Needles-Salt Creek District in the southern part of the park. Roads through Salt Creek and Horse Canyons are still primitive, but will lead to such wonderful names as Confluence Overlook, Beef Basin, Lavender and Davis Canyons, as well as Chesler Park. Angel and Druid Canyons are nearby, as well as a cowboy camp called Cave Spring. Chester Park has huge columns of sandstone and is a thirty square mile maze of convoluted rock canyons with tiny primitive dirt roads that, while harrowing, have claimed amazing power to change a traveler's state of consciousness entirely. Both Orrin Porter Rockwell's and Zane Grey's ghosts are said to haunt this area along with Bryce and Zion Canyons, their favorite places to vacation.

One interesting claim about Canyonlands National Park is that there is a joint alien-military base underneath the Druid Arch area. This belief comes from UFO organizations' and researchers' claims that there is a vast network of underground caverns stretching from the various southern Utah national parks to the Mojave Desert in California. While geologists say that the caverns are not connected, many not only believe that they are, but that dozens of top-secret military or alien bases are housed in these caverns deep under the earth and are connected by a vast subterranean highway. The unusual phenomena reported in the Druid Arch area include men posing as park rangers to keep people from going to certain public areas, many UFO sightings and manifestations, as well as high levels of electromagnetic energy that have affected all sorts of electronic equipment brought to the area. The craziest report says there are invisible military personnel that can only be seen as a reflection in a mirror. There are also people who believe that some of the projects from Area 51 have been moved to the Moab, Utah, and the Canyonlands National Park underground area.

While this national park houses both sacred beliefs and UFO conspiracies, it is also a gorgeous place to visit. The early Paiutes told tales of the Hav-musuvs, an ancient people who chose to dwell inside of mountains in deep caverns. There are stories told of Paiutes abducted and taken deep into these cavern cities never to return. One legend tells of a tribal chief's wife who died. The chief decided to take a spiritual journey to the underground dwellers to find his wife. After a long journey, he located his wife and led her out of the caverns. Although he'd been warned not to, he looked back at her. Because he broke this rule, he was forbidden by the cavern dwellers to bring his wife back from the dead. Apparently these ancient cavern dwellers abandoned their upper cities and journeyed even deeper into the earth to establish new dwellings. According to some, it is possible that the descendents of the cave dwellers still live deep under the earth. Others assume that not just aliens and military personnel live under the earth in this area, but also our own American brand of druids live deep under the arch to this day.

Newspaper Rock

The name Newspaper Rock came from the fact that this enormous boulder has hundreds of ancient symbols and writings on it. The petroglyphs depict various animals and scenes. Some of the animals have six-toed feet. They are, of course, considered spiritual or sacred writings to the Native American descendents who live in the area. The mysterious writings enthrall everyone though because no one has been able to translate what this rock has to tell us. Perhaps someday, the symbols will be translated. What it has to say may be no more than practical everyday messages of people passing by the area. It might be a signpost where travelers and nomads left directions for others, or even silly writings like those on a public restroom wall. On the other hand, maybe they are what they seem and have some great and profound messages for mankind, or at least information about how people lived then, long before any of us came to be. But no matter, this is still considered a sacred place in Utah.

Dead Horse Point

Valley of the Gods and Goblin Valley contain freestanding stones much taller than any human. The formations resemble people standing about in clusters. There is a series of three valleys where you can call out from the rim of one and hear the echo return loud and clear through all three. The point is shaped like a blunt arrowhead and is quite level. It's about thirty yards wide at the neck and up to four hundred yards at its widest. The two gorges on either side are about a thousand feet at their deepest point, but they narrow into nothing as one gazes out over the five hundred square miles of the reddish Colorado Plateau. Dead Horse Point Park I remember from my childhood because of the stories from my mother's uncles who were all cowboys, as was her father when he was a very young man out on the Kaibab Plateau in Kane County. They would tell stories about herding horses out on the range and tell us all about their experiences out in the Dead Horse Point area. I listened to these stories without a bit of the adult understanding that these were like fishermen's highly exaggerated tales. The stories got better and more outrageous as the afternoon went on. So it was a surprise to hear the real story behind Dead Horse Point because I had believed the story of the horses being literally herded off the cliff to their deaths. I thought of my uncles as awful men who had participated in the dirty deed. But this was a child's memory of things, and it became all mixed up in my imagination.

The real tale of Dead Horse Point makes a little more sense. It got its name from a band of wild horses herded to this point. The best of the herd or the "broom tails" were culled for cow service and the rest were returned to the range. The released horses were confused by the unfamiliar topography and found themselves wandering in circles until they eventually died of thirst. The irony was that the Colorado River was only a half-mile away but straight down. The park is on the rim of the Orange Cliffs escarpment, a line of wingate sandstone cliffs that winds between the Green and upper Colorado Rivers. Even in the 1940s, it was referred to as "the edge of a howling wilderness" because it was such a remote and primitive region. Nowadays, there are campgrounds, a visitors' center, and visitors traversing the dirt roads headed for river trips.

The legend of Dead Horse Point is the most interesting of all. It is said that the apparitions of the dead horses appear quite often to whoever stands there, especially on foggy or frosty days. They appear as distant shapes in the mist and then slowly form into horses that stare eerily and then slowly fade away from view. People claim to have heard their mournful neighs and cries out at the point but more often they are seen rather than heard. Some even claim that the horses have materialized right before them and have actually been mistaken for real horses. The misty horses intrigue me much more than the solid ones, as there is an unusual quality to this type of apparition.

Just recently there was an article in the local paper about Dead Horse Point. It explained all the new exhibits in an effort to entice more tourists to the area. There is a new visitors' center thirty-two miles from Moab. The exhibits are being filled with geology, wildlife, plants, and history of the area. This human pre-history will naturally include the legend of Dead Horse Point. The visitors' center's explanation for the name, Dead Horse Point, is the same as the others: that in the late 1800s, cowboys used the promontory as a natural corral for wild mustangs. While the best horses were broken, rejects were left to fend for themselves. Once, according to this story, a group of horses refused to leave, eventually dying of thirst. The visitors' center has plans for many interactive exhibits for children, and many people will want to see the place where Tom Cruise climbed, to the right of the point overlook, in the movie *Mission Impossible II*.

Nowadays, the point is used by hang gliders and was the site of Moab's World Invitational Hang Gliding Tournament in 1978. Hang gliders say it is like stepping off from solid ground into a gust of wind coming up the sheer cliff. The rim is only partially fenced off and the vertical drop is just a little over four hundred feet. People are constantly being warned to stay away from the edge of the cliff and several people have fallen to their deaths there. So the real tale of Dead Horse Point is not just about wild horses but about people who have tripped and fallen there, playing Russian roulette with the rim of the point.[2]

An interesting side story to the Dead Horse Point legend is about a little known canyon called Black Box on the San Rafael River. This deep gorge is located near Crescent Junction. "A man named Sid Swazy inhabited these wild lands in the late 1800s. A bit of a daredevil, he lept the chasm of the river on his horse at a point about three miles north of I-70's current path. The drop to the river was said to be about 100 feet at the time. Both man and horse survived to ride on to other amazing adventures. The spot is listed on some maps as Swazys Leap."[3]

Hovenweep National Monument

Hovenweep National Monument consists of six Anasazi ruin clusters with two of them in Utah and four of them in Colorado. The word *Hovenweep* means "deserted valley" in the Ute language. The area was occupied by the Basketmaker culture from about AD 250 and by the Pueblo culture starting around AD 1300. It is believed that the people left the area to search for better or more permanent water sources. What makes Hovenweep unique are its towers. There are two types of towers: isolated ones, often found in pairs and lighted by portholes or small windows; and integrated towers associated with a series of rooms or *kivas*. Speculations on what these towers were used for range from the practical to the mystical, from lookout towers, defense posts, granaries, and homes, to ceremonial and religious structures or celestial observatories. It was discovered recently that some of the portholes or windows do align during the solstices and equinoxes.[4]

Hovenweep is in the remote canyon country north of the San Juan River and was established as a national monument by a presidential proclamation in 1923. The main ruins are in Ruin and Cajon Canyons in Utah and in Hackberry and Keeley Canyons in Colorado. It is sometimes called the Sage Plains because of the thick stands of sage growing from three to five feet high in places. The missionary explorers Escalante and Dominguez passed through this area in the 1770s and by the 1870s the ruins had been rediscovered by fur trappers and traders roaming the area. The first settlers from The Church of Jesus Christ of Latter-day Saints, often referred to as the Mormons, reached the valley by 1880 and when many of them left, the stockmen remained in the area. The ruins had been thoroughly looted by around 1910 and the first archeologists to visit the area were hoping to protect them. Ruin Canyon contains the most ruins and clusters of buildings in the area and is sometimes called Square Tower Canyon. The towers all have very interesting names: Hovenweep House, Hovenweep Castle, Stronghold House, Boulder House, and Twin Towers. It has also been suggested that if some of the towers were used as solar observatories, perhaps the people worshipped the sun and carried out celebrations and rites within their kivas to both the sun and to mother earth.

Intuitives say that Hovenweep is indeed a sacred site haunted by the spirits of those who carried out these holy rituals. They say that certain towers were indeed used as astronomical observatories to determine when selected religious ceremonies were to take place, and that these beings still carry out these rituals either actively or as residual energy within the towers at Hovenweep. Native American holy men say that you can sit within or near a tower and feel the energy of the sun bringing its power into your being, so you feel energized and renewed to return to what lies ahead. They say that one visit to the towers can produce visions, to lead the way to new understandings and spiritual shifts. In the ancient times, it is said that "on the morning of the summer solstice, rays of light illuminate drawings of the sun, a snake, and a human twin figure. Different patterns of light illuminate the symbols at the spring and fall equinoxes" and that "the ancient ones' deep reverence for nature and the mystical heavens is easily felt in this serene national park."[5]

The road to Hovenweep is on Route 666, and although it has been newly named, it is still fraught with myths and legends of its own. And it is the only way to get there! It goes through all the bean fields by Dove Creek, Colorado, and then you wind around back into Utah from Cortez. Hovenweep has been compared to the medieval castles found along the Rhine River in Germany but without the moats. There is a new visitors' center for the 45,000 annual visitors to the park. The old center was a tiny log cabin, but the new one might bring many more tourists to the area, which is both good and bad. More visitors will provide much needed financial support but will also bring more tourists, making the area less secluded.

Hovenweep was highlighted in a recent article in *Utah Preservation* magazine. The debate continued on how to preserve the eight-hundred-year-old towers in the park. Archaeologists believe the Pueblos made the move to protect their water sources. In stories passed down through the generations, this meant moving into the openings in the earth that took the form of valleys. The Pueblos knew they could find water or seepage of water in the world below them. There is always an abundance of water provided for them under the earth. By protecting the earth's water sources, they would be closer to the next world. As the amounts of water dwindled in this world, they had to move closer to the next world by going deeper and deeper into the valleys. The square tower group is built at the head of the canyon seep while the highest tower, Square Tower, sits on top of a boulder. This is the highest point in Little Ruin Canyon, and the center of a little universe where water was of the greatest importance.[6]

President Warren G. Harding called these ruins the finest example of ancient masonry work in the United States when he dedicated the place as a national monument in 1923. The bricks were pecked into shape with stone tools and then stacked together with mud mortar and covered with mud plaster. The fingerprints of the ancient brick builders can still be seen in the mortar. Attempts have been made in the past to stabilize the towers before they fall. Steel reinforcements were placed in the 1940s and concrete walls were built in the 1960s. In the 1990s, erosion was discovered at the base of the towers and several plans were carried out to save the towers: workers modified the environment, reinforced walls, removed landfill, installed drainage tubes, and cleaned up surfaces. While a drainage crew was working on the south side of the tower, they discovered a previously unknown kiva and stopped their work immediately. This discovery further confirmed the spiritual nature of the towers.

All work currently underway is considered non-invasive measures to preserve the site without destroying it. One Pueblo elder finds this to be a paradox. The canyon itself, he explains, is a corridor between worlds. "Their ancestral kiva and tower which are, by the way, one and the same, are religious vehicles within these natural corridors that will run their course or live their lives depending on the will of the landscape." Hovenweep is "still living, it's still doing everything it was intended to do; it's just not doing it with people . . . The towers and kivas were built to connect to the world below. The seep is still interacting with those structures to the point that some of them are deteriorating, which leaves us in the National Park Service in the position where we intervene."[7]

Hovenweep's legends and myths are easy to imagine, although the ancients who left their signs are often misinterpreted. Hovenweep is far from anywhere. Houses on the White Mesa Ute Reservation dot the desert with a few goats and scrawny cows scattered about. It is an interesting drive through various cultures such as those of Moab, Monticello, Bluff, and Blanding. Way out there somewhere comes the turn off to Hovenweep where we drove and drove and drove through the desert wondering just how far each mile might be. When we finally got there, the staff was three weeks away from moving into their brand new visitors' center over the hill. The new center is an adobe-style dwelling with a parking lot and even a campground. It was about a hundred degrees or so even early in the morning. We took a very short walk around because visitors cannot drive around the forked arroyo. My husband did his video cam walk while I stayed in the shade and let the ancients talk to me.

These are the things that were said or given to me there. The usual buzzing noise in my ears, which tells me that I am in an active place, began much louder and stronger than most that I have experienced. A chant or rhythm came to me that I tried to write down or at least commit to memory. The number five figured prominently: five clans, five different eras or tribes, and five important towers. The wind got my attention several times and within it was a type of singing and the thought that the spirits often sang there. As I looked at the mortar or tiny pieces of clay wedged between the stones, and knowing that perhaps renovations have changed this, I was still shown a picture of little children putting in the mortar pieces. I was told that this was their duty and that they made it into a game that all the children played. They learned to count in this way.

I traveled in my mind's eye into the caves down below where the people lived. I could hear more chanting, a chanting that became so loud that it echoed down through the little canyon. I was told that this brought a welcome to me and that nothing evil was there and that every day messages would be delivered. I asked about the towers and they simply said they were built for defense but also for food storage to keep things cool, dry, and preserved. Only one tower was built to worship the sun, a large one wherein they sang and chanted to send a special echo up to the sky. This was also done as a warning to other tribes and was used as a defense to protect them from their enemies. Again the number five, five places that were of greater importance and interest than all the rest: Hovenweep Castle, Square Tower, Stronghold House, Unit House, and Boulder House. Boulder House and Boulder Tower were somehow connected with one meaning.

Present-day interpretations of these places from the experts yield the following ideas. The castle was build around AD 1200 and was the home of several farming families. It was also used for astronomical observations for seasonal planting information from the position of the sun. The square's functions are unknown, although experts speculate that they were for signaling, observing enemies, and making astronomical observations. All that is known about the stronghold is that it is larger than the rest of the towers and that its rooms were once connected by a giant log walkway. There were two rooms within each section. The unit-type house dates from the Pueblo period (AD 900–AD 1100). It is a single kiva with an additional room, which was used to indicate the dates of summer and winter solstices. The boulder formations consist of a home below and the remains of a tower above.

The community was built down the canyon that forks into two branches, one longer than the other. Side Canyon is the shorter fork and Little Ruin Canyon is the longer one. I stood by the end of the longer fork, but I didn't realize that this was the area where I heard spirits talking until I looked at the map much later. "In here we stood our last defense," they said. The towers were three stories high with a sort of ladder to each. There were hooks of some kind inside the walls with which to stand or hang things. "We did not leave of our own accord. The river dried up and left us," they said. There are eight graves of little children up the long canyon in the lower part of it and this is the town burial area. Three clans left and two stayed for a short while after. "We were weavers, only no one seems to know this," I heard. Then I saw in my mind's eye what appeared to be slices of dried bark or weeds that were to be woven into satchels and baskets. "The children are in the dry creek bed . . . eight of them. Find them, and honor them," the spirits pleaded.

As I stood there, three different spirits approached me from behind. It was as casual as passing other people at a shopping mall, only I was out of time and place here. The first was a middle-aged man who walked quietly up behind me and placed his hand on my shoulder to get my attention. I am assuming that it was he who spoke all of the words and phrases that I am writing here. Next, a curious little girl ran by me and then an old woman came and told me about the special ceremonial weaving. And last, more than one little child ran behind me and playfully tapped me on the backs of my legs. All of them whispered, but I only heard a little because the heat was getting to me. Delusions in the desert, some would say, though I know differently now. Spiris who said, "Sometimes we danced until our feet pounded the earth so hard that thunder could be heard as an echo."

Notes

1) Sams and Carson, *Medicine and Sacred Path Cards*, 133–35.
2) Roylance, *Utah: A Guide to the State*, 719–20.
3) Bennett, *Roadside History Utah*, 351.
4) Powell et al., *Utah History Encyclopedia*, 262–63.
5) Hauck, *Haunted Places*, 409.
6) Nystrom, "The Conservation of Hovenweep's Square Towers," 32–35.
7) Ibid., 35.

Anasazi Indian Village

Twenty-nine miles from Escalante, Utah, is the small grouping of farms and houses known as Boulder, Utah. Boulder was settled in 1894 and named for the volcanic rock on the slopes of Boulder Mountain on the Aquarius Plateau. In 1880, Captain Clarence E. Dutton wrote about this plateau in his book, *Report on the Geology of the High Plateaus of Utah*.

> The Aquarius should be described in blank verse and illustrated upon canvas. The explorer who sits upon the brink of its parapet looking off into the southern and eastern haze, who skirts its lava-cap or clambers up and down its vast ravines, who builds his camp-fire by the borders of its snow-fed lakes or stretches himself beneath its giant pines and spruces, forgets that he is a geologist and feels himself a poet . . . we are among forests of rare beauty and luxuriance; the air is moist and cool, the grasses are green ran rank, and the hosts of flowers deck the turf like the hues of a Persian carpet. The forest opens in wide parks and winding avenues, which the fancy can easily people with fays and woodland nymphs . . . Upon the broad summit are numerous lakes— not the little morainal pools, but broad sheets of water a mile or two in length. Their basins were formed by glaciers, and since the ice-cap which once covered the whole plateau has disappeared they continue to fill with water from the melting snows . . . It is a sublime panorama.[1]

In *Utah, A Guide to the State,* Ward J. Roylance describes the beginnings of the small town of Boulder.

> For years after settlement the tiny town was isolated from the world by towering walls of solid rock, 35 miles by pack train from Escalante. A man packed in a pickup truck, in pieces, reassembled it, and ran it eight years without a license; gasoline, also "imported" on pack horses cost seventy-five cents a gallon. In 1923, President Harding set aside 130 acres of public domain for a townsite, but a survey was neglected, and for nearly ten years the residents were legally "squatters," immune from taxation.[2]

For years, the stories of the *Moquis* or "little people" in the area persisted. In a very old Hopi legend, the Moquis were a race of people even smaller than the Hopi. While the Hopi stood four feet to five feet two or three inches, the Moquis were only three feet tall. Like Leprechauns or sprites, they liked to cause trouble for the tribal members. They were the poltergeists of the Hopi. Many stories, both funny and serious, were told about these little people. They lived in the local canyons, the people's storage granaries, and in the river bottoms in their own special Moqui houses. They were very mischievous and feisty. In the area around Escalante, they got to be such a nuisance that the local tribe waged war against them and won. The last of the Moquis were rounded up and run off the Kaiparowits Plateau, nicknamed Fifty Mile Mountain. They fell into the Colorado River, never to return. There is even one local cowboy story that says cowboys from the Nutter and Wilcox ranches gunned down the last of the Moquis who had survived the fall hundreds of years before.

Inside the city limits of Boulder is a six-acre state park that contains an ancient Anasazi village on top of a mesa. The word *Anasazi* means either enemy ancestors or ancestral Puebloans. A good water supply, fertile farm land, and a defensible area provided plenty of wood, rock, and wild game to sustain over two hundred tribal members for approximately seventy-five years on the 6,700-foot high mesa. Like all mysteries surrounding this ancient people, this village simply disappeared after AD 1300. There are a number of ideas as to what caused them to leave. It could have been exhaustion, wars, famine, climate changes, natural migrations to ancestral homes, or all these reasons combined. The Anasazi were recognized for their unique architecture and mysterious religion that involved, among other things, rudimentary astronomy and sun worship. Their main diet was maize along with beans, squash, gourds, berries, and wild game. They were also known as the Cliff Dwellers.

The first official investigation of this site was conducted from 1926 to 1927 by the Peabody Museum, although locals knew about the place for many years and regularly went out to the area to hunt for arrowheads and artifacts. The first report on the site was filed in 1930. Between 1958 and 1959, the University of Utah excavated the site and found eighty-seven rooms. Covered in plastic, the excavation remained incomplete until 1978 when the project was resumed. The village was made a state park in 1960; however, the site has never been fully excavated and work has continued on a small scale for years. The small museum was constructed in front of the site in 1970. When the villagers abandoned their homes, they burned them down. It is estimated that there were around one hundred dwellings on the site with approximately five people per dwelling. Before the repatriation law, there were several Native American skeletons on display in the museum and one in particular gained much interest among the locals and visitors. She was eventually nicknamed "the princess."

When they found the princess in the late 1950s, she was discovered to be around fourteen or fifteen years old. Since life expectancy at that time was the middle thirties, it is likely that she was already married and may have had children. The unusual thing about the princess is that she had been mummified. Female mummies were a rare find and her funerary finery was extraordinary. Amazing artifacts were literally piled over her, indicating that she had been of great importance in the tribe. The circumstances of the princess's burial engendered many stories over the years since. Had she been a great leader or holy woman? Or had she been the wife of a prominent man in the tribe? Had she simply had more wealth than others? Even more speculative, had the people buried so much on top of her to insure that her spirit would never make it to the surface? More and more tales were told about the princess displayed at the museum. People even claimed to have been there when she was found, to know what she looked like in life, and even to know that she had been buried in a bluebird feather blanket.

In the years that followed, her spirit began to be heard, felt, and even seen inside the museum walls. One man who led wilderness trips from Brigham Young University spent a night or two inside the museum while waiting for his students to return from their overnight survivalist experience. He had such a frightening experience that he decided to sleep outside from then on. He would not share what happened, but did say this experience made him look differently at such things. Tour guides also told stories, a favorite being that her spirit was tied to where she was buried until she was excavated, and then her spirit wandered the village, especially the museum, at night. A few have claimed to have seen the pretty, petite young woman with long black hair walking around the museum in the evening hours when most of the staff had gone. She became a legend to locals and visitors alike.

In 1990, the princess, like so many other legends of her kind, disappeared from the museum for a very good reason. The Federal Native American Repatriation Law was passed mandating that no Native American burial remains could be displayed in a public place and that if a tribal members wanted to claim their ancestors, they could. The remains could then be buried in a place of the descendents' choice. For the tribes in Utah who want to claim remains and do not have a place to bury them, the state has created an underground vault in Emigration Canyon near Hogle Zoo where such remains may be buried. However, what actually happened is that most of these skeletons, which could not be displayed, ended up in the basements or storage areas of local universities, lying there unclaimed and forgotten. The princess went into the recesses of the University of Utah and remains there until a local tribe wishes to claim her. Perhaps they will, if her notoriety is remembered and there is a symbolic reason to bury her elsewhere.

Lost Bird was one of the infant survivors of the massacre at Wounded Knee. She lay under her dead mother's body, sealed by her frozen blood in a warm air pocket, for four days after the massacre. Her faint cries were heard and she was rescued unharmed. She was adopted by the white Brigadier General Leonard W. Colby. The General was disappointed that he had not been associated with the massacre and thought this adoption would provide another notch on his political "belt." His suffragette wife, Clara Colby, knew nothing of the adoption until this little girl arrived at her doorstep. Lost Bird grew up with whites, but was displayed across the nation and even had an audience with the Queen of England in Native American costume. Her white father sexually abused her before leaving to live full-time with his mistress, whom he eventually married when she received her own inheritance. Meanwhile, Clara raised the child alone, occasionally sending Lost Bird off to private schools. Clara Colby was quite busy herself as a newspaper editor and women's rights leader. Later, she became an outspoken advocate against the exploitation of Native American culture, against the advice of her good friends, Susan B. Anthony and Elizabeth Cady Stanton. Eventually, Clara found Lost Bird just too difficult to manage and abandoned the child to an Native American school where more abuse took place.

Lost Bird's life ended at the tender age of twenty-nine after years of performing in the Buffalo Bill Wild West Show and silent films. She died on the streets of the Barbary Coast in 1920, after her first husband had infected her with syphilis and her second husband had physically abused her. She had three children, two died very young and the third disappeared into history, his fate unknown. Having never found peace or love in her life, Lost Bird searched for the fate of her real parents and relatives, but never found out who they were. To her ancestral tribe, she represented all of the adopted Native American children who had not been able to celebrate their own ancestry and culture. Renee Sansom Flood put Lost Bird's story in writing and eventually located her grave in a tiny California town. The sexton found no marker to indicate her burial, but Flood insisted that Lost Bird was in the plot. Finally, he poked a long stick several feet into the ground and struck something. It was Lost Bird's gravestone.

Flood wrote to the people Lost Bird had come from, the Lakota Sioux, and they responded with great interest. In 1990, her remains were flown across the country wrapped in a lavender star quilt and accompanied by a group of Native American holy men, tribal leaders, Wounded Knee Survivors Association members, and Lost Bird Society members. The Bigfoot Memorial Riders met the party at Porcupine Butte and carried the body in a horse drawn wagon to the burial site at Wounded Knee. A "release of the spirit" ceremony was performed for her and all her sisters and brothers who had lost their identities through white adoptions. A large stone covers her new gravesite at the Wounded Knee Memorial. As one of the few survivors of the massacre, she represents all of the lost children. Flood, wife of a Lakota Sioux, says that while she was researching and writing Lost Bird's story she had an inexplicable and repetitive dream. In the dream, a little Native American girl dressed up in her Sunday best with a white dress and a large white bow on her head was riding a carousel around and around. The author always woke up at this point, wondering what the dream meant. After the book came out, a resident of the neighborhood where Lost Bird had been raised told the author he remembered stories about the little girl from his mother. He remembered how his mother would watch the little girl ride the carousel in town for hours and hours. She had no friends and was sometimes made fun of, so instead of playing with the other children, she rode this carousel around and around until her mother came to get her for dinner.

The princess, of course, comes from a more ancient time when little about her life could have been recorded or even pieced together from the speculations of modern-day experts. She has no advocates or experts to research and write down her story because she is anonymous. On the other hand, she can also represent a group of ancient Native American people—those found over the decades and displayed in museums or later photographed like trophies in their glass cases. She has probably not been claimed by any particular tribe because no one is quite sure just who her descendents are. The legend of her royal birth has perpetuated the mysteries surrounding her. She can represent all the lost ancestors who are now being gathered in the Native American Repository at the mouth of Emigration Canyon by the various tribal councils. Perhaps someday there will be a memorial in her honor to guard the entrance to this place. Or someday she might be claimed and buried in a secret place so her spirit can choose its own destiny—either to walk freely on the ground or go on to where the rest of her people are. It seems while people claimed to see her and while her spirit haunted the museum and stirred up so much speculation, no one speculated on why. Perhaps, if her descendents are found, they will.

In 1996, a new museum was dedicated at the village site. It is interesting how things have changed in just a few short years. A Hopi holy man had blessed the museum some years before and he gave the curator a four-inch prayer stick with a piece of yarn and a feather on it. After the blessing, the holy man told the museum curator to hide the prayer stick somewhere in the museum. The curator placed it in a safe place not known to visitors and removed it while the remodeling was going on. He put it back after the remodeling and both Christian and Native American ceremonial blessings were performed. A ceremonial bowl and a new prayer stick or *paho* were also presented to the museum. The bodies of the dead found at the site are long gone, although there may be many more as yet undiscovered bodies there. So if the spirit of the princess was looking for someone, or attached to someone, or even just wanted to stay on the land, she will probably continue to be seen at this state park. Her spirit probably still wanders this museum on occasion, looking for the rest of her people, or remembering the time when she walked these grounds in physical form.

Notes

1) Dutton, *Report on the Geology of the High Plateaus of Utah.* Quoted in Roylance, *Utah: A Guide to the State*, 683.

2) Roylance, *Utah: A Guide to the State*, 683.

Book Two

Mysterious Creatures

The Bear Lake Monster

My uncle had an old log cabin on Bear Lake in the little town of Garden City for many years. We often held family reunions there. Eventually, he built a big fancy home where the cabin had been and moved there permanently. I have many fond memories not only of boating on the lake, but also of hiking and exploring some old mine shafts that I am sure we shouldn't have been in. The road to Bear Lake from Logan is a dangerous one, and many people have been killed or injured while traveling it. My uncle and aunt lost a son to this road many years ago, when he was driving with his girlfriend around those curves on his way home. They were both high school kids. She survived but he did not. Some people consider it a cursed road and it does have a feel to it, perhaps because Logan Canyon is one of the longest canyons in the state, extending more than thirty miles. It is part of the northeast end of the Wasatch Range, called the Bear River Range. My aunt and uncle are gone now. They raised a wonderfully close and loving family. Some of their children still have strong ties to Garden City, and at least one of them is raising his family there. At their mother's funeral, all of them spoke about how she always told them never to fight among themselves because they only had each other to get through life with.

Although I am not sure, Garden City is probably the only place that can boast of a huge monument to a grizzly bear. It is back in the woods on the way to Bear Lake, a short hike from a two-lane highway. "Old Ephraim" was the largest grizzly ever shot. Frank Clark got him in 1923 after tracking him for ten years. The bear's skull was placed in the Smithsonian Institute for many years and is now at the Logan Visitors Center. The monument to this grizzly stands as high as he did and is right near where he was buried, six miles in on Temple Fork Road, which is fourteen miles up Logan Canyon. It is an eerie place. When I went there, I had no idea the bear was buried there. I somehow missed this bit of information while reading the plaque. Now that I know this, I know why it felt so strange. It is a place where you have that feeling of being watched as you stand looking up at the large monument to the grizzly. The site is marked with an eleven-foot shaft to show the height of the grizzly bear.

There are other interesting sites along this canyon road even before one gets to the lake. There are the Wind Caves, a series of arches and rooms as one leaves Logan, only five miles out of the city along the canyon road. Over the years, other names for these eroded formations have been DeWitt's Cave, Sun Dance Cave, Witches Castle, and Devil's Cave, indicating quite literally the eerie feeling of all the caves that exist through Logan Canyon and even around Bear Lake. Logan Cave is a two-story cavern about two thousand feet in length. It's about fifteen miles from Logan. Tony Grove Lake is a secluded fishing hamlet about twenty miles from Logan. Beaver Mountain Ski Area is twenty-six miles from Logan. The Seeholzer family began the small ski area in 1939. They used to bill it as "one winter ski resort that's big enough to challenge the really good skier and small enough to include people who've never skied at all." The drive through this canyon is breathtaking and ends in a slow descent down to the crystal-blue Bear Lake.

Besides Old Ephraim, the canyon boasts some of the oldest trees in the world. There are two rather famous ones, although the old Jardine Juniper seems to have gotten all the publicity around the area because it is the oldest tree. Limber Pine is further up the canyon, just before Bear Lake. This tree was nicknamed the Mountain Monarch and it is a mile hike from the mountain summit parking lot to see it. In 1982, the tree was estimated to be around five hundred years old, twenty-four-feet around, and forty-four-feet high. These statistics are taken from a 1982 book, so I would imagine that the tree is even larger and higher now. Before 1978, it was thought this tree was two thousand years old. A professor from Utah State University determined that what appeared to be a single pine was actually five trees that had grown together, and that each was around five hundred years old. The trail to the Monarch provides high mountain views of the spectacular Bear Lake, which lies half in Utah and half in Idaho. Old Juniper is the largest known Rocky Mountain cedar tree. Early pioneers knew the abundant cedar tree as junipers, thus the confusing name. It is estimated to be 3,500 years old and the tree's trunk is now hollow and twisted. Only a few branches are still alive and growing. The tree is twenty-seven feet around and forty-five feet in height. There is some evidence that this tree might once have been two trees. William J. Jardine, who attended Utah State University and served as Secretary of Agriculture under President Herbert Hoover, discovered the tree in 1923. It is a steep mile-and-a-half walk to get to the site where Old Juniper is located.

Lake Bonneville covered all of Utah and parts of Wyoming, Idaho, Colorado, Arizona, and New Mexico between 12,000 and 14,000 years ago. Scientists say, however, that Bear Lake was never really a part of it. Bear River, on the other hand, was a major contributor to the Cache Valley portion of the lake and did play a part in the lake's development. Fossils have been found in Utah Lake and Thatcher Lake (in Idaho), but Bear Lake seems to have had its own separate development. The lake is twenty-one miles long and seven miles wide and has beautiful opal-colored waters.

Geologists estimate the lake to be 28,000 years old. It sits at an altitude of 5,900 feet. In the old days, the lake was nicknamed the Sea of Silence because as hikers crest the summit and behold the entire lake, its intensely blue and placid reflection inspires silence and awe. Overcome by its beauty and serenity, most people stop to gaze in silence for a few moments, especially if they are seeing it for the first time. People have always believed, no matter what the scientists say, that Bear Lake was once a huge glacial lake, even though it is a fresh water lake and not connected to the prehistoric Lake Bonneville in any way. Others continue to believe that somehow Bear Lake has to be a remnant of the huge glacial lake and that ancient sea life could still exist there today, especially with all of the underground caverns about.

Beginning in 1826, an annual rendezvous of mountain men and trappers, the biggest in the state, took place at the shores of Bear Lake. This is when the first Native American legends were heard. Stories about the Bear Lake monster seem ludicrous to many, but such stories have been told about Utah Lake, the Great Salt Lake, and even

Fish Lake in southern Utah. The likelihood of it being true is minuscule and yet, year after year, I hear this same story from my students who have heard it from their parents or grandparents. As the story goes, ancient sea dinosaurs from the Pleistocene era swam through underground sea canals to appear at various times throughout history in three widely separate lakes spread out all over the world. These three locations are Loch Ness in Scotland, Bear Lake in Utah, and Lake Champlain in New York State. These ancient sea monsters or dinosaurs have been doing this for thousands of years to visit their relatives and, perhaps magically, their descendents! No one has actually proven the existence of the monsters, but quite a few people have made their attempts at a lifetime career at Loch Ness and other great lake locations. So far, I don't know of anyone who has set up shop to look for the one in Bear Lake, probably because most of the sighting reports were many years ago. But that doesn't mean that the people of both Garden City, Utah, and Lake City, Idaho, don't capitalize a little on the legend of the Bear Lake monster with a new crop of stories appearing from time to time.

The legend of the Bear Lake monster began with the Native Americans who lived in the area before the white settlers ever saw it. They told of a monster that lived in the lake and carried off people who went swimming in it. It was described as a serpent-like creature that crawled on land for small distances. Steam was said to spurt from its mouth and it had two to four legs, each about two feet long. At that time, it had been named the devil fish by the local tribe. Many had stories of monster sightings or had lost loved ones when the creature appeared and dragged people down to the bottom of the lake. It was said that over the years several people had drowned this way. The creature had eaten children while others watched from the shore. Tribal members were warned not to swim in the lake. The Native Americans had not seen the creature since the buffalo had lived in the valley; however, they did tell the first settlers about the monster in the 1860s. They described the beast as having a very large mouth and large ears. They said the mouth was large enough to swallow a man whole.

A few of the first white settlers reported seeing the monster, but the people were always alone when they saw it, so no one took the sightings seriously. One writer offers the following story.

The group of men were camped near Bear Lake, and, having been warned of a monster, they were curious to verify or disprove the tale. Early in the morning, they discovered a number of mules missing, and Lieutenant Tillman set out to find them. The lake was overlaid with fog a few feet thick, making it impossible to see the water. Soon the Tillman heard noises that seemed to be coming from some sort of animals, and they saw water spraying into the air. Feeling he was about to discover the monster, he went closer to investigate. Soon he located two bulls standing in the water, charging each other. They struck their horns together with lowered heads, and when their nostrils filled with water, they lifted their noses and blew water into the air. The sounds of spraying water came not from some mysterious monster, but from the local cattle.[1]

But in July of 1868, Joseph C. Rich began the legend all over again with an article that appeared in the *Deseret News* stating there had been several sightings. Even Brigham Young provided a rope to use in snaring the monster. This was after Henry Walker of Lehi had reported a similar monster in Utah Lake in 1864 and after the *Deseret News* had accused two towns, Logan and Provo, of competing for the best monster stories. The *Daily Corinne* got into the action soon after by reporting a Great Salt Lake monster on the north side of the lake near their town.

About three weeks ago Mr. S.M. Johnson, who lives on the east side of the lake at a place called South Eden was going to the Round Valley settlement, six miles to the South of this place and when about half way he saw something in the lake which at the time, he thought to be a drowned person. The road being some little distance from the water's edge he rode to the beach and the waves were running pretty high. He thought it would soon wash in to shore. In a few minutes two or three feet of some kind of animal that he had never seen before were raised out of the water. He did not see the body, only the head and what he supposed to be part of the neck. It had ears or bunches on the side of its head nearly as large as a pint cup. The waves at times would dash over its head, when it would throw water from its mouth or nose. It did not drift landward, but appeared stationary, with the exception of turning its head. Mr. Johnson thought a portion of the body must lie on the bottom of the lake or it would have drifted with the action of the water. This is Mr. Johnson's version as he told me.[2]

The very next day it was sighted again by a man and two women who said that it swam faster than a horse could run on land, and soon townspeople and visitors were telling many similar stories.

On Sunday last as N.C. Davis and Allen Dais, of St. Charles, and Thomas Sleight and J. Collings of Paris, with six women, were returning from Fish Haven when about midway from the latter named place to St. Charles their attention was suddenly attracted to a peculiar motion or wave in the water, about three miles distant. The lake was not rough, only a little disturbed by a light wind. Mr. Sleight says he distinctly saw the sides of a very large animal that he would suppose to be not less than ninety feet in length. Mr. Davis don't think he (Davis) saw any part of the body, but is positive it must have been not less than 40 feet in length, judging by the wave it rolled upon both sides as it swam, and the wake it left in the rear. It was going South, and all agreed that it swam with a speed almost incredible to their senses. Mr. Davis says he never saw a locomotive travel faster, and thinks it made a mile a minute, easy. In a few minutes after the discovery of the first, a second one followed in its wake; but it seemed to be much smaller, appearing to Mr. Sleight about the size of a horse. A large one, in all, and six smaller ones had [headed] southward out of sight.

One of the large ones before disappearing made a sudden turn to the west, a short distance; then back to its former track. At this turn Mr. Sleight says he could distinctly see it was of a brownish color. They could judge somewhat of their speed by observing known distances on the other side of the lake, and all agree that the velocity with which they propelled themselves through the water was astonishing. They represent the waves that rolled up in front and on each side of them as being three feet high from where they stood. This is substantially their statement as they told me. Messrs. Davis and Sleight are prominent men, well known in the country, and all of them are reliable persons whose veracity is undoubted. I have no doubt they would be willing to make affidavits to their statement.[3]

Joseph C. Rich, a promoter of Bear Lake, never saw the monster, but that didn't stop him from believing. He said of the disbelievers,

> I am sorry they don't believe the story because they might come up here some day and through their disbelief be thrown off guard and be gobbled up by the water devil. There are few people even here who disbelieve the monster story, but as a general rule they have not prospered in what they undertake and their intellects are tottering; they are not considered competent to act as fence viewers; and no doubt the government will in time withhold from them the blessing of paying internal revenue.[4]

How nice it would be in our modern day world to have the so-called sane ones, those who bother us with their tales, be considered in a state of "tottering intellect" and "cursed in their undertakings." Fortunately nowadays, nothing in our world is considered safe or without question, and the line between the sane and insane is growing quite thin! There is an ancient Sufi saying that states, "Those who danced were thought to be quite insane by those who couldn't hear the music."

Joseph Rich even knew a man who had a plan as to how to catch the Bear Lake monster. Phineas H. Cook was hatching his plan to protect his family from the monster as they had had their own sighting. A woman named Marion Thomas and three of Phineas's sons had been out boating on the lake, fishing opposite Swan Creek, when they came near "his majesty." Brother Thomas describes his head as serpent shaped. He saw about twenty feet of his body, which was covered with hair or fur, something like an otter and light brown. It had two flippers extending from the upper part of its body, which he compared to the blades of his oars. He was so near it that if he had had a rifle he could have shot it."[5]

Phineas's plan involved

> using a barbed hook, attached to twenty feet of cable, which in turn would be fastened to three hundred feet of one-inch rope; at the end of the rope would be a large buoy with a flag-staff in a perpendicular position. The stars and stripes were to float from the top of the staff. To this buoy would be attached another one hundred yards of three fourth inch rope fastened to the switch end of a tree on shore. The hook would be baited by a leg of mutton . . . and allowed to sink twenty feet in the water, being held at that depth by a smaller buoy. Naturally, when the monster swallowed the hook there would be a great commotion in the water; but the flag would always indicate the position of the monster, regardless of where he went in the lake.[6]

Four years later, there were dozens of sightings and stories, such as this one that appeared in the *Salt Lake Tribune* in August of 1870.

> Brothers Milando Pratt and Thomas, son of Charles C. Rich, had a view of the Bear Lake monster July 19, south of Fish Haven. They reported that their attention was attracted by an unusual commotion in the waters of the lake, and looking in the direction, they presently saw a head and a portion of the body of a creature larger around than the body of a man, the head resembling somewhat the pictorial representations of the walrus, minus the tusks. The portion of the body out of the water was about ten feet long. Several shots were fired, but missed the creature. It swam away in the direction of the east side of the lake, its track being marked by a wavy, serpentine motion. Its entire length was apparently forty feet. The young men had a view of this denizen of the deep for about fifteen minutes. One enterprising citizen, determined, if possible, to capture one of these animals, had a large rope, to which is attached a strong hook, well baited, tied around a stout tree.[7]

In July of 1871, the *Salt Lake Herarld* reported that "information [had] been received of the capture of a young Bear Lake monster near Fish Haven. It [was] said to be about twenty feet in length, with a mouth sufficiently large to swallow a man without any difficulty, and [was] propelled through the water by the action of its tail and legs."[8] Apparently Phineas Cook had tried his plan, and according to the newspaper, caught a monster. But nothing further was heard about the captured creature, so either the story was untrue or Phineas and his sons decided just to let a sleeping dog (or monster) lie. In May of 1874, William Budge and three other respected citizens of Utah were traveling north about three miles outside of Laketown and saw an object about 20 yards from the shore. They described it as similar to an oversized duck with fur on its flat face. It had large ears and eyes and its face resembled a cross between a fox and a cow. It had a four- or five-foot long neck but did not seem to be traveling very fast (about the speed of a human strolling slowly around the lake). People speculated at the time that they had perhaps seen a large otter instead of a lake monster.

In 1881, an apostle of the LDS Church reported a sighting of a creature in the lake. This was when Phineas W. Cook came up with his plan to capture it. He failed to capture anything resembling what the local Native Americans called the devil fish, although in every attempt something had stripped the mutton bait on the hook. The same rope used in this endeavor was used a little later to ferry the Prophet Brigham Young up north on his tours of that region across the lake.

Around this time, Aquila Nebeker, a rancher in the area, had twenty of his sheep eaten by something that also swallowed a whole roll of barbed wire in the process. The Bear Lake monster was blamed because what else could have done so much damage in just one night so close to the lake? It never occurred to anyone that the whole monster could be a hoax. But then, who would do such a monstrous thing just to get attention? A mountain lion was the most likely culprit, although it would have taken two or three to do this in one night. Maybe a pack of wolves was responsible. This is one of the unsolved mysteries in the early days of Bear Lake monster sightings.

By the 1900s, reported sightings died out, except for one article in the *Logan Republican* that appeared on September 18, 1907. In this article, entitled "Bear Lake Monster Appears, Leviathan Comes from Lake and Devours Horse while Men Shoot at It," two cowboys said they saw a beast that looked part dragon, part bear, and part fish eat one of their horses, which they had tied near their campfire. The next day, they found bear-shaped tracks that were three feet long and two feet wide. At the end of the account, the newspaper's editor added this double-entendre comment: "The *Republican* would like to know who these men are and the brand they use."[9] While there have been occasional claims throughout the years of sightings on the lake, until recently, no one had officially stepped forward and said they saw a creature.

The legend of the Bear Lake monster is constantly being reborn. At the very least, it has been maintained over the years. Children especially like to tell stories of their visits to Bear Lake and all the stories they've heard about the monster in the lake. Children are fascinated by the prospect of finding a mystical creature lurking in the depths of this crystal blue lake. The plesiosaurus has a long neck and fins instead of legs. It is considered to be a plant eater, which would be inconsistent with reports of the monster eating meat. Over the years, hunters, campers, hikers, and boaters visiting the lake have tried to find evidence of a monster. People have talked about catching a glimpse of something big swimming deep in the water as they look down from their boat, but I would imagine that motor boats would scare such creatures even deeper into the lake or into the deep underwater caves that may be down there. For the most part, the townspeople ignore the stories except to use them to attract tourists to their towns on the lake.

Laketown was created on the south end of the lake a little earlier than Garden City. It was settled in the 1860s, but long before this, as early as the 1820s, a huge fur trappers' rendezvous was held here. Before this, Native American tribes used the area for camping as they moved further north on their nomadic routes. It was mostly the Shoshone tribes that camped here, although other tribes passed through the area. The Shoshone were still camping there as late as 1870. They often scared the few white settlers in the area because the camps were often three thousand people strong or more. Today, Laketown is an agricultural community although a state beach and development all along the lakefront is rapidly changing this.

A Latter-day Saint apostle, Charles Colson Rich, brought the first settlers to the shores of the lake to create Garden City. In 1864, there were just two little log cabins there, but very soon, the town began to prosper and the townspeople built a flourmill, a sawmill, a blacksmith shop, a picker, carding machines, and looms. By 1877, the town had been surveyed and an irrigation canal was completed. In the 1970s, another little town was created further north of the lake called Pickleville. Most people drive right through Garden City on the old highway to Idaho and into Pickleville without noticing much of a distinction. All kinds of developments along the lakefront, and the hills behind are rapidly changing the quiet little hamlet of Garden City into a summer home and water sports paradise. The winter months are nice and quiet, but the summer months are rowdy and there is some difficulty with burglary and vandalism, which shouldn't be a problem for a town of its size. The townspeople are working to keep the area from being destroyed by all this development. I hope their efforts prove successful.

Because there had been no actual sightings until just recently, no serious scientific research had ever been done at Bear Lake, like it has at Loch Ness. However, a "hydrologist with the U.S. Geological Survey, Robert Baskin, says an extensive sonar sounding of the lake two years ago found no evidence of monsters even in the 200-foot-deep waters along the eastern shore. The USGS sent a boat from the Woods Hole Oceanographic Observatory in Massachusetts to obtain a three-dimensional image of the lakebed. But, Baskin notes, any monsters could have eluded the sonar scanner because the boat could not cover the entire lake. 'Those lake monsters are wily critters. They're just too wily for us humans.' "[10]

Loch Ness is much, much deeper. A few years back, scientists swept through the whole lake with a fleet of boats equipped with sonar equipment hoping to get a picture of something, but nothing appeared. Bear Lake, being much shallower, would be easy to explore this way, proving once and for all there is nothing there. But even if such a sweep shows there is no monster, would anyone be convinced? There is also the theory that there are deep ledges on the sides of the lake where a monster could hide, or possibly even channels that go deep into the earth. These channels may join the Loch Ness, Lake Champlain, Lake Superior, and Bear Lake together in a sort of invisible (and probably impossible) underground rectangle wherein these same creatures can travel back and forth across vast stretches of ocean from one place to another.

There are tales of many similar lake monsters all over the world. There is even one in Sweden's fifth largest lake, Lake Storsjeon. What makes their monster significant is that while sightings have been reported since 1635, in 1986 their lake monster was placed on the country's national endangered species list. In 2004, a man filed for permission to hunt for the monster's eggs. Permission was denied by a Swedish environmental court because "it is prohibited to kill, hurt or catch animals of the Storsjoe monster species."[11]

Explanations for the Loch Ness monster, fondly nicknamed Nessie, are similar to those for the Bear Lake monster. The monster might really be a large log floating in the water, a trick of the light, another animal mistaken for a sea monster, or a leftover creature from ancient times. They could all be hoaxes or tall tales that people concocted to get attention. There is always the possibility that the sightings in the late 1800s were actually someone's early mechanical invention traveling across the water. Or they could be not of this world or at least not of this time frame, according to a theory that what we mistake for flying saucers or even sea monsters are, in reality, a brief time warp, whereby we see our future or our past and actually interact with it. They are brief moments of time that make little sense to us in the present. The easiest explanation is obvious: all of the stories were completely made up!

When I first heard of the Bear Lake monster as a child, I really wanted to see it. But in all my trips to Bear Lake, I never did. I imagined it as a giant bear coming out from the lake and then crossing it to hunt with her children in tow. She would then return the same way. I never imagined a serpent or anything devilish about it, probably because I took the name Bear Lake literally after seeing Old Ephraim's monument looming over me in the mountains. There is one major difference between the creatures in Loch Ness and those in Bear Lake: Native Americans saw the Bear Lake monster before the white settlers arrived. The Native Americans already had their own tales of the monster taking its victims. Unlike some deep lakes that lay claim to a monster of the deep, at least Bear Lake can support life. The lake is teeming with fish, plants, and other marine life. A few of these bodies of water have been proven to be unable to support any sort of life at all and yet divers go down anyway looking for the reported sea monster.

Perhaps sightings are rare because, as the Native Americans said many years ago, the monster only appears when it wants to. Some say that sightings stopped when civilization came to chase it away with all of its noise and pollution. In 1994, a general manager and four construction workers who were working on the multi-million-dollar Harbor Village hotel and restaurant, claimed to have seen a huge, agile object moving through the water. This sighting was dismissed as the active imaginations of business people trying to promote their new resort.

In the year 2000, Conrad Nebeker of Indian Creek created a sixty-five-foot replica that matches the size, coloring, and temperament of the serpent in the form of a cruise boat, which he christened the Bear Lake Monster Boat. At first, Nebeker used the boat to entertain his grandchildren, but later sold it to Brian Hirschi, a Coast Guard certified captain. For the last several years, Hirschi has ferried tourists around the lake in it. It was in the summer of 2002 that Captain Hirschi claims to have had his own experience with the Bear Lake monster. He was anchoring the boat at sunset a couple of hundred yards offshore when he saw two dark humps appear astern. They were quite large and caused a small ripple effect around each of them. The humps disappeared below the surface, and Hirschi figured they were nothing more than a lost pair of water skis. Suddenly, something scraped the bottom of the 8,000-pound Monster Boat, lifting it out of the water. Then, not fifty feet away, a huge animal shot out of the water and created enormous waves that rocked the boat violently. Hirschi relates his story in an interview for a newspaper article.

> "I grabbed the rail to keep my balance as I tried to keep an eye on whatever had just come out of the water," he reported. It was a serpentine creature about as long as his 65-foot craft. "It had a skin color of dark slimy green, beet-red eyes, and sort of a mist coming out of its nose," Hirschi claimed. "At first it made low throaty snarls and then finally a terrible squeal like a roaring bull as it submerged back into the water." The beast resurfaced some 200 yards away, racing toward the middle of the lake. Hirschi stood transfixed. "Did I really see what I saw?" he asked. "Was it going to come back?" As darkness fell he finally came to his senses, jumped on his SeaDoo and raced to shore, "almost beaching the watercraft with the engine still running" . . . Lacking any witnesses to his encounter, he decided to keep

the story to himself, lest people think he'd gone crazy. Civic duty finally compelled Hirschi to come forth and warn people "to be on the lookout for the Bear Lake monster because it is still alive and lurking."[12]

Brian Hirschi's grandmother, Charlene Hirschi, is the director of the Utah State University Writing Center in Logan and did a paper on the lake monster for the Utah Folklore Society just a few years ago. In her research, she found that Joseph Rich had admitted twenty years later that he was the one who had perpetuated the myth about the monster in the lake. In fact, he bragged about it, saying it was a "wonderful first-class lie." The whole thing had gotten out of hand and was entrenched in the minds and hearts of the people after so many sights. Charlene Hirschi also says that like all folklore, this tale has served several purposes over time. Pioneer parents used it to teach their children not to go too far into the lake. Hirschi also finds it amusing that the only sightings today are by businessmen who are promoting a business by the lake. As for her grandson's sighting, she says, "What can I say? I cannot discount anyone's experience."[13]

Regardless of the truth or fiction of the monster stories, there is one thing I think ought to be done. The most famous lake monster here in Utah ought to have a name, a name that everyone knows and can use, instead of just the Bear Lake Monster. *Monster* connotes savagery and terror, but we ought to look at these tales as a part of the mysteries of our state and give this legend our blessing by naming it. And here is my vote: I like the name Utahna after Utah or Bearinna after Bear Lake. Or even what some Utah children came up with: Shoney the sea serpent. The monster's popularity seems to be growing with a goofy tourist boat built to look like it and current sightings after all those years without any. Even the Cache Children's Choir has a song about the lake monster that says, "I've heard tell he's vicious. And children are delicious."[14] The Utah State Library in Logan has a painting that depicts the so-called terror of Bear Lake based on the Native American legends. At the local tourist places, you can buy a Bear Lake Monster sandwich that comes with fries for $3.99.

Many university experts say that Joseph Rich, the originator of these monster tales, admitted in his writings that he had made the whole thing up as a publicity stunt to promote Bear Lake. Will Bagley says, "I've never seen anything that indicated he didn't go to his death-bed believing in the Bear Lake monster." And Bagley ought to know, being a well-respected historian whose own private search for the Bear Lake monster links back to his own ancestry. Someone once said it is in the search that we find our own monsters, and not in the actual sighting of such beasts.[15]

Since lake monster stories are great fun and the local Native Americans had tales about this monster long before Joseph Rich entered the picture, I am hoping the locals will promote these stories even more. Being a dreamer, I prefer my "creative ideations" to the murmurings of intellectual humbugs! The greatest minds found both their monsters and their saints without the rest of us to help them. The latest article on the Bear Lake monster promoted a statewide drawing contest of what everyone thinks the monster looks like. It was mainly for school children and the winners were posted on the newspaper's website. However, I think they missed the point. There are many pictures of what the monster looks like already. It should have been a naming contest so the whole state could benefit from a name it could be proud of and from some publicity about our own nicknamed monster. Perhaps it would even catch the imagination of a team of monster hunters who would go to our lake and sweep it with sonar equipment with a fleet of boats. Then, even if nothing were found, at least we would have the documentary.

Notes

1) Bennett, *Roadside History of Utah*, 351.
2) Fife, "The Bear Lake Monsters," *Utah Humanities Review*, April 1948.
3) Ibid.
4) Parson, *The History of Rich County*, 330-31.
5) Carter, *Heart Throbs of the West* 2:53.
6) Parson, *The History of Rich County*, 330.
7) Carter, *Heart Throbs of the West* 2:53.
8) Ibid.
9) *Logan Republican*, "Bear Lake Monster Appears, Leviathan Comes from Lake and Devours Horse while Men Shoot at It," September 19, 1907. Quoted in Kristen Moulton, "Bear Lake Monster lives On," May 31, 2004.

10) Moulton, "Bear Lake Monster lives On," May 31, 2004.

11) Bagley, "Bear Lake Monster May Have a Long-lost Cousin . . . in Sweden," May 9, 2004.

12) Moulton, "Bear Lake Monster Lives On," May 31, 2004.

13) Ibid.

14) Ibid.

15) Bagley, "The Bear Lake Monster," interviewed by Hollenhorst, May 13, 2004.

Utah's Bigfoot Sightings

The Native Americans on the Ouray Reservation near Roosevelt have reported large Bigfoot-like creatures for years in a particular canyon. This place cannot be identified or investigated by anyone except for those designated within their own tribe. The Utes who live in the area consider this canyon to be sacred. Some Utes believe these creatures are Siants or old wrinkled female witches who can shapeshift into the large hairy creatures. Siants like to kidnap little children, never to return them. Others believe they are their own race living away from mankind for centuries, or that they are spirit beings and not made of flesh at all. The Utes believe that these creatures congregate in the Island Lake area of the high Uintahs. Sometimes there are reports of big rocks being thrown in the middle of the night around this area. Suffice it to say that Bigfoot sightings were around long before the white man came along.

David Thompson was a surveyor and trader for the Northwest Fur Trading Company and he is the first white man to officially report a sighting of a Bigfoot or Sasquatch. He didn't see the creature but discovered its tracks in 1810 near the Columbia River Gorge while on a surveying trip. The Bigfoot of our Western Hemisphere is considered the larger cousin of the Yeti or Abominable Snowman sighted in the Eastern Hemisphere. Bigfoots have been reported in Canada, parts of the Midwest, and even in Florida, although the major sightings have always been in the mountainous areas of the western United States. Here in Utah, the first reported sighting was in the 1960s near Beaver.

In the early 1970s, people in Clarkston, near Logan, reported some sort of creature taking a midnight trip through their community.

In 1998, a woman reported an incident that happened in 1968. She had not told anyone about it and still desires to remain anonymous. Apparently she was living in Ogden Canyon, specifically in Wheeler Canyon, at the time. Her husband was away one fall weekend and the ground was covered in leaves. She got up in the middle of the night to get a drink, went to the kitchen, got her water, and then turned to see two big, glowing red eyes staring at her through the living room window. She thought she was imagining it, so she turned back into the kitchen, got her thoughts together, and then turned around again to see the same pair of eyes staring at her. She described the creature as looking like a werewolf, and she was so shaken that she called the police and reported a prowler. The police showed up about forty-five minutes later while the woman hid in the bedroom where her small son slept. She could hear something going about from window to window rattling each one to see if it was secure. The police found nothing. When they questioned her about a description, she didn't tell them anything except that the prowler was quite tall.

Her husband laughed at her until he had his own experience about a month later. He got up early for work, heard a commotion out on the front lawn, and went to investigate. As he approached the diamond shaped window in the front door, he saw a dark, hairy face looking at him through the window. He thought it was a bear and ran to get his pants and his gun. When he got back, it was gone. It then occurred to him that a bear couldn't have gotten its face up close to the window like that because of its snout. Both the woman and her husband heard strange screaming where their horses were kept more than once. Their horses made strange sounds as well, as though sensing a mountain lion or some other large predator about.

The Bigfoot Field Research Organization posts on its Web site all of the reports and local newspaper articles about Bigfoot that people send them or that it garners on its own. The records go back as far as the 1960s and the organization is currently compiling more ancient and historical records of sightings from all across the nation. Frankly, I was surprised to learn that yes indeed, Bigfoot is alive and well in Utah! The first solid reports from our state were noted in the *Ogden*

Standard-Examiner and the *Davis County Clipper* from 1977 to 1980. The first of these was in August of 1977 and involved eight people who spotted a gorilla-like creature while hiking in the high Uintah Mountains. They estimated it to be about ten feet tall with a white mantle of fur over its shoulders and half way down its body. It walked on its hind two legs, stopped at a lake to stare at them from a distance and then ambled off into the nearby timber. Later, they talked to a sheepherder in the area who said he had been unable to get his sheep to graze in this same area; they would beat him back to his camp acting very scared. He also said this was the first summer he had not seen nor heard a single coyote in the area. On reaching the sighting area, conservation officers concluded that it was a grizzly though they did find a rabbit carcass skinned by human hands and partially eaten.

By September of the same year, two Davis County couples also reported seeing not one but three of these same creatures in the high Uintahs. They watched two of the creatures romp together in a clearing from a ridge about five hundred yards away from them. When the witnesses were interviewed separately, they all provided the same accurate details. They said the creatures had hands and feet with no hair on them and that their legs and arms seemed to be larger than or out of proportion with the rest of their bodies. The third creature stood at the edge of the meadow in some pines and watched the other two. When the creatures took off, they crossed the meadow at a very rapid speed walking on their hind legs. The couples said they did not have long snouts like bears and that they were unlike any creature they had ever seen. They walked upright not even in a crouched position and were between eight and ten feet tall. When the first hikers reported their sighting, the two couples who had actually seen the creatures a month before the others decided to come forth and report what they had seen. They had kept quiet about it because they didn't want to be laughed at. The couples had seen the creatures about seventeen miles northwest of where the hikers had seen them, a little southwest of Elizabeth Lake.

The Bigfoot Association in Mount Hood, Washington, was notified of the sightings and came down a few weeks later to investigate the site. Experts from throughout the nation descended on the Uintahs and stayed for about three weeks, scouring the area for Bigfoots. All the people who had seen the creatures came back to search and many local conservation officers and reporters joined, hoping to get a plaster cast of a footprint or find any sign of the creatures. Others reported hearing strange growling and howling noises in the area as well as crashing sounds through the brush. There was also a strange smell in the area. Officials were convinced it was a grizzly, although it was very unusual for grizzlies to be in this area. Not a single person found even a trace of the creatures in all of this time. All of the eyewitnesses were felt to be reputable and officers said they were not just going to write it off, but would keep looking in these extremely primitive and remote areas. Hunters that fall were advised to take their cameras along, but certainly the hunting season would frighten off any intelligent creature. All of this can either be a study in the human psychology of jumping on the bandwagon, or a real event with real creatures. To this day, no one knows what these creatures were or if they were real.

The next round of sightings took place beginning in February of 1980 in South Weber. A South Weber woman saw a strange creature on a ridge above the valley community in the middle of the afternoon. An interesting side note is that a horse belonging to a neighbor of the woman was so frightened by something in the night that it ran into a barbed wire fence and dropped dead below the ridge where the woman had reported seeing the creature the day before. A few days later, a man was arriving home from work in the early morning and stopped to feed his horses in his back pasture. For some reason, they wouldn't come to the fence like they usually did. He then heard something crunching through the snow in the field. He thought it was a husky high school kid in a big coat at first, but when he shined his flashlight on it, he realized how big it was. He then heard strange screams that sounded like a cougar only with a lot more volume to them. He hightailed it to the house and tried to find either his gun or his camera, but by the time he got back, the screams had stopped. The next morning, he went out to look for tracks but the horses had trampled over most of the area. The few tracks he was able to find were about six feet apart and had some toe imprints. Some of the officials and people from the first sightings went out into the area looking for tracks and eventually found some. The footprints were about fifteen inches in length and had toe markings and pads on the bottom of the feet. The strides were about four feet apart. Trackers believe that the creatures had returned to the headwaters of the Weber River where other sightings had occurred.

Although these sightings were a day apart and neither person could possibly have communicated with the other, one has to note that the man who saw the creature was the uncle of the woman who saw it. On the other hand, neither of them believed they had seen Bigfoot, just some strange creature that they could not identify.

People at the nearby Hogle Zoo were interviewed to see if any animals were missing. Forest Service officials said it was the wrong season for bears of any kind to be out and about. It is strange that the horses in the second incident didn't seem to be that disturbed by the event, other than the fact that a few days before the incident, they would only eat in the clearing and would not go near the trees. That same month, another man reported a large creature running in front of his headlights on an early Monday morning. The creature was ten to eleven feet tall with long, furry dark brown hair and weighed about six hundred pounds. He was about twenty-five feet away from it and only saw it for a few minutes before it disappeared into the trees in the same vicinity as the other sightings. Many others did not report what they heard or saw for fear of ridicule during this year of sightings. Others heard inhuman screams and one man who lived at the foothills saw a creature at his window one night. Another woman said many years later that she had heard the screams as well. Still another man said later that he had been camping in the area and left a pan of burned stew at his campsite to cool and when he came back it had been licked clean. A second report says that the pot was on was his back porch and that the animal had dragged it one hundred yards into the neighbor's backyard where they found it licked clean the next morning.

Other people living in the area reported strange happenings while camping in the Manti-La Sal Mountains in 1973. They had pitched camp with their horses and went out on an elk hunt. During the night, something very powerful had lifted off a three-hundred-pound horse trailer door and tossed it seven to ten feet away from the trailer. A local bear tracker and hunting expert checked an imprint that had been left on the door and he could not identify it as a bear's print. The next day while they were away hunting, something bit down into a beer can and split it. When the hunters returned they found teeth marks on it. The horses were also somewhat disturbed the next night and the hunters could find no cause for it.

The last thing that was reported that year was two Bigfoot prints, which were found in the backyard of a North Ogden residence in May. Plaster casts were made but officials could not determine just what they were. They seemed to be the prints of a three-hundred- to four-hundred-pound human and were thirteen inches in length and four and a half inches wide.

In 1997 an incident was reported that happened in September of 1976. Two hikers were in a place called Upper Docs Flat east of Brigham City. They noticed that they were not hearing any of the usual sounds of creatures about. This spooked them and they decided to head back to camp. One of the hikers had a hunting gun and heard some grouse or sage hens and decided to hike down a ways and look for them. The other hiker agreed to stay in place while the first hunted. They agreed to meet again at a certain time. The second hiker watched as the first one made his way down the draw. The man who stayed behind to hunt got stuck in some thorn bushes and as he worked to free himself, a huge rock came tumbling down towards him. His companion looked up to where the rock had come from and saw a creature running towards them from about four hundred yards above. The hunter below finally heard the creature and must have accidentally fired his gun, because the creature then turned and began running the other way. The two later described the creature as about seven to eight feet tall with dark reddish brown fur on its body and a white-capped or bald head.

In 1979, a couple went elk hunting near the Monte Cristo range, east of Ogden. They reported hearing an unusual, loud noise and smelling an awful odor. They then spotted a hairy creature about fifty yards away at a watering hole. They watched for several minutes and then rushed to their car when the creature moved towards them. Hikers at Flaming Gorge claimed that they had stumbled onto a sort of camp with a huge pine bed with a dead deer hanging nearby. Unearthly screams accompanying the scene, of course, scared them off. This particular report does not surprise me in the least as many a Vietnam combat veteran chose the woods over contact with human beings after their experiences both in Vietnam and returning home. Some of the veterans have chosen to live in the mountains permanently. Manufactured unearthly screams seem typical of someone who did not want to be disturbed by their own kind ever again. Although it might make more sense to go dumpster diving and campsite stealing at the various state campgrounds. I guess it would depend on the depth of the alienation from society and the degree of their survivalist skills. Having been married for twenty-nine years to a former hospital corpsman who served in Vietnam, I do indeed know what I am talking about. Bigfoot or "giant" survivalist, this is a valid point to ponder where unknown creatures walking on two feet are concerned.

In March of 1981, a Pleasant Grove man found giant footprints in the high Uintahs at his logging camp. He and his companions, professional loggers, scoffed at the notion of a Sasquatch or Bigfoot loose in the area. Still, the prints were unusual. There were two sets of tracks about six feet apart. The prints measured nineteen inches in length and eleven inches across and the stride measured fifty-four inches. The evening before they found the prints, they heard crashing through the willows, the sound of something being beaten, and a grunt or a growl. They followed the prints until they had no more time to do it. Two weeks later, they came back and found the old prints covered over in snow and some new prints near the carcass of a beaver that had been picked clean. Knowing that Park Service workers have reported sightings of hermits in the past, often assuming that these men are veterans, it is not hard for me to believe that not only would these individuals not want to be found, but that they might enjoy laying down a Bigfoot track or two or letting out a bloodcurdling scream, just for their own personal amusement. It's possible that others might have chosen this way who were never in a war but have what the veterans' magazines call the "wannabees." These people are usually survivalists who like to "play" at war. True veterans and Native Americans who prefer the woods would never be found and wouldn't want to be, except possibly by other veterans or Native Americans.

In the 1980s, various scattered reports of Bigfoot sightings came in from all over the state. A man in LaPoint in Uintah County was flying his small private airplane from Ogden to his home one winter and saw a large, hairy man-like creature walking through the deep snow in the high Uintahs. Another man was camping in the mountains above Ogden and reported that something stormed through his camp one night, frightening his horses. The next day he had talked to some hunters who had seen an unusual creature that had spooked them. A man on a dirt bike near the Francis Peak Radar Towers reported being chased by a large creature. A Vernal family saw the outline of a large creature outside their tent one night and then a large hand pressed against the tent cover. A thirteen-year-old in Washington Terrace in Weber County reported seeing a large hairy dark creature standing with its back to her only ten feet away in a gully near the Weber River. An Ogden couple went picking asparagus by the Weber River and saw an eight-foot tall black creature with glowing red eyes. They ran to their car and came back later and found dozens of tracks.

Teenagers reported hearing screams and smelling a terrible odor by the Weber River. Footprints were found later in the same area. A police chief in Garland in Box Elder County saw a huge creature run in front of his car and other residents reported sightings of a similar creature. Again, tracks were found in the area. Several drivers along Beck Street in North Salt Lake reported seeing a hairy creature run across the road in front of them. A jogger in Farmington saw Bigfoot near the city cemetery there, and campers in the Hoyt Peak area of the Uintahs reported seeing something strange as well. Several men in the Wheeler Canyon area near Snow Basin Road saw a large creature with glowing red eyes at about three a.m. Ranchers near Garland reported seeing two large Bigfoot-like creatures near their lambing pens right after dark and tracks were found all over this area. People followed the tracks for about two miles and then lost the trail. My favorite story from the 1980s involves a Bigfoot tape recording. A man from Layton, who is a long time Bigfoot fan, received a recording from another avid collector in Montana supposedly of Bigfoot's unearthly screams. One night in 1983, the man imitated the sounds from the recording as best he could outside his bedroom window, and the same sound answered back from the woods behind his house.

In 1989, reports of sightings stepped up again and they have been going on ever since. The first was in Grove Creek Canyon above Pleasant Grove. The hiker saw a large red animal up above him on the rim of the canyon. It looked as tall as a large man and was looking off towards Mount Timpanogos but then turned and walked away. In the 1990s, Bigfoot sightings began occurring continuously, but with much less publicity. An Orangeville, Emery County man reported seeing the Bigfoot creatures at least four times in the high Uintahs. He claimed that his family was with him on one of these occasions and also that his grandfather had reported seeing the creature in this area when he was a young man. More sightings were reported in the North Ogden area as well as screams and foul odors. Then reports started to come in from all over the Uintah Mountain areas including Scow Creek and Bakers Lake at the East Fork of the Bear Scout Camp, famous as well for the ghostly Hyrum Smith sightings and campfire stories.

In the summer of 1994 in Summit County, some boys were walking down a trail at night returning from a day of fishing at Scow Lake. Suddenly, a large humanoid creature appeared before them for a few seconds and then disappeared as quickly as it had appeared. It was either a very large man or a Bigfoot, the boys said. The creature walked across to an embankment and then up the slope and was gone. The boys attempted to hail it, but it did not answer or acknowledge their presence. They then heard a strange noise up ahead like two rocks clacking together. The noise scared them, so they headed back to camp. They had their knives out all the way back to camp. The creature was about six to seven feet tall and had a high crown and a stout build. Despite its size, it moved quite swiftly and gracefully. When the boys looked for tracks the next day, they found nothing.

In November of 1997, twelve miles North of Manderfield, Utah, a man, his wife, and his sister-in-law were looking for arrowheads across from Indian Creek. They found an unusual track, much larger than a human's. When the man put his ten-and-one-half-inch shoe into it, the track was a good seven to nine inches longer than his. The depth of the imprint was about one half of an inch and it was about eight or nine inches wide. The strangest part was that the track only had three discernable toes. A second track was over on the other side of the cedar trees, which might have meant an eight-foot stride. The two prints looked as if the person or creature had actually stepped over a five-foot cedar tree rather than going around it. But no one went back and reported it or tried to get an impression of the print at the time.

My favorite story comes from an article about how the wheels of progress are destroying South Weber. The biggest business in town, the gravel pits, is being threatened by plans to widen the highway. This would wipe the gravel pits out and most of the business district. The city of three thousand people was facing the end of a life they had known for many, many years. This is why, the article's author says, the legend of Bigfoot gave them something memorable to cling to. One man remembered how the hysteria resulted in a big picture of Bigfoot being posted in Riverdale and some kids blasting it with buckshot.

There were even self-appointed patrols all around the city and even the strongest of disbelievers admitted that it was quite a saga for the whole town. It became part of the folklore of the town, although others were embarrassed at the mere mention of it.

Wildlife officials say, as a joke, that if any of these things could be even the least bit substantiated, they would put a little more effort into locating the creatures and then managing their population through hunting. Of course if they are real, they might hunt us back and a few of these officials would find out the hard way just how intelligent these creatures might be, especially if they turned out to be human. People in South Weber tend to stand by the stories. Others say that when you're alone on a dark, moonlit night, you can make yourself believe almost anything. Two residents who followed some tracks took strands of the creature's fur to the state for analysis. It was passed off as cow hair, but the strands were never returned to them. The woods where the sightings originally took place have now been plowed and stripped to make room for more subdivisions. If the state went ahead with its plans, the author of the article suggested making plans to sell Bigfoot T-shirts and other merchandise.[1]

Sightings of Bigfoot in 2001 included one near Marysvale, Utah, and another near Strawberry Reservoir. Marysvale, where the Big Rock Candy Mountain is located, has always been considered a sacred area by the local tribes and ancient stories of Siants, a race of shape shifting giants, were perpetuated through oral traditions there. There were many sightings of this same creature near Beaver, Utah, in the 1960s and 1970s. The canyon has a drop of about sixty feet per mile. It is nearly impossible for a human to go down these canyon walls on foot; however, a Bigfoot could apparently traverse this canyon with ease. Large human-like footprints were found in the area after a family was besieged at their summer cabin one night with loud growls and howls that they could not identify.

Ryan Layton, Mark Woody, Derrell Smith, Rudy Dominick, and Brian Whitesides have been researching and hunting for Bigfoot for fifteen to twenty-five years in various parts of Utah. They publish their information and sightings on the www.aliendave.com website, an excellent site for any unexplained phenomena in Utah. Some facts that they put on the site include 160 known reports of Bigfoot in Utah as of the end of 2003. Nearly all are reported in mountainous areas with the beasts ranging in color from white to black. Reports describe a creature with anywhere from three to five toes. People have seen the creatures at as close a range as eight feet and the hot spots for sightings are Cold Water Canyon, Timpanogos, Logan, Ogden, the Uintahs, and just recently a report or two came in from the west desert. A few groups have organized locally to hunt for the creature in these areas. Most intriguing are reports of how these huge hairy giants run off with rabbits, pigs, and even pets for dinner. Just like any other state, there are files of reports, audiotapes, and even videotapes of these creatures along with casts of footprints, hair samples and photographs.

Bigfoots have been described as large and muscular, yet agile and elusive. They seem to be intelligent with psychic or telepathic abilities. The creatures have long brownish-red hair, a strong odor, large feet, and a piercing, eerie howl. Ryan Layton and Ron Mower founded the Western Bigfoot Society and besides lecturing, they put out a Utah newsletter on the subject. More recent sightings from 2001 to the present include an encounter at Red Mountain Pass in April of 2001. Two experienced hunters scouting for deer near Strawberry Reservoir smelled a foul odor that eventually dissipated. They had a strong feeling of being watched which sort of spooked them, something that rarely happened to these rugged outdoorsmen. They decided to head back for their truck when to the right of them they heard a large crashing noise, high-speed running, and eventually they saw the outline of a person walking from tree to tree following them. They assumed it was a person only because they could tell that he was walking upright. He was about six feet tall and made eerie sounds like they had never heard before. He followed them until the hunters got safely into their truck. This sounds like a Bigfoot sighting, but I have to wonder, with the reported size of the animal, if this wasn't a human.

In November of 2002, near Farmington, Utah, several witnesses reported hearing unearthly, high-pitched screaming for several nights in a row. It didn't seem to anyone that a human being could make these sounds. After a few nights, some of the witnesses went out to look for where the screams were coming from. Right behind the Farmington Power Plant, they saw something large plunge into the bushes. They went by the elk and buffalo cages on the Lagoon Trail where the Lagoon Amusement Park keeps them during the winter months and noticed that the animals were acting very unusual, all huddled in one corner, crying and restless. Then they smelled a foul odor and heard a loud piercing scream that startled them where they stood. They were momentarily frozen to one spot. As the sound drew nearer, they took off running. They went back again and again that month trying to find something. They finally gave up when the sounds stopped and were never heard again.

Reports of other types of giants found in Utah also continue, although most of them are probably hoaxes. Races of giants supposedly left petroglyph messages in remote canyons. These are the larger figures drawn with undulating lines that appear to be standing behind the more solid, smaller human figures in many examples of petroglyph rock art. While they can be interpreted in dozens of ways, some experts say that they represent either ancestors, ghosts, gods, or mythological siants of old Native American lore. Other believe that these pictures literally represent a race of giants. In one of these areas, a giant skull was found. Some made the logical connection that the skull was associated with the giants drawn in the petroglyph art. A six-foot six-inch skeleton was found in a Native American mound, raising questions since it is unusual for an early Fremont or Anasazi Native American to be that tall. Bigfoot reports are becoming more and more widespread in the mountainous areas of North America, and Utah is no exception. There are more and more Bigfoot sightings all over the state now.

As for me, I think anything is possible, although humans are really the most dangerous species of all. It would be hard to spot a Bigfoot. People are more likely to be so frightened that anything could be imagined, and probably is. Besides the usual ideas of what these sightings are (bears, moose, buffalos), perhaps Bigfoot is an undiscovered species from long ago or perhaps, as the Native Americans believe, they are spirits, mystical siants of the canyons. Or maybe Bigfoot is nothing more than a survivalist or old war veteran unable ever to come home again, wearing big clothes, and not caring much about his grooming. Or maybe these are beings taking a simple holiday from their own planet to visit these strange and ignorant beings called humans. Whatever they are, products of our own vivid imaginations or actual creatures, if we stop imagining those things both real and unreal, then we stop being human altogether. It's not certain what sorts of things the new century will bring in Bigfoot sightings here in Utah. Looking back at what happened in the last century, Bigfoot or Sasquatch will continue to live on in the woods and high country in places all over the Western Hemisphere, especially in the West's Rocky Mountains.

All of this reminds me of a scene in the movie *Close Encounters of the Third Kind* in which a large crowd of people shows up to chase the UFO lights. Later, local and government officials interview each one of them trying to figure out how it was possible for these people to know to come to the site when there were no lights or UFO media reports about the Devil's Tower location in Wyoming. The officials can't understand how these others got the word when everything else about the aliens landing there was kept top secret. As they interview groups of witnesses, one old guy stands up and interrupts the government officials to make his own statement. "I saw Bigfoot once, back in 1951 in the Sequoia National Forest . . . made a sound I wouldn't want to hear twice!"

For the record, however, I do want to state that I believe that something is out there that we do not understand and that all the confusion simply comes from mistaken sightings and hoaxes. The real Bigfoots are out there and someday those hunting them will solve the mystery of who and what they are.

Notes
1) Whaley, "Legend of Bigfoot May Be All South Weber Has Left: Town Can Cling to Bigfoot Legend," April 6, 1996.

Monsters and Folklore of the Great Salt Lake

Ancient Lake Bonneville occupied the Great Salt Lake basin for several million years, but the Great Salt Lake's birth began about twenty-five thousand years ago. The Salt Lake Valley today shows horizontal "bathtub rings" along all of the surrounding foothills. G. K. Gilbert was the first, in the 1870s, to survey and study the evidences of this prehistoric lake and describe its natural features. His map showed that ancient Lake Bonneville covered the southern portion of Idaho, all of Utah, the eastern portion of Nevada, the western portion of Colorado, the southeast corner of California, the northwest corner of New Mexico, and nearly all of Arizona. Through his various studies, Gilbert established that at its largest, the lake was at least a thousand feet deep and covered twenty thousand square miles. The lake flowed into a tributary of the Snake River that eventually flowed into the Pacific Ocean. Gilbert concluded that at one point in history, probably about fifteen thousand years ago, Lake Bonneville overflowed the rim of the Great Basin near Red Rock Pass in southeastern Idaho and scoured a channel out, down to the bedrock, which released a catastrophic flood down the Snake River. This event, the great Bonneville Flood, lowered the lake to a more stable level of about 4,750 feet above sea level. About twelve thousand years ago, dramatic changes in climate lowered the lake even more, and by ten thousand years ago, a second change made the lake only about fifty feet higher than the present level of the Great Salt Lake. What remains of this great lake has provided information about land formation, physical properties of the earth, and climate changes on the land.[1]

The first explorers thought that they had found the Pacific Ocean when they reached down in the Great Salt Lake and pulled out a hand full of salt water. The remnant of ancient Lake Bonneville is still the thirty-third largest lake in the world. Local Native Americans fished the fresh water rivers and marshes around the lake. They already knew that the salt in the water made swimmers itch unless the skin was rinsed off in fresh water. Jim Bridger, Kit Carson, John C. Fremont, and Captain Howard Stansbury are among the first white men to see the Great Salt Lake. Presently, it is seventy-five miles long and thirty-five miles wide, with a depth of only thirty feet, although its depth has varied twenty feet since the pioneers first came to the valley. Swimmers can no more sink in it today than in times past. A non-swimmer can even stay afloat because of the salt content, although the brine shrimp that blanket the surface of the water and the stinging salt make it mighty uncomfortable to do so. The constantly changing water level makes it difficult to describe the lake at any given time.

A lot of the experts credit Jim Bridger with discovering the lake, but he himself said he was sure that he was on the shores of the Pacific. Among others credited with discovering the Great Salt Lake before Bridger's time was Baron Lahotan. Exploring from Europe in 1703, he reported seeing the Salt Lake. The Dominguez-Escalante expedition wrote down a report from the local Native Americans about a greater lake north of the Utah Lake that made one itch all over upon getting even just wet from it. This expedition started the first myth about the Great Salt Lake by mapping a great river that connected the salt lake to the Pacific Ocean. For years after this, various explorers and settlers tried to find this river that would lead them to the ocean beyond it. When the Fremont expedition went through the area in 1843 and 1844, the explorers searched for this connecting river. This myth may have started the idea that lake monsters from Bear Lake, Utah Lake, and the Great Salt Lake could swim back and forth from the Pacific Ocean through underground connecting rivers. There are many people even today who perpetuate this myth but have no idea where the theory came from.[2]

Bridger brought other mountain men to the area and others saw the great lake before he did. It is unclear who first discovered the lake during this era. Bridger saw the lake in 1824 and a year later, four men from the Rocky Mountain Fur Company were the first to walk around the entire lake. They were looking for the river to the ocean but never found it. Several of the mountain men who first saw the lake were convinced that somewhere on the surface was a giant and fierce whirlpool. Existence of a whirlpool would explain lake waters flowing downward into subterranean passageways that led to the ocean. The rumors about the lake were passed down through the decades so that in 1870, boatmen who made regular runs on the lake with their City of Corinne steamer claimed to have seen the giant center of this whirlpool near Fremont Island. The Great Salt Lake waters were rushing into it at an alarming rate. They claimed they saw at least one schooner that was almost drawn into it, although no one knew of anyone who had disappeared this way.

When the Latter-day Saints came to the valley in 1847, Brigham Young and others visited the lake in July of that year and began to use it as their salt supply. Over the years, several resorts were built along its shores, the largest and most famous being Saltair. At present the "new," reconstructed Saltair sits quietly abandoned. Once they settled in the valley, even the Latter-day Saints began to tell stories of what dwelt in this lake, some say to compete with stories of the lake monsters in both Utah and Bear Lakes nearby.

The brine shrimp or "brine flies" blanket the beaches in every direction. They produce a tiny warm stinging on the skin along with the salty water and are often blamed for the steam that blows across the whole valley now and then. Sometimes locals wake up in the morning to a stench permeating the entire valley. People will joke that the lake is rising or falling again and letting them all know about it. As little children, we were taught to lick our fingers after being in the lake to keep our eyes from stinging from the salt. The joys of bobbing up and down in the water with absolutely no effort were irreplaceable. We went to ride the amusement rides and then went back out into the lake to float around a bit. Putting our heads under the water, however, was really not worth the awful stinging and murkiness that we experienced in trying to breathe when we came back up.

The Great Salt Lake also has several islands, the largest and most famous being Antelope Island and Fremont Island. There are a dozen islands with interesting names such as Bird or Hat Island, Egg Island, Mud Island, Dolphin Island, and Cub Island. Others are named after particular people like Gunnison, Carrington, and Stansbury Islands. Still others are named after a certain area such as Strong's Knob Island or White Rock Island. Antelope Island is being used as a recreational site now, although the local Native Americans remember a time when buffalo could cross from the mainland to this island without having to swim. Horses, cattle, sheep, and bison have all grazed there over time. The island's most famous inhabitant was a man named George Frary. He and his family lived there for over fifty years. Frary spent those years building various boats to explore the inland sea and his wife was buried there in 1897. His daughter was on the first passenger train to cross the Great Salt Lake using the Lucin Cutoff trestle in 1903.

Fremont Island's most famous but short-lived inhabitant was the grave robber John Baptiste, who was exiled there. John C. Fremont, who first discovered and explored this island, had his own name for it. He called it Disappointment Island because of its rocky terrain without trees and green carpets of grass like those found on Antelope Island. In 1848, Carrington visited the island in his boat called *The Mud Hen* and dubbed it Castle Island. Later, sheep were grazed there because there were no creatures to endanger the herds. During this time, they called it Miller's Island. The convict John Baptiste lived in the hut that the Millers had built to care for and shear their sheep until he disappeared a short time later. In the late nineteenth century, the Wenner family lived on the island for five years. Wenner was a judge who contracted tuberculosis. His family moved there from the city to provide him with needed fresh air and rest. The Wenners had a wooden home at first, called The Hut, and then built a two-story rock house, where they lived with their two children until the judge's death in 1891. He is buried on the island, where he was wrapped in a shawl and laid to rest in a homemade coffin.

Gunnison Island had an interesting short-term resident as well. Alfred Lambourne homesteaded on the island for a couple of years to write and to paint. His illustrated book *The Inland Sea* is based on this experience. He also planted a vineyard and left behind a beautiful legacy of descriptive thoughts about the island. Bird, Egg, and White Rock Islands are quite small and simply nesting places for the seagulls. In the 1930s, a family tried to homestead Carrington Island but did not stay for very long. Military aircraft used Gunnison Island for a target practice range after World War II. Mud Island is described as foul smelling, and Strong's Knob Island is considered an extension of Strong Knob Mountain. Dolphin and Cub Islands are tiny and barren and are located at the northernmost end of the lake. Stansbury Island, full of rugged mountain ranges, reconnected with the mainland in the 1870s because the Great Salt Lake dropped to its lowest level making Stansbury Island no longer an island.

In tracing the history of one little fishing boat, David Peterson gives a brief maritime history of the Great Salt Lake. Brigham Young commissioned the *Timely Gull*, which was launched on the Jordan River in June of 1854. The forty-five-foot vessel was used to transport cattle to and from Antelope Island. "Some say the boat was powered by horses that turned a treadmill, thereby turning a paddlewheel in the stern."[3] However, it eventually became a sailboat. The flat-bottomed vessel operated for four years and then was lost in a storm on the southern end of Antelope Island. Brothers Henry and Daniel Miller built two scows in 1859 and 1862 to use in their sheep ranching business on Fremont Island. Both were wrecked in the lake, the last one going down in 1876. Daniel Miller's son had a fifty-foot flat-bottomed boat built and christened it *Lady of the Lake*. The boat carried four secondary sails, two main sails, and had two main masts that were about fifty feet high. In the mid 1880s, Judge Wenner bought Fremont Island and moved his family there. The Miller's had to move their sheep operation to the mainland and Judge Wenner bought the abandoned *Lady of the Lake* that had been driven onto the western shore of Fremont Island in a bad storm. He repaired it and renamed it the *Argo* and used it to transport his family back and forth to the mainland. The *Argo* survived until at least 1909, when the new owners lost it on the rocks at Promontory Point.

At least two other vessels were built by the Millers, a seventy-five-foot boat named *Old Bob* and an additional vessel which was forty feet long and sixteen feet wide, but whose name has been lost in history. This second boat was sold to Captain George Frary who spent most of his time on the lake islands. He used this boat to transport the first dozen buffalo to Antelope Island in 1892. These boats were probably lost in the Great Salt Lake as well. Several large boats might still be sitting at the bottom of this lake, although the heavy salt content may have eaten away at them. There was one among these lost boats that went down with treasure aboard. This treasure was either in gold bars or gold coins and would have been able to withstand the salt. The money was most likely Brigham Young's, although the Millers might have had this kind of money or even the later owners of the four Miller boats. Captain Frary might also have been the owner of the money or it could have been in Judge Wenner's *Argo* vessel, which was used by others later on. Several books on legends of lost treasures name any boat from the *City of Corrine* to the *Argo* to the *Timely Gull*, as the one in which two large chests of gold went down to the bottom of the Great Salt Lake. However, the *City of Corinne* is most often referred to as the one carrying the gold and it never went down. I vote for the *Timely Gull*, because Brigham Young was most likely to be transporting that kind of money. After it went down, dozens of men were sent out to pole the lake where it had disappeared. The gold has never been found, one of hundreds of missing underwater treasures around the world. I suppose if someone researched it more, they could determine which vessel it was and approximately where it went down. If the legend is true, with the modern equipment we have now and the proper permission, this treasure could probably be found.

In 1868, when the first sightings of the Bear Lake monster began to be reported in the northern lake, the City of Corinne felt slighted. Corinne was the rowdy railroad city on the northern end of the Great Salt Lake, while the conservative Salt Lake City was on the southeastern side of the Great Salt Lake. These two cities competed for just about anything and on every level. For a time, because of the transcontinental railroad, Corinne was winning the battle to be the biggest city in the state. This changed when Brigham Young rerouted the railroad across the lake to Ogden City. At that time, even the prestige of having a lake monster was worth a competition, at least to the city of Corinne. Soon there were several reported sightings of a monstrous sea serpent near the shores of Corinne on the Great Salt Lake, and the citizens of Provo to the south began reporting monsters in their Utah Lake as well. For some unknown reason however, the Great Salt Lake never got very far in this media competition for monsters in the local lakes. Perhaps the serpent only liked the north side of the inland salt sea or the citizens of Salt Lake City weren't as enthusiastic to claim a monster in their lake.

When all of the resorts began to be built around the lake, Corinne decided to build a huge steamboat. The *City of Corinne* was launched in May of 1871. It was 130 feet long and twenty-five feet wide and weighed three hundred tons. Taking passengers from Corinne to Lake Point, Ophir, Stockton, and Salt Lake City, the steamboat ran only for a short period of time. It was then sold to a mining firm and in 1872 to the Lake Side Resort near Farmington, Utah. Its name was changed to *General Garfield* and the steamboat began to deteriorate. Finally, in 1881 it was sold to Captain Thomas Douris who expanded and improved upon the Black Rock Resort and used the steamboat only briefly. Finally, it became apparent that the *General Garfield's* seafaring days were over and "she was stripped of her machinery and paddlewheel, and used as a floating hotel, changing room for bathers, and a boathouse for the Salt Lake Rowing Club."[4] In 1904, what was left of the *Garfield* burned to the ground along with the resort. Douris ran two new small steamers called the *Susie Riter* and the *Whirlwind*. The *Susie Riter* went down only two years later in a storm on the lake.

General Patrick Edward Connor of Camp Douglas had two vessels built in 1868, the one-hundred-ton *Pioneer* and the six-hundred-ton steamer *Kate Connor*, named after his daughter. In 1869, he added a third schooner, the one-hundred-ton *Pluribustah*, to promote shipping on the lake. By 1872, he had sold the *Kate Connor* for use as a cattle ferry to Antelope Island and the *Pioneer* lay in a boat graveyard at the mouth of the Jordan River. The *Pluribustah* was wrecked near the tracks at Saltair and left to rot there. Saltair's only steamer was called the *Tulula* and it carried passengers back and forth to the various resorts or to the mainland. Saltair had one other small paddlewheel steamer called the *Vista* that began operating in 1907. The boat had been built in 1905 and was used from the Green River to the Colorado River near the boat's original namesake, the city of Moab. After being stranded many times on the sandbars there, the *Vista* was sold to Saltair.

Finally, in his Great Salt Lake maritime history, Peterson mentions the building of the great Lucin Cutoff train trestle across the Great Salt Lake. The story of this train trestle's building and demise is told in much more detail in one of my other books on railroad ghost stories. There were so many accidents and drownings both during the building of the trestle and through the many years that it operated, that hauntings on the Great Salt Lake could be numerous.

The Great Salt Lake has a history filled with all sorts of folklore. With about 2.9 million acre feet of water evaporating annually, the lake itself is a phenomenon of water in the middle of a desert, ever shifting and changing its face and character. In the early days, there were reports of terrible stenches that were thought to be deadly vapors that rose up from the lake when anything came near it. The vapors had been rumored to murder people on the spot. People would stay indoors hoping that the vapors couldn't reach them on such days. Today, between the pollution during the winter months that produces a gray smog and the overwhelming stench on certain days, one wonders if the early settlers weren't right about these vapors, maybe they could kill a person on the spot. During the 2002 Winter Olympics, residents were worried there would be a few days of this stench and that Utah's image would be ruined. Fortunately, the weather cooperated and our foreign visitors missed the dreaded vapors.

There was even a tale of the Great Salt Lake leaving its bed and sinking the city under fifty feet of water. This was quite an ironic tale, as a Nephite City was also rumored to be in its depths, just like the more famous city in Utah Lake. In those days, the early Latter-day Saints were intent on proving the truth of their book of scripture, the Book of Mormon. Finding artifacts or archeological sites where the Book of Mormon describes these ancient North American cities would have been a great discovery for any community. The idea of the lake rising straight up out of its bed and flooding the nearby city is not that far fetched considering how it has risen and shrunk over the years and flooded resorts along its banks. Another theory revolves around a giant earthquake that has been predicted to happen here in the Salt Lake Valley within the next fifty years. If it were to happen, the lake could surely rise up out of its bed to a certain extent like water splashing around in a bowl, and could flood some of the city.

There have been many strange sightings on the Great Salt Lake's shores and islands over the years. People have seen horses the size of dogs like the eohippus, alligator-like lake monsters, and even a race of giant Native Americans riding elephants along its shores. Strange creatures of the mythical type were said to sometimes drain the lake deep into the earth as an explanation for its shifting levels. Creatures would then release some of the water to the surface according to some unknown schedule. It has also been said over the years that there are underground passages to the Pacific Ocean. These subterranean passageways, like the ones that are supposed to exist in Bear Lake, conveniently explain the arrival and departure of ancient sea monsters that are seen only occasionally and disappear for long periods of time. Sightings of unidentified creatures from the ocean depths were sometimes rumored. Some claimed that they gained access to the lake via these caverns that have not yet been explored.

Between 1860 and 1880, it seemed as though there was a competition going on between all three lakes (Bear Lake to the north in Cache Valley, Utah Lake to the south in Utah Valley, and the Great Salt Lake) to see which could claim the biggest and most frightening lake monsters. Bear Lake had a corner on the market with many more sightings than the other two. Utah Valley residents were accused by the local newspaper, the *Deseret News*, of creating a character to compete with the one in Bear Lake. The Great Salt Lake was third when it came to lake monsters, although Corinne claimed in their paper, the *Daily Corrine*, that there were no monsters in either lake and the only real monster lived in the north end of the Great Salt Lake near their city. There were several reported sightings near Corinne during this time, although by the end of the 1880s, these newspapers claimed that the lake monsters had gone out of fashion.[5]

There have been a few real tragedies on the lake in the form of drownings, train wrecks, and car and small aircraft crashes. One rather famous aircraft crash involved a man who plunged his World War II plane into the lake and was found wandering around the shore several hours later with no memory of what had happened. But the biggest mystery is why the lake simply refuses to let anyone or anything predict its movements. Every attempt at establishing a lasting resort or recreational site has been discouraged by the constantly changing water levels, awful odors, brine shrimp, and myriad small disasters. The railroad trestles and roads have had to constantly circumvent new disasters to cross the lake. One of my favorite jokes a few years back was when Utah's state legislature and senate tried to legislate the lake's water level.

Beyond the strange and mysterious wildlife that simply could not exist, at least today, people have reported over the years a crocodile or alligator-like creature in the Great Salt Lake. In 1871, J.H. McNeil reported seeing a crocodile about five feet long but with a head that looked like a horse's. Since then, reports have described this crocodile or alligator creature as anywhere from five feet to seventy-five feet in length. Like Bear Lake and Utah Lake, reports of these creatures are rarely, if ever, heard today. The Great Salt Lake seems to have the biggest variety of creatures of the three lakes, the second most famous of which being the salt bears. These bears were pure white, and invisible too—an extraordinary feat in and of itself! They could blend into the background on the Salt Flats so well that only their little black eyes would be visible. They were responsible for tearing up the highways that cross the Salt Flats or startling a few lone drivers on the road. These little black eyes would stare, seeming to float in nothingness around cars as they drove past the lake or on the road across the lake to Antelope Island.

The size of the Great Salt Lake must have something to do with how many creatures it houses. There have been some real creatures in the area because of slightly strange circumstances. A sighting of a camel was reported near the lake's shores, which was very possible, as Grantsville also had a camel visit. The camel or camels might have come from either a traveling circus, or much more likely, military units in the area. The military used them in desert areas in the early 1800s. Neglected and suffering from the high alkali content in the soil, they often died, were sold to mine owners to haul ore, or ran off into the desert on their own. Pelicans and even a pink flamingo that escaped from the Hogle Zoo lived on the lake. One or more of these creatures could account for sightings of strange and mysterious creatures at the Great Salt Lake.

An 1890 article in a Provo newspaper told an interesting, if highly unlikely, story. James Wickham, a whale farmer, is said to have come up with the idea that the Australian whale could thrive in the environment of the Great Salt Lake. "He spent two years Down Under in a custom-built ship designed to capture the young whales without injury. The expedition seized two thirty-five-foot-long cetaceans in 1873 and shipped them to San Francisco in special tanks. The beasts were transported overland with 50 tanks of seawater to insure plentiful supplies of the natural element. His men fenced off a small bay near the mouth of Bear River to create a pen for the whales and Wickham journeyed from London to superintend the planting of his leviathan pets." At first lethargic, the two whales quickly became much more lively and "suddenly made a beeline for deep water and shot through the wire fence as if it had been made of threads." Within twenty minutes, they had disappeared and it was not until six months later that some of his agents spotted the creatures spouting and playing fifty miles away. They had grown to sixty feet in length and were followed about "by a school of several hundred young varying in length from three to fifteen feet." Unfortunately, Salt Lake whalers soon harpooned all of the beasts producing as much as twenty tons of pure oil each. The experiment was a success, but the whales became extinct due to whalers in the Great Salt Lake.[6]

No matter the mysteries of the most famous lake in Utah, the Great Salt Lake continues to mystify those who wish to predict its future. It is as unpredictable and ever-changing as any bodies of water found in nature. Its mysteries will continue to baffle us, although I am sure that the Native Americans might have the last laugh in all this. The Native Americans were the first to fish on its shores and the first to tell stories about it. They knew the water was extremely salty and harmful to the body. The lake was not a place that they advised their people to visit. Tales of the lake's creation were filled with warnings to stay away from her, but of course we white people paid no heed and here we are.

Spiral Jetty

In a last and fitting monument to the Great Salt Lake, we have *Spiral Jetty*. The *Salt Lake Tribune* has called it Utah's answer to Stonehenge. An interactive nature artist named Robert Smithson built the jetty on the lake in 1970. He had been looking for a place to make something out of rocks and earth in a dead sea. Smithson, with a little help from his friends, hauled some 6,650 tons of rocks out into the Great Salt Lake. He believed that art was to be demonstrative of ancient earth rituals and the environment. He also felt that works of art should have a lasting impact on the future. He built his monuments so that long after he was gone they would stand of their own accord in a natural environment. This is exactly what *Spiral Jetty* does. It is a 1,500-foot spiral that grows out into the water from the land and curls into itself. The spiral is a universal symbol that is found everywhere on earth from the tiniest flower to the pattern in solar systems and galaxies. On the shores of the Great Salt Lake, Smithson placed the most mystical symbol in the universe and in nature. When people gathered there for the so-called harmonic convergence, I was there watching the sand-building competition and thinking about the particle waves that surely rippled across the surface of our lake of salt near the city. Located on the south end of the lake, *Spiral Jetty* was hidden under the lake for years, just recently surfacing.

Black Rock

Nature's Black Rock is located near the old highway headed for Stansbury Park. While the resort and swimming place at Black Rock are long gone now, the huge black rock alternately rises out of the water and sits on the sandy shore. The area looks mystical and haunted, especially on foggy days. In 1881, the first Fourth of July celebration took place at Black Rock and a large homemade American flag was unfurled across it. Not far from this resort were the Garfield and Lake Point Resorts, which operated from 1881 to 1893. There was a railroad station, a lunch stand, a restaurant, bathhouses, and a pier leading to the dance pavilion. The pioneer steamboat *City of Corinne* was moored only one and a half miles west of there. The three-story hotel became the stopping place for overland stages and quite a few people spent their weekends at one of these resorts.

Of all the legends about the Great Salt Lake, the stories of the two families who lived on two different islands offer the most interesting details of life on the lake. The Frary family left no written records of their fifty years on Antelope Island. However, George Frary spent his fifty years there, along with his wife, building boats to sail on the lake or to explore the islands. His wife was buried on the island in 1897. On Fremont Island, Judge Wenner's wife kept a journal about the time they spent on Fremont Island and later these writings were published. Alas, this woman's tales are out of print and seemingly impossible to find. I hope that someone will pick up this journal again and publish it, as the passages are wonderful. Judge Wenner was buried on the island that he loved so much. His wife eventually settled in Canada.

Recently, a small plane went down in the Great Salt Lake. The two passengers were killed and the plane and its wreckage sat there in the lake until morning when a passerby happened to see it. Both men in the plane were good pilots with lots of experience. Authorities are still investigating this accident to figure out just what happened. The Great

Salt Lake swallowed up yet another mystery and two more wandering spirits were added to her roster of those who have passed beyond. Perhaps like the plane crash several decades ago, someone will spot a lone spirit wandering by the side of the road trying to find its way home. Or perhaps even two of them, for this ancient sea has a mind of its own.

There are three known ghosts that frequent the islands. The man and woman buried on Antelope and Fremont Islands are probably content spirits who wander the places that they loved, while the story of the third spirit, Jean Baptiste, is a much more grisly affair. (See book four). His ghost wanders both Antelope and Fremont Islands to this day. Only part of his story takes place on these islands; the rest takes place in and near the Salt Lake Cemetery. Baptiste's tale is the lake's ghost story that has gained the most notoriety over the years. Fremont Island and Antelope Island each boast two ghosts, although they share Baptiste as one of the spirits on both islands. But when I think of the number of skeletal remains from several large ships lying at the bottom of this lake, as well as the recorded drownings, and the early Native Americans believed to have been taken to their deaths by the lake's monster, I know that this much phenomena could account for anything strange happening on this large inland sea. There are probably a lot of apparitions on the Great Salt Lake that people will never encounter due to the lack of travel on the lake. The paranormal is unexplored territory there.

Notes

1) Powell, *Utah History Encyclopedia*, "Lake Bonneville," 313–14.
2) Powell, *Utah History Encyclopedia*, "Great Salt Lake," 233–34.
3) Petersen, *Tale of the Lucin: A boat, a Railroad, and the Great Salt Lake*, 13.
4) Ibid., 27.
5) Arave, "Mystical Beasts Lurk in 5 Utah Lakes," September 23, 2001.
6) Bagley, "Whale of a Tale Gives Great Salt Lake's Fabled History an Unlikely Spin," June 29, 2003.

Water Babies
and Golden Cities

Utah Lake is the state's largest freshwater lake. It is 150 square miles and drains into the Great Salt Lake through the Jordan River. Provo, Spanish Fork, and American Fork Rivers drain into Utah Lake. It is a shallow body of water with a depth of only nine feet. It is twenty-three miles long and about half that in width. There are trenches, benches, and deep slopes left over from ancient Lake Bonneville and many fossils can still be found today around the lake. It is now a three hundred–acre state park and marina and the most popular spot in the state for boating, fishing, and water skiing. But it can be dangerous in high winds. In addition to stories about river rafting or boating on the lake, there are also some ghostly tales about the Provo River.

One famous tale from 1850 involved a Native American named Old Bishop and some poachers. Old Bishop got his name because of his resemblance to a recently deceased Latter-day Saint bishop who had lived in the area. Old Bishop was a sort of game warden for his Native American people in the area. Three Mormon Battalion veterans had decided to go poaching near Fort Utah, the Provo settlement. When Old Bishop confronted them about violating the treaty, one of the men shot and killed him. In order to hide his body, they gutted him like a deer, filled him will stones, and threw him in a creek. Rather than sinking, Old Bishop's body floated downstream into the Provo River and eventually came to rest where the river meets the lake. The Utes found his body caught in a big cottonwood tree. This discovery contributed to what is now called the Utah War between the settlers and the Utes.

The Utes lost the war and many members of the tribe died in the process, including women and children. Apparently Old Bishop was murdered in either December or January because that is the time that his ghost is seen roaming the area. Ute lore says that every winter Old Bishop appears on the Provo River bank and can be seen removing the stones from his body one by one. He then tosses these stones one by one into the river. When he is done with this process he disappears, but soon reappears to reenacts this scenario over and over again. However, only Utes claim to have seen him. I believe it though, as it's likely Old Bishop is trying to get rid of the heavy stones he bears and deal with the men who never paid for their crime, but started a war instead.[1]

The United States Steel Corporation had a giant plant on the opposite shore of Utah Lake called Geneva Steel Works. It employed over five thousand workers from Orem and Provo and was constructed from 1942 to 1944 as a war plant by the government. It was sold after World War II for two hundred million dollars. Even though there were lawsuits over the years for emissions violations, the giant plant continued to pollute the air. Compromised plans for emissions controls were finally agreed to, but no one really knew the effect of the plant on the air, land, and lake. The plant has since been shut down, and the Geneva Steel Works, associated for so many years with the Provo Valley and the city of Provo itself, is deserted except for a few workers who guard the plant. No more pollution, no more jobs in the valley, and no more Geneva. The huge complex is still sitting there and perhaps another company will pick it up. It is certainly a striking contrast to the beautiful, deserted Saltair on the Great Salt Lake to see this huge, ugly plant and its many smoke towers sitting on the northern shore of Utah Lake.

Several resorts had short lives on the lake over the years, with Beck's Saratoga Springs Resort the biggest and best known. Beck's was built in 1884 on a thousand acres of land and promised wonderful medicinal properties for all sorts of skin diseases and joint problems. They even bottled the hot springs waters starting in 1897 and sold it as Saratoga Salvation. It promised to cure a variety of internal and external diseases. There was a train to the Utah Lake Pavilion and several other resorts came and went during the late 1800s, such as Woodbury Park, Old Lake, Geneva, Murdock, Lincoln Beach, American Fork Beach, and the Provonna Bathing Resort at the mouth of Provo River.

Saratoga Springs is still there today, although now it is called the Seven Peaks Water Resort.

Native Americans, who lived by the lake long before the white man came, told of water babies who inhabited the lake. They were of varying sizes, from the size of a hand to the size of a human. Water babies were considered dangerous, somewhat like mermaids, and could lead their victims to an underwater grave. They were like sprites that people would follow, as though mesmerized, into the depths of the water. They had long black hair and cried as a baby would, giving the appearance of creatures coming up from the depths of the lake.

In the 1860s, the lake monster fever caught on everywhere after the reported sightings at Bear Lake. A man named Issac Fox, while out hunting on the north end of the Utah Lake, heard strange noises. When he walked to where the noises were coming from, he saw a serpent-like animal about thirty feet long. He said that it had a head like a greyhound and black eyes that looked at him piercingly. Over the next few years, more sightings were reported. All of them agreed on the serpent-like body, the length, and the greyhound-like head. Then some fishermen from Springville stumbled upon a large and unusual animal skull. The back of the jaw had an approximately five-inch section of tusks. For many believers, this was proof of the Utah Lake monster. Even if it really was the skull of a much more ancient creature from ancient Lake Bonneville, this might have been a real find for the experts. But no mention or record was made of what happened to this skull, so it could very well have been a hoax.

In 1860, "two men reported splashing at the Jordan River and Utah Lake. They spotted a creature with a head shaped like a greyhound with 'wicked-looking black eyes.'"[2] In 1864, a man named Henry Walker of Lehi saw a Utah Lake monster shortly after the Bear Lake monster had been reported in Cache Valley to the north. Fearful and surprised at the same time, Walker described the creature as looking like a very large snake with the head of a greyhound. He kept this sighting to himself for four years until finally word got out and it was reported in the newspapers. In 1880, two boys spotted some kind of an animal on Utah Lake. Thinking it an otter, beaver, or even a dog, they saw it begin to swim towards them. Suddenly, it roared loudly and reared up from the lake with a head about three feet long and a long snout, like an alligator with lots of teeth. The boys, who had been swimming, turned around as quickly as they could and swam to shore. They were terrified and told their story immediately to those on the shore. At the time, the *Deseret News* accused the people of Utah Valley of creating a character for Utah Lake because they were jealous of all the publicity that Bear Lake was getting for its lake monster.[3]

There was not another report until 1921, when another fisherman near Goshen saw a strange animal in Utah Lake and tried to capture it so that he could exhibit it. He failed in his attempts and the Utah Lake monster has not been sighted much since then. It's possible that all the pollution might have killed the creature off or at least scared it away. Now that all the noise and confusion is gone with the closing of Geneva Steel, perhaps the lake's snake-like animal with the greyhound head, the giant alligator-like monster, or the small water babies will be back to their old tricks again. Or perhaps people will create sightings of them just to entice a few more tourists there!

Another interesting story about Utah Lake concerns the Nephite city. This story, told up until the 1940s, went that Utah Lake is extremely deep and has hidden caverns that are even deeper than the experts say. The story claims that the lake covers a sunken city from ancient times. According to the Latter-day Saints' book of scripture, the Book of Mormon, the Nephites were a civilization of pre-Colombian peoples who lived in North or South America. There are legends of sunken cities all over the world including the most famous one, Atlantis, although inland bodies of water in Europe seem to be the most common places for sunken cities. Such stories are extremely rare in the United States. Most sunken cities met their demise because of the wickedness of the people who inhabited them. It was usually some act of nature that did them in—an earthquake, erupting volcano, tidal wave, fire, or even a great storm. However, it is always God whose wrath brings down the natural disasters upon the wicked people and wipes them off the face of the earth. Even in Native American tales, there are stories about a wicked people who never got to the next world because of their greedy or selfish ways.

There are some Latter-day Saints who believe that a group of people known as the Nephites incurred the wrath of God that the ruins of some of these Nephite cities might still be found in the Americas somewhere.

An ancient sunken city is not so strange if we look at how this idea might have evolved from the beliefs that the Latter-day Saint settlers brought with them. These settlers named many places after people or places found in the Bible and the Book of Mormon. There was a Salem town, the Jordan River, a group of hills called Jacob's Ladder, and Mount Nebo. There are also canyons named after places or people that populate these two books, like Enoch or Israel. Many of the mountains and natural features of the various national monuments in middle and southern Utah have a combination of local Native American tribal names and names from the Book of Mormon or the Bible. There are very similar features of the land in Utah and the Holy land, such as the Dead Sea and the Great Salt Lake, the two River Jordans, and the Sea of Galilee and Utah Lake (both of which were important at one time for their fishing resources). The Latter-day Saints had to endure a great exodus after being exiled from a promised land and head for another one, just as Moses led his people out of Egypt.

When I heard the stories about the ruins of an ancient civilization, I was fascinated by the prospect that right here in Utah we have our own ancient ruins, a possible city of gold that all those miners over the years have been searching for, the nine vaults of gold, and the sunken city of the Nephites. I thought of the old Flash Gordon serials and Ming's floating city in the air. How fascinated I was by such stories, and that golden stairway in my illustrated Bible that showed all the people climbing its many steps and then disappearing into nothing at the top. New Agers are not any different with their magical and mystical lands and planets, although the idea of a huge ancient city under Utah Lake is pure fantasy. The mere idea of such a city from ancient times being discovered in Utah Lake shows how absolutely fascinating the history of my state is. We can always take this a step further and say that it is an invisible city, which would conveniently explain why no one has ever found any evidence of it. As you may already know, I for one will not discount anything, not even a city of gold under a neighboring lake.

Aside from mythical golden cities, there have been some interesting real events associated with Utah Lake as well. For example, there was a place called the Provonna Beach Resort that opened in 1889 as the Provo Bathing Resort near where the Provo River enters Utah Lake. The resort closed down, but boats were rented for excursions to the Saratoga and Geneva Resorts. Camp Riverside Resort came next, where boats christened the *Cleo, Martha Ann, Grace, Abba*, and *Minnie* took tourists out onto the lake. In 1911, Camp Riverside became the Riverside Boat Landing or Gammon's Resort. It was a quarter of a mile from Riverside to Utah Lake and in 1919, a large dance pavilion was built at Riverside, a quarter of a mile from Utah Lake. A driving bridge was completed in 1921 so people could cross the river to the resort. In 1921, huge piles of ice swept through the resort and swept the bathhouses into the lake as the storms destroyed everything in their path that winter. By 1925, the resort had been rebuilt and many improvements were made. In 1926, an airplane careened into the resort, hitting cars in the parking lot and narrowly missing two small boys on the beach. Seeing the boys at the last minute, the pilot made a sharp turn to avoid them and lost control of the plane. The plane tore off the roof of a car with a startled family inside it. In 1929, a dead body was found on the beach near the resort. However on closer examination, it was discovered to be a man made out of sand.

That same year, two teenage girls who had decided to swim out to a launch at the resort almost drowned. One girl became hysterical, while the other swam to her and grabbed her by the hair and began swimming for shore. A man on shore heard their screams and jumped in and swam to them just about the time that the swimmer was losing her strength to hold onto her companion. In 1930, a boat went out one evening with a brother and sister aboard. It made a sharp turn in the high waves and capsized. The sister went under and the brother grabbed her and began swimming for shore, but his heavy clothes began dragging him under just as they got close to the shore. By the time they were spotted and a boat was launched, the brother was floating unconscious in the water and the sister had disappeared into the depths. Her body was pulled from the lake a few hours later. She had left a husband and a one-year-old son behind. Also in that year, a huge Naval battle was staged at the resort on the Fourth of July with large models of several Navy vessels "at war" and a dramatic fireworks display. In 1932, the Provonna Beach Resort closed down forever.

The first notable excursion boat on Utah Lake was the *Eastmound*, which carried 125 passengers and was launched in 1886. The *Florence* was soon launched and it carried one hundred and fifty passengers. This boat later became the *Tulula* and made excursions to Saltair. The

Reanon W was built at the Geneva Resort with very powerful engines and took tours on the lake from 1913 to 1917.

A tragic event occurred on the lake on June 25, 1911, when the *Galilee* capsized. Captain Edward G. Brown, a native of Scotland who had been the master of a vessel on the Atlantic Ocean, was taking sixteen people out on an excursion in honor of his daughter's impending marriage. They were traveling from Geneva Resort to the Schneider Ranch near Saratoga Springs. The bride was twenty-one and the groom was twenty-six. High winds brought on a sudden squall that capsized the boat. The high waves made it impossible to cling to the sides of the boat. A father holding his five-year-old son in his arms drowned. The young groom tried to save his bride, but both drowned. The mother and father of the bride also drowned. A tourist boat called the *LeVom*, which was loaded down with fourteen young men came to their rescue. The bodies of Frank and Helen Brown were recovered and then the body of the bride, Vera Brown, who had been lashed to the mast by her father. Two days later they found Benjamin W. Raymond and his son, and the groom, Edward B. Holmes. Because of the tragic accident, the *Galilee* was sold. It became a fishing boat on the lake and was called the *Mary Jane* and later renamed the *Mina*. Superstitions that the boat was cursed did not prove true, because she spent her final years accomplishing several rescue missions on the lake. Perhaps this was the boat's atonement for what had happened before.

In 1932, a large excursion boat called the *S.S. Sho-Boat* was launched onto Utah Lake. On its first attempt to get to the lake, only a year before, the boat had settled on the shallow bottom of the river. After some minor adjustments, the boat was relaunched and followed in the lead of the other large vessels that had been on the lake. Two very creative World War I veterans designed and built the *S.S. Sho-Boat*, the biggest boat ever to run on the Provo River and Utah Lake. The two men began working on it and other nautical inventions in 1924. It was called the most luxurious boat ever to operate on Utah's "Sea of Galilee." The boat was ninety feet long and twenty-two feet wide. After the first launch in 1931, the boat immediately sank. People thought the inventors were crazy for attempting the entire project. There were all kinds of ingenious inventions on the boat, including two large rudders to keep the boat from drifting in high winds as it entered the lake. It had a full stage and dance band area with a large dance floor.

Benches lined the two sides and small rooms across the back of the boat housed a kitchen, bathrooms, a motor room, and a small gift shop. The *S.S. Sho-Boat* had a large observation deck that was surrounded by a heavy rail; benches were added to this area later. Over five hundred people toured the boat before its first launch. The owners and their wives always wore nautical uniforms, and the employees wore sailor outfits. Groups who rented the boat also hired their own bands and other entertainment for the trip.

The boat cruised at six to eight miles an hour down the river to the lake and then cruised to Bird or Rock Island six miles southwest of the river. Here the passengers would get off and go exploring on the island. Originally christened the *Smith-Strong Sho-Boat*, the name was shortened to the *S.S. Sho-Boat* somewhere along the way. It had an eight-person crew, including a bouncer for those occasional rowdy customers on board. On one trip, a man who had argued with his wife decided to drown himself but was rescued by one of the crew. This rescue went on for three separate jumps, until the crewmember told the man to go ahead and drown himself, at which point the man swam back to the boat. Another man tried the same thing and on the third attempt they knocked him unconscious and locked him in the closet until they could reach shore.

In 1933, the Provo River became very narrow and shallow from a long drought. The owners of the ship had to come up with a way to get the boat down the river to Utah Lake. They used a large water pump and telephone poles to accomplish this feat. The owners had a lot of trouble with vandalism during the long winter months when the boat was moored. This, as well as strong winds, caused the owners some financial difficulties. The boat was further damaged in a rather violent thunderstorm. Luckily, there was entertainment in the form of a former vaudevillian passenger who launched into his various routines to calm the nerves of the passengers.

In 1940, the owners built a new helm house on the upper deck and they and their families began performing aquatic feats for the passengers' enjoyment, such as "aqua-planing" using a small speedboat. Through World War II, the boat and its owners flourished. In 1946, the business ended and the boat was floated into its shallow grave, which was dug in a place on the Provo River close to where the *S.S. Sho-Boat* had been originally constructed. Vandals took a lot of the boat away, but the families managed to salvage some important items, like the ship's bell and siren. By 1958, not much of her was left, but the family salvaged the wood. A Latter-day Saint missionary called family members during those years and returned both of the anchors to soothe his own guilty conscience for having taken them. No one since has ever attempted another excursion boat of this size on the lake.[4]

In a recent article, Will Bagley added a few facts and thoughts in response to an earlier article on the Bear Lake monster called "Why Isn't There a Utah Lake Monster?" He apparently responded to some irate readers who knew all about the reports of monsters in Utah Lake over the years. While he was writing his column for the *Tribune*, Bagley wrote several articles about the Bear Lake monster and rarely mentioned the other lakes in the state. It is interesting that to this day there is a rivalry between the Bear Lake and Utah Lake fans for the best lake monster legends. Why the Great Salt Lake isn't included in this rivalry is a mystery, except perhaps because a salt lake or inland sea cannot compete with fresh water lakes. Maybe since it is near the largest city in the state, the Great Salt Lake doesn't need to compete with the two smaller lakes. There are enough interesting things going on at the Great Salt Lake, or at least enough strange and bizarre things, that Salt Lake City does not need to claim lake monsters so insistently.[5]

Apparently, the Utes have a story in tribal lore about a mysterious creature that swallowed a man whole near Pelican Point long ago. Issac Fox's sighting in 1864 stated that after he chased the monster, the fierce creature went back in the water and joined its mate. Fox saw two creatures side by side in the lake. Bagley also states that the monsters seem to prefer the northern end of the lake, where most of the sightings have occurred. Bagley added an additional sighting from 1866. "Two men cutting hay saw a yellow animal with black spots that repeatedly displayed a forked red tongue." He also adds more to the 1871 sighting in which "William Price of Goshen and two fellow travelers spotted the serpent on the west shore of Utah Lake in 1871. Standing about 6 feet out of the water like a giant snake, the beast's 60-foot long body looked like a section of a stovepipe."[6]

Bagley also names the two boys who saw the Utah Lake monster in 1880 as Willie Roberts and George Scott. His account provides just a little more description of this lion-like beast, which had four yard-long legs and alligator-like jaws three feet long. The boys also said that the creature chased them and made "savage gestures" towards them. The article also tells of an English traveler who wrote about this event, mentioning the "great snake" of Utah Lake and wondering if the Smithsonian knew about this "terror." An 1870 Springville discovery produced a skull with a five-inch tusk protruding from its jaw. The skull mysteriously disappeared after being shown around as proof that there were monsters in Utah Lake. Bagley theorizes that Geneva Steel's programs to upgrade the local air and water may have chased the lake monsters away.[7]

Since modern-day fishermen and boaters have never reported sightings of beasts in the lake. It's strange that there were so many sightings in the 1800s. Perhaps part of the reason is the rumor phenomena that takes one incident and adds on to it over and over until a fisherman's tall tale becomes a whopper. These sightings may also have been ordinary things mistaken for monsters. Fisherman on the lake think that, besides a log or something else floating in the river, they have an explanation for these sightings from over a hundred years ago. They suggest that what people really saw was a wild duck called a coot or hell diver around the lake. It seems that this duck flaps its wings furiously and "water skis" many yards before it is able to get airborne. The sight of this duck carrying out this process would be enough to scare anyone, these expert fishermen say, as it makes a lot of wild noises, enough to be mistaken for a sea serpent.

Despite all the talk of monsters, golden cities, water babies, resorts, boating tragedies, and fisherman's tall tales, what is of most concern to me is that structure that has resided near the lake since World War II. Geneva Steel was probably the real monster, silently polluting not only the lake, but also the entire Utah Valley. Remembering that gorgeous golden haze blanketing the highway and the entire valley, it seemed, I thought about golden cities and the writers who have mentioned this steel plant and its pollution in their novels. And while we all knew that we were driving through something deadly, the interplay of light and color was something we had never seen before or since.

Water babies and other sea creatures, whether real or imaginary, cannot survive in such a polluted place. I was relieved when I heard that the steel plant had shut down for good and its smokestacks would no longer pour out their filth. The plant's closure hurt the economy of the town and affected many, many people. Even though the plant is shut down, the pollution problem will continue for years to come, affecting many more cycles in nature. As for the monsters that live in the lake? They were either never really there, or decided to depart quite some time ago. Monsters can reappear at any time, be they fierce beasts rising out of the water or giant man-made steel plants that throw their pollutions into the sky, a sky that rains down both on the lake and the people who live by the lake.

Notes

1) Bagley, "Murdered Ute's Ghost Haunts Utah History," November 5, 2000.
2) Arave, "Mystical Beasts Lurk in 5 Utah Lakes," September 23, 2001.
3) Ibid.
4) Carter, "The S.S. Sho-Boat: Queen of Utah Lake," Winter 1997.
5) Bagley, "Maybe There Is a Monster in Utah Lake," March 31, 2002.
6) Ibid.
7) Ibid.

Legends of the Grand Lakes of the Badlands Cones

Ancient Fish Lake

While the monsters of Bear Lake, Utah Lake, and the Great Salt Lake receive most of the attention, there are a few other lakes in the state that have at one time or another laid claim to a monster. Panguitch Lake (which means big or heavy fish) is located twenty-one miles west of the town of Panguitch. A popular fishing and summer home area, it is on the Markagunt Plateau. The lake is at an eight-thousand-foot elevation and measures one square mile. It is a volcanic basin surrounded by ancient black lava beds that are rough and jagged. There are other ancient lava flows to the southeast and southwest. When I was in Kenya, we went to the Shatani Lava Fields, considered to be full of bad spirits; no locals ever went there for they believed it would bring them bad luck. A few of us got out and went leaping about on the long, high black lava rocks. It was eerie to see this ancient flow stretching for miles and miles in every direction as far as the eye could see. It is no stretch of the imagination that the Native American tribes in the area thought Panguitch Lake might have a few monsters in it, or at least caverns, crevices, or craters where ancient monsters might hide.

The other area that lays claim to monsters in its lakes is located near Gunnison and Salina. The high plateaus in the area and their history as active volcanoes connect all of the nearby lakes. The eastern foothills of the Sevier Valley rise up south of Centerfield, then continue on into Salina as the Aurora Cliffs. These cliffs on the Pavant

Plateau play reddish and maroon shadows on the desert floor as the sun crosses them. They are a "cluster of weird badland cones or gypsum hills, and rising above these the dark and massive hulks of other high plateaus—the Sevier, Fishlake and Tushar—all reach summits of more than 11,000 feet. Through the valley, in lazy meanders, flows the Sevier River, a murky stream of a modest size that belies its importance to thousands of people."[1] The word *sevier* is an anglicized version of the Spanish word for *severe*.

Fish Lake is near Richfield, so both Sevier and Wayne Counties can lay claim to it. South of Salina is Salina Canyon, part of the Old Spanish Trail. One fork of this canyon goes to Fish Lake in Grass Valley while another fork goes to Sevier Lake in Sevier Valley. Rich-field can be seen below the high Sevier Plateau, which rises 5,800 feet above the plains. The Sevier Plateau's upper third is a steep prec-ipice, while the lower two-thirds is a series of plunging buttresses. The Wasatch Plateau on the northeast goes clockwise to Fish Lake. Capitol Reef National Park is just next door to the Sevier Plateau on the east. These high plateaus are visible from miles away and have a dark and gloomy aspect to them. In every direction is a spectacle of tabular highlands from the Wasatch to Fishlake, Sevier, Tushar, and the Pavants.

Far from these shadowy plateaus are other high plateaus from the grand Aquarius where Boulder Mountain resides, to Thousand Lake Mountain, the Paunsaugunt and Markagunt Plateaus, and finally, the remote and rugged Kairparowits. Raised and lowered over the centu-ries by crustal forces, these sedimentary deposits are the result of great faults in the earth's surface. The ancient and extensive volcanic activity in the area is evidenced by all the trachyte, rhyolite, basalt, and various lavas coming up from inside the earth. The "vast erosion, faulting, and volcanic factors operating on this region have made it of fascinating interest to the geologist."[2] The whole area around Fish Lake has a spec-tacular view of endless highlands. The mineral deposits and the crustal forces show evidence of just about every form of ancient volcanic erup-tion. Fish Lake is representative of other smaller lakes in the area and is located in the Fish Lake National Forest at a nine-thousand-foot elevation. The lake is seven miles long and one mile wide and four dif-ferent streams feed it.

Fish Lake Stories and Tall Tales

When Brigham Young first sent an emissary to the Native Americans, he found an area abundant with fish, deer, bear, berries, and pine nuts. Because it was quite inaccessible in those days, it offered a perfect refuge or camping area for local Native American tribes. It was from these tribes that we get the first reports of monsters in the lake. In June of 1873, a group of white men with Chief Tabunia, or Sun-Dog, as guide and interpreter, arrived at the crest of the mountains and looked down upon a virtual paradise. They climbed down and reached Fish Lake on June twenty-third. The first Native American fisherman they saw had about forty fish lying on the bank. Fearful at seeing his first white man, he ran off, leaving the explorers to catch close to two hundred fish. Peter Gottfredson told of this incident in his journal, *Indian Depredations in Utah*, although the number of fish caught could have been a proverbial fisherman's tale. George Bean, another man in this party, wrote in his autobiography that they met with the main chief, Chief Pah-fa-ne-pa, or Fish Captain, who approached their camp fiercely, circling it three times, ceremoniously brandishing his weapons and then finally settling into a circle around their camp fire to talk. The white men made an appointment with all of the tribes in the area to meet in Cedar Grove in Grass Valley and later made a truce with them on July first. According to Bean, that pledge was never broken.

Soon settlers moved to the valley and lived by Fish Lake in the summer months, as the winters there were too harsh. Eventually they built cabins, where they fished the lake and collected the other abundant foods available during the summer season. The meadows soon had cows and calves, and the settlers were making cheese to ship down to Grass Valley. Dr. St. John was the first to build a house there, so the creek that ran into the lake was named Doctor Creek. The second summer he lived there, the roof caved in and killed his wife and two children. These three spirits are said to haunt the area around Fish Lake. Others began building along the various creek beds, establishing such settlements as Seven Mile, Frying Pan, Johnson's Rat, and Windy Hill. In 1886, a large steam-propelled boat was hauled in over the tiny, rough trails to ferry passengers around the lake.

An interesting side note to this Fish Lake story is that in the 1920s, several people had ambitious plans to make a huge resort as a gateway to what later became two national parks. The resort was to be called Wayne's Wonderland and was the brainchild of Joseph Hickman. There were seven committees from three counties involved in this enterprise. A two-day celebration in July of 1925 was to have kicked off the fundraising for this huge Wonderland resort. After months of hard work, Hickman took a well-deserved vacation at Fish Lake on Pioneer Day, a Utah holiday celebrated on the twenty-fourth of July with a second round of fireworks. Sometime during the day, his boat capsized with several people aboard. Hickman, who could not swim, was the only one who drowned. Only three days later, acreage was offered by the state for his Wonderland dream. After the old stories from the local Native Americans about how monsters in this lake could swallow a man whole, Fish Lake had claimed yet another life.

The Great Depression put an end to such dreams and by the 1930s, all schemes to build grandiose amusement parks along this lake were gone. In 1937, a Presidential Proclamation established Capitol Reef National Park, although no state parks came into existence until 1957 when the Utah State Park and Recreation Commission was established. The Wonderland dream was officially destroyed when the region was set aside as a national park. By the 1940s, Fish Lake did house two small resorts and one much larger resort and was a popular boating and fishing spot. Today, Fish Lake does not have as many fish, although it is still stocked. The pine nuts and berries it once had have dwindled. And while there are some deer, the bears are pretty much gone. But it is still considered one of the best places to fish in the state and is a gorgeously scenic place to visit.

The legends of Fish Lake in Native American lore are numerous, and nearly all of them stem from a time well before the white man had even seen the lake. One of the most intriguing tales comes from an ancient Native American legend involving a young warrior who, to this day, can be seen as an apparition creeping through the trees in spirit form, forever hunting and fishing on the lake. The young man loved the area and went there often to hunt and fish. One day he was found dead near the lake under particularly mysterious circumstances. It was never decided if he had been murdered or was killed by some sort of monster. So because he was killed on the shores of the lake that he loved so, his spirit hunts along the shores and can be seen, especially in the evening as he strolls along its shores looking for game.

Another legend tells of a monster that lives in the lake and that in years past grabbed some of those who ventured too close to its shores. The victims were never seen again they say, passing into a watery grave. Much like Utah Lake, these monsters are either described as water babies, often noted as looking and sounding like otters, or small serpent-like creatures that snatched people from the banks or pulled them under while they were swimming in the lake. According to Ute tales, water babies are said to be in Utah Lake, Green River, White River near Vernal, and in the lakes of the high plateaus. The Native Americans told stories of a typical trick the water babies used to lure their victims into the lake.

> Sometimes a young man would go to water the horses in the morning. If the water baby is female, the young man goes to sleep on the bank. When he wakes up he feels someone lying beside him. He looks and sees a beautiful woman in a green dress lying there. He sleeps with her. After a while she coaxes him to go with her under the water. His family will never see him again because he goes under the water to her people.[3]

Some of these stories are similar to siren stories or mermaid stories told on the high seas.

In other tales, the water babies are described as sounding like babies crying. First bubbles would come up from the lake or river and then the water baby would sit on top of the water. Water babies were about the size of a man's fist and had long black hair. It was also said that the "water used to be mean. When you tried to get the water, the hands of the water people would try to pull you under the water. A man was afraid to draw water." So the women drew the water. Throwing something at a water baby was dangerous. One man threw a stick at one and then began having dreams at night of the water rising up out of the lake and coming to get him. He got very sick and almost died. A story is also told of a man who went to drink from a river and saw a female water baby. She and another water baby quickly dragged him under the water. Once they were under the water, the girls' mother told the man that he had to tear the hills down around the river and make them flat. After he had filled her request, the two girls wanted to marry him. His response was that they were ugly and he ran away. The water babies also ran away, but their mother followed them. The girls threw some of their hair on the ground. Their hair turned into cactus thorns and stuck in their mother's feet. Their mother caught them and made them come home with her.[4]

In another legend, tribal people went to camp by the lake. A young Native American mother went to the edge of the lake to gather berries and laid her infant child on the shores. A monster snatched the child, and the mother mourns the loss of her child to this day. Her spirit can be seen wandering Fish Lake's shores, calling out and wailing for her child. Many Utes saw her over the decades, or at least heard her crying out for her child, but there are no records of any white men having seen or heard her. Some Native Americans would not go to the lake because of these legends. Although they gathered berries and pine nuts and hunted in the area, they stuck to the daylight hours, for night was when it was dangerous to be near it. It was believed that whatever monster roamed the area, besides the tiny water babies and the small snake-like serpents, hunted at night and never in the daytime.

When the white man came and settled the area, the sightings stopped. People heard the strange sounds, but there was no evidence of anything ever happening in the area. The spirits and monsters of Fish Lake were forgotten. Or were they? There is a sense of eeriness there in the early evening, although the "noise" of the white man seems to cover what might still lurk there. Interestingly, there have been no reports of the water babies or snake serpents for decades. When the white settlers came, they brought their own superstitions and legends that took the place of the Native American tales around evening fireplaces.

While the lake creature stories have stopped, there have been quite a few reports of Big Foot sightings around Fish Lake. In the old days, the Utes probably called these creatures siants, witches who cast spells on mothers and stole their babies or appeared at camp sites in the middle of the night. If one saw a siant, it was very bad luck because siants were only interested in stealing children to roast and eat them. Once a siant spotted people, it would follow the camp and try to get the children. Siants could not climb trees, so children were safe from such a witch by climbing and staying in a tree until the witch was gone or morning came. Siant stories were probably convenient for parents to scare their children into doing what they wanted, rather like the boogie man who could come and steal naughty children in the night.

I wonder if the Bigfoot reports in our modern day are just the latest evolution of monsters that live by Fish Lake and other lakes in this region. However, let's not forget that besides the water babies, snake-serpents, and creatures that steal children by the shores of the lakes, large-sized sea serpents were also reported in these lakes of the high plateaus. Although no one has ever described one, seen one, or hunted for one, rumors of sea serpents have somehow been told for decades. The tales probably arose from the idea that these lakes are actually ancient volcano craters and that such monsters could swim up into them from cracks and crevices under the earth caused by earthquakes. These are more tall tales of the high plateau lakes, which no white man would ever attest to as real, especially those fisherman who lived by and fished this lake for many years. While they might tell you how big that fish was, and exaggerate a little or even a lot, they will never tell you a tale about any monsters living in or around the lake except to scare other fishermen away from their favorite fishing spot. On the other hand, Bigfoot hunters have a different tale to tell. It seems that the area will always have its monsters of one kind or another.

The Fish Lake ghost story is probably a fabrication, although with so many tales of spirits by this lake, I do wonder. Michael Rutter writes,

> Folks say that Fish Lake is haunted, but don't you believe it! In fact, some have gone so far as to suggest that she (the ghost is female) even lives in the Fish Lake Lodge. In the late afternoon when the wind dies, you can hear her over the water, sounding mournful. Rumor has it she's lonely looking for fishermen to drown. You're supposed to get off the water fast before she tips your boat and makes you a ghost, too. The truth is, there's no ghost in the afternoon. It's a rumor started by some jealous fisherman who wanted the lake to themselves when the fishing was good. Seems they wanted to scare the competition away, and ghost stories were the best way to do it. Everyone around here knows the Fish Lake Ghost doesn't come out until midnight.[5]

We get a different story altogether from those staying at the Fish Lake Lodge. This ghost is not so much a mournful mermaid seeking to pull fishermen down into their watery graves, as she is a figment of the fishermen's imaginations. The lodge owners say there is no history of a ghost in their establishment, but do agree that there are old Native American tales about the lake. Most famous is the legend of the Aspen Heart, a grove of trees located above the old lodge, shaped like a heart. This grove, the largest on the hill, is always the first to turn bright red each fall and the first to lose its leaves before winter. Most aspens turn yellow, so the red leaves stand out from the rest of the hillside in autumn and the heart-shape of the grove can be seen clearly on the hills behind the lodge. The Paiutes told this tale long before the white man came to the area. The story goes that

A Paiute brave fell in love with the chief's daughter which was unfortunate for the Paiute princess for she was in love with him also. However, the chief had plans of his own for the daughter and they did not include the brave his daughter loved.

The two lovers disobeyed the chief and would sneak away at night and meet at a place high on the hillside above the lake. There, under the bright full moon, they made plans to run away with each other and live happily together, far from the chief and the people of the tribe.

Before the young couple could put their plans into action, the tribe went to war with the neighboring tribe and the young brave was called to fight.

Long after battle was over, the brave did not return to the Paiute princess. Heartbroken, and sure that the young brave was dead, the princess climbed the hillside to their special place and waited for her brave to come to her, either in life or in death. She refused food, shelter and comfort and there she died from her broken heart. The chief and his people buried her there at the lovers meeting place.

A short time passed and the Paiute brave did return to claim his princess. He had been delayed in returning because of wounds he had suffered in battle. But the wounds from the battle were nothing compared to the pain he suffered when he heard what had happened to his princess. He went to her grave and there he also died. Whether he died of his battle wounds, or a broken heart, who is to say. The chief and his people buried the brave beside his beloved princess.

It is said that the Aspen Heart grove grows upon the spot where the two lovers were buried and that every fall the leaves remind us of their love and devotion to one another.[6]

While there are plenty of opportunities for ghosts and spirits to roam this area, including this Romeo and Juliet couple who would surely re-enact their meetings over and over again in spirit form, the grove definitely has a mystical feeling to which hikers can attest. Occasionally, I stumble into such groves and I'm entranced by its special feeling of magic. I'm always reluctant to leave such places. The Aspen Heart grows such tales, although I have to wonder if this isn't another story started in the 1920s or 1930s to promote the lodge. In those decades, the romance of both the Native American peoples and the Egyptian culture were in high vogue and many a promoter made up such stories to entice people to visit his place of business. However, two things might weigh in against this speculation at the Fish Lake Lodge. First, the Native American tales were in existence long before white promoters, and second, while some people wanted to promote the lodge, many others did not. Fishermen wanted their special fishing spots kept secret and families didn't want the lodge to become too populated, ruining the beauty of the area.

Charles Skougaard built the Fish Lake Resort, also called Skougaard's Place. Skougaard had a dream one night prompting him to build a resort by the lake. In the late 1800s, Skougaard was the game warden at Fish Lake. By 1911, he had a total of twelve tents, six by the shore and six by the road. He had also ordered the building of twelve boats to be taken up to the lake by wagon to establish his resort. A white top buggy met the guests in Richfield to take them through Skougaard's Canyon to his tent resort. The first hotel had eight bedrooms and a dining room. It was built in 1912 with the help of a special sawmill in Pelican Canyon that was built just to make logs for the lodge. A thirty-foot launch christened *Jose* was put on wheels and hauled up to the lake by horse teams. By 1914, with only four automobiles in Richfield, Skougaard bought a *Pope Toledo* car and hired a driver to bring guests to the resort. By 1917, a new hotel had replaced the first one with guestrooms, a larger dining room, tent camping houses, an open-air dance pavilion, and the construction of individual camp houses. The new main lodge had fulfilled Skougaard's dream to match those built in Bryce Canyon and in the Grand Canyon. Skougaard's children operated the lodge until 1948 when they sold it. A series of managers failed to keep the lodge afloat until a group of businessmen formed the Fish Lake Resort Associates and bought the lodge in 1983. They have operated it successfully ever since.

But the heyday of Skougaard's Place was from the 1920s to the early 1950s. It took from 1928 to 1931 to complete the lodge. Those who lived in the area during that period fondly remember the wonderful dances held there. At the height of activity at Skougaard's Place, there were a hundred cabins, besides the main lodge, as well as a hundred boats. Then, in the 1950s, the Forest Service mandated that there could no longer be commercial or private cabins on the lakefront. This directive negatively impacted Skougaard's business, although the wonderful 1931 ballroom continued to operate through the 1950s, accommodating up to a thousand people comfortably. Fish Lake Resort Lodge continues to operate to this day, although not so grandly. Perhaps this is a blessing in disguise, as people nowadays want to get away from the crowds when visiting nature. The two smaller resorts that were built by the lake, Lake Side Resort and Bowery Haven Resort, also continue to operate to today. Early on, the lake was stocked by deep-lake fish by either John Long or Charlie Skougaard, although in the previous decades, Fish Lake had been known for its great fishing. As recently as 2002, a record Mackinaw weighing forty pounds eight ounces and measuring 40.5 inches long was caught near Bowery Haven.

One of the characters very likely to haunt the shores of Fish Lake could be Joe Nielsen, also called Joe Bush. The ghost began his career as a guide in 1911 and his love affair with Fish Lake began at about the same time. He set up camp by the lake as soon as the snow began to melt each spring and often walked the twenty miles to visit his family in town. He also built the boats that were used by all three resorts on the lake and was an excellent fisherman. He died at age eighty-six and would surely return, if he could, to the place he loved the most. Anyone who lived in the area would remember Joe Bush and probably a few people have a ghost story or two about running into his spirit somewhere along the lake or in the skeletal remains of one of the boats that he built.

Descendants of the Johan Gustave Jorgensen family also have stories about an early Fish Lake apparition. In 1879, Johan, his wife, and their eight children built a log cabin in a meadow by a creek that ran into the northern end of Fish Lake. They had a dairy and hog farm but usually spent the winter months in a small town called Koosharem, which is near Torrey and Bicknell. One of the buildings on their ranch had been constructed over the creek with half the flooring left open. It was built this way so they could store their milk and other foods in the cool stream. The local tribes left them alone, although relations with the local Native Americans were always tenuous. The story goes that

> One day when Mr. Jorgensen was away a young brave came running up the driveway and pleaded with Mrs. Jorgensen to hide him. It seemed the young brave had some romantic inclinations for the daughter of the Chief which was totally unacceptable to the Chief and his tribesmen and the tribe was currently forming a "war" party to capture and kill the runaway brave. Mrs. Jorgensen understood the young brave's plight and agreed to hide him. She quickly thought of the space beneath the flooring of the cooling house and gestured to the place to the young man.
>
> For several days a scouting party searched the Jorgensen Ranch and houses as well as the surrounding mountains for the missing lad and during these days Mrs. Jorgensen took food to the young Indian. When the search was abandoned Mrs. Jorgensen gave the young brave food and a warm blanket and bid him health and good luck. The brave told Mrs. Jorgensen he would have to live in the mountains forever, as he could never belong to a tribe again. One can well imagine the sad farewell to the then homeless boy.
>
> Years later in the late fall after the livestock had been driven to the valley one of the Jorgensen boys was sent back to the ranch from Koosharem to bring out the last of the fish and cheese before the winter set in. Soon after departing the ranch he found himself in a blinding blizzard

and became totally disoriented. Frantic and frightened he dismounted his horse and intended to wait out the storm in a grove of trees. Soon an apparition appeared from the grove. Young Jorgensen wasn't afraid for his life until the vision, covered in heavy furs, spoke. He revealed he was the young brave whose life had been saved by Mrs. Jorgensen. He then led the Jorgensen son and his horse safely through the forest, over the mountain to safety on the other side. When young Jorgensen turned to thank the Indian he was no longer there.[7]

Considering all the sources for ghosts, creatures, and apparitions, and even a modern-day hermit or two, Fish Lake is certainly a haunted place. Early deaths in the lake or near it, especially during the winter months, may have engendered these various tales. Early Native American tales of apparitions on the lake set the stage for later stories. The monster in the lake may have taken the form of the many Bigfoot sightings in the area. Or maybe, as the early Native American tales say, the water there is just plain "mean." The story of the wailing woman from the lodge may have arisen from the same sounds that the Native Americans attributed to the snake-like monsters, water babies, otters, kelpies, or other creatures. The Aspen Grove story and the Jorgensen story contribute to the idea that Native Americans lived as hermits and then died in the woods, later becoming what people considered apparitions of these same woods. Characters like Joe Bush may have returned to a place they loved. Perhaps there was even a woman who worked at the lodge and decided to return to it after she passed on. Perhaps the woman drowned there many years ago. Or perhaps, like so many times in my life before I became fully awakened as an intuitive, I was predicting a future event, which startled and awakened me more.

Over a twenty-year period, I had a favorite physician with whom I grew close to as her practice grew. She specialized in chronic ailments that are somewhat painful, and also treated my neuropathy. She was compassionate and caring with her patients, who adored her. One third of her patients were lower-income. She was a leader in her field of internal medicine, had four daughters, and was an adventurous spirit. She danced, bowled, hiked, biked, scuba dived, and raised her four daughters mostly on her own.

At the end of an especially chilly September, she went scuba diving with a partner at Fish Lake. They dove down thirty feet, and when her diving partner came up to the fifteen-foot mark, he could not find her. He went down and searched and then came up and went for help. A few hours later, her body was found floating on the surface of the lake. She was fifty-three years old. Apparently her breathing apparatus failed, although they were still investigating at that point. I went to her funeral and realized that I had had a much deeper relationship with her than I had comprehended. I am certain I will never find a physician like her again. She had scuba dived in many lakes around the state, but this was her first time at Fish Lake, a place considered too cold this time of year for swimming or scuba diving.

The autopsy revealed the official cause of death to be a "dry-lung" drowning. This is where extremely cold water enters the victim's mouth causing the throat to seize and strangulation occurs. Defective equipment or accidental dislodgement of her mask could have occurred, the coroner said, or she may simply have become disoriented in the dark water and removed her mask on her own. The air tanks contain a small computer that provides what is called a dive profile; this may have solved the mystery. Like all people with my gifts, I had to ask myself why I hadn't a clue just a week before her death, as I sat in her office for my doctor's appointment. She was in one of the happiest times of her life and it showed. I noticed the glow, but didn't know her well enough to know why, except to guess at a new boyfriend. Later, an article in the paper told of her two thousand patients who drove from all over Utah and southern Idaho just to have her as their doctor, probably because she not only honored the reality of their chronic ailments, but kept trying until she found a way to reduce pain levels and symptoms. After her death, the medical community was inundated with so many calls that a special meeting had to be called to help her many patients who were abandoned, grief-ridden, and lost.

A day after I heard the news, I began to have a recurring nightmare. I was inside her body, feeling her struggle with her hands and arms as the dark water and thick underwater plants entangled her arms to the point where she gave up the struggle and stopped breathing. I would wake up unable to breathe for a moment and quickly sit up and start breathing again. I realized she was trying to get her mask back on. For several nights I had this dream and then it stopped just as suddenly as it had begun. I had a strong feeling that she was asking me to do something for her. I just had to trust that this request would come floating back to me of its own accord in the future.

Mostly, I thought about how the Native Americans had warned their people to stay away from the lakes, especially as evening neared or winter approached. My doctor and her companion had entered the lake for the first time and were unfamiliar with its history and terrain. They had taken their dive in the late afternoon in a particularly cold fall. Experienced divers considered Fish Lake a dangerous place for scuba diving, especially as winter weather approached. They said the lake was too cold and too dark for visibility. Navigating in the lake is difficult year around. Experienced fishermen never entered the water there and locals knew better than to swim there in the fall. The spirits of this lake were both real and mythological. And no matter which they were, the warnings were the same.

I had to wonder if I had intuited this outcome. That would explain why no one had ever heard of the woman apparition I saw. I wonder now if there would be such a woman in the future. I saw her but only as an impression left behind, a photograph of an event. Her spirit wouldn't be there, but an imprint of her passing would be. I thought about the "mean" water and the stories of monsters that just might be the underground currents or darkness and weeds that could drag one down. I thought about my dream, the doctor's "spirit" request, and how it probably would not be honored for a long time to come. I wondered if I would therefore see or experience her spirit once I visited Fish Lake, or perhaps just dream a visit there. I only knew that now this story and this lake would also haunt me.

Notes

1) Roylance, *Utah: A Guide to the State*, 600.
2) Ibid., 603–04.
3) Smith, *Ute Tales*, 110.
4) Ibid., 110–11.
5) Rutter, *Utah: Off the Beaten Path*, 155.
6) Moulton, *Fish Lake Resorts*, "Legend of the Aspen Heart" chap.
7) Collester, *For Those Who Love Fish Lake and for Those Who Will One Day*, 85.

Book Three

UFOs and
Lost Treasures

Route 666
The Devil's Highway

Route 666 is a lonely, deserted stretch of road with a long history of accidents and apparitions. Because of the so-called bad luck along this stretch of road, state highway officials in all four states that it runs through have been asked to change the name of the highway at one time or another. The only state to respond to this demand at the time was Arizona. After repeated complaints from Arizona motorists, the portion of the highway running through their state was renamed Highway 191. Also disgruntled, a man from Indiana wrote one of his senators to ask why New Mexico didn't change the name of their section of the highway. In each state (except Arizona), the demands were noted but not acted upon. Eventually, however, much of the highway became Highway 191. Originally named in 1926, this highway was the sixth branch of the now defunct Route 66, and therefore became Route 666. However, people still didn't like having to drive on a road whose name references the antichrist.

Besides the many accidents along this stretch of road, many more than other, busier highways in this area, Highway 666 is host to many apparitions and tales. The most famous is the phantom car that appears out of nowhere during a full moon. Apparently, the phenomena along this road only occur during this part of the moon's cycle. The phantom car appears out of nowhere and attempts to run lone cars off the highway, especially at night. This car has killed at least five motorists according to paranormal investigators, if not more. There is also a truck driver who does the same thing. These tales were probably the inspiration for Stephen Spielberg's early film, a great experiment in terror, *The Duel*. In the film, a huge truck without a visible driver, chases poor Dennis Weaver. Weaver finally outsmarts it, and the truck tumbles over a cliff. When he climbs down to look he finds no driver in the cab. The 666 trucker drives back and forth on this specific highway, intentionally running people down. He doesn't give up on the first try either. Cars have to exit the highway to get rid of the mad trucker, and stopping along the way doesn't help at all!

Interestingly, my husband has his own tale of traveling this highway on his way to Texas, long before I ever met him. He used to drive very long distances by himself, being a country boy from southern Indiana. There wasn't much for small town high school kids to do there in the evenings except drive the old country roads, watch the fireflies over fields, gather in graveyards, go arrowhead hunting, or chase imagined UFOs. He was driving this highway (in the middle of the night) headed for Gallop. He was alone and hadn't seen a car for miles and miles. Suddenly, he saw a truck that looked like it was on fire heading straight for him, right down the middle of the highway. The large truck was going so fast that sparks were flying up off the wheels and flames were coming from the smokestack. It scared him so bad that he pulled way off the road and walked twenty feet or so out into the desert away from his car and waited for the truck to pass him. He estimated that the truck was going 130 miles an hour. He then got back into his car and continued on. If I had been there, the fear of rattlesnakes and other creatures would have kept me inside the car.

In addition to the mad trucker, packs of demon dogs have been seen on this highway as well. They attack at night with yellow eyes and sharp teeth, shredding the tires of those foolish enough to stop along this highway at night. Then there is a beautiful, frail girl in a long nightgown that roams the road. People see her walking along the side of the road, all alone in the dark out in the middle of nowhere. They stop to help her and as they approach, she vanishes. There are many other tales of people who either disappear along the route or suddenly appear out of nowhere. There are even tales of people disappearing at one point along the highway and then reappearing at another location miles away without any recollection of where they have been or what they have been doing.

The Native Americans tell tales of unwanted passengers appearing in the backseat of a car along such stretches of highway, but especially along Highway 666. It seems that skin walkers, or evil medicine men, can shape-shift into animals such as crows, coyotes, or wolves and appear out of nowhere in front of your car on the highway. This, in and of itself, can cause unexplained accidents along the road. However, this appearance is usually a warning and can happen several times before the evil shaman decides to appear in the backseat of your car, if you are driving alone. So it is advised that people drive in groups so the evil skin walker has nowhere to sit. This may work and it may not, for the skin walker can play all sorts of tricks on the eyes with his ability to shape shift. So it is good advice not to be driving all night or when tired, as this is when the skin walkers are on the prowl stealing souls.

Both police and funeral home records indicate an unusually high number of accidents along this road, as well as an unusual number of bodies being dumped near this highway or even along its roadsides. There are also far more kidnappings along this highway than in other places, although the statistics couldn't reflect the actual number as not all of the incidents would be reported. Apparently even murderers use this road to hide their deeds or to get rid of their evidence, probably because there are long stretches of absolutely nothing. The kidnappings also might occur because the road is so isolated in spots.

UFO lights are often reported along this stretch of road, usually the kind that move around in impossible directions, travel faster than any known human technology, or disappear and then reappear again. I have not heard of any UFO abductions, but who knows, since most UFO abductees keep their stories quiet for fear of ridicule. UFO abductions, or better still, dimension or portal doors to other realms or planets, could also account for the reports of people disappearing from one spot and reappearing in another.

Of late, the highway that runs into 666 in the state of Utah, Highway 6, has received some publicity for how dangerous it is too. Highway 666 runs from Shiprock south to Gallop, east to Cortez and finally north to Monticello, Utah. Highway 6 runs from Spanish Fork southeast to Price and then to Green River. It continues to Moab and on down to Monticello where 666 begins. If this is not confusing enough, add the fact that Highway 6 is also called Highway 191, or perhaps the original Highway 666, which a long time ago might have stretched farther. The little stretch that is left may only be a remnant of a much longer stretch of highway that is supposedly haunted. One would have to check very old road maps to find out for sure whether this was 6 or 66 or 666!

The entire stretch of roadway is treacherous and my husband and I have driven it ourselves a few times, though usually in daylight. It is long and desolate and boring enough to put a driver to sleep, distract him from paying attention to how fast he is driving, or at least cause a few hallucinations. Police are assigned to patrol the road in force and add extra day shifts to curtail accidents on the deadliest road in Utah. Last year, five people died in accidents along the highway; the year before, seventeen people died, and the year before that, ten people died in accidents there. People think it is because two-lane highways are a little more dangerous than four-lane highways, but officers say that this doesn't make much difference. They blame the accidents on people thinking they can get away with more on such a lonely stretch of highway, or tempers flaring when there is heavier traffic returning from weekend vacations. Motorists disagree, saying the road is too narrow and winding to be safe at any speed. Private citizens who have lost family to this road decided to do what they could by making bumper stickers and flyers printed with slogans such as "I survived driving Highway 6" or "I drive Highway 6. Pray for me."

Having unwittingly driven this road with a friend many years ago while on spring vacation from college, I do remember the eerie feeling we had being the only car on the road for miles and miles at night, watching Shiprock grow before us as we approached. As we drove all night with totally flat land around us, we could not see car lights, or anything else except an occasional giant shape which must have been rocks. The Navajo call the Shiprock the Rock with Wings because of the way it sometimes appears to be floating above the ground. One Navajo legend about the rock is that the "Slayer of Enemy Gods" killed two dragons that lived inside the mountain. The male and female dragons were changed into an eagle and an owl, two animals that represent the balance of a whole human being to the Navajo, a balance of the yin and the yang so to speak. To me, this rock has always looked like *The Flying Dutchman* schooner, appearing and disappearing in the mist.

The year we drove this road, which was still 666 all the way, as a short cut to the Grand Canyon, we could get only one station on the radio. We listened to a news broadcast of the fall of Saigon as we drove through this mystical land. My partner on this adventure was driving and trying to stay awake while I sat in silence listening to the sounds of a far away war. As I listened, I watched the sun set around us. I can remember crying as the women and children screamed. I saw the running and chaos and confusion in my mind's eye, just as I would see a replay of the real images later on TV. We were on an Native American reservation where people had been conquered and used in another economic war not so very long ago. We drove on in the dark quite lost. We were lucky to find our way at all.

I will never, ever forget this drive from Cortez to Shiprock and how frightened I was, hearing the screams and chaos of people trying to flee for their lives in a far away country. Here we were, two young girls, thinking of ourselves as adventurous and independent women, quite alone, driving along a highway in the middle of the night knowing nothing about its history. We did not see any apparitions, phantom cars, spark-yielding trucks, or anything out of the ordinary, perhaps because it was not a full moon or even more simply because these are all just stories, none of them true. Even the myth of the full moon, when put to the test, proves to be like any other day, although policemen, firemen, hospital personnel, and even teachers from the area will tell you differently.

"If you drive Route 666 at night, you drive at your own risk," the signs should say. Take a lot of people with you and don't leave any space for unwanted passengers who just might decide to appear in your back-seat. Pull off the road if a huge diesel truck comes bearing down on you from either direction. Don't be curious to see if there is a driver in that single car passing you in the night. Don't look for lights floating in the sky. Hope you don't see any young girls in white dresses. Never stop if you spot something peculiar and don't pick up hitchhikers. Lastly, if demon dogs approach you in the night, just keep driving.

Recently, there have been all kinds of articles on the mysteries surrounding U.S. Highway 666 because of a federal law that changed the entire highway's name in one fell swoop. Stories of satanic honeymoons, cars run off the road by ghosts, a disappearing girl in a nightgown, strange car crashes, skin walkers, and strange disappearances have all contributed to the biggest mystery of all: why the New Mexico Highway and Transportation Department wants to change the numerical designation for this highway. The Navajo Nation especially is plagued by the highway's bad name with negative connotations and references to the devil. The state of New Mexico is hoping to widen the two-lane, hilly road, which has several dangerous blind spots, to four lanes.[1] Apparently this old 666 road has been quite popular with tourists and heavy-metal songwriters and was even made reference to in the violent movie, *Natural Born Killers.*

The Ports of Entry agent in southeastern Utah was quoted as saying that some who drive in this area regularly are too spooked to drive on the highway. Besides the ghosts and the powerful, shape-shifting spirits that Navajo legend claims have been cursed and roam the area as skin walkers, there is an old lady who some claim they've seen wandering along desolate parts of this highway at night. A *Deseret Morning News* article mentions even more names for this highway including Purgatory Pathway, Lucifer's Lane, and Highway to H. E. Double Hockey Sticks. The road stretches 190 miles and the new highway will be named U.S. 491 or 393 in all three states. Each state will have to change the name on its signs and maps.

One of the problems that they had along the highway in all three states was the stealing of Route 666 road signs. These signs are in high demand by collectors. Since they are changing the designation of this highway, those road signs will be in even higher demand. Some people are upset about the name change because they enjoyed the notoriety, while others think it gives their area a bad reputation. The seventeen-mile portion in Utah has an average of 19.4 accidents per year, which officials say is not particularly high when compared to other two lane roads. One trucker who drives this route is a former man of the cloth and resident of Roswell, New Mexico, where alien visits are a tourist attraction because of the alleged 1947 UFO crash there. He drives the road daily and states that the supernatural stuff doesn't faze him. He says that nothing could bother him after Roswell, not even a highway named 666. The article says that with the name change, the road will no longer be the "route of all evil."[2]

An article from *Weird US* had even better puns and quotes about the new highway 491. The article even quotes an old Nat King Cole song from the 1950s but changes the lyrics to "the devil got his kicks on Route 666." New Mexico Governor L. Richardson officially designated the highway U.S. 491 in June of 2003 after all three states petitioned federal officials with the following justifications. "People living near the road already live under the cloud of opprobrium created by having a road that many believe is cursed" and "the number '666' carries the stigma of being the mark of the beast . . . described in the Book of Revelations." The petitions also claimed that "there are people who refuse to travel the road . . . because of the fear that the devil controls events along United States Route 666." They even claim that "the economy in the area is greatly depressed . . . and the infamy brought by the inopportune naming of the road will only make development in the area more difficult."[3]

Some worry that officials angered Satan with the new numerology. Others say it will always be the devil's road. Plans for christening the road include measures such as "to ward off any remaining evil spirits, a Navajo medicine man will bless the 'new' road after today's ribbon-cutting, cleansing it and bequeathing good fortune in times hence. A traditional Navajo feast of mutton and fry bread will cement the deal . . . the Navajo Nation objected to being bisected by a highway that bore a number the biblical Book of Revelations says is the 'sign of the beast.' " A spokesman for the Navajo Nation said that the name had a negative connotation. However, as reporter Christopher Smart interviewed locals and others who had crossed the highway often, he found mixed feelings about the change in the highway's designation. Some said the change was utter nonsense or that it was confusing for tourists. Others said they were messing with the wrong guy, that they had made the devil mad and they should have left the 666 alone. Still others like the novelty of having their shop along the so-called Devil's Highway and said that the change would be bad for business. Many had never heard of anyone afraid of driving on the road because it was named Route 666. Some locals liked the novelty of it and said that their claim to fame had been taken away. Others were glad about the change because they wouldn't have the tourists stopping to take pictures of the Route 666 signs that are stolen on a regular basis. On the other hand, replacing the old highway signs won't pose a problem because most of them are gone already.[4]

The best part for most people, however, is that they are widening the highway to four lanes between Shiprock and Gallup in hopes of cutting down on the number of accidents along this part of the road. "Still, many old-timers won't need signs to tell them what road they are on," explained Eldon Leffel, eighty-three, who still operates the Main Supply hardware store in Dove Creek. "The devil still runs up and down here," he said motioning to the roadway. "You can recognize him by his tail."[5] The irony being that in the other two states, the new road will simply be named Highway 491, while in Utah it will have the longer name of New 491/Old 666, not quite ridding the route of its former connotations nor any of its ghosts and legends.

Notes

1) Wharton, "U.S. 666 Linking Monticello with New Mexico Gets a Name Change," June 4, 2003.
2) Genessy, "Devilish 666 Name Is Going Down in Flames," June 3, 2003.
3) Moran and Sceurman, *Weird U.S.*, 227.
4) Smart, "Sixes Nixed on Devil's Road," June 30, 2003.
5) Ibid.

Utah's UFO Sightings, Abductions, and Underground Bases

Area 51, about ninety miles east of Las Vegas, is also known as Groom Lake and harbors a secret military facility. It is a "top secret" six-by-ten-mile block of land with a large air base at its center. It was set up in the early 1950s as a facility for testing what is called black budget experimental aircraft. Around this time, the UFO tales and conspiracy stories began. Area 51 has become a popular symbol for alleged United States Government UFO cover-ups. UFO encounters are broken into four categories. Close encounters of the first kind are those in which an object is seen at close range (meaning five hundred feet or less). These objects do not affect the environment. Close encounters of the second kind are UFOs that have a direct, physical effect on their surroundings. Close encounters of the third kind involve direct contact with the occupants of the spacecraft. Actual abductions by aliens are the fourth kind. There are other miscellaneous happenings such as cattle mutilations, crop circles, and government conspiracy cases involving aliens.

Researchers have proposed a new way of studying UFOs that changes the scientific model to a five level model:

1. Study of matter and physical evolution
2. Study of feelings and biological evolution
3. Study of thought processes and psychosocial evolution
4. Study of intuition and consciousness evolution
5. Study of spirit within a scientific model, going beyond evolution.

The study of UFOs would fit into this model with

1. Study of the crafts themselves
2. Study of UFO entities
3. Study of UFO messages and languages
4. Enhancement of our own intuitive abilities
5. Study of UFOs as a paradigm for cosmic consciousness.

Dr. Leo Sprinkle, a fifty-year veteran of UFO research, spoke at the 1998 Rocky Mountain UFO Conference. He proposed the idea that there are two general methods of gathering information or knowledge: maps, calculations, and statistics; and stories and oral histories. All of these, he explains, will become equally valid as research tools in the future.

The National UFO Reporting Center's state-by-state index on the Web contains dozens of UFO sightings in Utah. If we assume that one out of every ten incidents is never reported, the actual number would soar. People have reported lights shaped like disks, circles, fireballs, lights, triangles, ovals, spheres, cigars, flashes, and cylinders. There is also the classification "other" as various citizens describe their close encounters of the first kind. These sightings are scattered all across the state from Salt Lake City to as far southwest as Cedar City and southeast as Monument Valley. There have been a few in the Tooele area and as far north as Logan, Utah. There are no patterns to the sightings in our state, although in places like New Mexico or Nevada, patterns have been found. There are all the usual explanations such as meteorites, comets, asteroids, a flock of birds, a mirage of the sun, a cloud formation, a plane, a weather balloon, an experimental aircraft, and various other explanations for this phenomenon. Those who swear that it could have been none of these will always claim that it was a real UFO sighting.

There are many unofficial reports of UFO abductions in Utah. What I notice about these people is their sincerity. They truly believe in what happened to them, and I truly believe that something very traumatic did happen to them. Whether it was a UFO abduction or not, I don't know. I am of the opinion that the real tragedy lies buried deep in the subconscious. Being abducted by aliens can be a cover for something so terrible that the conscious mind or heart doesn't want to look at it. Or it may be that they have seen aliens, and I simply have not. Carl Jung would have said that what we are seeing are glimpses of our own future—tourists or scientists coming back to study us. This is a sad thought, as many of the abduction stories are negative, whether they are real or coming from some dark region of our own subconscious minds. I would hate to think that our descendents lack the compassion for others that many of us still prize today.

Abductions have been reported around the state, especially in southern Utah. Many of the abduction stories are very dark and negative. If it is aliens that have a hand in these terrible deeds, Heaven help us! However, since this is a part of the UFO world, I do want to mention a few of the abductions. One woman from Magna, Utah, claims her family had been seeing UFOs since the early 1970s and that she, her husband, and her son have all been "probed." The aliens who are bothering them in the middle of the night are called Grays. She says she is more intuitive because of the experiences, but it frightens her family to have their privacy invaded. Various Utah UFO web sites provide an abduction checklist for those who feel this has happened to them. Just a few of the clues of alien abduction include altered perceptions, human bodies inhabited temporarily for aliens' purposes, waking up with unexplained strange marks on the body, serious health problems that spontaneously appear, degenerated general well-being, extracted body fluids, injections of strange substances, hypnotism, examinations of human sexuality and reproduction, and visits to strange facilities. The most nightmarish claims involve terrible procedures, torture, experiments, abduction of children, creation of a hybrid race of alien-humans, and predictions of a holocaust wherein only a few select humans will be saved.

I prefer to believe in a better world. On the other hand, the people I have met who claim such abductions are always sincere and definitely traumatized. A few have an obvious mental illnesses, but most are very clear on what has happened to them and are as sane as you or I. On this level, I have to respect their claims, whether I accept what they say as truth or not. If I always say that you have to experience an interaction with a ghost before believing they exist, then I cannot dismiss what others say they have seen or experienced. I can only hope that aliens have a better moral system than ours and are intelligent enough not to need to experiment on us. I hope that they are way beyond us both in method of travel and in humanitarian concerns. We are all from the same crazy place and can never return to where we were before these events. Rather like a soldier returning home from battle, nothing is in its rightful place again.

The Dugway Proving Grounds

The center of suspected UFO activity and government conspiracy theories here in Utah seems to be the Dugway Proving Grounds. There are also relatively new claims of a miniature White Sands, or a new Area 51, near Green River, Utah, and another in the Uintah Mountains. The proving ground covers 800,000 acres of desert and is about eighty miles southwest of Salt Lake City. It is the most secretive of the facilities in the area and sometimes manages to be the most controversial. Dugway participates in technical tests and strategies concerning chemical and biological defense, as well as battlefield smoke and obscurant systems and environmental technologies. The staff also provides testing expertise in these fields for many foreign governments and customers throughout the United States in the private sector. In other words, Dugway is one of the major testing grounds for chemical and biological warfare in the United States.

Dugway has been deactivated and reactivated under various different guises over the years. At present, it is part of the U.S. Army's Test and Evaluation Command (TECOM). TECOM's headquarters are at the U.S. Army Materials Command in Alexandria, Virginia. It also manages another big facility, the Aberdeen Proving Ground, in Maryland. Dugway currently has about six hundred buildings on its site and is worth approximately 240 million dollars. What has people concerned, however, is the recent increase in activity at the facility both on the ground and in the air. Part of the concern relates to the building of a 15,000-foot runway for the testing of NASA's newest space shuttles. Residents also worry about the new experimental aircraft to be tested there. New and mysterious vapor trails have also appeared overhead. Security at the facility has been increased. Now if someone accidentally approaches the perimeter, mysterious black helicopters will appear. This increased activity may be due in part to the build up of war technology in the Bush administration to continue the war in the Middle East.

Just like Area 51, there are rumors that Dugway has an unusual facility on the grounds that houses experimental craft, including a possible alien craft. In the 1950s through the 1970s, the place was always under armed guard and convoy trucks were often seen entering the hangar with tarps over their cargo. One truck, accompanied by five armed guards, was spotted carrying a large, oval-shaped object about thirty feet wide. Three concentric fences were built around this particular hangar. Rumors about what this hangar held or did not hold persist to this day. One of the most popular rumors is that it holds an SIR-1 portable nuclear reactor, a very scary possibility. Many of the stories about this hangar, for those of a more paranoid persuasion, might simply be fabrications to distract us from what really lies within those three fences.

The most interesting story is about what happened to the five men who were guarding the truck with the tarp-covered metal disc. Rumor has it that all five men died within a year of delivering the cargo. Two died in a single-engine plane crash while flying from Chicago to Denver. The third died in an automobile accident; his car went off a cliff in northern California due to brake failure. The fourth man committed suicide by hanging himself with a necktie, although no one knew his reason. The fifth man left for work one day, but never showed up at his workplace. He has been missing ever since. Of course, I don't know what the evidence is for any of this or who saw the truck delivering its cargo in the first place, but it sure makes for an intriguing story. While there are UFO sightings all over the west desert, there are just as many sightings throughout the state.

It is the reality of what they are testing in our deserts that scares me the most. Only eighty miles from where I live, the site represents a constant danger of a chemical or biological laboratory accident which could wreak all kinds of havoc on civilians. One of these accidents could kill us all outright, yet we worry about nuclear waste being transported across our state. Now I have to worry about natural and unnatural disasters, all right here in Salt Lake City, a place where many believe our government would never make wrong decisions or do anything to harm its citizens.

In a recent *Deseret News* article entitled "Is Dugway's expansion an alien concept?," Joe Bauman talks about nerve agent contamination and alien hunters. The army's desire to acquire a huge 55- to 145-square-mile piece of adjacent land has sparked a flood of rumors. Many speculate that the army base, having become more and more scrutinized by alien hunters with telephoto cameras, wants to further secure its new anti-terrorism training facilities for the Middle Eastern war and home front guard. Security hassles at Groom Lake (Area 51) are amazingly difficult now, they say, with the on-going, intense surveillance by UFO enthusiasts. The New Mexico base is entirely staked out with high-powered technology and Dugway is fast becoming the same way due to its reputation as the most secretive and controversial facility in Utah. UFO watchers claim that there are mysterious vapor trails, increased military activities, unmarked black helicopters, and even housing of experimental and possibly alien craft at Dugway. Some even say that Dugway is the new military spaceport for alien crafts.[1]

The real news is that out in our own Area 51, there are real dangers, way beyond any strange UFO stories. These dangers are the chemicals we are all being exposed to from the army's Tooele chemical weapons incinerator. The chemicals are nerve agents that are already making workers sick and being guarded from public scrutiny. Only a few decades ago, we had a nerve agent accident right here in Utah that caused the deaths of hundreds of sheep. There are also claims that the transportation of chemicals all over the country is done at night and in low profile and that even our own local politicians know nothing about these secret maneuverings. Occasionally, we hear about one of them and there are fights to stop them from coming through a state or being dumped in certain areas. Words like *fugitive emissions* and *meteorological drift* are barely mentioned, while the threat of our own Three Mile Island accident seems to be skillfully downplayed with another term, *plausible deniability.* And then there are those "credible whistle blowers" who are still waiting for the rest of us to see or at least understand the dangers here in Utah and in other western states. If asked what I fear most, the UFOs in Utah or the chemical weapons being burned in Tooele, I would say the chemicals.

The chemicals are a clear and present danger today. But even decades ago, other dangers were present that are still affecting the land around Dugway. Descendents of Jesse F. Cannon, the original owner of the land around Dugway, tried to sue the government to force it to clean up the damage its activities have caused to their private property. The owners believe the government is trying to buy this land because it's cheaper to buy and fence it off than to clean up the contaminates. Apparently in the 1950s, an army project known as Project Sphinx

Linda Dunning

conducted its experiments on the leased Cannon land. The old mines on Dugway Mountain were used to see how lethal gasses would travel through the old tunnels. "They used our mining tunnels on our patented mining land," the Cannons claim. "They contaminated it with thousands of chemical bombs and mustard gas, phosgene, a shell that they call C-17. . . . Oh, there's lots of craters and fragments and old shells and stuff."[2] The area is full of old mining contaminations from the 1800s, 1950s contaminations, and modern-day army chemical experiments, so if watching the base for UFOs helps keep civilians distracted, then so be it.

Zack Van Eyck, a former staff writer for the *Deseret News*, has taken a special interest in collecting information about Utah's UFO sightings. Over the years, he has written several articles on the subject, but the most interesting is about a 489-acre ranch in Uintah County. In 1996, a couple was trying to sell the cattle ranch because they were tired of dealing with not only the constant UFO sightings and local media attention, but the other bizarre occurrences over the years. A millionaire philanthropist named Robert T. Bigelow bought the ranch and brought in a team of researchers with surveillance equipment. For years, he has been funding private research projects "on the far fringe of mainstream science." The ranch offered a secluded location to study all these phenomena. The projects are funded by his nonprofit National Institute for Discovery Science. The original owners had to agree to keep quiet about what had occurred on their ranch, such things as "the mutilated and disappearing cattle, UFOs the size of football fields, circular doorways that appeared in midair and floating bans of light that allegedly incinerated the family dogs."[3]

The *Las Vegas Sun* reports that

> The search for answers to one of science's greatest questions has led millionaire Robert T. Bigelow to an isolated cattle ranch in the heart of eastern Utah's Uintah Basin . . . the real estate magnate hopes his team of scientists can unearth roots of UFO folklore prevalent in this region since the 1950s . . . Last July, the Shermans [the original owners of the ranch] broke years of silence and went public with bizarre tales of strange lights and UFOs on their 480-acre ranch. Sherman said he and other members of his

155

family had seen lights emerging from circular "doorways" that seemed to appear mid-air, had three cows strangely mutilated and several others disappear. The rancher also reported unusual impressions in the soil and circles of flattened grass in a pasture. The Sherman's story appeared in the *Deseret News* and on a national radio broadcast. Several weeks later, Bigelow met with the Shermans.[4]

He eventually decided to buy the ranch. The Shermans moved fifteen miles away and Bigelow built an observation building and moved in scientists and a veterinarian. His National Institute for Discovery Science was formed, and John B. Alexander, a former director of non-lethal weapons testing at Los Almos National Laboratories in New Mexico, heads the research. Still other UFO researchers in the inter-mountain area say they are a bit disconcerted because Bigelow and his crew are being too secretive.

The institute dodges all media questions to this day and only says that it prefers to have solid scientific data. Bigelow does admit, however, that the strange phenomena are still going on, that he has assembled an impressive group of scientists. The institute directs all questions to its web site (www.nidsci.org). NIDS asks local ranchers and residents to contact them if they experience or see anything out of the ordinary at 1-800-433-6500 or by submitting a report at their web site. If an animal is mutilated, they may perform an autopsy and various other tests. Because Bigelow likes to maintain a low profile and has done so for many years, his granting an interview with the paper led to speculation that he has some sort of hidden agenda or governmental connections, although most UFO researchers have cause to be paranoid anyway with all of the unanswered questions floating around. Bigelow, however, does not allow photographs to be taken of him, although he has recently tried to reach out to the more mainstream scientific community in hopes of getting them interested in his research. Bigelow often wonders why the public and other factions in our society don't seem to take the study of UFOs and the possibility of extraterrestrials seriously.

Bigelow says he spends more than a million dollars a year on his research center because other institutions that should are not. He believes extraterrestrial contact is inevitable and that we should be preparing for it now. He maintains that the psychosocial effects on humans will be great, if we are not prepared to accept things we have never been exposed to. Growing up in the 1950s in Las Vegas, he has his own personal interest in the paranormal. His grandparents had a close encounter that they told him about when he was ten years old. A ball of light appearing to be in flames came right at their car; they swerved off the road trying to avoid the impact. However, there was no impact because the ball of light suddenly made a 180-degree turn and went the opposite direction. They were profoundly affected by the event, not only because it happened, but also because they thought they were going to die that instant. As a result of his grandparent's story, Bigelow became interested in UFO sightings around the Las Vegas area. He retained his interest while building his real estate empire. He wanted to answer the question of whether or not are we alone in the universe, but he also wanted to investigate the survival of consciousness after death. Throughout his career, he has maintained a low profile to ward off unwanted attention.

In the Uintah Basin, a former schoolteacher named Joseph "Junior" Hicks has been cataloging the over four hundred UFO sightings since the fifties. There have been hundreds of them, as well as suspicious lights and on-the-ground phenomena. As for the rest of the state, the National UFO Reporting Center web site shows at least one dozen reports in Utah yearly,[5] although local state reports average closer to forty or fifty such sightings. These national reports were filed from 1998 to the present. Three flying triangular shapes were seen near the San Juan River on U-261 in June of 1982, shining light beams onto the highway until the approaching car flashed its lights—then the beams were turned off. One of the objects flew over the car revealing eight lights underneath the craft. Hicks has heard several eyewitness accounts of living beings in the windows or portholes of UFOs. He estimates that over ten percent of the population in the area has seen a UFO, including a neighbor of the Shermans' (former owners of the land Bigelow purchased) who claims he saw rays of colored lights shooting from the underbelly of a craft in two separate decades. In 1996, the Shermans and others had also reported the appearance of an orange ball of light above the ranch they assumed to be a wormhole of some kind, also called a dimensional vortex. Out of this wormhole came dark-skinned beings as well as a boxcar-like craft; immediately afterward the ranch suffered a series of cattle mutilations.

The Shermans reported a lot of incidents once they were no longer living on the ranch. For example, they said their son and daughter had seen three types of UFOs many times: small box-like crafts with white lights, forty-foot-long objects in the sky, and huge ships the size of several football fields. One craft emitted a wavy red ray and others had lights that emerged from orange, circular doorways that appeared in mid-air. In addition to these sightings, crop circles marred the ranch's fields. The three circles of flattened grass were about eight feet across and thirty feet from each other. Other three-foot-wide and two-foot-deep soil circles were found as well. Lights from the sky followed a family member home one night. The family members then heard voices in the field speaking an unfamiliar language; their dogs barked and growled and suddenly ran from the fields into the house, too frightened to go back out. Seven of their cows disappeared, although later three were found mutilated. Over time, the Shermans came to associate the increase in sightings of crafts with cattle mutilations. They say there have been many more cattle mutilations in the area, but the ranchers either did not report them or when they did, the authorities told them reporting would be a waste of time and effort. When the local sheriff's department was contacted, they said they had not received any reports in the last two years.

The Shermans have safely moved away, but they continue to tell stories of the things that happened to them on their ranch. All of the family members suffered from spontaneous nausea, night-sweats, and nosebleeds. In UFO circles, the former Sherman ranch, now Bigelow's investigative center, is considered one of the most impressive cases ever studied. One theory is that a tear in the electromagnetic fabric has taken place there, a separation between the electromagnetic spectrum and our gravity. This tear allows an interdimensional doorway between worlds. While many people in the area are not sure they believe the Shermans' stories, there are plenty of others who have had their own experiences around the area and do talk about them. Neighbors have seen UFOs, veterinarians have worked on cases involving strangely mutilated animals, and others have seen things they cannot explain. All of this intrigued millionaire Robert Bigelow.

There are other areas of the state where UFO sightings are being reported. They are not quite as active as the Great Basin, but sightings are still recorded and analyzed. In 1962, a fireball raced across the Salt

Lake Valley and on into Nephi. Although it received national attention, many believe it to be a hoax. A man recently claimed to have seen a UFO in 1964, but kept quiet about it for years. He says that he was driving down Emigration Canyon early one morning and saw an oval-shaped craft hovering above him. He claimed the beings inside it peered out at him from in front of his car and gave him a telepathic message. When they asked him to come with them, he thought of his wife and children and told them he could not. They left politely.

In the 1970s, some men from West Valley City working in the Wyoming oil fields said over 250 workers saw a UFO over the rig, which subsequently exploded. They were told not to mention the ship. The ship was transparent with multi-colored lights and a particle beam. In 1972, a driver in Provo reported seeing a bright cloud that turned into a silver saucer and shot across the desert. A Tooele resident, driving to work around midnight in July of 1993, saw four stoplight-green, glowing orbs hovering over the Kennecott Copper Mine. The lights then flew northward at extreme speeds. In January of 1997, a bright object emitting a yellow-green light changing back and forth from a beam to a floodlight dissolved into a cloud of light near Moab. People at a star party for the Hansen Planetarium spotted a moving star near Alta that hovered, darted, and moved in different directions for more than three hours. In Emery County, a teenager from Huntington saw a green streak over the night sky lasting five minutes in May of 1997.

A Navy warrant officer took photos of flying discs over Tremonton in 1952 that received national attention. However, one of the earliest reported Utah UFO sightings happened in 1947 over the Salt Lake Valley. Earl "Skip" Page, his wife, Beulah, and their nine-year-old son, Ronald, were in a two-seater plane flying from Las Vegas to Salt Lake City. At 3:30 p.m. they spotted a group of silver-colored, disc-shaped objects zipping past their plane at the same altitude. Some came within fifty feet of them. Earl has since died, but Beulah, who is now eighty-two, and Ronald, who is sixty, say they still vividly remember the encounter. Beulah now lives in Washington State, but she and her son still talk about seeing what they first thought to be birds. She says when her husband turned the plane towards them, the discs zoomed away at high speed. They just disappeared, she says. The Pages only told relatives and friends but never the media for fear of ridicule. They also say the sighting made them feel nauseated, although there could have been another reason. Earl Page worked in the secret plutonium processing plant in Hanford, Washington. Two disc-shaped UFOs visited the Hanford Plant in daylight in 1953. There are many black and white photos of the discs the Pages saw over the Salt Lake Valley so many years ago, although there isn't any detail on them and they really do look fake.

One of the most intriguing of all Utah UFO reports is the one that happened in Utah's Gadianton Canyon by a railroad crossing near Modena, on the edge of the Escalante Desert in 1972. UFO researchers call this type of phenomena Highway Space Warps (HSW). The legend about the canyon claims that freighters passing through the canyon greatly feared the Gadiantons, who the Book of Mormon describes as a secretive brotherhood or sect of assassins during the Nephite/Lamanite wars. Freighters told stories of rocks closing in on them and blocking their way through the canyon, or of the canyon literally folding up to entrap them. In this same place, full of its rich lore of evil, four students from Southern Utah University were driving back to Cedar City after spending the day at the rodeo in Pioche. At 10:00 p.m. they arrived fourteen miles east of Modena. Spotting the railroad crossing with a forked road ahead, the girls mistakenly took the wrong turn and entered the red rock canyon instead. Suddenly the blacktop road disappeared and they were driving on white cement; realizing they were lost, they backed up and turned around. Instead of seeing the desert highway, they were surrounded by grain fields and ponderosa pines. They continued to retrace their path to the highway but could not find it.

Suddenly, they saw a roadside tavern with a red neon sign, but they could not read what it said. Some men came out of the tavern and the girls decided to stop and ask them for directions. Sticking her head out of the car window, the driver suddenly screamed, slammed the car into reverse, and lurched forward at top speed. The other girls were now terrified too, as the driver exclaimed that those were not men. Four egg-shaped vehicles, appearing to be mounted on tricycle wheels, began to chase them. They made a whirring or buzzing sound as they moved along, and one bright light shone from the top of each of them. Minutes later they roared out of the canyon in their old Chevy at eighty miles an hour. The white cement road suddenly vanished and they were back in the desert again. The car went into an arroyo and they ended up with three flat tires and a crumpled bumper. The girls stayed with the car until morning and then walked two miles south to Highway 56 and flagged down a state trooper. They told him their incredible story, but he did not believe them.

In this case, there were several things that could not be explained. There were the tire tracks showing where the Chevy had left the highway in Modena. Tire tracks from the wrecked Chevy extended only two hundred yards back into the desert and then ended abruptly. No one could explain just how the car had gotten two miles north of the highway without leaving any physical traces. And the car's right hubcap was never found. The girls could have made it all up to explain the wrecked car; they also could have been scared by something they saw, but did not understand. Unless someone confesses to a hoax, or new evidence is found, which is not likely, this mystery will probably never be solved. The articles I read about this event, seemed to agree something happened, although the girls might have embellished it.

My favorite quote is from an article by Joseph Trainer. "If Utah's Gadianton Canyon is, as some people claim, a gateway to another dimension, then perhaps Janna's missing hubcap is a prime exhibit—an 'alien artifact'—on display in a museum on that parallel Earth."[6] The Gadiantons from the Book of Mormon are somehow becoming confused with evil aliens from another planet. Who knows, perhaps the Gadiantons, who were essentially robbers and thieves, could have been aliens too! In the old days, they were the most feared among those who carried freight through this canyon. Linking these old tales to present-day alien interference is not that far a leap either way you look at it.

For all the fun or terrors we have with these sightings, there is always the flip side of that coin: we should never be presumptuous enough to think we are the only living beings in this vast universe. Just recently scientists discovered what they think is another solar system. It is fairly close to us and some of its planets have the ability to support life. "My personal opinion . . . is that the Universe is teeming with life," says Patrick Wiggins, a spokesman for the Clarke Planetarium. "There are more stars in the sky than there are grains of sand on planet earth. The notion that anybody would say that out of that incredible number of stars there is only one planet that has life on it, that's ludicrous. That's egocentric to the max."[7] Local cult filmmaker, Trent

Harris (*Plan 10 From Outer Space*) says he has heard all sorts of stories from Utah, especially while filming a movie in Zion's Canyon. He recently sponsored a UFO film festival in Bicknell, Utah. "You can't throw a rock in southern Utah without hitting somebody who's been abducted,"[8] he says.

However, I think the Midwest had a corner on sightings long before Utah got onto the scene. My husband, born and raised in a very small southern Indiana town, spent hours and hours along with hundreds of other young high school and junior high school kids, UFO hunting in the country. One of our first dates was UFO hunting. In high school in the early sixties, my husband perpetrated one of the best hoaxes I've heard of. He bought several metallic space blankets from the army-navy store and made himself a suit and helmet. Then, at a very skinny six foot five, he jumped out of a cornfield in front of an old farmer on his way to town for a drink. He raced through the fields and got to the tavern before the old farmer did, shedding the evidence on his way. The old guy came in and told everyone about his encounter with a seven-foot reed-thin alien being. Over a few beers, my husband got to hear all about it with the rest of the guys.

Skeptics say two things. First, there is no solid evidence to prove we have ever been visited by alien beings. Second, they too believe that we cannot be alone in the universe; we just haven't met any of these aliens yet. As for myself, I think if aliens were here, we wouldn't know it anyway. They would be so advanced in their technology or natural abilities that we would be totally unaware of their visits. Another view is such travelers could be human just like us, but from a hopefully more advanced civilization. This reminds me of the movie called *Disaster in Time* with Jeff Daniels. In the film, people from a very cold and boring future culture on earth, return to the past as tourists. They are looking for a little excitement by arriving just before known disasters take place and then watching them take place as observers on a paid tour to several historic places. As an idealist, I prefer to believe that if aliens are here, they are trying to help us advance a little rather than experimenting on us like lab animals or, even worse, not really caring about us at all. Or perhaps *we* are the aliens and don't know it yet. Regardless, science fiction and scientific research predict our possible futures for us. We ought to at least listen to what they have to tell us.

Recent updates in the field have produced more Utah UFO sightings, one in West Jordan in August of 2000, one in Layton in 2001, and several in the Clearfield area in 2001 and 2002. The West Jordan sighting involved what people thought was a flock of geese, but as they watched, they saw the formation do some unusual things. They watched the flight of these "vehicles" from Corner Canyon near Bountiful until they disappeared around the Point of the Mountain on the south end of Salt Lake Valley. They reported the large vehicle was pulsing with luminescent lighting and waves of color and looked to be about the size of several football fields. Five or six smaller craft made a semi-circle in front of the large vehicle and seemed to escort it until, in a sort of starburst, they arced out and disappeared in luminescent trails.

In Layton, a gray triangular-shaped air vehicle was spotted traveling very fast around town, and then disappeared into a nearby canyon. The Clearfield sightings have happened several times with formations of small lights flying in groups of seven. The odd thing was they were not flying in any sort of recognizable formation. They were also traveling so fast that they were going from one area to another in less than five seconds. Two groups of seven vehicles were seen, but then they divided up and flew over various parts of town in sets of three. The lights, the speed at which they were traveling, and the lack of formation convinced everyone who saw them that they were not flocks of geese. When three of the crafts flew very low over a local gas station, it shook the ground. Some thought them to be experimental aircraft from Hill Air Force base.

Of late, there has also been much speculation on where the new Area 51 is going to be located. It seems that the government is either moving their top-secret base to another location or breaking it up and establishing several new underground bases around the West. Some think a main base will be in Colorado and others think it will be in New Mexico. However, quite a few have speculated that Utah has been housing the main and very secretive underground military base since 1999. Others say that all three locations, Utah, New Mexico, and Colorado, are housing parts of one big underground network of military operations. There has always been speculation about an old abandoned site in this desert area of Utah. The base was supposedly shut down years ago. But now speculation centers around this as only the tip of the iceberg in Green River. The recent war in the Middle East could also be contributing to stepped-up secret military operations and research underground, as well as the constant surveillance of Area 51 by UFO watchers. New and more secretive operations are probably needed to avoid the high-tech capabilities that many of these UFO groups now use to monitor the activities at Area 51.

If the government facility is indeed already in Utah, it is rumored to be called Area 6413 and is located in the white sands area. Its original name was the White Sands Missile Range Utah Launch Complex, and it is in an even more desolate and forbidding area than the original White Sands New Mexico Complex. Experts say it is located east of the Green River and south of the town of Green River on highway Route I-70. They also say if you wanted to hide something well, this would be the place. The Pentagon's interest in the real estate there and consistent spotting of unusual government transports with blue tarps thrown over them in the Green River area fuel rumors of the secret base. "Part of the public's fascination with the original Area 51 is its rich collection of stories about crashed flying saucers, alien bodies and unexplained lights in the sky. The relocation of Area 51 does not necessarily mean those tales will be left behind when operations begin here in Utah, perhaps as early as 1999."[9]

The latest reports as of 2004 indicate quite a few alien bases in underground locations. Besides the Crossroads Mall, Little Cottonwood Canyon, and various other caverns under Salt Lake City, there are several towns where UFO researchers say alien-military bases might be located. These towns include Draper, Salem, Spanish Fork, Payson, Modena, and Vernal. Apparently all of these towns have exits from underground installations and between Salem and Thistle there is a suspected joint underground venture involving Masons, Nazis, and alien Reptilians. Salem has all the legends of Hyrum Koyle's Dream Mine, an ethereal all-white Buddhist temple, and has been the site of UFO gatherings over the years. Thistle has become a ghost town after being wiped out by a giant mudslide with apparitions of its own. Both locations seem ideal for an alien base. There are also supposed to be other such installations buried deep within mountains such as Mount Nebo, Bald Mountain, the Monroe Mountains, Sleeping Ute Mountain, Twin Peaks, and several others along the Wasatch Mountain range. There are also installations supposedly under Lake

Powell and in Dark Canyon (Manti-LaSal National Forest) as well as in the area of Zion National Park and Druid Arch in Canyonlands National Park.

There are old Ute and Paiute legends about their ancient ancestors who moved into deep caverns inside mountains. These ancient cavern dwellers abandoned their upper cities and journeyed even deeper into underground caverns to establish new dwellings and sometimes abducted people from the surface, people who never returned. Some even believe that the descendants of these people still live there. There are also stories of farmers in small towns with giant boulders that they needed to have moved in their fields. When the boulders were moved, the farmers found tunnel openings descending underground. Upon entering the tunnels, the farmers came face-to-face with serpent-like creatures presumed to be aliens. The story goes that the farmers turned right around, ran out of the tunnels, and re-blocked the entrances with the boulders so no one else could find or enter them. This would be a convenient way not to have to prove the stories.

According to the latest Utah UFO Sightings Map, put out by the Utah UFO hunters at www.aliendave.com, a comprehensive web site for anything strange in Utah, there were around fifty reported sightings in 2003. Most of these were clustered around Salt Lake City, Ogden, and Provo. This is quite a change from the scattered previous sightings in the Uintah Mountains, out near the Dugway Proving Grounds, and in southern Utah, although these areas continue to report sightings too. The various details about these sightings are available on the web site in addition to the latest goings on at the National Institute of Research Science at the now locally famous Sherman/Bigelow ranch in the Uintahs. There is even one report of a Beck Street tunnel exit in the industrial part of Salt Lake City that produces the high amounts of electromagnetic energy there is constantly fouling up of all sorts of electronic equipment. All things associated with UFOs (cattle mutilations, alien abductions, chemtrails, sightings, reports, videos, photos, and updates) can be found on this web site. Suffice it to say that the aliens have arrived in Utah, although we wouldn't want to say that we didn't have a lot of aliens before all the publicity. Whatever you believe, the alien menace or the paranoia will never go away. Who will ever know what is truth and what is fiction? The scary thing is, that perhaps we aren't ignoring or chasing fantasies, but realities instead.

Notes

1) Bauman, "Is Dugway's Expansion an Alien Concept?," November 4, 2004.

2) Ibid., 3.

3) *Las Vegas Sun*, "Nevada Millionaire Buys 'UFO Ranch' in Utah," October 23, 1996.

4) Ibid.

5) http://www.nidsci.org.

6) Trainer, "Utah's Time/Space Warp Gadianton Canyon Encounter," May 26, 2000.

7) Van Eyck, "Frequent Flyers? Those Aliens Do Get Around," June 30, 1996.

8) Ibid.

9) Wilson, "The New Area 51," 1994.

Exits and Doorways
Mythical Tunnels and Subterranean Highways

Some will find this story a bit hard to swallow. Truth and fiction has been intermixed in the tales told over the years. I look at this tale as being a fantastical journey down into the tunnels beneath Salt Lake City and Ogden. It is also a journey down into the natural caverns under the state of Utah or even into the vast expanses in our underground west. In writing this story, I could not help but think of all the stories in fiction that I had heard. Such stories as those of the mythical city beneath the ground in the *Beauty and the Beast* television series. There are stories about the underworld in classical literature by H.G. Wells and Jules Verne, visionaries who saw the future and invented their own personal interpretation of things to come, with many of their inventions eventually coming to fruition. L. Frank Baum told a much more interesting tale of Dorothy's visit to the underground city, where instead of following the yellow brick road to "somewhere over the rainbow," Dorothy and her friends slide down glass tubes to get from one place to another. The tale of the *Hunchback of Notre Dame,* in which the poor and misfits of the Paris live in their own city in the maze beneath, is a touching portrait of the class system and society. Having seen people's faces as they emerged from the depths of the catacombs, I was surprised that anyone would even try to get to the bottom of these underground tunnels. Looking exhausted, frightened, and somewhat mystified, the terror of their decent into such a place and the fear of being lost down there had really gotten to them. The spirits of so many dead easily overwhelm the few living travelers in such a country.

There have always been futuristic tales in science fiction of nuclear holocausts, which then cause the survivors to move underground, creating whole cities beneath the surface. In the mythology from many countries and cultures, the underworld is alive with terrors and legendary creatures that threaten mankind. In *Lord of the Rings* series, there is a character that leads people up from the darkness of this underworld using an illuminated crystal. And of course there have always been tales of the underworld of hell from which people must be rescued, or to which souls are condemned for eternity. "Beowulf" was a seventh or eighth century English poem that involved the rescue of human souls from an underground labyrinth by an epic hero. *Dante's Inferno* even had various levels of hell moving down to the core of the earth. In Native American lore, many tribes believed that souls must keep emerging from one underworld to the next in order to advance themselves and their people. They saw their souls as moving upward from the known into the unknown. All of these tales implied that the underworld was usually symbolic of lost souls, darkness, despair, and even evil. Like the unexplored depths of the ocean or the far reaches of outer space, the area from the earth's core to the surface is another unsolved mystery to man. It has also been a source of fear and terror, both in the world's literature and in centuries of tales and stories of what we speculate is under the earth beneath our feet.

Then there are the true tales of underground tunnels, tales of sewer systems, subways, and other labyrinths that cities slowly create beneath themselves, sometimes loosing track of just how many they have. There are also the real tunnels most often built by the local railroad station in many cities and leading to the local hotels, brothels, and gambling houses. During Prohibition, underground bars and tunnels bloomed. Quite a few cities today offer a tour of these tunnels. Visitors can see how the wealthy, soldiers, and even the poor got their entertainment unobserved.

But unlike other major cities, Salt Lake City has a unique myth. It is said that its first tunnels were built for Brigham Young to get from the LDS temple to his various homes as a protection and in inclement weather. Later, the tunnels were used to avoid the authorities during the years that polygamous husbands were hunted down and made to serve prison terms. There is quite a controversy even today over whether or not these tunnels ever existed. The truth is that there are indeed a few tunnels, long ago closed off, under the city near Temple Square. Private citizens have photos of them before they were closed. Apparently they were quite nice and lined with wide brick arches. They would have provided the ideal place to hide when the federals came looking for polygamous husbands. The old Latter-day Saint Nineteenth Ward House, where the Salt Lake Acting Company now resides, has a tunnel in its basement. It is sealed off now and rumor has it that it is directly connected to the Capitol Building and Temple Square. The houses down the street from the Lion and Beehive Houses are also said to have had connecting tunnels. One of these tunnels, under the Lion House, is still used for storing restaurant supplies. The tunnels under Temple Square are still being used. While many people believe them to be a myth, they actually do exist. However, the extent of the tunnel matrix under the city is greatly exaggerated.

On the other hand, residents of Ogden hint at the possibility of a few more tunnels down Main and State Streets in Salt Lake City. The tunnels in Ogden were dug for those involved in prostitution, operating gambling establishments, and running opium dens in the 1800s. Later, in the 1920s and 1930s, Prohibition led to even more underground establishments with accompanying tunnels to get patrons to these illegal places unseen. It is very likely that a few such tunnels existed in Salt Lake City's commercial district. It is known that Ogden had quite a network of them as a result of its raucous atmosphere. From the late 1800s through World War II, sixty to seventy trains arrived each day at the Union Station and brought in all sorts of emigrants, travelers, and con artists. In the early 1900s, there were opium dens, bootlegged alcohol, and quaint underground bars that offered their hidden fare, gambling dens, and houses of prostitution along this street and several others in the vicinity. Rumors of a vast network of literally underworld tunnels all over Ogden persist to this day. The closed up entrances and exits in the basements of many buildings along Twenty-fourth to Twenty-sixth Streets can still be seen today.

A few years back, the mayor of Ogden came out with a great statement about the tunnels, perhaps thinking about all the tourism revenue that tunnels in Nevada have brought to the state. However, many residents of Ogden are in denial about these tunnels, feeling the city's image would be tainted by it's sordid past. A new generation in Ogden feels that these tunnels ought to be documented and turned into a downtown tourist draw. That is just what the mayor of Ogden had done, setting city planners to work locating these tunnels along Twenty-fifth Street as well as Wall and Grant Streets. So far, they have found bricked up archways linking certain buildings together, but no long tunnels. The Bigelow-Ben Lomond Historic Suite Hotel on Twenty-fifth Street has such a tunnel under its hotel because I have actually seen it, remnants of an old bar and all. How far it went onto Twenty-fifth Street is anyone's guess, because it is closed off now. The Union Station, on the other hand, had several such tunnels for many years so passengers could get to their trains faster. It is said there was also a tunnel that ran from the bank on Twenty-fourth Street to Union Station on Twenty-fifth, to allow money to be transported safely between the bank and the train station. Exit passages were found in the basement of the old Egyptian Theatre and other exits were found underneath sidewalks. The city planned to tap into this mystique with above ground displays in the area with photos and interviews with long time residents who remember the tunnels, that is if they can find them. The city wanted to open the tunnels and make sense of the maze. Old timers talk about railroad workers who dug tunnels to conceal opium dens. They also tell of underworld figures that ordered tunnels dug to stash illegal booze during Prohibition-era raids.

Historians say there were probably opium dens but no tunnels, although they too have heard the rumors and are curious to see if any of them are true. Retired police officers claim to remember the basement passageways. A lookout would buzz the gamblers in a poker game to warn of a police raid and all the evidence was quickly removed via a hidden passageway that the police could never find. One long-time Ogden resident whose father owned a business in this area says that he remembers a steel door in their basement which led to pathways that stretched at least half a block north and half a block south. "I know what I saw . . . and they were definitely tunnels," he says. If businesses give the city permission, they may go so far as to knock down a few walls to find the tunnels.[1]

As I explored the tunnel myths along the Wasatch Front, it never occurred to me I would find stories about tunnels or caverns that are actually underneath the typical mazes of sewer systems under any city and the other debatable tunnels in the areas. I consider these stories the modern-day version of the ancient mythological stories of underground worlds deep within our earth. These alien stories are an utterly fantastic matrix told by those who believe that aliens are living in the earth. UFO watchers believe these various alien races are visiting our earth and have been for centuries. They also believe the alien cultures have constructed a nationwide underground shuttle network or something called the subterranean highway. In the past, the state of Utah was nearly always left out of UFO or alien conspiracy theories, unlike our neighboring states that supposedly house endless exits and entrances to these deep underground caverns. So when an anonymous eyewitness of several such bases was asked if there were any underground alien bases in Utah, he surprised everyone by answering yes. He said that Utah lies directly over one of the largest natural cavern systems in the United States. This system reaches deep into the western Rockies as well as under the Bonneville Basin. Scientists agree that these caverns exist, but they do not agree that all of these caverns are connected together, thus providing a network for travel.

There are indeed many alien installations in the Wasatch Mountain area according to the Mutual UFO Network, the Center for Study of Extraterrestrial Intelligence, and other UFO organizations. In fact, there are claims of several of these secret underground installations all over Utah, of both alien and human origin. These installations are claimed to be under downtown Salt Lake City; under downtown Ogden; in the Lake Powell area; in a place called Dark Canyon due west of Monticello; in the Canyon Rims Recreation area of the Manti-LaSal National Forest; near Modena; almost directly west of Cedar City near the Nevada border; under the town of Vernal; and at the Dugway Proving Grounds out in the west desert. There is a connection to the Dugway Proving Grounds because of the biological warfare research going on there, which could be a real threat to the city, if not the state and the nation. It is here that former employees claim to have seen Reptilians masquerading as humans and working along side human workers. Perhaps these are disgruntled employees, or maybe just imaginative ones. Then there are the alien wars being witnessed in the Uintah Basin by many ranchers over the years. These incidents are being studied, observed, and recorded, making Utah a hot bed for those investigating alien encounters, abductions, and speculation that have always existed here.

The stories, however, get even better. Several people have spoken of ancient tunnel systems that were discovered when excavating the land for the downtown Crossroads Plaza Mall in Salt Lake City. The stories surrounding these tunnels, which are supposedly under other tunnels, are amazing! Simply telling them, I feel as if I'm in a science fiction novel, but for the absolute certainty of the people who tell them. For example, people exploring these deep caverns say that some people who either came with them or went in alone have never returned, or that "lizard people" have been encountered in these tunnels at deeper levels. These explorers describe various types of aliens from planets and cultures far away. They describe the "Grays" or those little aliens with the long fingers, bald heads, pointy chins and big black almond shaped eyes who inhabit the tunnels, work side by side with humans on electronics and massive building projects for other underground caverns. Believers describe the "men in black" or "M.I.B.s" who have been seen in these caverns carrying Uzi machine guns. Other believers claim to have seen walls between these passages that can be walked through or walls that vibrate and give off a greenish glow. People who have entered these places also claim to have seen discs emerging from the exit points of these tunnels fly up and defend the valley against UFO attacks.

Other stories involve Dungeon and Dragon fans that have entered these tunnels and claimed to have found hundreds of maze-like passageways stretching for miles and miles. Some say that the sewage drainage system under Crossroads Mall leads directly to the deeper tunnels, and that the whole state of Utah is providing a connecting highway for more facilities in Nevada and New Mexico. There are two versions of a story about a worker at the Latter-day Saint temple who saw tunnels under the ones he was working on. In the first version, the worker accidentally broke through to an underground tunnel below Temple Square and traveled some distance into it. Soon he encountered a lizard man that tried to attack him as he made a hasty retreat to the surface. Because the man talked about his experience, government officials soon arrived and closed off the entrances to these tunnels. In the other version, a customer entered the tunnels near the cinema area of the mall and followed them across the street and on up to Temple Square, discovering that there were more tunnels there. Now that The Church of Jesus Christ of Latter-day Saints has bought the whole area including the Crossroads Mall with plans to incorporate the area into the grounds of their worldwide headquarters, the rumors in UFO circles will become even more fantastical.

There is also talk about the facility under the mountain in Little Cottonwood Canyon where the Church keeps its records in case of a natural or manmade disaster. It is said that the record storage facility is only the upper levels of a vast network of tunnels, and that the Grays took over the lower tunnels, ordering the vault workers out of forbidden areas, telling them it was their patriotic duty to keep it a secret. Apparently the FBI and local police sealed off these tunnels and the vault workers are not allowed near them. These stories reminded me of Cheyenne Mountain in Colorado Springs where the North American Aerospace Defense Command (NORAD) has an underground city similar to the vaults in Little Cottonwood Canyon. It is claimed that both places have the same giant springs built under them so that the buildings will bounce in an earthquake. We had a friend who worked on installing these giant springs at NORAD. He said that they were about the size of semi-truck tires.

Anonymous internet stories tell of a woman from Boston, Massachusetts, who claimed she was abducted by aliens and taken to a stolen farm beneath the Salt Flats in Utah and held there for three weeks. Other stories from various sources have described strange subsurface phenomena associated with the Salt Lake or Great Basin subnet. The wildest stories make reference to a system of tunnels and catacombs below the Salt Lake Valley, said to exist long before any settlers came to the valley. Early stories claim that early polygamists discovered and expanded these caves to escape from government prosecutors. Some of the early pioneers who entered these tunnels never returned, a convenient way of explaining mysterious murders and disappearances in the early days of settlement. These are the most intriguing tales to me—those that tell of early pioneer settlers discovering and exploring these ancient tunnels and finding creatures from other planets in them. Some stories go on to tell of settlers actually joining with the creatures to create underground colonies below the Salt Flats, within the Salt Lake Valley, and in the Western Rockies. Bottomless shafts are said to exist beneath the city, as well as huge passages that lead from downtown Salt Lake City to both Big and Little Cottonwood Canyons.

Other stories actually give names to all of these various alien groups. There are the Mayan-Telosian aliens who have a large base with tunnels that lead to the Latter-day Saint and Masonic temples downtown. This would make the early Mason and Mormon settlers in cahoots with each other! One lady claimed that a blond man in a black astronaut uniform, who showed her a *Star Wars*-like scenario taking place above the Cottonwood Canyons, took her one night from her house in Salt Lake City. She saw cloaked disks emerging from Twin Peaks to fire beams of energy at incoming UFOs. The beams hit what appeared to be the force shields around the incoming craft, and the energy crackled around the UFOs, many of which seemed to lose power and drift away.[2]

There are several other stories about the Crossroads Mall area. One is about men who used their truck and a heavy chain to rip open a manhole cover and go exploring. They made their way through the sewer system and eventually came to a shaft that descended downward through five small rooms, one on top of another. When they got to the bottom room, there was another shaft to a larger room where it seemed that there was a bottomless pit, as well as other tunnels with very high ceilings and many footprints from some sort of bipedal, three-toed creatures. These underground systems are said to run from under Trolley Square into the old Sugarhouse district. One man stated that he was taken from just north of Sugarhouse, had his leg operated on, removed, and then reattached. When he woke up in the morning, his leg gave way beneath him. Another woman claimed that she was abducted and taken into a huge chamber west of the Sugarhouse Mall. In an altered state, she met a tall, dark-haired man who was with a Gray and was given instructions she cannot remember. As the whole Sugarhouse area has become a hive of various "aliens" to the Utah way of life, none of this surprises me! Once a model for the small-town fifties lifestyle, Sugarhouse is now the hub of myriad counter cultures in Salt Lake City. It is the perfect place to meet aliens of every sort, both from our planet and beyond.

Another great tale from the Crossroads Mall involves a woman working with the mall's night cleaning crew. Mopping the floor in an area all by herself, she looked up to discover a creature coming around the corner. It slowly wobbled up to her and snarled. She was frozen in terror, as the creature or "demon" as she described it, simply passed her by; it was one of the lizard people who supposedly live underneath the city. Another night, a worker claimed to have placed his hand against a wall and discovered a tunnel behind it. He went down into this tunnel only to find his hand went straight through the next wall, an experience he described as totally unnerving. Later, he went back and tried to do it again. The wall was solid this time, suggesting the theory that the aliens could shift molecules within an underground passage, passing through hidden chambers undetected. Others have reported passing green luminescent rooms or locked rooms with ancient wooden doors and metal gates across them.

I find the early history of these various alien groups as written down by the alien believers not far removed from, or at least parallel to, ancient esoteric writings. Here is a synopsis of this history of the aliens here on earth or under it. The groups who inhabited the underground during these early days were called the Telosian-Agharti-Melchizedek-Mayan. They lived in an underground network of cultures and kingdoms. It was among these early alien groups that the great wars occurred inside the earth. The majority of the fighting took place in these caverns between the 1920s and the 1940s. Wild rumors about other alien races here on earth say that the greatest enemies are the Reptiloids and the Grays. The Grays are trying to get the Reptiloids to experience human emotions, as they are normally emotionless creatures. However, the Grays apparently blew it by allowing the Reptiloids the opportunity to use the collective consciousness of humans. The Reptiloids abused this power by sending subliminal messages to the humans, trying to control their minds. I imagine that to avoid collective mind control, a person would only have to use a little self-control and street wisdom to keep from being brainwashed, even temporarily.

This history of the alien races on earth reads like a not-so-good science fiction novel. Although the novel's chapters are somewhat disconnected, the tunnels are supposedly not. Some people laugh when I read this history to them, others sing their own version of *The Twilight Zone* theme song, and a some say, "Really? I've seen a UFO myself!" It is said a few people even believe that when the end of the world comes, spaceships will land to collect the faithful over the hills behind the State Capitol Building! However, my favorites are those stories that can top even this one. My husband, for example, says, "None of this could be true because creatures from other planets would have developed the technology to dig their way through the underground in tunnels that are burrowed as one goes. They could disappear as soon as one presses forward through them! They do not need a labyrinth because they themselves are a labyrinth." But then, he is a good science fiction writer. Another science fiction buff said that aliens didn't need tunnels at all because they could just walk among us. We wouldn't see them because we are either hypnotized or they can disguise themselves as humans simply by shape-shifting. Perhaps it is like the movie *They Live* where the aliens had hypnotized everyone into seeing only what they wanted them to see and the heroes had to wear special sunglasses in order to distinguish the aliens from the humans. The movie created a sort of tunnel vision of the "us" and "them" variety. Beyond human prejudices, don't we all sometimes wish we had such sunglasses to discern the evil that we see around us every day, or that the "Men in Black" really did wipe out our memories of such "aliens" among us.

Apparently, Utah is awash with various alien bases occupied by Reptilians, Nordics, Grays, secret societies, giant subterranean humans, Oranges or hybrid humans, and even natural-born humans who are being held prisoner in Reptilian strongholds. It is rather like the ghosts of our past, present, and future coming back to haunt us. The various government agencies have their own collection of "fools file" letters from people, for example, asking about submarine cities under the Great Salt Lake or warning the officials about the explosive alien rocks placed about the city by those who live under them. These letters are but a few of the wild theories, besides the usual UFO sighting reports, collected weekly from about the state. I found that collecting these stories was as confusing and fantastical a journey, as are the endless lost Utah mines and treasures stories. The modern-day urban myths are far surpassing their predecessors.

All of this reminds me of my childhood when I used to walk past empty cars and wonder just who had been in them. I never thought that I was seeing glimpses of people's pasts or their futures, and that I was seeing people's essences in them. It was a sudden realization that those parked cars along the street on both of sides of me really did have people inside them or at least the shadow of their former selves from either a few moments ago or perhaps weeks, months, or even years before. Those shadows could also represent future events. I thought it was my vivid imagination and never thought that perhaps I was in that small group of sensitives who could see them! Now I understand that energy and matter connect everything and that someday we just might also concede that the soul and the mind are connected. When that day comes, these ideas will usher in a new era of brain and soul research and a new kind of technology that will connect man to nature. Many of the great geniuses of our history eventually found out that a child-like fascination with the universe brought about new discoveries and inventions. They also believed that we were not alone in the universe.

So I say, prove these people who believe in such things wrong. People laughed when they first heard of humans being able to fly and now we do. Claims of underground lost treasures hidden in these caverns just might be true as well.

Notes
1) Dirr, "Ogden Digs Into Stories of Tunnel Network," July 29, 2001.
2) http://www.thinkaboutit.com/branton/secrets_of_ the_mojave11. htm.

Cache Valley Crop Circles

Hoax or Providence Found?

Crop Circles are usually imprinted in a single night in fields of wheat or corn. However, they have also been found in barley, oats, grass, canola, trees, and even snow and ice. They happen in the spring and summer seasons and have been reported all over the world except in two countries, China and South Africa. Thousands are reported each year. The most complex ones are usually reported in the United Kingdom, where mass markings of the ground in the form of circles swirled clockwise or counter clockwise began to be reported in the 1970s. Scientists and others around the world started to research this topic. Although the reports reached their peak in the 1970s. Crop circles have been reported since 1647 in England and other countries around the globe. In the 1990s, crop circles began to appear with complex pictograms composed of straight lines, angles, and spiral rings. They became a form of land art and theories of their origins became a popular topic of discussion.

The mystifying element of crop circles is why these formations are studied at all and why they aren't believed to be manmade. The answer may lie in how we look at it. Are they hoaxes, a form of long distance communication from outer space as claimed, or a new, quite beautiful art form appearing on our lands? On the other hand, they are not legal and often anger those whose crops have been ruined in their creation. Are they manmade or alien-made? Among the peculiarities of true crop circles is a molecular change in the plants and the soil involved in crop circles. Such things as enlarged cell walls, expulsion cavities in the nodes of the plant stalks, extended node lengths, and changes in the composition of the soil itself are scientifically significant. Farmers also report an increased yield in their crops where the crop circles were in the years following their appearance, or they report that nothing will grow in or near the circles for at least a season or more. Some of the stalks are actually woven like cloth to the floor of the formation and patterns swirl in multiple directions with complex woven patterns. Multiple layers of plants are often swirled in various directions, one on top of another. Sometimes stalks from the middle of unaffected groupings of plants will get pulled into the formation.

Other odd phenomena have been reported in the vicinity of crop circles such as farm equipment malfunctions and compasses spinning out of control in planes flying over the area. Other equipment affected includes cell phones, batteries, cameras, and watches, although pacemakers seem to operate just fine. There is a distinct emission of energy at the sound frequency of 5 KHz for a few days after a new crop circle has been formed; witnesses describe it as a trilling sound. Physical reactions are also reported during or after a visit to the crop circle. Nausea, headaches, dizziness, tingling sensations, pains, and giddiness have all been reported. At their centers, the circles emit ten times the radiation level of a normal field measured by a device called a flux gate magnetometer. Witnesses have also reported strange light phenomenon similar to an electrical storm. The circles seem to consistently appear over underground water supplies and land situated above chalk beds; the supposition is that this is because water is a good electrical conductor. The theory is that whatever is responsible for the circles may be trying to detect electromagnetic currents.

Formations often, but not always, appear inside restricted areas in fenced-off military installations. Parts of the formations are made without affecting the surrounding tramlines left behind by the tractors. Without any sorts of intrusion, are the stalks bending themselves? The plant stalks also bend in unusual ways, although in hoaxed crop circles, the plants will be bent to the ground and then will eventually straighten themselves to reach for the light. But in those crop circles that cannot be explained, the plants are bent at various junctures along the stalk or nodes in small groups or individually, bending every which way, which is considered by scientists to be extremely unusual. Crop circles tend to be aligned with the physical features of the land, tramlines, and already darkened features of the land. To form so perfect a pattern, the architect would have to be viewing the whole formation from above. That's the only way these elaborate designs with such symmetry could be made. Most importantly, "researchers have discovered layers within layers of information contained in the crop circles themselves. There are sacred ratios, such as pi, that governs the growth process of all organic life."[1] Some researchers make the supposition that further study might reveal messages or a higher intelligence behind these works of art on the land.

There are nine basic theories as to what creates these crop circles. These theories can be divided somewhat into two camps. On the one hand, those who don't base their beliefs solely on the scientific process say that they may be hoaxes, secret military experiments, or manifestations of a God force, or signs from extraterrestrials past, present, or future. On the other hand, the scientific explanations range from whirlwind vortices and plasma gravitational vortices to chemical applications and just plain good planning on the part of those who make them. Some theorize that natural earth energies are the cause, although most scientists, while admitting to the possibility of such things, say that they cannot thus far be proven. New Agers say that these natural earth energies are simply things that we do not understand yet. It's odd that in researching crop circles, these two worlds (the scientific community and the esoteric and ecological one) seem not only to occasionally agree, but also to continuously collide with one another. Perhaps such a simple phenomenon as crop circles will be one of the forces to bring these two worlds of thought closer together, unless most of these crop circles turn out to be hoaxes. If these land designs are hoaxes, time itself will stop their appearance as the media loses interest and removes the hoaxers' motivation. A future scientific discovery may make crop circles easier to create and therefore more common. Or people may simply move on to another fad or a newer, and therefore more interesting, phenomenon.

The plasma-gravitational theory simply means the land is being microwaved although this still does not answer the question of whether these waves are being spontaneously generated or generated by an outside source. The whirlwind vortex theory is similar to the plasma theory; only in this theory, the vortices are caused by natural atmospheric phenomena. The anomalous light phenomena that many witnesses have experienced cannot be explained by the self-electrification that occurs in crop circles with electromagnetic properties similar to tornadoes or even dust devils. The theory is that the earth's magnetic and electrical fields interact to create the circles. Because of recent scientific research, the chemical applications theory has all but been abandoned in explaining the formation of crop circles.

Natural earth energies might be considered the crossover theory for scientists and New Agers because it includes the theory of a grid of what they call ley-lines on the earth that could one day be proven scientifically. This network of earth energies is supposed to provide an energy grid for the many sacred sites of the world. The idea is that over the centuries, man has divined or stumbled upon these power spots and placed his sacred sites over them because of the special energies that they provide. This theory holds that it was two brothers who essentially planned and helped to build most of the great cathedrals of Europe. Their original plans were passed along from city to city either by chance or by design. Either on purpose or by accident, they built conduits to receive power from the earth and beyond at maximum frequencies. Others took the brothers' plans and intuitively built these huge edifices on junctures of the so-called ley-lines, not only to draw people, but also to produce powerful energies to awe and inspire. This is similar to the theory of the pyramids that are said not only to store energy but also to rejuvenate or even restore life. It is theorized that the Egyptians also built their pyramids over ley-lines. It's possible that these natural earth cycles were understood and manipulated by ancient peoples in ways that we do not understand.

Crop circles, at least those not considered hoaxes by the scientific community, will probably be scientifically explained someday. However, just who is involved in their creation and what they want from it, is another matter for speculation. Even the scientific explanation does not include where the waves are coming from or why. It is rather like the theory of the universe; there is always another unexplained layer, below the one that may have found explanation. The spiral shape found throughout nature seems to be a basic principle in many of my intuitive dreaming and visions. Perhaps crop circles are a mere cosmic artist's whim, created in ways that our earthly artists cannot even conceive of at present, and sent here from light years away to intrigue us and amuse them.

The universal symbol of the spiral has appeared in several of my intuitive readings. In on instance, the woman had asked me what her mother's death had been like. As soon as she asked the question, I began falling in my mind's eye through a huge tunnel that at first looked like a well. Soon I realized that it was curving around and around like I was inside a snail's shell, only the insides were smooth and connected by dark brown rings between light brown sections. Suddenly, I pulled out of the ride and saw the huge spiral from some distance away. It was a coiled shell like a French horn although more natural in color, like the inside of a giant snail shell. People floated out of one end of it, their bodies stiff, straight, and perfectly vertical. The woman's mother came out the other end of this spiral ride and then I realized that I was seeing many shells and that people were floating out of the others as well. All of the people were floating feet-first towards an immense, curved shape that was dark on the surface and yet at the same time emitted a bright white light all over it. It seemed as if the people were arriving and being assisted into parking stalls all around this shape. When I described this image to the woman, she told me her mother had been in a coma for several days before she died. I can remember thinking, had I really seen where people's minds go when they are in a coma state or just what this particular woman was hallucinating as her brain shut down? Or even stranger still, had I seen what it felt like to be dying where people were held in some sort of way-station before moving on to whatever came after this?

Later, a friend of mine who works in the medical field had an explanation for me. She said that I had perfectly described what the brain is doing when it is shutting down, or possibly when the person is going into a coma state, although not as much is known about this. The part of the brain at the back of the neck begins to collect memory, and as the brain dies, the person goes to a last area where a bright light is seen, traveling through the convolutions to get there. In other words, I was traveling through the convolutions of the brain with her as she passed away. There is both a metaphysical explanation and a scientific one that may at some point come together to explain the process of dying itself. Yet I still wonder if perhaps I wasn't seeing something else there, something we do not understand, as yet beyond the scientific explanations. What interested me the most was there was the spiral again, a scientific and esoteric symbol of eternity found in so many places in nature as well as in mathematics.

For three summers, starting in 1996, unusual crop formations appeared in the Cache Valley, two hours north of Salt Lake City. The patterns were similar, with the largest stretching approximately 316 feet from end to end. The first formation appeared in an eighty-one-year-old farmer's barley field a few miles outside of Providence. The crop circle was dubbed the "Glyph." It appeared in August of 1996 in Seth Alder's field about fifteen miles south of Smithfield. It was 240 feet long. Mr. Alder called the police who determined it had been there about a month and suggested that gophers had made this perfectly symmetrical design. It was photographed by a local pilot flying over the field. Alder believed in life on other planets, although he did not venture any theories of alien communications. The police also drew a map of the design saying it looked like a long-necked, long-tailed turtle on skis. Locals visited the field and made their own speculations and businesses nearby capitalized on the popularity of the field. Kate's Kitchen across the road from the field began advertising with a slogan that read: "You know what they say? The food at Kate's Kitchen is out of this world." Scientists who are also crop circle enthusiasts came and examined the field; they felt the crop circle could be authentic and not a hoax.

The next one appeared July of 1997 in the Hansen family's wheat field near Smithfield. The formation was accompanied by unusual beeping and buzzing noises. The Hansen's were having a birthday party outside when the alleged crop circle was being formed. It was dubbed the Smithfield "Joe" crop circle and was much smaller than the Glyph at a mere seventy-five feet in diameter for the larger circle and thirty-one feet for the smaller one next to it. Then came the "College Ward" or "Cove" crop circle in July of 1998 that appeared in a wheat field in the little town of College Ward, right next to Providence in Cache Valley. This one measured 102 feet in diameter and was made up of a circle, rings (the largest of these being forty-six feet in diameter), and several pathways. Scientists came to study this one too. Pilots took photographs from the air, and the police believed that pranksters were involved but did not have enough evidence to book anyone. People who visited this crop circle did report some unusual reactions however, such as becoming weak and dizzy or even very ill and having to immediately leave the area. Many rolls of film that people shot of the crop circle did not develop, and they were told that it was a shutter failure. People also found some sort of green luminous substance on their cars or vans that there was no explanation for.

Calvin and Carol Funk woke up one morning to find a crop circle in their barley field four miles south of Smithfield that same month. This one was dubbed the "Funk" crop circle and some people were beginning to suspect a hoax as all of the circles were appearing in the middle of the summer, while many others began to take them more seriously because of the number that were appearing in the area. This design was the most intricate yet and resembled a Jewish menorah on one end with a line connecting to a backwards cursive *E* on the other end. A shorter line crossed the other line in the middle with two oval shapes on either end of it. The Funks wondered why they had been picked on but felt better when they heard about all the other incidents. Scientists who studied this design found that structural changes had taken place in the barley due to high heat and declared the formation authentic. The Hansens and the Funks had to put up with a lot of E.T. jokes everywhere they went. Photographers came and so did a lot of newspaper reporters. The Cache Valley police stuck to their original assessment of the situation, theorizing pranksters or gophers, although they had no suspects, and no humans or rodents were arrested.

In 1998, the "West Approach" crop circle appeared near the Cache Valley airport but was smaller and not as ornate as the others. Another appeared in a field near Cove, Utah, near the Idaho border. All in all, seven crop circles appeared over the course of the late 1990s. They brought in not only scientists and researchers from the local area, but also a few from the international community. There had been a few previous crop circles in other parts of Utah, but none as spectacular as those in Cache Valley. The formations in the Cache Valley were the most intriguing and received the most publicity. After conducting all of their experiments, researchers felt that Cache Valley's circles fit all the criteria and were indeed of unknown origin. The second year they occurred, the Cache Valley formations made it all the way to *The Art Bell Show* and were featured on the show's website where they were touted as encoded messages from beyond this earth. Meanwhile, the local sheriff and his force felt they were close to arresting the pranksters who were involved, but they did not have enough evidence to charge them.[2]

A year to two later, after three years of crop circles appearing, a Nibley man (another little town in Cache Valley) and his buddy took credit for creating the first year's circles in 1997 as part of a class at Utah State University in Logan, Utah. They said they used boards and strings to create them. The farmers involved in these hoaxes were not the least bit amused, claiming at least five hundred dollars worth of damage. However, the two men said they had not created the formations that appeared in the second year, nor the third year. However, they believed that copycat crop circles had been created by bored Utah State University students on their summer vacations, which would explain why crop circles were appearing in Utah, Idaho, Oregon, and Washington over the summer months. Why only Utah State University students in the Cache Valley? Because apparently one hundred and fifty students had all taken the same class at the university in which the physics professor had taught everyone how to fake a crop circle that would seem to be real. Apparently they all went home for the summer and tried their own design out just to see if they could fool the experts, which in some cases they did. The crop circle researchers said the experts in these cases had been too quick to jump to conclusions and should have conducted more tests before confirming them as authentic crop circles.

This would have closed the case, if not for a few more words from the farmers and the researchers. One woman, whose family owned the land where one of the crop circles appeared, said she did not believe for a moment that they were hoaxes. The next year, her husband planted the same field and nothing would grow in or around the formation. She also said that there were no tracks anywhere around the circles, and it was unclear just how the students were able to create them. Another family, who had a crop circle in their barley field, found no tracks and, after seeing it from the air, questioned just how such a perfect circle could be made in the dark. College students would have been having a good time, and the families believe they would have heard something or found evidence of something at the scene. Some of the families took samples of the soil and sent them to labs out of state. The labs sent people to investigate. The farmers sent samples because several of them got sick when they were in or near the formations. All of the theories were called into question when former college students, Mike Norton and Joe Parker, admitted to an elaborate hoax in the local fields. They claimed the crop circles they created that first year clearly spell out "Mike" and "Joe."

The local sheriff never did press charges because, as he said, it was all hearsay with no evidence to back any claims. Those taking responsibility for the first year's crop circles said they knew who had done the other ones. They also said a large crop circle in the middle of a field really doesn't cause much damage because crops like wheat, barley, and hay are not that profitable in the first place. This statement probably did more damage with the local farmers than anything else the two young men could have said. In the meantime, other crop circles began to appear near Boise, Idaho as well in Star and Tampa, Idaho. Others showed up in Hubbard, Oregon, and near Pasco, Washington. While radio and TV stations reported they were all hoaxes, the Mutual UFO Network researchers said the media was trying to protect the property owners from further damage to their property either by curiosity seekers or copycat crop circle makers.[3] Crop circles, on the other hand, are still appearing all over the world. Can all of them, every single one, be a hoax? It's possible . . . or is it?

Jill Marshall, the professor whose class learned how to make crop circles, said she thought it was embarrassing to the scientific community that scientists continue to try to prove something she believes is always a hoax. The researchers from other universities who came to Cache Valley claimed that they had discovered the same abnormalities in many crop circles throughout the world. They found internal, physical changes to the plants inside and outside the formations. They found some electromagnetic radiation in the Providence pattern and some of the others indicated a spontaneous energy vortex of some kind. Marshall countered that at least ten percent of the crop circles which these particular scientists had investigated since 1989 turned out to be hoaxes. Ten percent proven to be hoaxes, however, still leaves ninety percent out there somewhere that are still unproven as hoaxes.

In Europe and especially in England, the craze is still in full swing. Many reputable scientists study them there and all over the world. It will be interesting to one day learn the truth about these phenomena, or perhaps there will be several "truths" when we understand them. But as I said, the spiral pattern is what intrigues me most. Spirals are found everywhere in nature and are the most complex of mathematical equations. They can be seen out in the solar systems, galaxies, and all around the universe. We are born from a spiral and we go to one in our last moments before death.

After the crop circle phenomena in Cache Valley, no other such phenomena was reported for several years. However, in 2002, there was an unusual occurrence at the Sherman/Bigelow ranch, the site of the National Institute of Discovery Science. In the middle of winter, a perfect circle around six feet in diameter appeared in the ice of a pond on the ranch's property and was reported to the Utah UFO Center. While this could have been another hoax, some scientific experiment being done at the ranch, or a natural phenomenon of some kind, there is always the slight possibility it was a real crop circle. However, ice circles, while reported all around the world, are a pretty rare phenomenon and much more unusual than the crop circles found in farmers' fields.

June 24, 2004, a new crop circle was discovered in Paul Prior's barley field just outside of Spanish Fork, Utah. Besides the news media that took aerial photographs, one local investigator who had just returned from crop circle investigations in England measured the design but found it wasn't symmetrical—a necessary requirement of a true crop circle. The farmer thought it an amusing prank by local kids, but was a bit upset about loosing his barley crop. It was a very good crop circle however, with one large double ring with a sort of stick figure overlay on it. There was a head and neck on one end and two legs in a triangle coming out of the center smaller ring. One of the figure's feet had lines coming off it like a sun and the other foot had only one line coming off its slightly bigger circle. There have been only ten crop circles reported in Utah over the past ten years, but I would imagine that we will hear more about crop circles in Utah, now that they are a national craze.

Notes

1) http://www.paradigmshjft.comlpecs.html.
2) Van Eyck, "Baffling Crop Formations Appear in Cache for 3rd Year in a Row," July 12, 1997.
3) Van Eyck, "Prankster Say They're Hoaxes; Others Say Nope," August 1996.

Aztlan
The Mythic Aztec Homeland

Quite a few scholars have searched for the historical location of Aztlan, the first homeland of the Aztecs. Like Atlantis, Aztlan may or may not exist, although many believe this great empire was once located somewhere in Mexico. However, many scholars believe that historical clues point to somewhere in Southern Utah as its location. Among them is University of Utah ethnic studies professor Armando Solorzano, who says that the Aztecs left Aztlan to build a civilization in the Valley of Mexico. "Since the 1960s and '70s civil rights movements, chicano activists have used the name Aztlan to describe the American Southwest as the northern homeland for Americans of Mexican heritage."[1] People around the world have been trying for generations to find the precise historical location of the legendary place the Aztecs left behind.

When he and his wife went to Paris, Mexican-American Roger Rodriguez ran across a map drawn in 1768 by a Spaniard. The couple believes that this map, drawn by a man named Don Joseph Antonio Alzate y Ramirez in 1768 and authenticated by experts, contains clues to a North American location. According to this map, "where present-day Utah would be, and next to a large body of water called 'Laguna de Teguyo,' are the words: 'From these desert contours, the Mexican Indians were said to have left to found their empire.'"

Roger Blomquist, a doctoral student at the University of Nebraska at Lincoln, believes that the evidence of Aztlan's location in Utah is very compelling. The article cites that cryptic message as "one clue among many—a petroglyph etched on a sandstone wall in eastern Utah's Sego Canyon, an 1847 United States map highlighting the confluences of the Colorado, Green, and San Juan rivers in southern Utah, a mound and more petroglyphs just outside Vernal—that have researchers considering a new angle on the history of the southwestern United States."[2] Blomquist says, "Some don't believe Aztlan was true, like Atlantis or the Garden of Eden, but I'm convinced it's in Utah."

To many Mexicans and Mexican-Americans, the search for Aztlan is literal, figurative, and sometimes even spiritual. They say their people are often told to go back to where they came from. Wouldn't it be ironic if they *were* back and living in the very place that their ancestors came from? Many feel their work to find Aztlan is about whether they belong or not. Scholars, Catholic clergy, Chicano activists, and a lot of everyday people have been searching for Aztlan for centuries. The mythical part of this five-hundred-year-old story revolves around the tale of a people emerging from the bowels of the earth through seven different caves and settling on an island called Aztlan meaning "place of the egrets" or "place of whiteness."

A spirit commanded these people to leave Aztlan and migrate south until they found an eagle devouring a serpent. They encountered such a scene and settled in the present location of Mexico City. Historical records indicate that the city of Tenochtitlan was founded there in the fourteenth century. According to this tale, in 1433, Aztec leaders burned any books or accounts of this migration, leaving only the oral traditions to tell of the existence of Aztlan.

Motecuhzoma was the first Aztec king to look for Aztlan. In the 1440s, Motecuhzoma sent sixty magicians to the north to search for the lost city. The tale became a legend when the trip ended with a spirit being appearing before the magicians and turning them into birds that then flew away to Aztlan. When the Spanish conquered the Aztecs in the sixteenth century, they too began to study the Aztecs' origins. A Jesuit priest in the late 1700s, Francisco Clavijero, wrote that Aztlan lay slightly north of the Colorado River. Many others placed Aztlan in Florida, California, Wisconsin, and the Mexican state of Michoacan. The most widely accepted theory comes from Alfredo Chavero, a Mexican historian. His theory was proposed in 1887 after he retraced Nuno de Guzman's 1830 expedition north from the Valley of Mexico to an island off the coast of the Mexican state of Nayarit called Mexcaltitlan.

Modern-day scholars who favor Utah instead for Aztlan's location study oral histories to support their theories. They point out geographical features in the Salt Lake Valley, in the Uinta Mountains, and on the Colorado Plateau that match the descriptions in the histories. They even use the Treaty of Guadalupe Hildago as a clue. Rodriguez and his wife, Patricia Gonzalez, gathered so many clues and information that they have written one book on the subject already, with two more on the way. They call the research and project "Aztlanahuac." They have gathered oral histories from Native Americans and, believing that Laguna de Teguyo was indeed the Great Salt Lake, they came out several years ago to visit the lake's Antelope Island. When they asked a park ranger about the caves on the island, they were told there were precisely seven of them.

Blomquist is studying the Aztec origins in Utah for his dissertation in American Frontier History. He believes it was the Aztecs who advised seventeenth century Spanish prospectors to look for gold in northeastern Utah, based on stories from the oral histories of more ancient people. Blomquist claims there is a natural Aztec temple site in the Uintah Mountains near Vernal. It is a two-hundred-foot-high mound with footsteps carved into it and an altar-sized boulder at its base that looks a great deal like Aztec temple locations in Mexico. On a rock at this site are petroglyphs of a warrior and his family. These petroglyphs look nothing like the other Fremont rock art found in the area. The warrior carries a long sword-like object that looks similar to a Mesoamerica weapon called a *macana*. My brother, a paleontologist, made it clear that rock art can be interpreted in as many different ways as the Bible can, and that these petroglyphs and rock art formations are also multilayered, having been added onto in culture after culture over centuries of time. This makes it difficult to interpret any given symbol within a certain time period.

Cecilio Orozco is a retired education professor from California State University in Fresno. He has studied petroglyphs in Sego Canyon, thirty miles east of Green River, and believes these petroglyphs correspond to the Aztec calendar's mathematical formula of five orbits of Venus for every eight Earth years. One of the canyon's sandstone walls shows what some believe to be ancient calendars made out of knots and string, one has five strings hanging down and another has eight. Alfonso Rivas-Salmon is another researcher who theorizes that southern Utah is not the location of the Aztlan, but instead, is the location of Nahuatl or "the land of four waters" where the Colorado, Green, and San Juan rivers pour into the Grand Canyon. A Belgian scholar, Antoon Leon Vollmaere, believes the precise location of Aztlan is where the Colorado and San Juan rivers meet under Lake Powell on either Grey or Wilson Mesa. All of these researchers and many more cite the close connections and similarities between the Aztec and Ute languages. They also note the strange coincidence that the Anasazi culture began to decline at the same time the ancestors of the Aztecs were supposed to have left Aztlan.

More often than not, it is archeologists who are most skeptical of the theories about Aztlan. They say that while there are clear linguistic and economic connections between the Aztecs and Utes, the Aztecs might have moved north before then moving south. Many archeologists believe that these people moved to Central America more than five thousand years ago and then spread out north all over the American West, including Utah. Out of this multitude of cultures, some could even have migrated south to northern Mexico, ending up in the Valley of Mexico. One man, who listened to his grandmother's stories about his people coming from the south, is Forrest Cuch, a member of the Northern Ute tribe. As Director of the Utah Division of Indian Affairs, he says he is open to the idea that the Utes and the Aztecs could have lived in close contact once. Although archeologists note the multitude of cultures over the West, they say that proving the existence of Aztlan would be nigh to impossible.

Some researchers claim that finding one exact location is nowhere near as important as the search itself. The search for identity is far more valuable in the higher scheme of things. Modern-day Mexican-American leaders say that their ancestors' back and forth migration would mean a great deal to people now moving from Mexico to the United States. It would be validating to know that their ancestors had lived there before.

Professor Armando Solorzano agrees it is the journey more than the trail of clues that makes the idea of a Utah Aztlan location intriguing.

When he arrived in Utah twelve years ago from Guadalajara, he considered the Wasatch Mountains and the Great Salt Lake to be Aztlan. "I felt a spiritual unity with the land, something that I had never felt in Mexico," he recalls. He compares the concept of Aztlan as a sacred land of harmony with the concept of Zion in the Latter-day Saint tradition. One similarity is that both cultures are searching for a common goal. Solorzano calls his Utah adaptation of Aztlan *Utaztlan*.[3] He shares this sense of importance with many others migrating from one homeland to another and considers this a journey to return to the land from whence his ancestors came.

There is, however, one thing that both skeptics and researchers agree upon—the search for these mystical lands will go on forever. Whether the legends are true or not doesn't seem to matter, for it is the search itself that counts. Proof of both religious and cultural origins are of great importance to many, although sometimes I think we miss the point. Up until now we have been living by separating and destroying things. In the future, it will become imperative that we come together as integrated communities caring for each other as well as for the planet. Going back to where we came from, as Mexican-Americans have been told for generations, means returning to our own origins, which in the end are all the same. If Aztlan truly exists and Utah once housed the ancestors of a mighty civilization, this would make the history of my state even more enthralling.

Notes

1) Sullivan, "Bits Of History Suggest Utah Is Location Of Mythic Aztlan," November 17, 2002.
2) Ibid.
3) Ibid.

Book Four

Ghost Stories

Ghosts of the Salt Lake City and Mount Olivet Cemeteries

The Salt Lake City Cemetery

The Salt Lake Valley High Council of The Church of Jesus Christ of Latter-day Saints established the Salt Lake City Cemetery in 1847 and the first person was buried there in that same year. The city set aside two hundred and fifty acres and as of March 2000, there were 105,325 people buried there. When the cemetery opened there were plans for 140,000 plots, so now only a precious few are still available. The cemetery is completely surrounded, so buying more space would be impossible. I have noticed of late what I call miniature high-rises or small mausoleums being installed so that those who choose to be cremated can be stacked upwards, conserving space. For many years, the Salt Lake City Cemetery was the largest city cemetery in the country.

There are quite a few famous people buried in the city cemetery. Archibald Gardner, the man responsible for building many of the mills around the state and for pursuing Elizabeth Lewis Raglin, who became his childless, non-Mormon wife and continue to sing in churches and saloons. She was buried here along with several of his other wives. Several outlaws are also buried in the cemetery including Jack Slade, Lot Huntington, and Hiram BeeBee. Lot Huntington was a tall, handsome young outlaw who was probably just as notorious as the reports say. Orrin Porter Rockwell shot Huntington down and left him to bleed to death over a rail in a stage station barn in Skull Valley in 1862. I could find nothing about Hiram Beebee and so I hope someone else will come forward with his story. It is known that Rockwell married one

187

of the daughters of Isaac and Olive BeeBee in 1832 in Independence, Missouri. Luana Hart Beebee Rockwell left her husband around 1846 to marry another man. It is possible that Hiram Beebee was a relative or son of Orrin Porter Rockwell and therefore a cohort of his. Orrin Porter Rockwell, the most famous protector of Brigham Young, is also buried there. He is said to have killed over a hundred men, although his descendents say this is very much exaggerated. He killed people both legally as a stage line marshal and illegally as the private body-guard of his friend Joseph Smith and then later as the protector of Brigham Young. He was also a member of the Council of Fifty and of the Danites who protected the early Church.

Jack Slade's story is more eloquently seen through the eyes of his wife, Virginia, as most of his story took place outside the state of Utah. The mysteries about Virginia Slade are her ties to Utah and Salt Lake City. Many wonder if perhaps she was a Latter-day Saint who had run away from Utah as a young girl, but no one seems to know where she came from or what the story of her early life was. Then known as Maria Virginia, she arrived in Virginia City, Montana, in 1863 having previously been a hurdy-gurdy girl and gambling woman. No one knows for sure how she met Jack Slade, but rumor has it she saved his life in a gambling brawl. Virginia was an excellent cook and seamstress. She was also a very handsome woman of negotiable virtues who felt that Jack had saved her from a life of which she was not fond. Jack Slade was a small, red-faced man who worked as a freighter from Montana to Salt Lake City. When he was drunk, however, he turned into a wild and violent demon that no one could control. Rumor had it that he had killed at least twenty-six men and was a member of the Vigilantes, a committee formed to protect the Virginia City community from out-laws. He married Virginia, making her a respectable woman, and set her up in a house eight miles from Virginia City in Meadow Valley where she was able to order elegant furnishings from Salt Lake City.

When Jack was sober, they had a pretty normal life. They enter-tained friends and were respected members of the community. Virginia was also an excellent dancer and while the other wives wore cotton dresses to the community dances, Virginia would wear her own hand-made fancy silk dresses. The Slades liked to ride together out near their home, and Virginia probably knew some about her husband's clandes-tine activities, but she never said anything to anyone about them. She would just pray he would come home safe, and if he came home drunk, she would help him off his horse, put him to bed, and wait for him to sober up. Slade began to drink more and more and was finally expelled from the Vigilantes for being dangerous to the public safety. Virginia knew nothing about this or that Jack had been arrested for disturbing the peace. On March 8, 1864, Virginia was waiting as usual for Jack's return, but hours after she expected him, he still hadn't shown up.

While Virginia waited, Jack was getting in trouble again in town. He was warned to return home and sober up or this time he would be in danger of losing his very life. Jack did not return home. The Vigilantes held their own assembly and decided on death by hanging even though his best friend, Jim Kiskadden, argued for simple banishment from the territory. It was Jim who sent a message to Virginia when he could see that all hope was lost for saving his friend. As soon as Virginia got the message, she saddled her horse and rode for town. She was an excellent shot and very persuasive with the town's people, but she got there too late. She probably could have saved her husband, at least that time, if she had arrived in time. Jim wept bitterly as they held Jack Slade at gunpoint and hanged him. Maria Virginia Slade had these words to say to her friends and neighbors upon facing them in town: "Why, oh, why didn't one of you shoot him and not let him endure the shame of being hanged? If I had been here, I would have done it. No dog's death should come to such a man. He did not deserve to die on the scaffold."[1]

The story continues that "from that day forward, Virginia felt hatred for the people of Montana. She purchased a zinc coffin and preserved Jack's remains in alcohol. He was temporarily buried across from the rock house, where she could look out at the site. Later, Virginia had Slade's remains taken to Salt Lake City and interred in the Salt Lake Cemetery. She did not want her husband to rest among his enemies." Because Jim Kiskadden had been there to comfort her, she ended up marrying him. Their marriage did not last long as Jack Slade had been her only real love. Soon Virginia Slade was gone from Montana forever. No one knew where she had gone. A few years later, she was discovered running a brothel, but again, no one seems to know just where this was, although rumor has it that Virginia ran a brothel in Salt Lake City for a brief period of time. Reason says that having been able to choose from any cemetery in the West, Virginia must have had a reason for choosing the first major cemetery in Utah for her husband's burial. She claimed it was the only way to keep his enemies from finding his grave and desecrating it. In those early days, Mount Olivet Cemetery tended to be the cemetery of choice for wealthy non-Latter-day Saints, while the Salt Lake Cemetery was mainly for Latter-day Saints of means. It is my belief Virginia had come from Salt Lake City or lived in the city at some point in her life, perhaps having strong ties there, and this is why Jack Slade ended up being buried there.[2]

The Salt Lake City Cemetery is huge and covers several city blocks. It is crowded with all sorts of interesting and ornate headstones and crypts that are really worth seeing. Most cemeteries have their tales. I'm interested in the ones that are ghostly, or at least mysterious. The Salt Lake Cemetery houses the famous grave robber, Jean Baptiste, but strangely, he has never been sighted there like he has on the shores of Fremont Island on the Great Salt Lake. The cemetery also contains Imo's grave. Imo's is perhaps the most infamous crypt in the city, especially to decades of high school kids who try to visit it year after year. The details of the legend of Imo's grave are sketchy. The story says that a man with the initials I.M.O. was executed for practicing witchcraft in this very cemetery and in an unnamed canyon, possibly Emigration Canyon. The truth is a little more realistic and certainly makes more sense. Imo's real name is on the graveyard registry as Jacob Moritz and his claim to fame sheds some lights on the legend—he was the first person to have been cremated in the Salt Lake Valley. Back in those days, there were two terrible sins relating to cemeteries: grave robbing and cremation. Cremation itself was enough to start the rumors of evil and witchcraft. The location of Mortiz's grave could explain another legend. Moritz was buried across the lane from his bitter political rival, Utah Governor Simon Bamberger. Perhaps Imo haunts the cemetery because he is angry about his proximity in death to his enemy.

Imo became quite famous locally and even nationally, although in a word-of-mouth sort of way. At one time the urn with Imo's ashes had been sitting on a platform in the middle of the crypt inside a small grated area of the monument. Unfortunately, it was within reach of anyone brave enough to reach through the grate, and while it could not be stolen intact, it could be vandalized and smashed with some effort. Various stories say it was removed because of the continuous vandalism, or that someone smashed it and scattered the ashes, or that a gate over the opening had been removed. In my mind's eye, I perceive a light blue or turquoise urn with gold veins in it that had darkened over the years. The little platform on which this urn sat now stands empty. I can see how all the rumors of evil doings might have gotten started.

There are decades of high school and college kids who have visited the grave in the middle of the night. Various groups have used the place for their own rituals, be they fraternities, high school clubs, or individuals who want to try their hand at raising spirits. While I can't tell much more about Imo from the stories, I can tell you what you are supposed to do upon visiting the grave. Of course you have to go at midnight and then you have to chant around the grave hoping to see him. You can see his reflection in your car windows or in your rear view mirror as you drive away. You may also stick your arm into the small side opening of the little mausoleum. The further you go or the braver you are, the more likely Imo will grab your arm and try to pull you in with him. It is said he can only be seen in the correct slant of moonlight. He will also talk to you if you wait long enough after the midnight hour. There is some sort of mirror behind where the platform once held the urn and this would account for the stories of seeing either your own reflection or that of Imo's as you dance around the tiny mausoleum. I have even been told that taking jello along helps to raise the spirits. People will do just about anything to get a glimpse of Imo!

Jacob Moritz became more famous in death as Imo than he was in life. In 1875, he bought the brewery whose only remaining building, the administration building, was The Old Salt Lake City Jail Restaurant on Fourth South until recently. He owned this brewery, which covered several acres, until 1878. When Moritz died, he was buried in the Jewish section of the Salt Lake City Cemetery and was the first person to be cremated in the city. Most interesting, however, was the feud between Governor Bamberger and Jacob Moritz. They were both very powerful men and were constantly at odds over politics and liquor laws. The grave is said to be haunted because Jacob Moritz was buried right across from Governor Bamberger and neither of these men's spirits will rest until someone is moved!

There are probably dozens of other versions as to what visitors must do when they visit Imo's grave; I have heard several. While many know where the grave is located, others do not and I wouldn't be surprised if many a high school or college student visited the wrong grave thoroughly convinced it was Imo's. It doesn't really matter because the high school kids of tomorrow will surely add to Imo's mythology just as they have to the story of the so-called Gravity Hill, located not far from the cemetery.

Gravity Hill can be found "at the intersection of B Street and 11th Avenue, just east of the Capitol, a little one-way road drops down into the mouth of City Creek Canyon. After descending the east side of the canyon, the road turns and goes back up the west side . . . While going up, you can shift your car into neutral, and it will continue to coast right up and out of the canyon." While there are many reasons given for why and how this happens, "in truth, it's an optical illusion. The hillside on the right side of your car gradually decreases in height, giving the illusion that you are cutting a path 'up' the hillside. The laws of physics have not been suspended; the road does in fact slope downward."[3]

The original story is that in the earlier days of Salt Lake City, a man was driving a tractor down the road and, becoming confused as to whether he was going forward or backwards, turned it over on himself. This man's spirit supposedly haunts the road. Later versions had the man driving a tractor over the edge of an overpass on the interstate and dying, although this doesn't seem to fit with the location of the road. Anyway, if you put your car in neutral on the incline of the hill, it will just stay in that position. The car will then be pulled up the hill on its own and will never roll backwards. I tried it when I was young and it is a very odd feeling. It did happen, although it may have been helped along by our belief that it would.

The more modern versions involve a family that died in a car accident on this hill. The story goes that their car broke down and they were all out pushing it when a semi-truck came along and hit them. Cars go up the hill in neutral because the spirits of this family are pushing them. Another version is that while you are looking through your rearview mirror and being pushed by invisible hands, you might also see the "Hoppity Lady." The story goes that a couple was killed in a car accident there and only one leg was found on the woman's body. She roams the street at night looking for her other leg on Gravity Hill. The mystery of Gravity Hill's spirit hands has been around for decades, but the story of the Hoppity Lady is certainly a new twist on an old theme.

A recent tale that surfaced on the web about the Salt Lake City cemetery is that of the grave marker of a woman named Lily. Engraved on the front of the tombstone is "Victim of the Beast 666." Supposedly just reading it gives one the chills. The history behind this grave marker is definitely intriguing, although legend has it that the poor woman was possessed by the devil. Perhaps there is a much simpler explanation considering the magical and mystical beliefs of the times in which this woman lived. She may have died of some unknown illness that would have seemed evil to the people of the times, or perhaps she succumbed to the "evils" of alcohol or drug addiction, or even broke one of the Ten Commandments. Ghost hunters have visited the grave on several occasions to place tape recorders beside it or take photographs of it in hopes of receiving some sort of communication or visual evidence at this supposedly haunted grave. So far, no one has come forward with any concrete evidence of its being haunted.

An interesting side note to these cemetery stories is the fact that in 1952, a catastrophic series of rainstorms caused several mud slides that ran right down through the Salt Lake City Cemetery from the hills above. A winter of record-breaking mountain snow pack and then sudden high temperatures made parts of the valley floor look like a flood plain. Homes were vacated all along the creek beds. The Jordan River over-flowed its banks and sent a wall of mud and debris down through the city. The water was six feet deep in fifty west-side blocks and 1300 South had to be sandbagged all the way through the city. Governor J. Bracken Lee had to seek federal relief funds. As the walls of mud came down into the cemetery's grounds, hundreds of coffins floated up from their graves. One man, who was in high school at the time, remembers riding down the hills on the tops of coffins, surfing down the gentle mud slopes with his other prankster friends past the cemetery limits and on down the streets. The pranksters were never caught because they did it in the middle of the night. Coffins floated right into people's basements and fell open on their basement floors; others became lodged in the debris on the city streets.

The city workers had a difficult time reburying coffins in their previous resting places. Following the complicated cemetery maps was only half the problem; identifying the remains of those from years past was an impossible task. To this day, many coffins are probably not where they should be as a result of this catastrophe.

It is the largest cemetery in Salt Lake City with many decades of burials crowded tightly together over a huge area of little hills and valleys. Even with tight security, there are all kinds of pranks, both by younger kids and college kids who live near the University of Utah. My own favorite memory of this place happened when I went to the university, fondly dubbed the "U," in the 1970s. One of the other renters in our old South Temple mansion apartment was a lead actress in college plays. She was writing a paper on the fine line between madness and creativity and she would often come down to our apartment to talk about the progress she was making on this big project. She always wore either white or black ball gowns that she obtained from Desert Industries, similar to Goodwill Industries. She rarely wore shoes even in the winter and had a huge styrofoam ball hanging in the middle of her one-room apartment that she filled with flowers stolen from the city graveyard a few blocks away. She was always taking trips up there late at night to collect her flowers and stick them into her styrofoam graveyard flower artwork. One evening she came up the stairs with two police officers in tow and knocked on my door. She had been arrested for disturbing the peace in the graveyard and wanted to know if I would take care of her cats while she was away.

Apparently, and this is her version of the story, she had been collecting her flowers in the early evening before the play she was to perform in that night. She was wearing her black shawl and gown for the performance. She spotted some high school kids vandalizing a grave. She spontaneously decided to take the law into her own hands and raised her black shawl above her head with arms outstretched like a big black crow. She then ran down the hill towards the kids cackling loudly as only a good actress could do. The high school kids made so much noise screaming and stumbling into graves trying to get out of there that several neighbors had called the police. Since she was to appear in *Marat Sade* that evening as the lead, several of her friends bailed her out just in time for the production. She had given us some free tickets to the show and so we went, not expecting it to be an interactive play where the mad residents of the insane asylum crawled between the seats and under our legs, popping up whenever they wanted to startle members of the audience. I can remember thinking at the time that perhaps she was just getting intensely into her part like many actors and actresses do. To this day I do wonder, however, if she was just being dramatic or if she herself was dealing with the issue of the fine line between reality and madness.

The City Cemetery, as many call it, probably holds many other stories behind its gates and I will probably hear more of them as the years roll by. There could be numerous other spirits that dwell there and it is a very interesting area to research. I don't mind doing the research because the atmosphere is friendly. On whatever particular anniversary I wish to commemorate, I place a red rose upon a friend's grave. No one would ever know when this occurred, as I vary it as I choose. Sometimes I go alone, sometimes my husband comes with me, and sometimes if a friend from out of town is visiting, she and I go there together. There are plenty of spirits to haunt the place and as the Electronic Voice Phenomenon (EVP) investigators have discovered, the ghosts in this cemetery talk back to you.

Mount Olivet Cemetery

Mount Olivet Cemetery was started in 1874 when a group of citizens petitioned the U.S. government for a non-denominational cemetery where people could be buried at a reasonable cost. At that time, Camp Douglas had 10,525 acres. At several later dates, the camp gave land to the University of Utah, the Shriners for a children's hospital, the Utah Pioneer Trails and Landmark Association, the National Guard Annex, and the Veteran Hospital grounds. The very first federal land transferred to anyone was fifty acres for this non-profit cemetery to be established by an Act of Congress signed by Ulysses S. Grant in 1874. In 1909, the Mount Olivet cemetery acquired another sixty acres from the military post. Today Fort Douglas retains only fifty-eight of its original acres.

The cemetery has 55,154 burial plots and as of October 1999, there were 26,100 people buried on the grounds. The first actual burial wasn't until 1877. The secretary of war at the time, a man named Cameron, was put in charge of the cemetery. He established the rules and regulations for the protection and operation of the cemetery and then turned it over to a non-compensated board of directors with a salaried superintendent. Half of the money from lot sales is put into a fund for perpetual care of the cemetery. There are many more interesting gravestones in this cemetery than there are in the Salt Lake Cemetery, with elaborate verses and "magnificent statues of lambs, horses, tree trunks, temples, angels, and muses. There are photographic portraits on some, symbols of a person's hobby or profession on others,"[4] probably because more money was spent on the headstones and the elaborate memorials.

"Markers for government officials, businessmen and bankers reflect the development of Utah—the Keiths, the Kearns, Penneys, Clarks, Walkers and many more . . . The discoverer of Lehman cave in Nevada was buried in a pauper's area. A troop of Boy Scouts who visited the cave placed a flat marker honoring him . . . Trees of 88 varieties shade the paved roads, which are strolling paths for nearby residents, and for family, and friends who reminisce among the beauties of nature. The cemetery is historic and beautiful where the past is unfolded, and the beauties of the seasons enjoyed."[5] Mount Olivet Cemetery offers a refuge to many deer who come down at night from the foothills, cross the busy street, and stay to graze in the cool grasses and wander under the many shade trees until the next night. There are deer crossing signs all along Fourth South and the people who run the cemetery allow these deer free reign.

Mount Olivet has its share of prominent people buried there, but most interesting to me is the story of silent film star John Gilbert and his family. His mother's grave is in Olivet. She was born Ida Adair Apperly in Logan, Utah. Her mother had been a survivor of the Mountain Meadows Massacre, and according to family stories, she was one of the babies never given back to her relatives in Arkansas. Her family is sure of this, but may not realize the earthshaking bit of new history this might be for some historians in Utah. Only one such baby from this massacre has ever been officially recognized as having been raised in Utah and never sent back to her Arkansas relatives. There are several more such stories passed down through the families by oral tradition, but none of these can be officially proven through the historical records available. Gilbert's grandmother was named Lydia Mangum by her adoptive family and was raised in Washington City where family history says she felt like a bond servant and ran away from home several times. She married a young man from Logan, William Apperly, who took her back live with his family. She had seven children with him and ran away several times until finally she actually got away and her husband could not find her. No one in the family has any idea where she went or where and when she died.

Apperly put all the children in a wagon and went about the state temporarily pawning them off on relatives while he looked for his wife. He kept only one child at home with him, his prettiest and favorite daughter, Ida Adair. William Apperly had two wives after Lydia ran away and they are buried beside him in the Logan City Cemetery. Apparently Ida was just like her mother Lydia, a real handful. She ran off at an early age to become a stage actress. Ida was everything that would have been considered sinful in those days. She was independent, addicted to alcohol and prescription drugs, self-centered, and had quite a few boyfriends, two of which became husbands. A terrible mother, she often left her son, John, with strangers or sent him home to her father's house in Logan for long periods of time. John, born Cecil Pringle, was always miserable in Logan, having been bitten by the acting bug himself since the age of two or three when he was with his mother performing on stage. He is quoted as saying that the only thing to read in his grandpa's house was the Sears & Roebuck catalogue or The Book of Mormon. He was definitely a city kid trapped in the country, although at the same time, his stays in Logan were probably the only taste of normal family life that he ever experienced.

Ida had only one child with her first husband and she said that this had been a mistake. When she married her second husband, who stayed with her a little longer, he changed poor John's last name to Gilbert after his own, and thought of a better first name for a boy than Cecil. Walter Gilbert remained an extra in the movies, but never had anything to do with his stepson until in 1925 when John Gilbert was filming *The Merry Widow*. His stepfather was an extra in the movie and approached the famous silent star asking for money. John Gilbert was furious and threw him off the set. Both mother and son probably suffered from what is now called bipolar disorder. They may have medicated this uneven temperament with several addictions in the days when there was no diagnosis for extreme emotional highs and lows. But these same qualities, coupled with a brilliant mind and a vivid imagination, were what helped Gilbert not only survive into adulthood, but also to become a famous actor in his day.

When John Gilbert was fourteen, he was called home from a military school in California to attend his mother's funeral. The last time that he had seen his mother, she had been readying herself for a performance at a theatre in California and was dead drunk and didn't recognize him. By 1911, Ida had performed for the last time at the old Orpheum Theatre in Utah, which was later torn down and made into a parking lot and business offices. She got very ill, probably with tuberculosis or pneumonia or both, and came home to Logan where members of her family took care of her for about three years before she died in 1915. After the funeral, John Gilbert was given his inheritance, which consisted of two little make-up cases, some posters of plays that his mother had been in, and a ten-dollar bill.

His grandfather gave him his inheritance at the Union Station in Salt Lake City when he put him on a train bound for California. He told his grandson that any money his mother had was used to care for her and to pay her funeral expenses. He also told John never to return to Utah again. And he never did. To soften the story a bit, one of John's aunts from Logan did give him additional money to go to Hollywood and pursue his dreams. Gilbert's daughter, Leatrice Gilbert Fountain, says that Gilbert had a terrible mother and spent most of his life looking for an ideal woman he could possess as a wife and a mother. Gilbert often rewrote the mother's part in his films to show that the loving mother's son would rather return to her than to his own sweetheart. It is easy to see why he tangled with Louis B. Meyer, who adored his mother and idealized her in his films. In one of their run-ins, John Gilbert had gotten sick of Louie talking about his mother and announced that his own mother had been a drunken whore or something to that effect, at which point Louie threw him out of his office. It is often thought that Meyer had something to do with ruining John Gilbert's chances in the talkies by sabotaging his voice-overs, but no one has ever proved this and many of the experts doubt there is any truth to this rumor. Skeptics say that he had a wonderful and commanding voice that just did not translate well into the talkies. Meyer and Gilbert had another run-in when Jack tried to get Greta Garbo to the altar for the second time and she bolted. Gilbert went in the men's room to compose himself. Meyer was in there and asked Gilbert why he didn't just sleep with her instead of marrying her. Gilbert lost his temper and beat Meyer up. Meyer swore to ruin him in Hollywood, which he could easily do. This is another Hollywood legend which some say happened and others say did not. It could, however, explain Gilbert's fame as the great silent movie star whose own voice ended his career.

John Gilbert died tragically young just like his mother. She was forty-three and he was only thirty-six. He was and still is one of the most maligned of the great actors in Hollywood. He is considered the twenty-eighth most influential actor of all time and starred in over a hundred films before his death. A private nurse caring for him as a recovering alcoholic gave him an accidental overdose of a sedative causing a heart attack. His lover at the time was Marlene Dietrich and she went on to be somewhat of a second mother to his daughter, Leatrice, whose mother was also a famous silent movie actress, Leatrice Joy. John Gilbert lived with a lot of tragedy. The day after they broke up, he lost his first great love to a stage accident in which the young starlet was the only person killed. He had to live with that guilt too. I became a fan after seeing a few of his films, especially *The Big Parade*, a World War I story that really showcases his talent. This is how I ended up finding Ida Adair Gilbert's little headstone under an old tree on the corner of Maple Street in the Mount Olivet Cemetery in Salt Lake City.

Both of these cemeteries are just loaded with people's stories. I have only told a few of them. I imagine that there are dozens of apparitions as well, floating among the many deer allowed to graze there. Visitors would probably hear things a great deal more than see things, with all those snatches of conversation that EVP recordings have picked up. Ghost hunters in Salt Lake City say they usually investigated much smaller cemeteries where they will not be overwhelmed by so many inhabitants. The smaller cemeteries give a more detailed emotional impression to the ghost hunters, anywhere from very friendly commentary to downright evil demands to get out. The larger cemeteries are just too overwhelming, and it is difficult to isolate just one grave and one story. I have not heard anything about either of these cemeteries, although I do know that ghost hunters have been to the Salt Lake City Cemetery many times and at least once to Mount Olivet. It may be that getting permission to go in there at night is tough, especially with the history of vandalism particularly at the Salt Lake City Cemetery, which, because of its size, seems to be more accessible to trespassers. While other cemeteries in the state have apparitions or strange phenomena reported in them, these two major cemeteries have remained unscathed except for Imo. This doesn't mean, however, that phenomena don't exist there; it just means we have not heard about or seen anything yet. With so many people buried there, it would take some doing to separate all the ghostly happenings reported. EVP is quite prevalent at the Salt Lake City Cemetery and multiple groups have recordings collected.

Someone once asked a famous ghost hunter why he chose to stalk the dead. His reply was that he was not stalking them. They were choosing to stalk him, and he wanted to know why.

Notes

1) Towle, *Vigilante Woman*, quoted in Seagrave, *Soiled Doves, Prostitutes in the Early West.*
2) Seagrave, *Soiled Doves, Prostitutes in the Early West*, 119–23.
3) Stanley, "Utah's Believe It or Not: Gravity Hill," 80.
4) http://www.arosnet.com/~/~fee/web_page/olivet/.
5) Ibid.

The Story of Jean Baptiste
The Graverobber and the Outlaw

Around 1860, Jean Baptiste, nicknamed John the Baptist, was one of the first gravediggers in Salt Lake City. He was a quiet loner who worked hard and was always on time during the three years that he worked for the City Cemetery. He probably would have continued this way if not for a visitor from the East who had come to claim the body of his brother to have it reburied in the family plot. Unfortunately for Jean Baptiste, even the potter's field graves turned out to be risky to rob. The irony was that even in death, one robber was about to meet another.

The potter's field grave contained the body of Moroni Clawson. Moroni Clawson was not an unknown vagrant and was most assuredly someone who would be recognized by name. Clawson had been one of three robbers on his way to California after robbing an Overland Mail Company employee around 1863. Clawson was also wanted for an incident in which he had beaten the former federally-appointed governor of Utah, John W. Dawson, at Ephraim Hank's stage station on New Year's Eve in 1861. Dawson was waiting for the eastbound coach that evening. He had traveled from Indiana as the newly appointed governor of the Utah Territory and had made his grand entrance in Zion Canyon only a few weeks before. In just three weeks he had managed to alienate everyone. This was during a time of intense conflict between The Church of Jesus Christ of Latter-day Saints and the federal government. Dawson, who was not a member of the Church, had been courting a respected Latter-day Saint widow. He was accused of "improper advances" towards this lady and was actually fleeing for his life from the territory. He had hired a group of six young men as his bodyguards, although everyone else saw them as drunken hellions. While waiting for the stage, the young men turned on him and beat him senseless. It is said that they also castrated him, although no one really has ever known for sure. Clawson was one of the six young men.

Two weeks passed after warrants had been put out for all six of these men, but no one knew where any of them were or at least no one would tell. Then Giles Mottin, an Overland Mail Company stableman, reported that eight hundred dollars was missing from a tin box that he kept hidden in the stable where he worked. Two of the six who had beaten the former governor were suspected of the crime. Lot Huntington and John P. Smith were the two suspects. They were also suspected of taking Brown Sal, a local prize horse. A few of the local men formed a posse and set out to chase the two young men who had been seen in the settlement of West Jordan and were heading west. Moroni Clawson joined the other two fugitives on their ride west, although he had had nothing to do with the stable robbery. A full day ahead of the posse, and not suspecting that they were being followed, the three young men rode leisurely into the west desert. Lot Huntington was tall and good-looking and probably the leader of the group. Moroni Clawson was also a charmer with the ladies.

Other young men working a cattle ranch in the area rode out to join the three when they saw the campfire. They ate dinner with them about twenty miles west of Camp Floyd in the Skull Valley. It was these unsuspecting cowpokes who told the posse that the three young men were at the Faust Stage Station. Weary from riding, the posse borrowed a stagecoach for the remainder of the journey. When they got to the stage station, the four members of the posse hid their stage and took positions around the station. It was about four o'clock in the morning in the bitter cold of a January day. They waited until sun-up and when the station owner emerged, they waved him over and asked what the young men were doing. They were eating breakfast. The leader told the stage owner to go back in and tell them to come out with their hands up. Instead, Lot Huntington emerged with a pistol in his hand and headed straight for the barn to get Brown Sal. According to some accounts, the leader gave Huntington several warnings as he sat on his stolen horse before they began firing at each other in the barn. Huntington took eight bullets and lay bleeding to death on a corral rail. He was only twenty-seven years of age.

Clawson and Smith surrendered without a fight. On the way back in the stagecoach next to their dead friend, the posse stopped to talk with the cowpokes the robbers had eaten dinner with the night before. It was later learned that the three robbers had planned to rustle these men's cattle and drive them on to California. When the posse pulled into town and turned the other two over to the police, it was only minutes later they heard shots. When they arrived at the scene, both young men lay dead in the street. They were told that they had tried to escape, and the policemen were forced to shoot them.

Bill Hickman, who was both outlaw and lawman during his lifetime, had an opinion on the young men's death. When he heard about these shootings in the Skull Valley and on a Salt Lake City street, Hickman pretty much pronounced the truth of the matter. Having been almost shot and killed two years before by Huntington, Hickman said there had been foul play in the deaths of these young men. Lot's men and Hickman's men had started a gun battle on the steps of the Salt Lake Tabernacle right after services the day after Christmas. The gun battle moved down the street and ended in front of the old Townsend Hotel. The only other man wounded in this fifty-bullet fight was a man named Butcher who accidentally shot himself with his own gun after the battle ended. Hickman was quoted as saying the claim by the city police that Clawson and Smith were killed while attempting to escape was utter nonsense, and most citizens, although they kept quiet, believed the same thing. "They were both powderburnt, and one of them was shot in the face. How could that be, and they running?"[1]

Another man, T.B.H. Stenhouse, wrote in his journal,

> All the bad and desperate Mormons were not brought to judgment, but the pretext alone was wanting for carrying more extensively into execution the general [police] programme. Resistance to an officer, or the slightest attempt to escape from custody, was eagerly seized, when wanted, as the justification of closing a disreputable career . . . The Salt Lake police then earned the reputation of affording every desperate prisoner the opportunity of escape, and, if embraced, the officer's ready revolver brought the fugitive

to a "halt" and saved the county the expenses of a trial and his subsequent boarding in the penitentiary. A coroner's inquest and cemetery expenses were comparatively light.[2]

Relatives claimed the other two bodies, but Clawson went to the potter's field at the Salt Lake Cemetery. The sheriff personally bought his funeral suit and paid for his funeral. Hundreds of people went to Clawson's funeral probably because of his notoriety and the fact that no one had claimed his body. A few days later, Clawson's brother arrived from the East. When the body was dug up, Clawson was found stripped naked and lying face down in his coffin. This was the final insult in a series of events that call into question whether or not Moroni Clawson was ever really guilty of any murders at all. Perhaps at the very worst, he participated in the beating of the former governor and joined up with the other two after they had robbed the stage employee. Moroni Clawson paid for his "bystander" participation with his life, and perhaps he was less guilty than Jean Baptiste.

Clawson might have been face down in that coffin for a reason, maybe because the graverobber could not bear to look at his face. Perhaps Clawson was the one shot in the face and disfigured. But it was Moroni Clawson's last act after death in Salt Lake City to identify the graverobber, Jean Baptiste.

The police began surveillance on the cemetery after Clawson's grave was opened. They soon caught Jean Baptiste hauling away a wheelbarrow load of clothing from the cemetery. When they went to his home, they found a vat in his basement for boiling all the clothes, mounds of clothing, and furniture covers and drapes made of clothing. Checking the records of a local pawnshop, they discovered he had sold most of the jewelry and watches he had dug up. His wife answered the door when the police first came calling. When one of the policeman saw all the boxes of clothing stacked around, he became irate. He had just buried a daughter a few weeks before in the cemetery this gravedigger was robbing. Baptiste vehemently denied defiling the grave of the policeman's daughter and thus saved himself from execution on the spot. Police found he had kept nearly everything he had taken inside his home. When he was taken to the cemetery to identity those graves he had robbed, such a crowd of irate citizens gathered that he begged the police to take him back to jail.

In the end, they figured that Baptiste had robbed the graves of more than 350 people in three year's time. Charged with robbing the dead, a horrific crime in 1860, he was unable to tell which coffins he had ransacked. Some families had the bodies of their loved ones exhumed to see if their graves had been vandalized. The police buried all the clothes and personal effects that could not be identified, which was a considerable amount, in a big pit inside the cemetery. The debate over Jean Baptiste's fate carried on within the city's new police force for a long time. The distraught townspeople were reassured that God would sort it all out for them. One of the interesting mysteries about the case is that no one seemed to think his wife was guilty too. If the vats and personal effects of the dead were piled all over the house, what was his wife doing all this time? Could she really be innocent of any criminal activity herself? Records of this incident are sparse and even records of a supposed trial and conviction were eventually destroyed or lost.

Jean Baptiste was apparently tried and convicted, although there are no records left to confirm this. It is rumored his ears were either cropped, notched, or cut off entirely. According to various versions of this tale, he was also branded on the forehead with a hot iron with the words *Branded for Robbing the Dead*. He spent three months in jail where his fellow prisoners either shunned him or tried to attack him. For his own safety, he was then taken in the middle of the night in a boat to Antelope Island, which was pretty desolate in those days. Eventually, he was moved to Fremont Island because the water was deeper there and he had less chance of escaping. Citizens had been worried that he could escape and return to town to seek retribution against those who had branded and disfigured him. It is generally thought it was Brigham Young who suggested this punishment with the added warning that if the man ever returned to Salt Lake City, he would be killed on the spot.

The Great Salt Lake covers 2,300 square miles in area, but is only twenty-seven to thirty feet at its deepest point. It is a desolate place even today, and back in Baptiste's time, no one lived on either island, with the exception of a few sheep that grazed there. On Antelope and Fremont Islands, there is some vegetation and wildlife, but everyone believed then that escape from these islands was impossible. Three weeks after his exile, sheepherders went to check on their sheep and noticed that the banished convict had vanished. They found Baptiste's campsite and thought that perhaps he had taken his own life. Others thought he had somehow built a raft and escaped. Rumors were that the hut on the island had been stripped to make it look like he had built a boat of some kind and escaped. Other versions say they found his body and he had been murdered, possibly decapitated. The little hut that had been used by the sheepherders was the only building still there, but it had been abandoned for some time as the sheep farmers had left the island long before this. Jean Baptiste may have used this little hut for a home while imprisoned on the island. Some said it was still there, while others said it had been stripped and not enough was left for someone to live in. The Wenners, who lived on the island for five years from around 1886 to 1891, never made mention of seeing Jean Baptiste's ghost there. Although Mr. Wenner is buried there and might have run into another apparition besides himself . . .

Nearly thirty years later, some hunters found a human skull, but the rest of the body was not found. Three years after that, a headless body with a ball and chain on the leg bones was found. However, authorities insisted they had not shackled Baptiste. Some thought the body was the remains of an escaped prisoner from the state penitentiary, while others claimed the authorities were lying about the shackles and were sure Baptiste had built a raft from the wood from the hut on the island and drowned attempting to escape. No one ever suggested another more logical reason for Baptiste's disappearance—perhaps he had been murdered and even tortured by those who felt they had the right to act as his judge, jury, and executioner. The ball and chain may have been part of the torture; by throwing the man into the lake with this apparatus around his ankles, he would drown. The ball and chain may also have been used to get rid of any evidence by weighing the body down in the water.

The records on Jean Baptiste are almost entirely absent, which has caused much of this speculation. Perhaps someone was trying to hide something. Perhaps, as rumors to this day say, no trial was ever held. Perhaps he was put on the island to inflict this solitary confinement as an appropriate punishment or more likely, to isolate the prisoner from prying eyes so matters could be taken care of underhandedly. Perhaps a distraught relative of someone buried in the city cemetery went out and murdered Baptiste on the island. Or, as I propose, a group of vigilantes got it in their heads to finalize the matter when the sentence that was pronounced wasn't satisfactory to them. But it makes no sense at all for a prisoner from the Utah State Prison, which was miles and miles away from the Great Salt Lake, to choose to escape across the Great Salt Lake. Escaping across the water in shackles would be an amazing feat to say the least and not a very smart plan by any means. With no forensic science in those days, who can say if the bones found were those of Jean Baptiste anyway? For all we know, the remains could have been some other poor murdered man's from a deed done either by citizens, authorities, or by the Great Salt Lake itself. Even the record of Brigham Young's speech in which Baptiste's sentence is pronounced in detail cannot be found. No one knows how long Baptiste was jailed or if he ever actually had a trial. So the biggest mystery here is, why did all the records so conveniently disappear?

Baptiste's own history is confusing. Some records say he was from Ireland, while others say he was from Italy. Still others say he came from France via Australia. And even his first name changes from story to story. It would really be significant to find out if he was a Latter-day Saint or not, why nothing was ever done to his wife, if he had any children, and if he was really suffering so much that the poor man felt he had to turn to a life of crime, especially a crime so abhorrent to people in those times. Perhaps he was doing fairly well and just saw a good opportunity when it came along. What is interesting, however, is his ghost has never been reported to haunt the Salt Lake City Cemetery, where he committed all his dirty deeds in the middle of the night. Although, as an intuitive, I would guess that many other ghosts do. Most certainly Moroni Clawson is one of them if his body was never moved. If his body was moved, then one has to wonder how his brother felt, knowing Moroni might have been innocent, gazing at the final disgrace to his body by another man possibly more guilty than Moroni.

Instead of haunting the cemetery where he carried out his terrible work of robbing the dead, John the Baptist's ghost haunts the beaches of two islands in the Great Salt Lake, especially Fremont Island where he is said to have met his demise by decapitation. Either way, his ghost has been reported for decades roaming the beaches at night, carrying a lantern or torch in one hand and a bundle of rotting clothes in the other. Some people have seen just a light approaching their campsite from the beach and then suddenly disappearing as it draws near. Others have actually seen a shadowy shape coming towards them. Still others claim to have actually seen his full apparition without a head walking on the shoreline or as far away as the mouth of the Jordan River. They say that he is searching for his lost head on the beach where the body washed ashore. And since head and body were never proven to be from the same skeleton, even this is suspect. Those who claimed to have actually seen Jean Baptiste say he always walks headless, carries the clothes stolen from graves, and is either seen from a distance or walks toward the campers, disappearing slowly the closer he gets to them.

I prefer to think Jean Baptiste got away or at least had a peaceful ending, although I am sure many of the relatives of the dead hated him enough that murder is very likely. He would never have been safe there as long as private citizens were willing to take the law into their own hands. Everyone knew where he was, alone and certainly vulnerable. One has to wonder at Brigham Young's sentencing, rather like one that King Solomon would have given, making it rather convenient for a murder to take place. If by some slim chance Baptiste did escape, that would have been quite a miraculous feat even more so in those days. Living alone on the island would be enough to drive anyone mad and Baptiste could have taken illogical chances. On the other hand, murder was more likely for the heinous crime that Baptiste had committed. A crime so horrible in those days that even rape and murder could not equal it.

I have been on Antelope Island, but never at night and never when one of those sudden storms erupts there. I have been told that a storm can suddenly blow in with high gusts of wind and waves pounding the shore. Perhaps this is the only time that one can see Jean Baptiste, thus making the sightings few and far between. As for the spirits on these islands, I am sure that they are real and walk those shores either at peace or, in Jean Baptiste's case, not at peace.

Notes

1) Hickman, *Brigham's Destroying Angel*, 149, quoted in Harold Schindler, *Orrin Porter Rockwell: Man of God/Son of Thunder*, 315–19.
2) Stenhouse, *Rocky Mountain Saints*, 419, quoted in Harold Schindler, *Orrin Porter Rockwell: Man of God/Son of Thunder*, 315–19.

Denver and Rio Grande Station

The Purple Lady

In 1909, George Gould constructed the Rio Grande Railroad Station to service the Western Pacific Railroad. He combined two types of architecture—Beaux Arts Classicism and Italian Renaissance—to create one of the most interesting and inviting structures in town. Originally, the depot housed a men's smoking room and a women's retiring room. There were several meeting rooms on the second floor where company parties were sometimes held. Railroad officials' offices were on this floor as well. It is on the National Register of Historic Places and today houses the Utah State Historical Society's museum library and the Utah State Antiquities Division. In the downstairs north wing is the popular Rio Grande Cafe, which serves southwestern cuisine. The entire atrium was once a museum and one of Utah's most famous characters had a display there—Eugene Jelesnick, a talent show host for many, many years on local television. The atrium is now an art gallery.

The Rio Grande also houses the most famous ghost story in Utah, although many less famous sightings and haunting events have happened there. The story goes that the "Purple Lady" had an argument with her boyfriend, a soldier possibly in World War II, though others say World War I. The two lovers had come to meet each other from separate trains. The argument ended with the soldier throwing her engagement ring out onto the railroad tracks. When she ran to retrieve it, she was struck by a train and died instantly. She is often depicted in a 1940s suit of light violet with a hat, veil, and matching shoes. People often visualize her with darker skin. Others say she wears a long purple dress from an earlier era, though most agree she has black hair. She is said to haunt the hallway passage between the main station floor and the entrance to the Rio Grande Cafe. People sense something there, and others have seen a light, cloudy shape. Sightings of her, however, have not been reported since the late 1950s.

In the 1940s, train crews talked about her constantly and sightings were numerous. There have been two recent sightings from the security guards, who keep a log of the different unusual happenings around the building. In the first, a woman was eating at the cafe and went into the restroom. When she came out into the hall, she saw a ghostly figure with a purple dress and black hair. She told the waitress about it and the waitress had to tell her about the legend. In the other, which happened about ten years ago, a customer came into the library upstairs and told the clerk about her experience one night while on a date. She and her companion had gone to the cafe for dinner. She went into the restroom and a lady in a purple sequined dress with black hair was sitting on the couch and she seemed very angry. It scared the woman, and she quickly went back out. She later heard the story of the Purple Lady. A maintenance worker in the station apparently reported seeing her and quit his job because of it. A recent version describes the Purple Lady with long red hair instead of black and says she can be heard singing not only near the women's restroom, but at other locations during the night, especially out on the tracks that no longer exist.

Other events have been reported in the last few years. Construction crew members could always hear a lady singing in the bathroom. An employee of the restaurant was mopping the floor and the lights went out. When he went to the switch box, something was standing there, and it told him to leave the building, and boy, did he! The women's shower was on and running when they opened the doors up one morning. This has happened twice and both times it was just the cold water. One night the alarm went off at the Rio Grande. The security officer came to check it out, and when he went to turn the alarm off, footsteps started up in front of him and then ran on down the hall. At three o'clock in the morning, State Capitol security received a phone call from the elevator phone at the Rio Grande, and there was no one on the other end. The elevator phone is for anyone stuck in the elevator to call security at the State Capitol. Right after the phone call, the officer heard footsteps but could not tell whether they were coming from the Capitol or the Rio Grande.

In the 1980s, a custodian heard a phantom party going on in the cellar in the middle of the night. In fact, maintenance workers have checked more than once to see why lights were going on and off down in the cellar, but one worker says he saw a party of people and heard voices and music. When the custodian walked in on them, they all vanished instantly. Employees who work in the basement lab go over artifacts found in sites all over Utah. They say they will not work down there alone late at night. When they have, they describe eerie feelings. They have heard footsteps leading up to the door, and when they answer, no one is there. One person even felt a tap on the shoulder when no one was there to do it. In my opinion, housing ancient artifacts in a building already reputed to be haunted seems unwise. But then, like I said, I am a "spiritual creationist." Like a lot of Native Americans, I feel that spirits follow their possessions around.

More than once, security guards have heard someone walking on the upper balcony at night. One security guard heard someone walking up there at the same time every night. He hid nearby to watch but never saw anything, though he did feel something brush past him each time he did it. As for myself, I was allowed to go there years ago, on the weekend, when it is much quieter, especially upstairs and down. There were so many layers that it was difficult to determine which was a newer event and which had happened long ago. Where the Purple Lady is supposed to be, I felt nothing. But in the lady's restroom and outside by the tracks, there was activity. Downstairs was a hive of energies and less-than-positive feelings. Upstairs in the southern end where large meeting rooms have been made into tiny individual offices, I had the same feeling of long ago parties taking place. I did not go into the basement because I really did not want to—the feeling was too negative.

At one point, our mayor was considering moving the State Historical Society and the antiquities section and making the old Rio Grande into a light-rail station for the Olympics in 2002. He wanted a better, more colorful place for visitors to our fair city to see as they boarded the various UTA Traxs trains bound for various parts of Salt Lake City. He envisioned we would need a gathering point for all of these city trains, but nothing was said about where the wonderful book shop, the museum that covers all of the first floor, the state historical library, the offices, and all of the rest would be relocated. I liked the idea of it being a train station once again, but I hoped if these plans become a reality, all of the things there would find a good home.

Some years ago, a local psychic was invited by a local television station to go to the depot late in the evening of Halloween to try to either speak with or even exorcise the Purple Lady. In hindsight, the psychic now says it was probably presumptuous of her to attempt this. Once she got there, she immediately realized two things. One, that there were many more spirits in the building than just the famous one, and two, she and her companions had taken on more than they could handle not only in terms of the number of ghosts, but also in terms of the media circus that it became. Many people showed up to watch, and many members of the media were there to document. As she walked around, she could tell that all of the noise and confusion were disturbing the ghosts, especially in terms of being made fun of by the living.

There were two teenage boys in the crowd who had brought an over-sized plastic bat and ball. They were playing with them as the crowd surged forward to hear what the psychic was saying. There were plenty of witnesses to what happened after this, and it was pretty obvious the boys were not responsible for what happened. As the psychic finished up her work and came out of the ladies bathroom into the hall where the crowd was, the boys were in the background playing with their bat and ball. Suddenly, without warning, the bat was pulled out of the boy's hands, flew over the crowd, and whacked the psychic hard on the side of her face. It was as though invisible hands were directing the bat. The force of the blow was so hard it almost knocked her down. It was lucky, she said, that it had been a plastic bat and not one of the wooden ones. With that, the psychic and her companions left the building and the Halloween ghost hunt was over. She says the lack of respect for the ghosts in the building caused the whole thing. I am of the opinion that presuming to clear old ghosts from buildings they either love or are attached to through some tragedy would certainly not be safe.

As for the various ghosts in the depot, they will continue haunting and being reported by the many employees. As new ghosts appear or are connected to an older story, the information desk people keep copies for anyone interested in reading them. It is probably a good thing that some of the security guards are not believers, because they can walk right through all this and never experience a thing. However, others do believe, and they keep track of every event quite accurately. Even the Rio Grande Cafe has a few ghost stories on its menu. If the depot were to be made into a train station once again, it would change one thing—passengers, as well as an employee or two, would be alone in some area of the building once in a while in the middle of the night. Ghostly phenomena would surely frighten a few of them. I, for one, would not want to stay there overnight—too scary. Because you can be sure of one thing anyway, nighttime at the Rio Grande Depot must be a hopping place—and not something for the faint of heart!

Eventually, the Rio Grande was not made into a train depot. Instead, the Utah State Historical Society had such severe budget cuts that they lost their bookstore, several employees, and their exhibit space in the main hall. The Rio Grande Cafe was saved by concerned citizens in the community that went all the way to the former governor's office for help. Governor Leavitt protected the cafe from being closed down. The old heating and power plant building to the south of the station has been modified to house the historical society and the city is presently in the process of moving everything into the building. In the shuffle, a new ghost story emerged relating to an old underground tunnel that used to connect the two buildings. It seems that a construction worker was killed during the initial construction of this tunnel, which would have been soon after or during the building of the new depot in 1909. His ghost supposedly haunted this tunnel area for years and railroad workers reported numerous sightings. Employees did not like walking through this tunnel alone.

Years ago, the tunnel was filled in and that ended the ghost stories in the tunnel. Employees since, however, believed that the man's ghost still walked around in the basement area. This would account for footsteps outside the doors of the basement work areas where the tunnel would have come out into the rooms. Now that the society is moving many of its offices to the old remodeled heating and power plant whose smokestack is still standing, plans are in the works to build a new underground tunnel between the two buildings. Many wonder if it will be, by accident or by design, located in the exact same place. If so, will this ghost decide to make more appearances as his old "home" returns? It is said when employees were alone working in the basement and heard these footsteps stop right outside their door, they gave up checking for the phantom and instead would wish him a happy holiday according to whatever time of year it was. One man, who had run back to get something he had forgotten, was down in the basement alone with his dog. The dog stared at something in a specific spot and kept barking insistently and would not follow his master's command to come to him. Being a total skeptic, this event was odd enough for the man to then take notice of the other stories told about the area.

It might be that plans are still in the works to make this a railroad and light rail station sometime in the future. The Rio Grande Cafe would fit right in if passengers like Mexican food. With the building being full of people all the time, there would be less likelihood of people noticing ghostly activity. On the other hand, I thought it very intuitive of the scientists to put on display the "haunted" shower that was removed from the governor's mansion when a new, more modern shower was installed. The shower was located in the same hallway by the woman's bathroom where the Purple Lady is often sighted. One of the common ghost stories about the building also involves showers, women's showers at that. The cold water insists on coming on in the middle of the night and the custodians have to turn it off. It would be interesting to know how close the women's showers are to this women's bathroom, or perhaps location doesn't matter in these instances.

The governor's shower, temporarily on display in the Purple Lady's hall at one time, was used in a couple of horror movies filmed in the governor's mansion when it was the home of the Utah State Historical Society in the 1970s. Many of the governors did not like this shower, and in its day it was considered a "man's" shower because only a strong man could take all the jet streams hitting from every direction. It is a large metal contraption with water jets aimed at you from all angles and it really looks like some sort of torture machine. One governor almost drowned in the contraption and another could never regulate the temperatures correctly. In a scene from one of the movies, a woman was killed in this shower and ever since it has been considered to be haunted. It is usually stored in the basement with the other artifacts and only brought out for garden party events or fundraisers. It was interesting to me that the scientists and historians had not only displayed it in the most haunted hall of the depot, but also made a sort of subtle comment on their budget cuts. It was probably subconscious, but you never know.

There have been several paranormal investigations of the old depot. In one of these investigations, a man had an Electromagnetic Field (EMF) meter and a 35 mm camera but only got a few orbs in his photos. However, he did mention one interesting detail in his Web report. He had encountered a visitor to the depot who had worked in the depot restaurant in the 1940s. This person said the train crews who came into the restaurant often talked about the ghosts they had encountered on their train rides as well as those spirits who inhabited the depot. He said it was common knowledge in those days that the Denver and Rio Grande Depot was haunted.

The Home of Unusual Events

Phenomena Reported by the Shop Owner

An antique shop has been housed in a particular pioneer home for quite a few years. It was apparently a vacant, run-down little house for many years before the owner rented it. The owners had renovated it, entirely redoing the outside of the home. It is one of the original pioneer homes from the late 1800s and nothing spectacular to look at. It has been my experience, however, that little, unknown, tucked away places are usually more haunted than the bigger mansions that are famous for a haunting. The renter intends to hang onto the antique store as long as possible, hoping the little house will be protected from being demolished. Almost immediately after the renter began stocking and decorating the store, she began to realize she was not alone in the home. And for many years the phenomena has continued. Closet doors that had been left open would be shut the next day. Items such as lace pieces or pillows would be rearranged when the shop was opened the next morning. There were cold spots and many customers reported feeling a presence at the top of the stairs. Clocks hung throughout the shop would all be stopped at the same time even though they had been set at different times or not set at all. The sounds of people moving around or walking up or down the stairs could be heard when no one was around. The original stairs were located in another part of the store and footsteps and other odd sounds could be heard coming from the now phantom staircase.

When working late at night, the storeowner would get the feeling she was not wanted at the shop and needed to go home, as if a presence was saying to her that the night was not for the living. Her teenage son brought friends over to watch movies late at night in the store, and they got the same feeling: they were not wanted there and needed to go home. To get them to leave, the presence literally shoved the "intruders" with invisible hands right by the room where the spirit seemed to stay. On one occasion, the son and his friends were watching a video when suddenly the upstairs windows all flew open at the same time. This frightened them so much that they shut and locked all the windows and then left the house. As they were piling into their one car, they looked up to discover that all the upstairs windows were wide open again. No one volunteered to go up there and shut and lock them again.

However, employees and visitors feel the house spirits are friendly and warm and not threatening at all. Over time, the storeowner began to feel there were two distinct spirits in the house that probably didn't even know each other. She believed one was a reclusive man who stayed in one of the upstairs rooms and the other was a female apparition who goes all over the store as though guarding the other spirit from entering the rest of the house. The female spirit is warm and loving and has been both sighted and photographed at the top of the stairs. She appears as a long twisting string of light moving in the photographs. The woman has also been seen standing in the window of the front room downstairs and also near the front door. Those who have seen her describe the woman spirit as being dressed in long dark clothing with her dark hair piled on top of her head, as a Latter-day Saint settler woman would have been dressed in the late 1800s. Others have only reported seeing a white mist that sometimes forms into the general shape of a woman in a long gown.

Ghost Hunter Investigations

Sightings and photos by ghost hunters in the shop consist of orbs, streaks of floating or twisting light, and an actual human shape—a pretty dramatic and unusual ghost picture. The shop owner said each of the spirits seemed to have its own little idiosyncrasies and each could be identified by these little habits. For example, the male apparitions like to have their closet door shut, and if no one remembers to shut it before they leave for the night, it will be shut for them the next morning. Sometimes employees will even get a reminder in their thoughts to just go up and shut the door. It is the female spirit who rearranges things and just loves the antique dolls. She does not like people to touch them or pick them up and when customers come into the shop and exclaim over the dolls, they report that something gives them the feeling not to touch the dolls or attempt to pick them up. The dolls are very old and are displayed in a cradle. One morning one of the rockers on the cradle was found broken off with no explanation. Sometimes the dolls are found undressed in their cradle when the shop is opened in the morning, and the clerk will have to re-dress them.

It is the female spirit that stops the clocks to indicate her presence in the home. The female spirit has been sighted gazing out of the front window with her hands pressed against the glass. Passersby have reported seeing her there when the shop is closed. The woman will also appear as a faint image in the mirrors in the house, and while her face is not distinguishable, her clothing is much clearer and appears to be late nineteenth century. She wears long skirts and her hair is pulled back and piled on top of her head. People report seeing her out of the corner of their eye as she whisks down the stairs and around the corner. Photos of streaks of moving light have been taken below the ceiling at the top of the tiny, narrow stairs. Ectoplasm has been seen in these two areas as well as in an upstairs window. The large-sized orbs that the ghost hunters photographed were in the room where the reclusive man stays and one rather large orb was photographed in front of the open closet door.

On the preliminary ghost investigation visit, the investigators captured, totally by chance, one of their most dramatic ghost pictures ever. It was a week before the actual investigation and the photo was taken in broad daylight. During their official investigation late at night, they obtained many EVP recordings, nearly all of which were upstairs and many in the room where the reclusive man seems to stay. Just to see what would happen, they opened the closet door and left it open while they were recording. At the end of the session they shut the door. When they went back to the lab and analyzed their tape, they heard a clear voice say "Thank you" right after they shut the door. Electromagnetic fields were really high all over the upstairs and especially at the top of the stairs and in the stairwell. They also heard the name Julie, which is strange because Julie is a modern name. The investigators photographed many light streaks and orbs. While the orbs might be explained in some other way, the moving waves and streaks of light cannot be camera anomalies or reflections, as they clearly stand out from the ceiling and walls and move as if floating in space.[1]

Our First Visit

The first time my friend and I stopped by, the owner of the shop was not there. We had only just discovered the location of the place and went to visit on a whim. We were immediately overwhelmed by the strong presences in the house and the residual energy from the antiques. I walked up the stairs and stood at the back window on the north side of the house. This was where the woman's presence was the strongest and I felt as though she had stepped into me or I into her. I felt her sadness, her reminiscences of the past. I also felt the way she looked out into the empty fields as though she were waiting for something, looking towards the old train tracks as though someone were about to come home to her any day soon. I realized later that I had been looking at a different time and place, a place where this woman had spent her childhood. However, the woman I saw was very old. She was little and round with her gray hair in a bun. Her vision was dim, and I saw what she saw at the small window upstairs as though through milky glass or layers of gauze. The apparition was one of the most interactive that I have ever encountered and one of the strongest presences that I have ever felt. Her essence was powerful, loving, and easily identified as a higher level being there to teach rather than warn or play games.

The female presence was clearly pleased with having a shop of this type in her home. She was very protective of the shop and the woman who ran it, and was loving her chance to see others after so many years of being lost and forgotten. She obviously had a strong relationship with the renter, even though the store proprietor was not present when we were there the first time. This entity seemed to think of the store manager as a daughter or a sister. The other intuitive with me became quite overwhelmed by the energy of the many antiques that carried stories and impressions of their own. Both of us felt the heady atmosphere in the place immediately upon entering the store and we were soon dizzy. We wondered how anyone could concentrate with such a strong presence from the past in both the antiques and the woman's essence in the home.

Our initial combined thoughts on these entities were that the young man had either died there or had gone away suddenly. We saw him in each of our mind's eyes in a uniform of some kind, which has never been explained. Then we saw an older man as well who seemed to be recalling some sort of trauma as he paced the floors at night unable to sleep. We could not tell his relationship to the woman, although we leaned towards son or father rather than husband. The closet door had to be shut because it reminded him of some past traumatic event. The older woman seemed to present images of herself at different ages in her life; it is a common theme for a spirit to travel in mirrors and be seen in them as she travels at different times in her life. However, I felt that there were two women apparitions, a mother and a daughter. When people are there admiring the house and the antiques, both spirits are especially warm and loving presences. When the place is empty, they become melancholy and search at the windows for both memories of times gone by and for someone who never returned home.

I also felt that the female entities often recalled their growing up years in some other place where they had a finer life, and this kept them going as they suffered the lean and stark pioneer life. Wherever they grew up, probably in some foreign country, what was outside that upstairs window was rich and green and humid and very unlike what they saw as adults from this little house. In other words, they had and admired fine things when they was growing up, and it pleased them to have a second chance at these things when the antique shop was opened. I believed that I was seeing England or some Scandinavian country because I saw tea sets, dolls, and other European things. The environment was conducive to a very wealthy family and a happy childhood. My impression was that the mother had to leave her home when she grew old and did not die in the home, but the minute she died she returned to it to stay, as had her daughter. Both were buried in the local cemetery. As to the name, I didn't think either one was named Julie. I feel that one of their names sounded phonetically like this or that Julie was a middle or last name and not a first name. The young man was buried somewhere else for some reason, perhaps a family plot elsewhere or at least not next to the family.

We both sensed two little girls in the home, but could not figure out whether they were attached to the people who had lived in the house or to some of the antiques. Every time we passed a little black and white print of two little girls huddled together, the picture either turned, moved right in front of us, or fell. Some of the people with me felt the movement of objects was attached to the antiques. I had a strong feeling the image of the younger woman in the house was showing us herself and her little sister when they were growing up. Apparently the sisters were each other's main support. We felt that the female apparition missed her lost infants tremendously, as well as her lost son. At this point, we knew nothing of the history of the house and its various owners. We did not know its tragedies and only felt the warmth and beauty of its present surroundings.

The apparitions were definitely aware of us. They seemed to like us and at least one of them was trying to communicate in little subtle ways by moving things around as we wandered, hoping we would notice. We probably did not notice all the subtle movements because we were so overwhelmed by the overall feeling in the place. We had to hold onto things because it was making us so dizzy. The person who had come with me wandered into another room and spotted a large French music book on a music stand. As she stood there, the music stand began to twist back and forth as though being manipulated by invisible human hands. The stand stayed straight and unmoving, while the holder for the music moved back and forth with the heavy book on it. My friend stood away from the stand and checked to see if some air currents from the door or a fan might have been moving it. She could not locate anything that could move the top of the stand. Fearing the book would fall off, she grabbed for it and the music stand stopped swaying.

The shop owner's young son had been playing in the front yard with the clerk's son. The clerk, who we were spooking anyway, called him in and introduced him to us. She asked him if he had ever noticed any ghosts in the shop. He said no, but that he had seen things move before. The boy was sitting inside right across from the music stand as my friend watched it moving back and forth. She asked the boy if he had also noticed it and he confirmed this with a rather nonchalant nod of his head. He told her again he had noticed other things move on their own around the shop. But it all seemed rather matter-of-fact to him. My friend wondered if the entity was moving the stand to get her attention or if the woman's son had moved it, as he seemed quite intuitive and cases have been recorded of young children having such an ability with objects. Were the boy and the spirit working in tandem? Or was my friend just seeing things? Perhaps things were being presented as an illusion just to entertain us. Was it the two little girl sisters who sometimes played with the two dolls in the house as well?

Our Second Visit

This time we were much more prepared for the atmosphere in the place. I brought a notebook to write down what I experienced there and arranged to meet the store owner and talk to her personally. She had told me over the phone the history she knew about the little house, which was very little, but mentioned that she would find a folder of information taken from a local book on the history of the house. She also mentioned that after several years there was a strong attachment between her and the spirit. She was remarrying and moving to another town nearby and she feared the apparition was upset with the changes. She didn't want the ghost following her to her new home. She was fine with the ghost remaining at the shop, and she intended to keep the shop for as long as she could. We set up a time and date for our second visit.

I had chosen to go back to the shop only because of something the shop owner had told me on the phone. I had taken most of my information about the ghost from the ghosthunter's videotape, but in the course of telling me many of the same things, the store owner told me something new. I had come to the house with the attitude that this was the research for the story and then I would be done with the book. So I was in a hurry just to get the information and leave. However, as an intuitive I was not going to get to do this. I received a strong feeling from this female spirit that she wanted to talk to me. Her urgency and desperation made me feel that I had to try meeting with the shop owner one last time. While the ghost hunters were making their EVP recordings, they heard another phrase on their tapes after they asked, "What is it that you want?" At that moment, their tape player malfunctioned and the answer was erased from the videotape. It was only been the people present who heard a voice say, "Won't anyone talk to me?"

When we got there, the shop owner had totally forgotten our visit and never showed up.

Our Third Visit

I continued to feel compelled to go back and talk to the apparition in case she had something important to say to us, the shop owner, or her descendants. It was as if she were calling to me across time and distance, and I could hear her when no else seemed to. She had found me in this big city and kept bothering me until I went to visit the shop one more time. This time everything on our visit worked like clockwork, as though it was just meant to be. The owner had forgotten our appointment once again and was not even scheduled to be there, but that morning she had been called to fill in for someone at the last minute. After so much trouble connecting with her, I was about to give up. The urgency of this esoteric calling kept me determined to visit before the school year began. That morning, I told a friend that we needed to go, whether the renter was there or not, because this would be a last chance for the two of us to go together. My friend had forgotten we were suppose to go and really did not want to accompany me. She told me later that I had such a commanding voice about it, that she had felt obligated to go with me. We arrived at the shop, walked in, and there was the owner all alone in the shop. We continued to be the only three living people in the shop all morning long.

I asked the shop owner if I could just wander about and take notes and then sit down with her and go over these notes. She said I was welcome to do this, and she and my friend stayed downstairs talking. I went upstairs and started writing down my impressions. The very first things that came were two names, Elizabeth and the owner of the shop's first name. After several pages of notes, I was interrupted by the renter who came up the stairs and leaned over the railing to talk to me. My friend had come up the stairs and was wandering about in the other rooms. The owner made it clear that the spirit was attached to her and that when she left, it would leave with her. She also admonished us not to touch the two antique dolls in the little rocker. Her whole demeanor changed and her melodic voice changed to one that seemed older than her years and much more commanding. My friend and I looked at each other guiltily. We found out later that we had both not only touched the dolls, but had picked them up and examined them. It was as if the woman apparition had seen us do it and was scolding us like two little children through the owner's words. I went on to finish my notes after the other two went back down stairs, but the owner had been right. The atmosphere changed almost immediately. I then realized that the spirit had gone downstairs too and there was nothing more I could write down. So I went downstairs to the room where the shop owner believed the spirit spent most of the time. Surprisingly, it was like a little sitting room and the four of us, one apparition and three women, sat around talking.

The last thing I had expected was to do an intuitive reading in this little shop, but we spent the next three hours together, myself as interpreter and my intuitive friend, who lives much more in the present than I do, as a sort of grounding force for my other worldliness. Before this, I had always kept my intuitive world separate from both my work life and my book writing life, mainly to keep focused but also because of the way people treated me when they found out I had the second sight. I was hesitant in this instance because I knew I was an interloper on this scenario that had gone on for the last several years between the owner and the female spirit. I was wise enough to recognize the spirit of a "Mother Theresa" when I felt one and I knew I was out of my league. It was best to just listen, interpret, and try to communicate to the shop owner what I was getting. More than once during the three hours, I would see the shop owner's whole demeanor, body posture, and facial expression change enough that it felt as if the apparition was speaking directly to me from the shop owner's body. It felt just as crazy as it sounds. I also felt obligated to do the best that I could since the apparition was much older than I, much more aware than I, and so far ahead of me that I was running in my mind to keep up with her. The notes on my pages flew, and I did all that I could.

I began to realize as the reading continued that it was the land that had mattered in all of this. It came down to the apparition's love of her home, the land, and the farm that her father had built out of nothing. It was the land that had meant everything to all the family members, but especially to the father who had emigrated there with his family. He had homesteaded the land and then gone far off to work to feed his family and to keep his land. This was the land on which the poor house had been built, where one of their children was buried, and where cornfields and other crops grew from the hard work and sweat of their brows. The loss of the land was a tremendous factor in why these spirits were there. Apparently, over the years, more and more of the acreage had been sold off and little remained of the original 160 acres that the family had homesteaded. Suddenly the shop owner asked me to ask the apparition just what it was that she wanted. Once again the woman's whole demeanor changed. She sat up straight, her rounded shoulders disappeared, and her hesitation and melodic voice changed into a deeper and more commanding voice. "My father loved this land. He was the farmer and he was the most attached to it. Go and speak to him about letting go of the land. This will be a big sorrow for him. Go to father's stone and tell him about it." I wrote it down word for word, not realizing at the time that I had been the only one to hear it. I had simply written down what I had heard in my head, but it felt as though the woman stood over my left shoulder, watching me write it all down. I could feel the tingling on my left arm like someone was touching my arm and watching carefully what I wrote down. While the owner spoke, I had heard only the apparition's answer.

I read it back to the shop owner, whose long dark hair framed her delicate features. She had happened to wear a long dark skirt that day, and the apparition she had described seeing in the mirrors of her shop was near her age with dark hair and wore dark gowns. At this age, they did look like sisters, or even mirror images of each other. A bit fearful, but also determined to be as intuitive as possible, the shop owner listened quietly to my words, and the whole room changed as though some sort of veil of time had been lifted between all of us. The lightness was gone, the heaviness returned, and the seriousness of what I was being told to tell her became evident. I felt there was more to this than just the land and that I needed to tell the woman all of my impressions and notes as we sat there immersed in this reading. Absolutely no one had come into the shop to disturb us. These impressions made little sense at the time, but they seemed vital to the apparition in this home. And they also seemed to be vital information for the shop owner. These scattered, but eventually understood, impressions are what I told the shop owner that day.

The apparition's father, the original homesteader of this home and land, needed to know what the land would be used for now and why so much of it was gone. The lost infant needed a ceremony down by the knoll near the river. It was to be performed by the living, both relatives, and the "new family" in the shop. The infant, whose mother I was not sure of at the time, had lived in the house for a short while a very long time ago. Next I was told that the mother and her daughters, whoever they were, needed family to come for them. The family descendants included a genealogist from a branch of the family that consisted of three sisters, one having passed on, who needed to fill in the family history spaces. The larger part of the family was buried separately, and they needed to be told where the two family sides now resided. The sides of the family were far apart from each other, the other side possibly in a Scandinavian country. The shop owner was asked to go to the grave of this apparition's father in the town cemetery, although at the time I didn't know who he was, and talk with him about the loss of the land. She was to ask him to also make restitution for whatever had happened in this house.

Although they were certainly scattered thoughts, I still felt compelled to give these impressions to the shop owner for whatever purpose they would serve in the future. The reading ended, we chatted, and the shop owner went one last time to find the folder with the history of the house in it. She said she had been looking for days and just couldn't find it. She walked back out of her office with a startled look on her face and handed me the folder. "It was right there on top of the other papers on my desk. I swear it wasn't there when I looked before," she said. I asked if she trusted me to take it. She said yes, that she wanted me to read it and see if more would come to me.

I had come to write a last ghost story for my new book, and three hours later, with my friend as the grounding force, I had done the most powerful reading of my life. During those three hours, no one had come into the shop. The shop owner had almost seemed possessed by this apparition as she spoke to me commandingly. Her demeanor and body language had changed dramatically. I was running in my mind to keep up with this powerful spirit as she spoke through me. I was well aware of the power of unconditional love that was in the room that day. Would the owner see this too? I wouldn't know for a long while to come. There were themes of redemption, loss, guilt, forgiveness, and even promises not yet kept. There was much this house had to heal from. It was guarded and protected by spirits waiting for this healing process to complete itself, both on the land itself, within this home, and within the hearts of these people who were sharing life stories across dimensions and time. I hoped that the history would provide some continuity to my various impressions.

The Pieces Fall Together: The History

Hannah Krants grew up on a very wealthy farm in Denmark that her mother had inherited from her German relations. The estate was located in a fertile district of Denmark and was named Fuegholt (the Home of the Birds). It was Hannah who read the Bible and converted to The Church of Jesus Christ of Latter-day Saints unbeknownst to her husband, Christian Beck, who learned about her conversion when someone in town "asked him if it was true his wife had joined the despised Mormons." Initially opposed to the idea, her husband eventually had a change of heart, and he went with her to America and converted two years after he came to Utah. They sold everything and in 1866 crossed the Atlantic Ocean on a sailing ship. They had four children with them, Christina (age fourteen), Carl (age eight), Dorthea (age five), and Christian (age three months). During the voyage, little Christian became sick and died. He was wrapped in a little sheet and slipped into the ocean, buried at sea. They took the train to Omaha and then walked across the plains to Utah, suffering along the way as all the hardy pioneers did. They arrived in Salt Lake City and then went on to a smaller town where they lived for two years. They then moved to another small town in Utah to homestead 160 acres of land. It was here that Christian and his son Carl built a little one-room adobe house with a dirt floor. Hannah Beck cared for her three surviving children in this house. She had lost either four or five infants (accounts vary according to whether she had eight or nine children) within days or months of their births.

In 1869, Christian Beck left the family to find work to help their destitute condition. He went to Echo and Weber Canyons to work on the Union Pacific Railroad for six months and was present at the joining of the railroads ceremony completing the east and west railroad connection at Promontory. He also did some mining in American Fork Canyon. He made the long journey home after this and worked hard to cultivate his land. Christian Farmer, as he was called, was soon the owner of a very prosperous farm, and in time, the home was remodeled to add two rooms. As they grew older, Christian and Hannah lived in this little pioneer home with their only remaining son, Joseph Hyrum Beck, and his wife, Bernetta McDaniel. Joseph, or Joe, had little formal education and spent his youth helping his father on the farm. At twenty, he married his childhood sweetheart, nicknamed Nettie, who was just eighteen. Within a period of three years, Joe and Nettie had two girls and a boy. All of the babies died within a few days of birth. Their fourth child, a boy named Joseph Karl, survived. By this time, Joe had added four additional rooms to the little pioneer home, two of them upstairs. Joe was known in the community as a kind man who cheerfully helped his neighbors.

Nothing is said about where the rest of Hannah's lost children are buried, although the cemetery is most likely. One was buried in Denmark and one was buried at sea. Hannah and Christian's oldest son, Carl Jacob, took sick at the farm in January of 1872 and died of diphtheria just a few days short of his fourteenth birthday. This was a great trial and sorrow for his parents. "It was a terrible blow to them as he was a very trusty boy. They had come to lean a great deal on him as he readily learned the English language and to partake of the customs of this country, which they were slower to grasp because of their matured age. It took them years to overcome this sorrow."[2] Christina and Dorthea's parents died within six years of each other and are buried side by side in the town cemetery. I feel that at least one daughter is buried on the farm property, but the question remains as to whether this is one of Hannah's lost daughters (records do not show that she lost any daughters, but the number of children she had is in question), Nettie's lost daughter, or even Hannah's daughter Christina's lost daughter. I am guessing it is Hannah's daughter or at least a child connected to her in some way, simply because of information gained about her as this story unfolds. However, this part of the story will probably remain a mystery.

Hannah's eldest daughter, Christina Beck Peterson, lived in the home from ages fifteen to age twenty-one. She and her husband, Louis Peterson, moved into a little log cabin on the south part of town shortly after their marriage in 1874. Christina had six children, but one boy died at two years of age and one girl died in infancy. She lived in her little home well into her nineties. Her first husband died after fourteen years of marriage, and she became mother to her second husband's four children, all in the same little home. Christina loved the finer homemaking arts and did beautiful needlepoint. She loved flowers and always wanted her surroundings to be inviting. She loved her home very much and stubbornly refused to leave it until the last two years of her life when she went to live with two of her daughters. She was the oldest of the eight children and always took care of her younger siblings. Between husbands, she earned her living weaving carpets and doing farm work. Her house was torn down in 1955.

Dorthea Marie "Tear" Beck was Christina's younger sister. She married Joseph William Watkins in 1877, and they moved into their one and a half acre homestead about half a mile southeast of town and then built their own larger place east of this. Dorthea Maria Beck was Christina's younger sister born in 1860. She died eleven years before her sister in 1929 at the age of 69. While her sister and mother took care of the house, Tear herded her father's cows, often barefooted. When she got older, she worked in a mining town boarding house. One family story is about how she got caught in the boarding house one evening with a crowd of drunken men. One man from her hometown was worried about her, so he grabbed his gun and took Tear and walked all night with her to her home many miles away to avoid these men who were looking for them. Tear and Joseph had five healthy babies, four sons and one daughter. In March of 1888, Joseph became ill with pneumonia and died a week later. Six weeks later, Tear's fifth child was born. During this time, Tear and all her children lived with her parents. It was pretty crowded. After her uncles worked tirelessly to build a little two-room adobe house on a lot that she and her husband owned in town, Tear was able to move into her own home on Christmas Eve of 1888. Later she married "Frank" Francis Farquharson. They raised her children and lived together for thirty-seven years. Her second husband died just six weeks before her death in May of 1929.

As his parents grew older and their health deteriorated, Joseph Karl, their youngest child and only remaining son, ran the farm and cared for his ailing parents. In the last eight years of her life, Hannah was blind. Nettie and their son, who was born in 1893, worked the farm alongside Joe, who was always busy with other town jobs as well. Only one year after the death of Hannah, the Becks moved out of town. Joe had held several local offices, including town councilman and watermaster for the local district. In 1906, he was elected to the office of county assessor for a term of four years. The position required him to move to the county seat. He kept the farm, however, renting the land and keeping stock on it.

Joseph Hyrum Beck died in 1931 and Nettie McDaniel Beck died in 1958. It is unclear if anyone lived on the farm as renters between

Joseph's death and Nettie's or if their son, Joseph Karl, managed the farm. However, Joseph Karl became a doctor, and it is unlikely that he managed the farm as well, unless he worked very long hours. The home was then sold to three different dairy farmers in succession. Tear's second husband ran a creamery, and this was probably the connection between the three subsequent owners of the small pioneer homestead. These three men later built dairy barns. The first owner, Alvin Rieske, built one in the 1940s. He was milking thirteen cows when he sold his place to George Heaton between 1947 and 1948. Heaton and his son increased the herd to one hundred, milking eighty cows. Alvin Heaton sold the home to Harvey Hutchinson, who also built a dairy barn. The Heatons were the last people to live in the home before the house became an antique shop.[3]

From this point on, things are not as clear. The current renter says that a family with thirteen children bought the home and lived there in the 1940s and 1950s. This would have been an amazing feat since the house is tiny even with a second story. This family may have been the Rieskes or the Heatons. Another family bought the home later. This was either the Heatons or the Hutchinsons. While one of these families was living there, two of their teenage sons were killed. The owner didn't know the circumstances, and there is no mention of the deaths in the written histories of the town. I could find no other details concerning the last family to live in the home. Perhaps the stories of these three families intermix with the ones that I did find, and perhaps the details pertain to some of them instead. Perhaps they too left not only residual energy but also active spirits. After this family moved out, the home stood vacant until the antique dealer decided to fix it up and open her shop.

The mysteries of the ghosts in the house were somewhat clarified for me when I read the original homesteader's history. I feel the primary spirit is Hannah Krantz Beck, but both of her daughters and her daughter-in-law visit upon occasion. Even in the house today, the theme of sisters is very strong. Perhaps Hannah felt that all three of these younger women were her daughters. The two little girls are another matter. Were they sisters, or just attached to objects in the store? The shop owner, who is very intuitive, has reinforced this theme of sisters throughout her store with paintings and lithographs, probably without realizing it. There is even a large painting of two sisters in embrace in the room where the renter says this spirit spends a lot of her time. It is also my feeling that actions of the man upstairs are those of a teenage boy. I don't know if it is fourteen-year-old Carl or one of the boys supposedly killed later. Since these rooms were added much later, perhaps this would explain the addition of two extra bedrooms and a likely one to three spirits.

However, I also felt that the original homesteader, Christian Farmer, was the most likely visitor to this east room upstairs, although four men lived in this home after him, including his own son. The man who is occasionally seen there seems older and a little stern and grumpy, which a hard working man who had suffered some disappointments in life might be. Perhaps it is the father of the boys rumored to have been killed in an accident. Perhaps it is Joseph Hyrum mourning the infants he and Nettie lost. Or most likely, it is his father, Christian Farmer, mourning the loss of his elder son, Carl Jacob. Do spirits move into areas of the house that did not exist when they were alive? Or do they stay in the house that was familiar to them? Most psychic investigators agree that more often the spirits continue to walk through the original areas. There is a famous photo of a group of ghost monks walking into an old church in England. They are seen only from the waist up because they are walking on the old original foundation of the church. However, records of the house seem to indicate that the second floor might not have been built until much later. The second floor may have been built by Joseph Karl when he lived there with his family and parents.[4]

As I took my notes and read the history of this family, it was easy to see why Hannah would be there. It also sheds light on the residual energies of the others that could be there too. These additional apparitions could be real or memories from Hannah's and the house's consciousness, like an old eight-reel film being run again and again. The last of Hannah's son, Carl Jacob, had made her a permanent mourner in this home. This loss had been deep and devastating. The most startling discovery from the history was an explanation for the strong reprimand from the renter never to touch the two little antique dolls sitting side-by-side like two sisters in the upstairs cradle. I have a rather large doll collection myself, and I know what it feels like, even as an adult, to have one of your most precious dolls damaged. It would be devastating to a child not only to have the doll damaged, but to have to give it away to survive. Perhaps the two little sister spirits in the house had similar experiences with their dolls.

It seems that Hannah's daughters, Christina and Dorthea, had brought a beautiful porcelain doll with them from Denmark. It had been given to Dorthea when she was five years old. At Omaha, as they prepared to embark on their wagon train trek across the continent, all excess baggage had to be left behind. Dorthea's doll was considered excess baggage, but she put up such a fuss that they allowed her to keep the head. She was made to rip the head off on the promise that they would make a new body and outfit for it. Dorthea kept the doll's head safe all across the plains. When they got to the settlement, she had to trade her beautiful doll's head for a big black hen so that the family could eat. At five, Dorthea had learned sacrifice as her sister and mother would learn throughout their lives. All of these women, related by birth or marriage, mourned deep losses and managed to maintain a deep love for each other.

Theories and Thoughts

Dorthea's doll was a symbol, a last remnant of their wonderful childhood years in Denmark at the House of Birds farm. I think it is Hannah who guards these dolls from being both handled or sold, as they represent her two remaining daughters, daughters that she had somehow been unable to protect from the trials of life. Regardless, the two little dolls were the heart of the house because they represented sisterhood, great losses, a beautiful childhood, wealth, idealism, and even the many babies lost by Hannah, Christina, and Nettie. They represented the women who lived and worked and played in this house. Although the losses were replaced by great faith and sacrifice, these women still lost many things that were irreplaceable, both solid and spiritual. Beyond this explanation, there is still the mystery of why Hannah saw these two little dolls as representative of both a lost home and a lost innocence. I also wonder why the other women who had lost children in this house, or were simply attached to the dolls of children who had perhaps died, would come to this house as well.

I had already realized before reading the family history that things would just begin to fall into place. Inside that folder were the keys to the mystery of this house and land. Perhaps there would also be reasons for these women to be linked across time, both to the house and the present owner. Theories came with these mysteries. Did the present day owner remind the apparition of her own sister, one of her daughters, or perhaps someone's mother? Upon viewing the old photos of a young Christina and Dorthea, the resemblance to the shop owner, as well as the ghost she described in the mirrors, was startling. Perhaps Hannah had looked exactly like this when she was young. Believers in reincarnation would say that the shop owner *was* the apparition's sister or daughter reincarnated and being protected and guided. Others would say that the shop owner merely reminded the apparition of herself or a daughter and she had grown fond of her and wanted to help her. Why else would such a theme of sisters and mothers and daughters permeate the shop? Either theory would fit, yet I still did not fully understand what I had stepped into, only that it was beyond me but, at the same time, needed me to be complete.

The old woman who stood at the top of the stairs and stared out that window was Hannah waiting for her husband or others she had loved to come home on the railroad tracks that no longer ran along this old bed on the hill. She also stood there thinking about her lost children, especially her teenage son whom both she and her husband had so loved. Just as Nettie, who had lived in that home for a quite a while too, might have stood there thinking about the little ones that she had lost. And perhaps other women, who had come later in the history of this house had gazed out that window waiting for or mourning the loss of something or someone that I would never know about. Life had been slow and unhappy for them all in this tiny house that was indicative of its poor inhabitants who probably knew that their dreams might not ever be fulfilled. But it was especially Hannah who often reminisced about her lost idyllic life on their comfortable and wealthy home in Denmark. There was Hannah with her lost children, and standing within her was her older daughter, Christina, who stood at the same window, thinking of her lost children, just as Nettie mourned those that she had lost. But all of this was connected to Hannah, who had not been able to protect them from some sort of family storm. Whatever these storms were, Hannah was at the center of their secrets, and her strong spirit had survived through time. Even the fact that everything was hazy and distant as I stood at that window for the very first time fit with the fact that it was Hannah who had slowly gone blind in the last eight years of her life.

The names Catherine and Elizabeth came up and did not belong to any of the original dwellers of the home. The shop owner had been told by psychics and other visitors on several occasions that the name of the woman apparition who followed her around was Catherine, so this was the name that the store owner had chosen to call the ghost. I suddenly understood what was going on, even though others would think me balmy. The women spirits were trying to tell me that Catherine was the adopted name, but the phonetic name was Hannah Krantz Beck or what I had misunderstood as E-liz-a-beth. Unless Elizabeth, or something that sounded close to this, had been the infant's chosen name unbeknownst to anyone but her parents. When I asked for the number of years that the apparition had lived in the house, I heard the number forty. When I read the history, I figured out that this was exactly how many years Hannah had lived there. What I had heard that very first day, when no one else was there, were two names, Elizabeth and the shop owner's first name.

That same day, I was shown pictures in my mind. I saw the daughters, the young man in the room with the closet, and a very poignant image of a woman, probably Nettie, holding her infant in her arms and saying that something was wrong with this particular little girl when she was born and they knew she was going to die. It then began to dawn on me that there were several spirits: the mother and her two daughters, the young Carl Jacob who had died at age fourteen, Nettie, the two little girls, and possibly spirits from a later time. Some of the lost infants and small children from these original settlers could also have been in the home. There were others spirits here as well. Three families had lived in the home later. One of these families had thirteen children, and the other had lost two of their sons to tragedy. This house was filled with spirits of the dead, but it was Hannah who had lived the longest in the home and seemed to dominate the activity taking place.

While others came and went, it was Hannah who was the active spirit. She arrived with a drop in temperature like the swish of a long skirt and made her presence known by gliding past the others and standing to the left of me as though looking down or even reading the notes I was taking as we sat there. She announced herself with a warm tingling sensation in the whole room, eventually touching my left arm like a kindly old aunt would do. I had never felt such love and warmth in one room, and I knew that I was in the presence of a very humbling spirit whose wisdom and knowledge were way beyond my own. She was not in this home to frighten or cajole but to advise and guide the shop owner, who for some reason the ghost didn't feel was listening. I was the interpreter, and yet, I felt that I too would not be listened to. Hannah was small and round and with gray hair pulled back at the nape of her neck. She smiled both kindly and bitterly at the same time. She had been very wise in life. In the afterlife, she was extraordinarily loving, although she seemed to be in constant mourning.

The Last Piece Falls into Place

When the storeowner realized that there were two or possibly three female spirits in the home, everything seemed to make more sense to her. On the other hand, it both frightened and intrigued her. Being intuitive herself, she needed to own everything in the house, including the apparitions. What had started as a simple visit for a story became the defining of a house and the people who had inhabited it. To the unaware or non-intuitive, all of this sounds crazy. But to me, the pieces of the puzzle fell together. I know that land remains, no matter what we, the living, decide to put on it. A history of the people on this land also remains in the hearts and minds of their descendents. Although these descendents are often oblivious to where they came from, they still carry the memories and family histories inside them. Spirits are often mere echoes of the land and the dwellings built on it. The labor and sorrows of the original pioneer family combined with their losses and hardships make up a part of those who come after them. No matter the belief systems, customs, or cultures, apparitions remain to remind us of what we often forget to honor within ourselves. Time will take the dwellings, and new dwellings will replace them, but the land itself remains, holding on to its secrets. The descendents are meant to seek out and understand these secrets, pieces of a family puzzle that will provide information for the future of that family. The old adage is true, that if we do not know our own history as a people and nation, then we cannot learn from the past to improve our future for our children.

When the last piece fell into place, I was astonished. Had what I heard as Elizabeth, really been Hannah Beck or even Bernetta or Nettie Beck? Was there another name that I knew nothing about? Had some of the lost infants been given a name? Was it one of the little girls attached to a doll? Separations, intuitive children, and issues of protection made me understand that Hannah, Christina, and Dorthea had also dealt with these same issues, as well as anyone else who had lived in this home since this. It was what many women deal with in any generation. Decades come and decades go, styles change, belief systems rearrange themselves, and generations become different in how they view themselves and others. But they are all the same, call it karma or reincarnation or simply linear time. Women bear children, lose or guide them, deal with the world into which they are born as best they can, and then die and move on, or choose not to move on, coming back for unfinished business of their own. This was the last piece of the puzzle, and either the shop owner would listen or she would not. Hannah was back to visit, to make restitution, to undo or maybe redo, and perhaps she hoped she could do this through those living in the home now. My job was to try and pass the information along to those who either couldn't hear it or didn't want to hear it. That was all that I could do in this house where one of the most miraculous experiences of my life had taken place. I was to do my best, no matter how crazy it might seem to me or to anyone else reading this unusual tale.

The Last Visit

The shop so far has not been razed. The manager called me one day after I had sent her my notes, just to tell me that the activity had increased at the shop since I had been there and she wondered what to do. Apparently some paintings had flown off the walls and things were being hidden from the employees. I can remember thinking, *Just listen!* But I knew that fear, lack of trust in herself, and a dozen other things stood in the way. I knew that the apparition was still just trying to get her to listen. Hannah was trying to help the shop owner in her own life so that she could put the puzzle pieces together for herself. I had done all that I could and now it was up to her. An interloper, I was not the one she needed to talk to. I was just the interpreter. This "spirit soap opera" would end itself on its own.

And it did. Two weeks before school ended, I suddenly decided to take a personal or mental health day off from school. A friend and I were delivering books to some small towns and decided to stop in at the shop. The owner had assured us that she would hang on to the shop, but she had not. A huge going out of business sign declared that only one week was left, and much of the merchandise in the shop was gone. I walked in, and the sadness was so overwhelming that I just stood there frozen. I walked around and found one of the two dolls in the shop, the one I had been attracted to, sitting in the upstairs window. The cradle was gone, and according to the owner, the other doll had not been sold but had disappeared the day before and they could not find it anywhere. She thought that perhaps the ghost had taken it and hidden it to keep it from leaving the shop. All the people were downstairs, so I went upstairs and stood crying by the small window where the train tracks used to be. The rest of the day became a blur, and I bought the doll for way too much money but a great deal less than it had been marked.

The owner was on her way to a new life and adventures elsewhere, but she had to make sure that she was going alone without the apparition following her. She told us a story. She said that she had gotten a phone call only a week or so before from an East Coast psychic. She didn't know how he had found out about her shop, and she did not know him. He had located her and called to tell her that she had a strong spirit in her shop who had called to him from across the country. According to her, he had searched for the shop psychically and found it. If this is how it happened, perhaps he had seen the same video tape that I had purchased. Or perhaps he really was that intuitive. More likely, the owner had called him for reassurance. Once more in trying to help out in the situation, I had instead frightened her. This psychic assured her that the apparition would not follow her to where she was moving because the spirit was attached to the land through a lost child and the spirit would stay there. So even if the house was destroyed, the apparition would stay on the land because of the lost child. He also told her that the spirit had lost someone who was violently murdered, even hacked up. There are no records of any such thing in the town.

The psychic told her that the spirit was an old woman and not young like she had supposed, as if this were new information for me. I realized that all my intuiting and information had meant nothing. It had not helped, but had frightened instead. The shop owner was really only concerned with confirmation that the spirit would not follow her to where she was moving. The other psychic's information, on the other hand, had confirmed all of the information that I knew in my heart to be true. The information was best left where it was—in the heart of this house. So at least for me, I now understood the generations of women who had lived there and their thoughts on their lost children. I understood how some of these women, especially one very strong spirit, Hannah, could be mourning those losses so strongly that they could return to visit. I could not leave that doll sitting forlornly on the same window sill from which all these women had stared out beyond it while mourning their losses. I offered a price I could afford since the doll had always been outrageously priced and impossible for me or anyone else to want to buy. The proprietress let me buy the doll for more than I had offered but at a price I could swing with a little balancing of the budget. I knew that if I did not buy the doll, I would regret it for the rest of my life. At the same time, I felt foolish for having to live a life that most others would never understand. The owner said that she would call me if the other doll turned up somewhere before the shop closed for good. She said that the shop would not go down because some other woman was already interested in renting it for a retreat of some kind. Perhaps the other doll would reappear then, but I doubted it. It didn't matter, really. The dolls had been separated, and the tie between owner and apparition was permanently broken.

I knew why I was there but was mystified that I had not obtained both the dolls. As I left the shop, I felt as though I had just been through World War III. I was drained emotionally, and all my energy was swept away in just the few minutes I had been in the shop. I had a sudden headache, and I could distinctly hear the woman sobbing as I stepped out the door. It was an internal cry, the type that brave pioneer women in Utah became experts at. It was the silent look, the grimace on the face, and the mourning in the eyes through a half smile that hid their tears. This was the spirit that the owner had assured me was not there anymore. The psychic had told her to do something—something she did not reveal—and had assured her that then this spirit would move on toward the light and not come back. Was it the other doll whose negative energy needed to depart? I would never know. But Hannah had not moved on, and I felt terrible that things had ended this way. I had known that they would when I first said that the shop would go down. I also wondered why I was to have the doll and why it fit in my living room perfectly. Would I be visited too? It was the larger of the two dolls and the one that I had held and admired while in the shop before. I had over five hundred dolls, but few antique ones and never one this expensive. On the other hand, I had grown used to such visits from the other side and knew that I was not afraid of such things. I was pretty sure that I would never have to rip its head off or trade it for a big black hen.

If I had not had a witness on this journey with me at every visit, I would have sincerely thought myself crazy, especially with everything gone now. But I had a witness. I also had the confirmation from some unknown famous psychic that what I had told the owner long before this just might be true. The apparition was an older woman who could appear at any age in her life or who had a daughter or even daughter-in-law who also had dark hair and wore long dark dresses like the older woman had when she was young. She had lost someone in that house in a terrible way. Perhaps the so-called murder had been of a kind not spoken of in those days when the baby wasn't right or came unexpect-edly. The hacking that the psychic has also told her about was of a different kind, much more symbolic and easily misinterpreted. Hannah had lost a son in that house as well, an older son, whom she and her husband had adored. She had lost many children, and she had guided her surviving ones in losses of their own. The house was a shrine to lost children, as so many others were in the pioneer times. The house was full of great love, but love that involved great mourning and loss.

I could stay in the house no longer. We walked out around the little house and down to the small canal to look for a big old cottonwood, of which there were several. The picture in my mind of the burial spot was different from what was there now, but I knew that I stood near it. The owner had done none of the things the spirit had asked her to do. She did not remember any of what I had told her, or if she did, she told me something different, I guess to impress on me that she was done. I wept again down by the little canal, knowing I was standing near the child's grave. I felt ridiculous, but my friend assured me that she had been on this entire journey with me and understood why I would feel the way that I did. Who would believe any of this and why was I believing it? I was so affected because I had felt, seen, and been touched by something

I might never experience so strongly again in my life. I had felt the all-encompassing love of a powerful spirit who had only wanted to teach those among the living what we could of course not understand. I had gone just a little ways on the path, but that was enough.

I sometimes look at this little doll now and wonder about its connections to all of this, knowing that I will probably never find the second doll. The two dolls were never to be touched or separated, the owner had said. Knowing in my heart that the story is now finished, I wonder why it all happened. What drew me there and why did nothing come of it? Or did something occur that I will never comprehend? Is this the end of the story or will there be more? The little children haunt me. And I see the spot where this child is, knowing she will remain there like so many others we walk or build or drive over in our mad rush to cover every acre of land that remains open. The development even on this property is evident. Will her little grave be found accidentally as they build new homes, or will it remain hidden? Will the new renter suddenly find the other doll placed just so in the old home? Or as I had originally supposed, was the house soon to be razed instead? Was the desperation I had felt when the apparition first called me down there, that of the spirit knowing she would lose the house soon? Had she been desperate to get the messages to the right people? At least I had done what I could, even though I realized, as time went on, the hopelessness in these attempts. There was always the thought, however, that maybe something had been accomplished and Hannah had helped yet another woman, the manager of the shop, to do what she needed to do to move on.

The Doll's New Home

Another intuitive friend of mine made a suggestion upon hearing this whole story. She said she was sure that the time had come for the dolls to be separated, that the other doll had negative energy around it. There had indeed been two little sister spirits around the place, but they had nothing to do with Hannah and her family. Instead, they were attached to their respective dolls, each from a different European country. She felt that the two little girls had died young and found each other in death. My "witness" agreed. She remembered the same negative energy around the other doll, a bad feeling, she said. The doll

I had purchased felt very positive to her. My intuitive friend said that the little girl apparition had died of a high fever at ten or eleven. All the information that I had on the doll so far was that she was made in Normandy in or around the 1920s. Could the doll's owner have died in the great epidemic in 1918? Or had she died of the very thing that Carl Jacob had, diphtheria? The coincidences may or may not be there, yet I still was not sure how my home would do with this new doll inside it.

My intuitive friend suggested that not only was my doll a gift, but I had rescued it from a somewhat domineering situation and the doll was now free. She also said that now I had a spirit that would not only visit me, but would assist me in my own work to help those grieving for lost loved ones or even a loss of their own souls. She felt the biggest tragedy in that house had not been the little one buried on the property—which she concurred was there—but the loss of the Beck's older son. She said the couple came back to mourn him and the land that they had so loved. The doll's attached spirit would now be in my home upon occasion, and it would bring great gifts to me in return.

She asked if there had been a Jake or Joe living in the home. I said that there had been several Josephs and Jacobs living in that house at one time or another. For Hannah, there was Carl Jacob, the fourteen-year-old who had died in the house. There were two additional Jacobs who had died as infants in that house. Their only surviving son, Joe or Joseph Hyrum, had married Nettie McDaniels and run the farm and lived in the house while caring for his parents. For Nettie, there had been two infant sons who had died in the house and might have been named Joseph or Jacob. Finally, there was their only surviving son, Joseph Karl, who had grown up there. I remembered the name that the ghost hunters had mistaken for Julie. In my mind, this was quite close to Jacob, Joseph, or even Joe. I also realized that Hannah had not lost any daughters, only sons. Nettie was the only one from that first family who had lost a daughter. Hannah's oldest daughter, Christina, had been living in her own house when her infant daughter died. The child on the property was a mystery that might never be solved. But for Christian and Hannah, it was the great sorrow for their eldest son that had kept their spirits returning again and again to the farm. I had opened the door, and more than one spirit had walked in, leaving me a bit confused forever.

I understood now that my doll had been a gift for my attempt to try and communicate for this apparition. It was a response to a promise I had made on my third visit to the house. I remembered picking up the doll and talking to the air around me, assuring whoever was listening that I would be careful with it, that I collected dolls myself and really loved them. I said that I would never harm it but just wanted to admire it, just making sure that no one would be angry with me for having picked it up. When the owner came up and gave us the strong warning not to touch them, I had already done so, and a connection had been made without my being aware of it.

Perhaps I had succeeded in bridging these two worlds; I would never know. I had once again been called down to the house without knowing why. I was there to rescue something hard to understand and certainly crazy to those who read this story. I had walked up those stairs immediately, and there it was all alone in the middle of the windowsill as though waiting for me. I argued with myself. I hesitated. I walked about, asking in my head if this was what the little girl wanted me to do, and finally I bargained for it. Within minutes, the doll was mine at last. I knew that every time I looked at this doll in my living room, I would know that this was the first gift I had ever received from an apparition.

Notes
1) Meyer and Rogue Entertainment, *Ghost Hunting in the Unknown Zone.*
2) *Beck Family Book*, 54.
3) Adams, "Alpine Creamers," 1982, 257–58.
4) *Beck Family Book*, 53–65.

Maggie Coyle and
the Beaver Island Prophet

With so many layers of history and so many conflicting groups of people, is it any wonder that a visit to Beaver Island can be haunted? Between the battles and skirmishes on the island, unjust treatment, and secret murders, there are many apparitions who would have great cause to come back in spirit form and lodge a few protests, or at least produce occasional reenactments of the events of their demise. Even if only orbs and mists inhabit these abandoned or long-gone places, the islanders and visitors would still experience occasional unexplainable phenomena. Having seen some travel shows about the area, I know there are indeed other ghosts on these islands. Even those followers of James Jesse Strang, the famous prophet who stayed for the winter on Beaver Island, found themselves troubled by these earlier apparitions.

Old lake sailors told tales of what really happened on Beaver Island during the Strang occupation. Besides the members of the Strangite church who drowned in storms, their own prophet and his strong-fisted henchmen murdered some of Strang's steadfast followers. Lake sailors also claimed that others joined in the conspiracy to murder Strang. Some say that Strang and his men murdered sailors for their plunder. "Old lake sailors told stories of vessels disappearing in the vicinity of Beaver Island in mid-summer, and that neither they nor their crews were ever heard of again. It was expected that some vessels would 'go missing' in the fall, but it was nearly unheard of in the summer. The sailors claim the Mormons boarded the vessels, killed the crews, stole the cargos, and then burned or scuttled the ships to assure there was no evidence. Dead men told no tales about Beaver Island."[1]

This is the stuff of which ghostly tales are made—lost sailors and their captains wandering the shores of an island where they lost their lives with no one to witness their executions except the deep lakes. Stolen goods and plunder were moved about the island when government officials came to look for it. Some disgruntled Strangite men simply disappeared, never to be heard from again. If the tales are true, then Strang, with his visions, prophecies, and plates of Rajah Manchou and Laban, did indeed become the man Thomas Paine described when he said, "He takes up the trade of a priest for the sake of gain, and in order to qualify himself for that trade, he begins with a perjury. Can we conceive of any thing more destructive to morality than this?"[2]

Jesse Strang was never in Utah, but he had a strong connection with the area because he was one of the supposed "false prophets" of which Joseph Smith and Brigham Young warned. Some may say that Strang actually only copied what Smith had done with the same powers of prophecy and charisma. Speculation is that he switched his first two names in order to avoid sounding like the outlaw, or because King James sounded better than King Jesse. However, it became clear as time went on that he did not have the same powers of leadership and sound judgment with which Brigham Young was endowed. Joseph Smith baptized Strang in the winter of 1844 and asked him to head up a Latter-day Saint colony in Wisconsin. Strang was then thirty-one years old. He was a lawyer and an articulate speaker. When Joseph was murdered four months later, Strang, who had only been a member of the Church for five months, tried to take over the Church by producing a letter that he claimed Joseph had written appointing him as the new prophet. He also produced his own encoded tablets, which he claimed had been created by God.

At the time of Joseph Smith's martyrdom, there were five parties attempting to take the helm of the newly inspired church: Brigham Young, Sydney Rigdon, Emma Smith and her young son Joseph Smith Jr., James Jesse Strang, and a charismatic brother of Joseph Smith who died from digestion problems not long after Joseph. John D. Lee claims in his writings that Joseph Smith's brother was actually poisoned by the head of the Nauvoo Legion, a loyal follower of Brigham Young. However, Sydney Rigdon was Brigham's only real threat to the presidency. Emma and her son went off and started the Reorganized Church of Jesus Christ of Latter-day Saints, and both James Jesse

Strang and Sydney Rigdon were excommunicated and took followers with them. President Young called Strang a "wicked liar," and Strang was excommunicated on the spot. As one of the leaders of the Church, Rigdon had a great deal more power. A debate or speech competition was held between Rigdon and Young. Rigdon lost when the spirit of Joseph Smith seemed to enter Brigham's body and nearly all of the followers were convinced that Brigham was the true prophet of their church.

Strang was as charismatic as Joseph Smith and could outshine Brigham as a divinely inspired prophet, but he had not been around long enough to garner the power he needed from the people. However, some claim he did manage to eventually take two thousand church members with him, some of which had been powerful in the early Church. Strang started his own version of the Latter-day Saint Church after he was excommunicated, and one of the factors that made him so appealing was his renunciation of polygamy. Even though Strang was in an entirely different part of the country, he still became Brigham Young's chief rival for the first three years after Joseph's death. At one point, he even petitioned the United States government to make him the new governor of the Utah Territory when he was in the Michigan House of Representatives. One Smith brother left to follow Strang, although he too fell away and disappeared into history.

People speculate that Strang was actually an atheist who thought Smith a fraud but was interested in the power that he had over people. Even as a young man, he had plotted a way to marry young Queen Victoria so that he could take his place as British royalty. Strang had also studied Napoleon and Caesar extensively and considered them his own personal heroes. Strang continued to take more and more church members away from Brigham Young until the first body of followers of the original Church started their trek west to Utah. There were other converts who were affiliated with neither church who came to the island on their own. Many of his followers went on missions to share the gospel, including Strang himself. In 1847, Strang persuaded some of his followers to set sail for Beaver Island, Michigan, just as Brigham Young was heading west to Utah. The island had only a few Irish fishermen on it at the time and was perfect for settlement.

The local Native Americans, the Ottawas, reported seeing small fishing villages in many of the bays when they arrived on the island in the mid-1700s. Father Baraga came to the island in 1832 to convert the "Odawas" to Catholicism. He came ashore at what is now called Baraga's Landing, on the north shore. The Native Americans who renounced the white man's ways lived near what came to be called Whiskey Point. Baraga managed to convert 199 natives on nearby Garden Island, which is the site of over three thousand Native American graves. White trappers and traders soon came, and by 1850, there were three hundred people living at Whiskey Point. Some claim that a few Latter-day Saints were already there. This fact may partially explain why James Jesse Strang chose the island. Perhaps the Latter-day Saint settlers already there had told him or others about the island. Others say that no Latter-day Saints lived on the island until Strang brought his sect there and that Strang had chosen the island for its cheap land values, few inhabitants, and isolation from the mainland. Still, the mystery of their real reason for settling there remains.

By 1848, Strang and his followers were settled on the island. They hoped that its remote location would offer them peace and isolation, something that they longed for after so much persecution for their beliefs. Strang knew exactly how many settlers were on the island before he and his followers arrived and the mostly Catholic islanders became newly christened "Gentiles" on their own land. The previous settlers, at first friendly to the Strangites, soon were in conflict with these new arrivals. By 1850, Strang claimed to have some 2,600 followers on his island, although experts tend to agree that there were probably only about eight hundred Strangites on the small island, which was only thirteen miles long and six miles wide. Soon the Strang's followers made up seventy-four percent of the island's population and took over the local elections. Although Strang claimed to have received directives and visions from God before coming to Beaver Island, he began to have many more prophetic visions and produced numerous brass plates from the ground. By 1852, Strang had his followers elect him to the Michigan Assembly, the state's Lower House, where he served for two years. Whatever his strange habits at home, he served in the assembly as an outstanding government official, without any strange or bizarre proposals. One of Strang's wives later related that at home he was a quiet, gentle, loving man, except that his word was law and never to be questioned.

As early as 1850, however, Strang had proclaimed himself a king and sat on a throne with a crimson robe and a paper crown. Strang had red hair and was five feet four inches tall. He had absolute power over his subjects and their property, and the Irish fishermen found his kingdom to be very bizarre. On the other hand, Strang published a local newspaper and was a nationally prominent naturalist and an accomplished musician. He established a school for Native Americans on the island and opened his homes to them. At first, the island's previous inhabitants and Strang's followers got on well together, helping each other out, especially through the harsh winters on the island. But as Strang's rules became more complex and more harshly enforced, his own followers began to fear him.

Elizabeth Williams asked a young man who boarded with them after the Strangites's departure about Strang's so-called secret society, which the young man had been forced to join when he was eighteen. His answer was,

> If only these stones could talk they would tell you of some things that would horrify you, and though I am free from [Strang's] rule, I would not dare tell you some things which our band was sworn to do. We were trained for our work . . . It meant sure death to any of us to betray anything pertaining to our business . . . At first the orders were given our captains by the King, but it was not long before we never waited for orders from headquarters. We did what we found to do. It was the intention that Strang should own and rule the whole territory about these islands and mainland as fast as he could get his people scattered about to possess the whole.

The young man "often had spells of great sadness and many nights walked the floor because he could not sleep."[3]

As things worsened on the island, some of Strang's followers with means to leave departed the island, while others, newly converted, were just arriving. Still others completed his orders either against their will or with great loyalty to their leader. A few were left to the elements on the island as a way of assuring their eventual return to the sovereignty of "King James." Many minor conflicts took place between Strangites and the other islanders, and local government officials were eventually summoned for help. The local government was unsuccessful and sought federal assistance. All of these conflicts had created fear and mistrust between the Strangites and the rest of the island. Most important, however, was the fact that both groups lived in mortal fear of Strang. For a member's disobedience to his rules, a man was lashed between two trees and publicly flogged. Disobedient women were shunned, left to the elements to repent, or manipulated into submission.

At first, Strang did not practice polygamy, but when he translated his brass plates into *The Book of the Law of the Lord* and asked his followers to accept it just as they had the Book of Mormon, he felt that God approved of the practice of plural marriage. However, it was only the many leaders of Strang's church who began to take multiple wives. Strang's second wife was asked to dress as a man, and worked as his assistant until the plates were translated. His first wife, Mary, would have no part of the law of polygamy, and she and their three children soon departed the island to return to Vorees, Wisconsin. Strang eventually wanted all of the women to dress in bloomers and have short hair, but he had not counted on the women banding together to resist the newly revealed law. The women leaders spent hours and hours in the temple reading scriptures and debating with Strang that God would not reveal such a thing. In his anger, he tried to subdue the women with more and more stringent manipulations. Many felt that "Strang got too busy making laws that did not suit many of the women, which was one cause of the ill-feeling among his people."[4]

Strang went on to have four or five more brides and fifteen children, according to varying accounts. Two very beautiful young teenage sisters were preparing to wed Strang just days before his assassination. There are four known brides, but there were probably others that were kept secret. Apparently what started as normal behavior on the part of Strang became more and more strange as each year passed on the island. He had already established himself as a tyrant with his own militia forces, although not well organized, controlling the island. His militia, however, could not have been capable of offering armed resistance without his leadership, and few guns were known to be present on the island. While the other islanders spoke of their wounded, missing, and stolen property, it was actually the Strangites who had more casualties before the whole period had ended. The

Strangites felt persecuted for their beliefs, and the other islanders felt frustrated by Strang's strong authority on the island.

The Irish on the island, who also had their own injustices perpetrated against them, sometimes fought back with violence by gathering forces from the mainland. In one such battle, called the War of Whiskey Point, Strang's militia fired from the southwestern edge of the harbor toward Whiskey Point, but only three shots were fired. All the boats approaching the island sailed farther and farther from shore. No one died in the battle, but blood was reported to have soaked the bottoms of the boats from those wounded, although it was Strang's men who suffered the most injuries in these skirmishes.

> Rightly or wrongly, Strang's band gained a reputation for thievery and piracy. Some Gentiles referred to them as a "band of forty thieves" or "Society of Illuminati," who sailed boats ready to assault any lakeside town should they discover the men gone and their families left unprotected. Once, when some Gentile fishermen were driven ashore on Beaver Island by a storm, a group of Saints suggested killing them outright. After much discussion, they were just robbed and set adrift.[5]

On the other hand, "During their 8-year occupancy, the [Strangites] cleared and cultivated the ground, built roads and houses, and changed the island from a wilderness to a moderate outpost of civilization. But fate conspired to keep them from reaping the benefits of their toil."[6] Strang had taken an active role in establishing lighthouses as well. He had one built on the island and another built at St. James Harbor to the north. He had no influence, though, on the decision to build the Beaver Head Lighthouse on the southern end of the island. This made the island more attractive to passing steamships to help generate trade and currency. He had his own men elected as the lighthouse keepers, key positions not only to defend the island but to monitor any activity on or around the island.

In 1851, President Millard Fillmore had Strang and his main lieutenants arrested due to the internal discord with the other island settlers. A federal steamer took them to Detroit, where they were brought up on any charges the federal government could think of. Strang defended himself and his men brilliantly with the same charisma and charm that had led people to follow him in the first place. The jury believed him and acquitted all of the men. The nation's anti-Mormon feelings reached their height in 1856, and while Brigham Young had successfully moved his mainstream group far away, Strang's offshoot group was easily reached and isolated on Beaver Island. Many said that this was why things began to fall apart. Others say that it was Strang's heavy-handedness, along with the mainland and islanders' suspicions that Strang and his men were practicing piracy on the high lakes around his island.

Some historians claim that early on, Strang managed to get a key position for one of his men as the lighthouse keeper for the Aux Galets Lighthouse on a small island named Skillagalee, east of Beaver Island. From its vantage point, the lighthouse on Skillagalee Island could control the waters all around Beaver Island, as well as the surrounding islands. "Lake captains complained that the man would turn off the tower light and display false ones in an effort to entice vessels onto the rocks and shoals so they could be plundered by the Saints."[7] Others say, however, that Skillagalee Island, also called Isle du Aux Galets, was too far away from Beaver Island to exert any control over boats in the area.

By this time, Strang had instigated all sorts of strange rules as dictator of his island. He began to have dissenters among his followers who were tired of floggings, stringent dictates, and heavy-handed leadership. Strangely, what brought about his downfall was his dress code requiring women to wear a bloomer costume that he had designed himself. He thought that this would give women more equality, less difference in adornments, and would free men from the power of sexual temptation.

Mrs. Thomas Bedford refused to wear the costume, and Strang had her husband publicly whipped. Thomas Bedford was already in a feud with Strang and had had many sanctions by his church placed on him already. Mrs. Bedford had a friend who also refused to wear the costume, and they convinced their husbands to plot revenge. The other man, Alexander Wentworth, was afraid that Strang had designs on his wife, and this was not an unusual thing to suspect. His wife had complained about the unwanted attentions whenever Strang visited their home. Strang was ambushed near the boat docks and showered with bullets and then clubbed. He was taken to his home in Vorees, Wisconsin, against doctor's orders, where he died six days later on July 6, 1856. He wanted to be with his wife Mary and their three children. He called her his "real wife" and knew that she would take him in, even though she herself had left the island for good because of his vision about polygamy. As he lay dying, his best friend asked him if he wanted to appoint a successor, and he turned his head with little reply, possibly realizing that the whole thing was over and was only desirous of seeing his wife Mary once more.

With the death of Strang, fear of retribution vanished. As soon as they got word of Strang's death, fifty to eighty armed men, mostly Irish, descended on the island. On July fifth and sixth, the remaining Strangites were driven onto ships and allowed to take only what they could carry; many left bundles and suitcases on the shore. Strang's followers scattered all over the Great Lake ports but mainly ended up in Chicago and Detroit. The people near Beaver Island reoccupied the area, moving into the Strangites' homes and taking over all their possessions. One of the ironies was that the leader of the invading group, A.P. Newton, had been contracted by the government in 1870 to make lighthouse improvements and would have worked directly with Jesse Strang had his group survived.

While the Latter-day Saints in Utah went on to a modern-day membership of twelve million people, Strang's followers dwindled rapidly. Today there are two hundred members left of Strang's church residing in either Wisconsin or New Mexico. Many of the modern day islanders resent any historical attention paid to Strang because they consider him a tyrant, a charlatan, and an immoral fornicator with no right to a place in history. There are others who consider him a man before his time, promoting equality for Native Americans and women. As a self-educated journalist, schoolteacher, postmaster, naturalist, musician, and lawyer, he treated his people well for a long time. They say that, unlike The Church of Jesus Christ of Latter-day Saints that became a worldwide religion and can defend its own history, Strang cannot defend his place in history. People can say anything they want, and James Jesse Strang cannot speak from the grave.

The Irish took over the island and developed their own
unique identity. Beaver Island was blessed to be near some

of the best fishing grounds in the world. The Mormons had excluded the Gentiles from partaking in this bounty, but once the Mormons were gone, Irish fishermen began to appear. They came from Gull Island, Mackinac Island, various port cities on the mainland and County Donegal in Ireland. Once they settled in, they wrote to their families and friends about "America's Emerald Isle."[8]

The Beaver Island fishermen, notoriously independent, weathered laws and restrictions, maintaining some of this independent streak to the present day. The islanders were especially isolated during the winter months, but most of them seemed to enjoy this isolation.

The first priest to live on the island was Father Peter Gallagher in 1865. He mainly dominated the island after the departure of the Strangites. With a long white beard and commanding presence, he was an avid hunter and fisherman. He was also an excellent marksman and started a lot of fistfights. Once he challenged a man to a fight in the St. Ignatius Chapel and could not be forcibly removed. Controversial but highly respected, he died in 1898. Another island character was Feodor Protar, who had been a newspaper editor and actor on the mainland. He had embarked on a spiritual quest to Beaver Island. There he became Dr. Protar and began providing local medical services. This elderly immigrant loved to read Tolstoy and was considered a saint by the people on the island. He is buried on Bonner's Bluff in a special stone and iron tomb.

There were also the women who ran the lighthouses, such as Elizabeth Whitney Williams, who spent her youngest years on St. Helena Island in northern Michigan where her father was a ship's carpenter. The family then moved to Beaver Island because her father wanted to try commercial fishing. She grew up to become one of the most famous female lighthouse keepers of the Great Lakes and went on to write *Child of the Sea; and Life Among the Mormons.* Her books are considered by some to be colored by the times, while others consider them the best record of this tumultuous period on Beaver Island. Her family was among the last residents forced from the island when the Strangites took over the island. Elizabeth's family was given ten days to convert to Strang's religion or leave for good. When they refused, they were rousted from their beds in the middle of the night at gunpoint and allowed to take with them only what they could carry.

Elizabeth wrote in her book about her last thoughts as her family left the island, setting sail for Charlevoix. "The sun was just coming up in the east and as we looked back we could see the door of our house stood open as our doors had always been to strangers or any who needed help. None had ever gone away cold or hungry. And some of the people who now stood on shore with guns pointed toward us had been fed and cared for by my people."[9]

Elizabeth met her first husband, Clement, on Beaver Island where he made barrels for the fishing industry. They later moved off the island when he was appointed by the government to teach Native Americans on Garden Island in 1865. In 1869, the position of lighthouse keeper for the Harbor Point Lighthouse became vacant; this was the former St. James Lighthouse whose name was changed after Strang's departure. Elizabeth and Clement operated the lighthouse together. The light was visible for nine miles and a taller tower, forty-one feet high, was erected in 1870. When Elizabeth's husband became ill, she took over his duties on the lighthouse. She recalls how "in long nights the lamps had to be trimmed twice each night and sometimes oftener. At such times the light needed careful watching. From the first the work had a fascination for me. I loved the water, having always been near it and I loved to stand in the tower and watch the great rolling waves chasing and tumbling in upon the shore. It was hard to tell when it was loveliest. Whether in its quiet minutes or in a raging foam."[10]

When she lost her husband early in her marriage, Elizabeth was grief stricken. He and another man launched a small boat to go to the rescue of a sinking schooner. Neither of their bodies was ever found and she was heard to say more than once, "Only those who have passed through the same know what a sorrow it is to lose your loved one by drowning and not be able to recover the remains. It is a sorrow that never ends through life."[11]

When the Strang era ended, Elizabeth was quoted as mentioning the ghosts that still inhabited the houses and roads that were constructed by the Strangites when fear ruled the island. While many of the dwellings were made use of, King Strang's cottage "was allowed to go to ruin, with some of it carried away as souvenirs by summer visitors." People who see or sense such things as spirits, as Elizabeth did, refrain from talking openly about them. However, in her self-published book, Elizabeth Williams spends several pages on the ghostly houses and streets left behind in Strang's people's exodus. When Elizabeth and her family moved back to the island, she and her friend visited the places she had heard stories about from the people who had experienced these events. Her journey around the island was so sad and so haunting that she found herself in tears on several occasions. "I looked a long time, seeing it all in my mind as the woman had told me her story," she writes. "We hurried home as the sun was sinking in the west, and I wanted to get away from all these empty houses, for every one seemed like an open grave."[12]

The old print shop was turned into a hotel for visitors to the island, and the two lighthouses are still standing. None of the other homes exist today. Any other evidence of the Strangite years has all but vanished. However, from ancient tribal relics to the Strangite occupation, from the Ottawa to the Irish fishermen, and even from the turn of the century to the present, there are ghosts everywhere on Beaver Island. Besides all these ghosts and apparitions, there are also the ghosts that a lighthouse can hide or those who were lost in the waters of the lakes. One wonders if they too walk the shores near where they were lost, drowned, or murdered.

The most interesting ghost story is the tale of Maggie Coyle, who haunted the island for many years after Strang and his followers were driven out. This legend transitioned with ease from a Strangite story to an Irish Catholic folktale. Maggie Coyle was living in Baltimore when one day a Latter-day Saint missionary came by her front yard on a Sunday afternoon. Maggie and her friends pelted the poor fellow with tomatoes and any other fruits and vegetables they could find in their yard. The missionary just kept talking, and finally Maggie dropped the ammunition from her apron and invited him back to talk with her parents. Eventually the whole family converted at the insistence of Maggie's mother. In the spring of 1851 or 1852, the family took a ship to Beaver Island to join Strang's sect. The minute Strang set eyes on Maggie, he took a special interest in her, for Maggie Coyle was a great beauty and fiery to boot.

A marriage was arranged for Maggie with an elder of Strang's church. Maggie's new friends, either teasingly or with direct knowledge of how Strang worked things on the island, warned her that the elder was a stand-in for Strang himself. They told her that the elder would slip out to pray while Strang entered the bedchamber on her wedding night. At first she did not believe them, but she soon changed her mind when she saw how the island functioned. She decided she would have no part of it.

The wedding date was set and all the arrangements made, while Maggie secretly plotted her escape. The wedding day arrived and Maggie had vanished. The St. James community searched high and low, but Maggie was nowhere to be found. However, she had left a note stuck in the rough log work of the unfinished tabernacle. She said she could not go through with it; she said she was not worthy of such a high honor. She wrote that by the time the note was found, she would have already taken a ship for the Eastern Seaboard.[13]

Three Strangites, deputized and ready to search for her, spent the next seven weeks looking, but she was never found. She had not actually left the islands because she had no money for passage. Instead she had asked a young convert fishermen from Texas to help her. She had gone to Egg Island to hide out. The young man's father sent his son on a long errand that delayed the son by almost a month. When he came back from his month-long absence, the young man spent every free moment trying to find Maggie but never did. By this time, the Strangites were being chased off the island and Strang was dead. The young man pleaded with the new leaders of the island to search one more time for Maggie. Denied his request, he told them the whole story, only confirming all the rumors about the tyrant Jesse Strang. The young man was put ashore with the rest of Strang's followers, perhaps having secretly cared for Maggie himself.

The returning Irish settlers told Maggie Coyle's story over and over. They told of her perishing in the wilderness at the hands of the Strangites and mothers used her tale as a moral to warn little ones from wandering off too far. Later, Maggie's story took on a new twist. As other young brides planned their weddings, of which there were many in this new land, they claimed to see Maggie Coyle in her wedding dress. If a young bride saw Maggie Coyle's ghost, it meant she was destined for a bad marriage. The first young bride to see Maggie's apparition claimed, after her unhappy marriage, that Maggie Coyle had appeared to her in a wedding dress on the young bride's wedding day. She claimed that Maggie had tried to warn her before she married.

For the next twelve years, Maggie Coyle's spirit, in complete wedding array, was thought to attend weddings performed on the island if the apparition thought it necessary to warn brides-to-be of an impending disastrous marriage.

> For a period of over twelve years at least seven brides shuddered or fainted and refused to go on with their wedding ceremony, claiming they had been warned of inevitably dire consequences by the ephemeral waif. It might have been a ploy, about which there was as tacit agreement not to delve too deep: these women needed an acceptable way to say no. In any event, the spate of broken vows attributed to the sudden appearance of the dead lost girl seems to have come to an end when the brother of the father of the last known immanent bride to try evoking this excuse simply refused to hear of it, saying something like, "A spirit? Nay, I think not! Tis mere foolishness got into the lass's head. The quicker the knot is tied, the quicker her husband can teach her correct thinking."[14]

There have been no new appearances of Maggie Coyle's ghost in modern times. The situation from which Strang's people came and the persecutions and the violence that they had endured left unanswered questions as to the disappearance of Maggie Coyle.

It is very possible that Strang sent some of his men or even went himself to find the disobedient Maggie Coyle and dispose of her secretly. She could have drowned while waiting for her young man to return or gotten away with help from others. She could have fallen into the hands of Ottawas, although they seemed quite peaceful, or even been found by sailors of an unsavory kind. She could have made her way off the island on her own. What is not likely is that Maggie was on a ship bound for the eastern seaboard as her note claimed. This was probably written to avoid any suspicion of foul play but certainly is not believable, as most of the people were very poor and stranded on the island because they had no way of leaving. Besides, with such a story, no one would look for her. If she did perish from the elements or from starvation or was murdered, an apparition certainly is possible.

Whatever Maggie's fate, her appearance at weddings as a young bride come to warn of impending dangers in a disastrous marriage would fit even better if she had been unjustly murdered for refusing to accept her fate. It is not a far stretch of the imagination for Maggie Coyle's ghost to wander the shores of Egg Island or Beaver Island or both and the old town that was once called St. James. There are ghosts and spirits of many men all over the state of Utah from this era, men who disappeared without a trace, having little in possessions and seeking help from those passing through. Just as there are ghosts and spirits in Utah, there are probably such ghosts on Beaver Island from Strang's piracy on the lakes and dominion on the island. In Maggie Coyle's case, she had something to warn other young brides of, a fate far worse than just simply tying the knot.

Beaver Island is a fascinating place to visit with its quaint Print Shop Museum, unique shops, the north and south lighthouses, and all the boating one could desire in an absolutely beautiful setting. There are other ghosts on the island besides the earlier Native American spirits and those of the Strangite and Irish settlers who came and went there. One such ghost apparently occupies the south lighthouse, which has been restored and made into a cooperative organization between the local school district and the islanders. It is called the Beaver Island Lighthouse School and is used for students to experience the history of lighthouse operations in addition to being a tourist site. According to legend, the ghost is a young boy named Clarence. Just a few decades ago, he became depressed. Unable to live up to his father's expectations, he hanged himself in the lighthouse. He is apparently roaming the south lighthouse to this day and the staff refuses to stay overnight in the building for fear of the footsteps, noises, and other phenomena that precede or follow this lighthouse ghost's appearances. The boy's ghost has been described as quite handsome, with short blond hair and a great smile. He was apparently quite young when he committed suicide.

Notes

1) Stonehouse, "Women and the Lakes: Untold Great Lakes Maritime Tales," quoted in *Great Lakes Boating Magazine*, October/November 2001.
2) Paine, *The Age of Reason*, quoted in Van Noord, *Assassination of a Michigan King*, 229.
3) Williams, *Child of the Sea; and Life Among the Mormons*, 198–99.

4) Ibid., 199.

5) Stonehouse, "Women and the Lakes: Untold Great Lakes Maritime Tales," quoted in *Great Lakes Boating Magazine*, October/November 2001.

6) Ibid., 82.

7) Ibid., 83.

8) Cashman, "A General Overview of Beaver Island's Rich and Colorful History" 3.

9) Williams, *Child of the Sea; and Life Among the Mormons*, quoted in Stonehouse, "Women and the Lakes: Untold Great Lakes Maritime Tales," 80.

10) Ibid., 86.

11) Ibid., 89.

12) Ibid, 80–87.

13) Cashman, Beaver Island Historical Society, email interview, November 28, 2003.

14) Ibid.

Bibliography

Above Top Secret. http://www.abovetopsecret.com.

Adams, Jennie Wild. "Alpine Creamers." *Alpine Yesterdays* (1982).

Angus, Mark. *Salt Lake City Underfoot*. Salt Lake City: Signature Books, 1996.

Arave, Lynn. "Mythical Beasts Lurk in 5 Utah Lakes." *Deseret News*, September 23, 2001.

Associated Press. "Gathering Marks 125th Anniversary of the Site Where Four States Touch." *Salt Lake Tribune*, July 13, 2000, Sec-A.

Associated Press. "Hopi Researchers Objecting to Study that Anasazi Practiced Cannibalism." *Salt Lake Tribune*, September 30, 2000, Sec-B.

Bagley, Will. "Bear Lake Monster May Have Long-lost Cousin . . . in Sweden." *Salt Lake Tribune*, May 9, 2004.

Bagley, Will. "Does Monster Lurk Beneath Bear Lake?" *Salt Lake Tribune*, March 4, 2001, 8–2.

Bagley, Will. "Family Found Shangri-La on Fremont Island." *Salt Lake Tribune*, January 28, 2001, A.

Bagley, Will. "In Utah History, When It's Nature vs. Money, the Buck Usually Wins." *Salt Lake Tribune*, September 21, 2003.

Bagley, Will. "It's Monster Season Again, So Take Care on Shores of Bear Lake." *Salt Lake Tribune*, April 20, 2003.

Bagley, Will. "Lake's Waves Whisper a Love Song." *Salt Lake Tribune*, February 4, 2001, A.

Bagley, Will. "Living Planet Aquarium Needs a Monster to Lash It 'Into a Terrible Foam.'" *Salt Lake Tribune*, May 2, 2004.

Bagley, Will. "Maybe There Is a Monster in Utah Lake." *Salt Lake Tribune*, March 31, 2002.

Bagley, Will. "Monster Tale Haunts Shore of Bear Lake." *Salt Lake Tribune*, April 1, 2001, A.

Bagley, Will. "Murdered Ute's Ghost Haunts Utah History." *Salt Lake Tribune*, November 5, 2000.

Bagley, Will. "Recent Witness Says Bear Lake Monster 'Is Still Alive and Lurking.'" *Salt Lake Tribune*, October 5, 2003.

Bagley, Will. "The Bear Lake Monster." Interviewed by John Hollenhorst. KSL-TV News, May 13, 2004.

Bagley, Will. "Utah Territorial Politician Was the Wellspring of Many Scandals." *Salt Lake Tribune*, February 15, 2004.

Bagley, Will. "Whale of a Tale Gives Great Salt Lake's Fabled History an Unlikely Spin." *Salt Lake Tribune*, June 29, 2003.

Bannan, Jan. *Utah State Parks*. Seattle: The Mountaineers, 1995.

Bauman, Joe. "Is Dugway's Expansion an Alien Concept?" *Deseret Morning News*, November 4, 2004.

"Bear Lake Monster Appears, Leviathan Comes from Lake and Devours Horse while Men Shoot at It," *Logan Republican*, September 19, 1907. Quoted in Kristen Moulton, "Bear Lake Monster Lives On," *Salt Lake Tribune*, May 31, 2004.

Bennett, Cynthia Larsen. *Roadside History of Utah*. Missoula, MT: Mountain Press, 1999.

Bigfoot Field Research. http://www.bfro.net/GDB/CNTS/UT/SM/ ut_ smool.htm (page no longer posted).

Blodget, Gary R. "Big Foot in Uintas: Nothing Conclusive." *Davis News Journal*, September 15, 1977.

Boren, Kerry, and Lisa Boren. *The Gold of the Carrie-Shinob*. Springville, UT: Cedar Fort Publishing, 1998.

Brandon, Jim. *Weird America: A Guide to Places of Mystery in the United States*. New York: E.P. Dutton, 1978.

Buttars, Lori. "Back From Sleep in the Deep." *Salt Lake Tribune*, August 28, 2002.

Buttars, Lori. "Living Window on Early Utah History." *Salt Lake Tribune*, April 1, 2000, B.

Buttars, Lori. "Road Accidents Claim 7 Lives." *Salt Lake Tribune*, July 26, 2002, Sec-C.

Cannon, Anton S. *Popular Beliefs and Superstitions from Utah*. Salt Lake City: University of Utah Press, 1984.

Carter, D. Robert. "Fishermen Find Utah Lake Monster." *Daily Herald*, May 13, 2006.

Carter, D. Robert, "The Meanderous Monster Migrates to Utah Lake." *Daily Herald*, May 6, 2006.

Carter, D. Robert. "The S.S. Sho-Boat: Queen of Utah Lake." *Utah State Historical Quarterly* 65, no. 1 (Winter 1997): 64–87.

Carter, Kate, ed. *Heart Throbs of the West*. Vol. 2. Salt Lake City: Daughters of Utah Pioneers, 1940.

Cashman, William. "A General Overview of Beaver Island's Rich and Colorful History." Beaver Island Historical Society, 2002.

Cashman, William. Beaver Island Historical Society, email message to author, November 28, 2003.

Cecil the Librarian. "This Week In Salt Lake City History." *Expanding Your World*, KCPW, May 18, 2001.

Cecil the Librarian. "This Week In Salt Lake City History." *Expanding Your World*, KCPW, July 27, 2001.

Clifford, Mary Louise, and J. Candace Clifford. *Women Who Kept the Lights: An Illustrated History of Female Lighthouse Keepers.* Alexandria, VA: Cypress Communications, 2001.

Collester, Jo. "For Those Who Love Fish Lake and for Those Who Will One Day." Family history, 2001.

Cronin, Mike. "Young Activist Channels Passion." *Salt Lake Tribune*, December 6, 2005.

Crop Circles. http://www.paradigmshift.com.

DeJong, John. "Deniably Clueless: Whistle Blowers from the Army's Nerve Energy Incinerator See the Big Picture, Unlike Those Who Are in Denial." *Catalyst* 12, no. 2 (February 2000).

Deseret News. "Bigfoot Sightings in Utah." April 1, 1993.

Dirr, Leo Tyson. "Ogden Digs Into Stories of Tunnel Network." *Salt Lake Tribune*, July 29, 2001.

Dutton, Clarence E. *Report on the Geology of the High Plateaus of Utah.* Quoted in Roylance, Utah: A Guide to the State (Salt Lake City: Utah Arts Council, 1982).

Fife, Austin. "Bear Lake Monsters." *Utah Humanities Review* 2, no. 2 (April 1948).

Flood, Renee Sansom. *Lost Bird of Wounded Knee: Spirit of the Lakota.* New York: Scribner, 1995.

Fountain, Leatrice Gilbert. *Dark Star.* New York: St. Martins, 1985.

Gad, John D.C. "Saltair, Great Salt Lake's Most Famous Resort." *Utah Historical Quarterly* 36 (1968): 198–221.

Genessy, Jody. "Devilish 666 Name Is Going Down in Flames." *Deseret News*, June 3, 2003.

Genessy, Jody. "Wow! Heavenly Light Widens Eyes." *Deseret News*, October 7, 2002.

Gibby, Julie Anne. "Boaters Beware: Loch Ness Has Nessie—Do Utah Lakes Have Monsters?" *Get Up and Go*, June 1999, 8–9.

Goodman. Jack. "Hovenweep Apartments Offer Much to Contemplate." *Salt Lake Tribune*, June 16, 2000.

Harrington, John. "Did Bigfoot Visit Small Town?" *Ogden Standard-Examiner*, February 12,1980.

Hauck, Dennis William. *The National Directory of Haunted Places*. New York: Penguin Books, 1996.

Havnes, Mark. " 'Gap' May Be a Key to Past." *Salt Lake Tribune*, June 22, 2002, Sec-B.

Hickman, William A. *Brigham's Destroying Angel: Being the Life, Confession, and Startling Disclosures of the Notorious Bill Hickman, the Danite Chief of Utah*. J.H. Beadle, ed. (New York: 1872). Quoted in Harold Schindler, *Orrin Porter Rockwell: Man of God/ Son of Thunder* (Salt Lake City: University of Utah Press, 1966).

Hill, Christie L. "Ghosts Lend Spookiness, Spice to Utah Sites." *Deseret Morning News*, November 10, 2003.

Horrocks, Rodney. "Timpanogos Cave: The Origin of the Word and Name." Timpanogos, UT: Timpanogos Cave National Monument, 1996.

Holzapfel, Richard Neitzel. *A History of Utah County*. Salt Lake City: Utah State Historical Society–Utah County Commission, 1999.

In Memory of the Becks: History of Jacob Stephenson Beck, His Three Sons: Stephen, Christian, Frederick, and One Daughter, Lucy, and Their Sons and Daughter. Compiled by Stephen F. Beck. Arranged and typed by Cora Beck Adamson, Maybelle Beck Mills, and Sharon Stoddard Beck. Reference provided by Lois Shepherd Beck.

Jackson, Richard H. "Great Salt Lake." In *Utah History Encyclopedia*. Salt Lake City: University of Utah Press, 1994.

Kelleher, Colm A. "Final Report: Investigation of the Unexplained Death of a Cow in N.E. Utah on October 16, 1998." National Institute for Discovery Science. http://www.nidsci.org/articles/ucd_report1.html.

Keller, Colm A., and George Knapp. *Hunt for the Skinwalker: Science Confronts the Unexplained at a Remote Ranch in Utah*. New York: Paraview Pocket Books, 2005.

Las Vegas Sun. "Nevada Millionaire Buys 'UFO Ranch' in Utah." October 23, 1996.

Leonard, Glen M. *A History of Davis County*. Salt Lake City: Utah State Historical Society–Davis County Commission, 1999.

Logan Republican. "Bear Lake Monster Appears, Leviathan Comes from Lake and Devours Horse while Men Shoot at It." September 19, 1907. Quoted in Kristen Moulton, "Bear Lake Monster Lives On," Salt Lake Tribune, May 31, 2004.

McCormick, Nancy D. and John S. McCormick. *Saltair.* Salt Lake City: University of Utah Press, 1985.

McOmber, Robert. *Zion's Lost Souls: Utah's Most Notorious Urban Ghost Legends.* Lincoln, NE: iUniverse Inc., 2004.

McPherson, Robert S. *A History of San Juan County: In the Palm of Time.* Salt Lake City: Utah State Historical Society–San Juan County Commission, 1995.

Meyer, Alan. "Ghost Hunting in the Unknown Zone." VHS. Ogden, UT: Rogue Entertainment, 2002.

Miller, Layne. "Slowing Down on Highway 6." *Salt Lake Tribune*, May 10, 2002, Sec-C.

Moran, Mark, and Mark Sceurman. *Weird US.* New York: Barnes & Noble, 2004.

Morgan-Larsen, Kathryn. "A Desert Within a Desert: The Great Salt Lake." *Salt Lake Tribune*, June 1999, 14.

Moulton, Kristen. "Bear Lake Monster Lives On." *Salt Lake Tribune*, May 31, 2004.

Moulton, Stephanie Lewis. "Fish Lake Resorts." Fish Lake, UT: Fish Lake Resorts.

Mount Olivet Cemetery. http://www.arosnet.com/~/~fee/web_page/ olivet/ (page discontinued).

National UFO Reporting Center. http://www.nidsci.org.

Nystrom, Jan. "The Conservation of Hovenweep's Square Tower." *Utah Preservation Magazine* 4, Millennial Issue, 32–35.

Ogden Standard-Examiner. "Man Says Marks Are Yeti Tracks." March 5, 1981.

Ogden Standard-Examiner. "Prints Human-like Big Foot? Hard To Tell." May 4, 1980.

Onet, George E. "Animal Mutilations: What We Don't Know." National Institute of Discovery Science. http://www.nidsci.org/ articles/anima1/html.

Paine, Thomas. *The Age of Reason.* Quoted in *Assassination of a Michigan King* (Ann Arbor: University of Michigan Press, 1997).

Parsons, Robert R. *A History of Rich County.* Salt Lake City: Utah State Historical Society, 1996.

Petersen, F. Ross. *A History of Cache County.* Salt Lake City: Utah State Historical Society–Cache County Commission, 1997.

Peterson, David. *Tale of the Lucin: A Boat, A Railroad and the Great Salt Lake.* Trinidad, CA: Old Waterfront Publishing, 2001.

Powell, Allan Kent, et al., eds. *Utah History Encyclopedia.* Salt Lake City: University of Utah Press, 1994.

Powell, Allan Kent, and Miriam B. Murphy. *Utah Trivia.* Nashville, TN: Rutledge Hill Press, 1997.

Roberts, Richard C., and Richard W. Sadler. *A History of Weber County.* Salt Lake City: Utah State Historical Society–Weber County Commission, 1997.

Rutter, Michael. *Utah: Off the Beaten Path.* Fourth edition. Guilford, CT: Globe Pequot Press, 2004.

Schindler, Harold. *Orrin Porter Rockwell: Man of God/Son of Thunder.* Salt Lake City: University of Utah Press, 1966.

Schulthies, Valerie. "Two Bigfoot Sightings in South Weber." *Deseret News,* February 12, 1980.

Seagrave, Anne. *Soiled Doves: Prostitutes in the Early West.* Hayden, ID: Wesanne Publications, 1994, 119–123.

Seifert, Chris. "Alien Dave: A Look Inside One Man's 'Waking Dream.' " *City Weekly,* December 26, 2002.

S.L. "This Is The Place! Do You Know Your Utah Geography?" *Salt Lake Magazine of the Mountainwest,* October 2002, 78–84.

Smith, Jason Matthew. "True Ghost Stories: Ten Haunted Locations." *The Event,* October 28, 1999, 6–7.

Stanley, David. "Utah's Believe It Or Not." *Salt Lake City Magazine,* February 2005, 77–84.

Stenhouse, *Rocky Mountain Saints.* Quoted in Harold Schindler, *Orrin Porter Rockwell: Man of God/Son of Thunder* (Salt Lake City: University of Utah Press, 1966).

Strand, Bert. " 'Bigfoot' Sighted Now in Riverdale." *Ogden Standard-Examiner,* February 27, 1980.

Strand, Bert. "8 Hikers Spot Elusive 'Big Foot' In High Unitas." *Ogden Standard-Examiner,* August 25, 1977.

Strand, Bert. "Search Party Tracks 'Big Foot.' " *Ogden Standard-Examiner,* September 3, 1977.

Sullivan, Tim. "Bits Of History Suggest Utah Is Location of Mythic Aztlan." *Salt Lake Tribune,* November 17, 2002.

Trainer, Joseph, ed. "Utah's Time/Space Warp Gadianton Canyon Encounter." *UFO Roundup* 5, no. 21 (May 2000). http://ufoinfo.com/roundup1.

Parson, Robert E. *The History of Rich County.* Rich County, UT: Utah State Historical Society and the Rich County Council, 1996.

Roylance, Ward J. *Utah: A Guide to the State*. Salt Lake City: Utah Arts Council, 1982.

Sadler, Richard W., and Richard C. Roberts. *Weber County's History*. Ogden, UT: Weber County Commission, 2000.

Sams, Jamie and David Carson. *Medicine and Sacred Path Cards*. Santa Fe: Bear and Co., 1990.

Smart, Christopher. "Sixes Nixed on Devil's Road." *Salt Lake Tribune*, June 30, 2003.

Smith, Annie M. *Shoshone Tales*. Salt Lake City: University of Utah Press, 1993.

Smith, Annie M. *Ute Tales*. Salt Lake City: University of Utah Press, 1992.

Smith, Barbara. *Ghost Stories of the Rocky Mountains*. Edmonton, AB: Lone Pine Publishing, 1999.

Smith, Barbara. *Ghost Stories of the Rocky Mountains*. Edmonton, AB: Lone Pine Publishing, 2003.

Stonehouse, Frederick. *Women of the Lakes: Untold Great Lakes Maritime Tales*. Gwinn, MI: Avery Color Studios, Inc., 2001. Reprinted from *Great Lakes Boating Magazine*, October/November 2001.

Think About It. http://www.thinkaboutit.com/branton/secrets_of_the_mojave11.htm (site discontinued.)

Thompson, George A. Some Dreams Die: Utah's Ghost Towns and Lost Treasures. Salt Lake City: Dream Garden Press, 1984.

Thompson, Ian. The Towers of Hovenweep. Mesa Verde National Park, CO: Mesa Verde Museum Association, Inc., 1993.

Thompson, Paul, ed. Indians of Utah. Alpine, UT: North Mountain Publishing, 1984.

Towle, Virginia Rowe. Vigilante Woman. South Brunswick, NJ: A.S. Barnes, 1966.

Utah Humanities Review. "The Bear Lake Monsters." (April 1948): 100-107.

Van Eyck, Zack. "Baffling Crop Formations Appear in Cache for 3rd Year in a Row." *Deseret News*, July 6, 1997.

Van Eyck, Zack. "Family Saw Silver Discs Zipping through Utah's Skies." *Deseret News*, July 6, 1997.

Van Eyck, Zack. "Frequent Flyers? Those Aliens Do Get Around." *Deseret News*, June 30, 1996.

Van Eyck, Zack. "Prankster Says They're Hoaxes: Others Say Nope." *Deseret News*, date unknown.

Van Eyck, Zack. "Private UFO Study Takes a Public Turn." *Deseret News*, August 10, 1998, Sec-B.

Van Noord, Roger. *Assassination of a Michigan King: The Life of James Jesse Strang.* Ann Arbor: University of Michigan Press, 1997.

Vaughn, Valerie. "Deadly Cold, Jim Bridger, Brigham Young, and FDR Shape the Human Imprint on Logan Canyon." *Hard News Café*, November 11, 1999.

Wagner, Stephen. "Bigfoot and the Cherokee Hill." About: Paranormal Phenomena. April 8, 2007, www.paranormal.about.com.

Walker, Calvin. "The Legend of Timpanogos." Private paper, no dates.

Warren, Steve. *Drat! Mythed Again: Second Thoughts on Utah.* West Valley City, UT: Altair Publishing, 1986.

Whaley, Monte. "Legend of Bigfoot May Be All South Weber Has Left: Town Can Cling to Bigfoot Legend." *Salt Lake Tribune*, April 6, 1996.

Wharton, Gayen, and Tom Wharton. *It Happened in Utah.* Helena, MT: Falcon Publishing, 1998.

Wharton, Gayen and Tom. *Compass American Guides: Utah.* Fifth edition. New York: Fodor's Travel Publications, 2001.

Wharton, Tom. "U.S. 666 Linking Monticello with New Mexico Gets a Name Change." *Salt Lake Tribune*, June 4, 2003.

Wild, Jennie Adams. *Alpine Yesterdays: A History of Alpine*, Utah County, Utah 1850–1980. Alpine City: Blaine Hudson Printing, 1982.

Williams, Elizabeth. *A Child of the Sea; and Life Among the Mormons.* Harber Springs, MI: E.W. Williams, 1905. 1905 edition reprinted by Ann Arbor, MI: Edward Brothers.

Wilson, Jim. "The New Area 51." *Popular Mechanics* 6, 1997.

Wharton, Tom. "Hovenweep Monument to Get New Visitor Center." *Salt Lake Tribune*, June 6, 2000, 8–2.

Wharton, Tom. "Mountain Is a Sacred Place and a Home." *Salt Lake Tribune*, June 24, 2000, Sec-B.

Wharton, Tom. "U.S. 666 Linking Monticello With N.M. Gets a Name Change." *Salt Lake Tribune*, June 4, 2003, B5.

Woodward, Don C., et al. *Through Our Eyes: 150 Years of History as Seen Through the Eyes of the Writers and Editors of the Deseret News.* Salt Lake City: Deseret News Publishing, 1999.

Wright, Jim. "Uncovering the History of Fremont Island." *Ogden Standard-Examiner*, April 11, 1996.

UFO Folklore Center. http://www.qtm.net/-geiba/catmute.html (site discontinued).

UFO Resource Center. http://www.angelfire.com/movies/UFO/page 3.htm/utah.

Utah County Sasquatch Investigative Society. http://www.sasquatch.i8.com.

Utah Gothic: Weird and Wonderful Utah. http://www.utahgothic.com.

Utah UFO Hunters. http://www.aliendave.com.

Utah UFO Sightings. http://www.geocities.com/Area51/Labyrinth/6897/sightings/uta/uta.htm (site discontinued).

About the Author

Linda Dunning has taught school for thirty-two years and has gone to school herself for approximately twenty-two of those years. She has taught children ranging from severely handicapped to resource to gifted and talented.

As a writer, Dunning has always searched for that perfect story. She has won several Utah Arts Council writing awards: first place short story in 1980, honorable mention for a collection of short stories in 1987, second place non-fiction book in 1992, and first place autobiography book in 1995. For the last twelve years, she has been on a quest to gather stories about the strange, weird, and ghostly happenings of Utah before they are lost forever. She is also the author of *Specters in Doorways*, and she contributed to the book *Weird U.S.* She is presently working on two books: *Haunted Dance Halls, Amusement Parks and Theatres of Utah* and *Early Stage and Screen Stars from Utah*.

For the last eighteen years, Dunning has done intuitive readings to help those searching for a spiritual path. In her mother-daughter memoir, *Light on a Sensitive Surface*, Dunning investigates this spiritual journey that she and her mother shared.

Dunning and her husband, John, live in Salt Lake City with all of their animals.

0 26575 70589 8